THEY WALK IN THE CITY

BY J. B. PRIESTLEY

FICTION

FARAWAY
ANGEL PAVEMENT
THE GOOD COMPANIONS
WONDER HERO
BENIGHTED
ADAM IN MOONSHINE

PLAYS

BEES ON THE BOAT DECK
DUET IN FLOODLIGHT
CORNELIUS
EDEN END
DANGEROUS CORNER
LABURNUM GROVE
THE ROUNDABOUT

MISCELLANEOUS

ENGLISH JOURNEY
FOUR-IN-HAND
I FOR ONE
TALKING: AN ESSAY
OPEN HOUSE
APES AND ANGELS
SELF-SELECTED ESSAYS
THE BALCONINNY
THE ENGLISH COMIC CHARACTERS
MEREDITH (E.M.L.)
PEACOCK (E.M.L.)
THE ENGLISH NOVEL
HUMOUR (E. HERITAGE SERIES)
BRIEF DIVERSIONS

THEY WALK IN THE CITY

THE LOVERS IN THE STONE FOREST

By

J. B. PRIESTLEY

"They walk in the city
That *we* have builded."

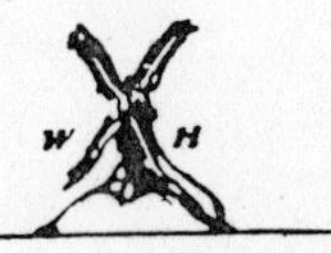

WILLIAM HEINEMANN LTD
LONDON :: TORONTO

FIRST PUBLISHED, JULY 1936
REPRINTED, JULY, AUGUST 1936

PRINTED IN GREAT BRITAIN
AT THE WINDMILL PRESS, KINGSWOOD, SURREY

TO

H. G. WELLS

in ever-renewed

exasperation, admiration

and affection

I

HALIFORD, in the West Riding of Yorkshire, is a textile town. A hundred years ago it was of no importance at all; merely a little market town, with a few small mills dotted about the hillsides. It grew steadily during the Fifties and Sixties; then came the Franco-Prussian War—a godsend—and Haliford made money, or rather, some people there made a lot of money and the others were able to buy an extra joint of meat now and again and perhaps risk an annual four days' holiday at the seaside; and after that, in spite of a slump or two towards the end of the century, the town grew and prospered, until at last there came the Great War—and what a god-send that was—and Haliford men still at home and with their wits about them began to make fortunes, and slaved away trying to get rid of their excess profits; and the town, though a little lacking in brisk young manhood, reached its peak. It started slipping and sliding down the other side, towards nobody knows what, early in the Nineteen Twenties. The world seemed to take a sudden dislike to Haliford and its undeniably excellent products. Now, most of the mills have begun to look old. Some of them—grim black stone boxes though they are—have even begun to look pathetic. You feel—as they say round there—that they are "past it." In the watery sunlight of the Pennines, their windows sometimes look like the eyes of a blind beggar. The tall chimneys that are still smoking do it now in a leisurely fashion, like retired men making a morning pipe last as long as possible. Many of the chimneys have stopped smoking, not having known the heat of a furnace for years. The air above Haliford ought to be clear by this time, but somehow the old haze still lingers, perhaps out of kindness to the bewildered townsfolk below, who would feel naked without it.

There is only one big factory in the town that does not look old. It is at the top of Toothill Lane. You cannot miss it. There it shines and glitters, an almost brand-new, five-storey building, all glass, metal, bright paint. It belongs to the Keep-Yu-Kozee Underclothing Company, Limited, which owns four other and similar factories in this island, and, thanks to an ingenious system of mass production and clever advertising, does very well out of them. This Haliford branch is a fine up-to-date affair, very different from the grim barracks of the older textile companies. It looks more like a giant greenhouse than an honest mill. The elderly folk of the town do not know what to make of the place. It has no tall chimney, no paved yard, no battered hoist doors. Old mill hands, pondering over it, cannot believe that the thing represents a solid commercial enterprise; a parcel of women might have put it up. If they had found their way inside (and they never did, for no old mill hands were wanted there), they would have been still more surprised and possibly contemptuous. All the older working folk in Haliford talk at the top of their voices, even in their own tiny homes, because for most of their lives they have had to make themselves heard above the noise of the machinery in the mills. Foremen and overlookers have the loudest voices of all; stentorian to a man. But inside this newfangled Keep-Yu-Kozee place there is no roar of machinery, no shouting, friendly or unfriendly. There are no foremen and overlookers. There are no huge machines. Every floor is filled with long rows of girls and women, attending to trumpery gadgets that merely hum or whine a little. It is nearly as quiet, and just as busy, as an ant-heap. Without any fuss, any obvious supervision, vast piles of underclothing, stockings, knitted jumpers and dresses, contrive to get themselves properly made and finished, labelled and packed in dozens in bright green cardboard boxes. Even the boxes are mysteriously coming into existence all the time on the fourth floor, and sticking labels on themselves, with only a few girls to see that they do it neatly. The only people there who seem to know exactly what is going on, how it all happens, are five or six youngish men, fellows with rimless eyeglasses who seem to alternate between a brisk business air and a vague scholarly one, who brood and chuckle over blue prints, elaborate charts and schedules, in a central office. The Keep-Yu-Kozee factory in Haliford is, in short, a successful example of the modern method of mass production. Even American manufacturers (there was one of them on the board of directors) would have approved it. Russians of the Party would have cried in ecstasy at the sight of its smooth, efficient working, its stupendous powers of production, and would have promptly organised meetings of thanks, processions and theatrical displays, in its honour. Haliford did not know what to make of it, though it welcomed the regular money that the hundreds of girls brought out of the building each Friday. Among the older and graver citizens, who still attended service at the square, gloomy little chapels, there was a conviction, mysteriously arrived at, that work in the Keep-Yu-Kozee place somehow undermined a girl's morals, started her off on lipstick, bare arms and legs, riding behind dissipated motor-cyclists, cocktails in gaudy roadhouses. But that older, disapproving Haliford was rapidly vanishing, dying of malnutrition, cancer, senile decay. Probably Haliford itself was dying. But the Keep-Yu-Kozee establishment was not part of Haliford. It was merely camping there.

The men who made most money out of this factory did not even camp there. Mr. Welkinghurst, for example. He was managing director of the company, had to keep an eye on all its five factories, but he lived in London and spent most of his week-ends at a nice little manor house in Hampshire, where Mrs. Welkinghurst was busy pretending that she was a member of the landed classes, and even grumbled at the very conditions that enabled her to live down there at all. Mr. Welkinghurst, this summer afternoon, had just inspected the Haliford branch. He had walked briskly through every room, attended by some of the fellows with rimless eyeglasses, had remained some time in the central office, talking sharply, even angrily, and had then hurried away. He was not staying long enough in Haliford even for a cup of tea, but was going to spend the night in Harrogate, where he thought there might be something for his occasional twinges of rheumatism. So he popped into a long black Rolls-Royce, leaned back and yawned for a moment, then, remembering his position as a managing director and the awful state of the world, he opened a dispatch case, buried himself among its papers, tried to think about figures, succeeded in thinking about his twinges and about his son, now in his second year at Oxford and a most promising spin bowler; and did not think at all about Haliford or any of the people in it. Yet what he had just said, so sharply, in that central office, would have its effect on certain Haliford lives, and perhaps if he had not spoken so sharply we should have had no story to tell. We shall not see Mr. Welkinghurst again, nor know if Harrogate did him any good, if his son ever got his Blue, if his wife was secure with the "county"; he is merely a name attached to a wraith; but just as surely as he and his fellow-directors set going the organisation and machinery that turn wool, rayon silk, cotton, into underclothes, stockings, jumpers, at the top of Toothill Lane, so he has set going the action of this tale.

The men in the central office had been abashed and repentant before Mr. Welkinghurst; but now that he had gone it was their turn to be angry. They had been given a fright, and now, recovering from that fright, they were all noisily and not unhappily angry together. They were all afraid of losing their jobs, much more afraid than all but a few of their workpeople. They were the brains and nerves of the organisation; and, unlike the crowd of working girls and women, they knew what was happening in the place, knew how the bales of raw stuff came to be turned into neatly labelled dozens of pants and vests; they enjoyed putting their charts and schedules into operation; they were not uncreative in their work, had to tackle new problems all the time, and so they were interested and worked with zest. Here they were more fortunate than the horde of routine workers. But they all had this terror of losing their jobs, and so were frightened of Mr. Welkinghurst, who could turn them out at a month's notice. And Mr. Welkinghurst had some reason to be annoyed, for the Keep-Yu-Kozee method of production depends upon an alert and foolproof routine, with nobody missing a single beat, and this afternoon—of all afternoons—there had been a hold-up in the cutting department, only of a minute or two, but long enough to throw the whole intricate organisation out of gear, to keep sewing, binding, trimming, labelling machines either congested or empty. We should not have noticed anything wrong, but Mr. Welkinghurst, who knew his business, spotted it at once. So did all the executives, of course. To them, it was like seeing a running blot on the exquisite page of a copy-book. They were bewildered and hurt then, and now they were angry.

"That cutting department," said Mr. Spencer, the oldest of them and the manager, "has been going like clockwork for months, right up to the tick, and now of course, just when Mr. Welkinghurst walks in, they go and get clogged up."

"It was just one damned girl that did it, wasn't it?"

All five were agreed on that. One damned girl. Which one? Well, Young Walker was finding that out.

"And he can send her in to my office," said Mr. Spencer. "I'll fire her this very afternoon." He was not an American, but when he was feeling brisk and rather brutal, he liked to use these American terms, which made him feel like one of those dominating rasping chaps you see on the films. "All right, you fellows."

Young Walker arrived, looking rather despondent.

"Well, which damned fool was it?" he was asked.

"It was Rose Salter," Walker replied unhappily. "I can't understand it. She's a bright kid as a rule. You'll remember her. Good-looking."

"I don't care if she looks like Greta Garbo," cried Mr. Spencer angrily, "she goes. Putting us all in the cart like that! Is she there? Send her in."

Enter Rose Salter, wearing a green overall. Mr. Spencer, glaring away, remembered her at once. She was a young and very pretty girl, with fair and wavy hair and darkish brown eyes, an odd and attractive combination. The general effect was a dusky golden one, unusual, very nice. Mr. Spencer promptly condemned it to blazes. She ought to have been tearful, at least. Here was a girl, a brainless kid, one miserable unit in the grand design, who by not attending to her silly little job properly had slowed up the department, ruined the time they had worked out to a fraction of a minute, darkened Mr. Welkinghurst's afternoon, made him suspicious of the whole Haliford branch technical staff, and therefore menaced the well-being of Mr. Spencer, his wife, his family. She ought to have been crying her eyes right out. Instead of that, she was simply sulky. Pretty and sulky.

Even her good looks were annoying. He barked a few sharp questions at her.

"I began thinking about something," she said.

Could anything be more idiotic? "What's that got to do with it? The point is, you weren't looking after your machine, and so you went and threw the whole department out of gear. And do you know who that was who walked in just when you'd held everything up? Only Mr. Welkinghurst, that's all." The terrible irony of this lifted his voice almost into a scream. "Only the managing director of the whole company, that's all."

The girl looked at him with round, sad eyes. They were dark now, whereas a minute ago they had been quite light. "I'm sorry," she said, mumbling a little. "You see I saw something out of the window."

"You'd no business to be seeing something out of the window."

"It was nothing much," this in extenuation. "A bird—or something. And then I began thinking. And—and—I forgot for a minute."

"Well, you'll have something else to think about now. Another job. Because you've lost this one." And the thought that she had gone and lost it, so stupidly, wantonly, when men like himself fought day and night to hold on to theirs, made him angrier than ever. "Just thrown it clean away by your own damned stupidity and carelessness, d'you understand?"

Yes, she understood. There was a suggestion of tears now. Probably his raised voice, his reddening face and glaring eyes, had done it.

Recovering himself, Mr. Spencer glanced down importantly at a scribbling pad (though all it said to him was: "See abt Bridge markers—sherry—new magneto?"), and in a cold official tone: "Take your card to Mr. Dimsdale and ask him to pay you off."

"Yes, sir," said Rose Salter meekly. She lingered a moment. She was about to say something apologetic.

Mr. Spencer looked up. Suddenly, unaccountably, he thought how extremely pleasant it would be to take this girl in his arms and console her, and then was annoyed with himself for entertaining such a thought, was further annoyed with the whole troupe of enticing young girls who troubled a man during business hours, and said gruffly: "All right, all right. That's done with. I'm busy." And pretended to be.

In the cutting room some were indignant and said it was a shame, others were not a bit surprised at all because they had seen it coming; and Rose, a little dazed, still rather dreamy, as if that bird she had seen had not been quite of this world, said good-bye to both parties with the same abstracted air. Then, without the green overall, her card stamped, herself paid off and done with, she walked out of the Keep-Yu-Kozee factory for the last time. Toothill Lane was warm, rather close; the late afternoon sunlight lay heavy upon it. The girl walked slowly, not without grace, as if the air had more substance than usual and she were wading through it. Her face was quite calm; her eyes clear, untroubled. Like fish passing through the lighted section of an aquarium tank, little thoughts, of no importance, went in and out of her mind, which was as easy and contented now as it had been when she was staring out of the window. She had not deliberately thrown away her job, for she was not that forceful or reckless kind of girl, but now that it had gone sliding away from her, she did not care, was even pleased, for she was tired of Haliford and the safe monotony of the Keep-Yu-Kozee. Her great friend of the moment, Alice Hargreaves, a dashing character, was always saying that the two of them ought to leave Haliford, find work—mysteriously adventurous sort of work—in Leeds, Manchester, or even London. Alice always said she was ready to throw up her job, at Whitley's the draper's, at any moment, and now, as it had turned out—and Rose put it to herself that it had merely "turned out"—Rose was the first to be free, out of work, ready for an adventure in one of the big towns. She thought of all this, idly, as she walked slowly down Toothill Lane, towards her home in Slater Street.

This girl should not have been as wholesome, comely, even beautiful, as she was. The fact runs counter to all our accepted knowledge of what is good and bad for human beings. All the conditions of her twenty-year-old life had been monstrous. From earliest childhood she had been denied sunlight, good air, proper food and exercise. She ought to have been a premature hag, with a crooked spine, gummy eyes, rotting teeth. Yet somehow out of this dreadful mess of rubber teats, sinister teething powders, dirty linen, over-heated rooms, pastry, fish and chips, dubious laxatives, dreadful patent medicines, ignorance, swinishness, savagery, had emerged this healthy and handsome young creature. Nature had found a way to circumvent the idiocy of half-civilised Man. Or perhaps this was a legacy from her ancestors, Salters who had been hard moorland shepherds or labourers on the great wheat farms in the plain of York, whose wholesome red blood still flowered—it might be for the last time—in this evil industrial soil. Feminine beauty ought to be the prerogative—as so many other things are—of the privileged and carefully nurtured classes, yet, as the records will show, it has an odd trick of springing from the nameless mob beneath, suddenly blossoming in perfection out of stinking ghettoes, bug-ridden tenements, dockside lodging houses. Rose was not one of these astonishing beauties, who now so often coin their straight little noses, the fine curve of their cheeks, into millions of dollars in distant Hollywood; nor was her home in Slater Street, a respectable dingy street, the Yorkshire equivalent of those ghettoes and tenements; but nevertheless she was a surprise, a stroke of luck, a happy chance we do not deserve.

It would be easy and impressive to show the girl, workless now in a community where work was hard to find, returning to a home of despair and slow death, a family of tight-lipped suffering proletarians. But it would not be true. The Salters were not like that. As a family they had a notable capacity for enjoying themselves. They belonged to that section of the workers which is the despair of the austere revolutionary, who can understand neither their hoggish blindness nor their ability, which he lacks, to come to easy terms with each passing day.

He sees them swallowing with evident enjoyment each new dose of capitalist dope. They seem to thrive on it. There is no persuading them that under these present conditions life is not worth living because obviously the fools are having a good time with it. Including Rose there were six Salters crowded into the little house—two rooms below, three above—in Slater Street: father, who was a warehouseman, a cunning bowls player, and a figure at the East Haliford Working-men's Club; mother, who was fat, jolly, and a very sketchy shopper and meal preparer; George, who was in a dyeworks by day and in the sporting life by night; Fred, who did a variety of jobs and just now had wangled something mysterious for himself at the Greyhound Racing Track; Nellie, in a toyshop in Market Lane, for ever getting herself engaged and then disengaged and telling you all about it with tears in her eyes and laughter on her lips; and Rose herself, the youngest, considered the quiet and rather deep one of the family, who had been known to sit with a book—not a picture or racing paper but a real book—for a whole hour together. Every meal at the Salters was a long-drawn-out noisy picnic. There was more shouting, more hustle in this little house than there is at most railway stations. Every member of the family had friends who continually popped in and out. The wireless set worked at full blast. The females were always making one another cups of tea; the males were always opening bottles of beer, or slipping out for a jug of old ale. Every week-end with them seemed like Christmas. One or other of them attended all football and boxing matches and other sporting events, the one local music-hall, the more important films of the town, all public celebrations; and one or other of them tried a hand at all the competitions run by popular papers or commercial firms, so that the postman might bring a fortune at any hour. The family finances were so complicated, everyone borrowing from everybody else, that they could never be straightened out. Sometimes George and Fred were existing, in shirt-sleeves, with half-closed eyes over a cigarette and the sporting columns, on their mother's and sisters' bounty; and at other times they burst in like millionaires from the gold mines, slapping dirty pound notes and heaps of silver on the kitchen table and proposing to take everybody to Blackpool (their favourite resort) for the week-end. Rose did not set herself against all this; she was fond of her family; but there were times, and there had been more and more of them lately, when she found herself wanting something different, not quite so noisy, so Halifordish. She never protested, unless she wanted to be quiet and was not left alone, never sneered; but more and more, inspired by what she saw in picture papers or at the films, she entertained thoughts quite foreign to the other Salters.

She arrived home to find her mother, large, hot, dishevelled, doing some of her sketchy cooking. The fact that it was a warm day and would be a close evening had not deterred Mrs. Salter from attempting a very hot and heavy meal, for she took no notice of the weather but catered by immediate inspiration, so that in January she might offer you cold pork pie and tinned pineapple, in August fried steak and a suet pudding. This seemed reasonable to all the family, except Rose, who was—they said—"a bit pernickety."

"Mother," she announced at once.

"Yes, love?"

"I've got the sack."

"Well, you silly monkey!" cried Mrs. Salter, lifting her large round red face from the low oven. "Whatever for?"

Rose told the story of the afternoon as well as she could, blaming neither herself nor the company. Her mother did not clearly understand what it was all about, but by this time she had given up trying to understand what all these things were about. Every other day one of them brought home some fantastic tale. But she was neither cross nor worried. She was even pleased. This was drama of a kind; and the Salters liked drama.

Fred, who was off duty, had been dozing upstairs, and now came down in his shirt-sleeves, and collarless, the inevitable cigarette smouldering at a corner of his mouth, had to be told. He took it very calmly.

"Now listen," said Fred, with a mysterious conspiratorial air, easily acquired in sporting circles, "I believe I could get you in up at the Track."

"Whatever doing?" roared Mrs. Salter. "What could our Rose do wi' them dogs?"

"Don't they have girls paying out at the Tote?" Fred shouted, quite amiably.

"I don't know. Do they?" his mother shouted, with equal amiability. They were only two yards from one another, but they liked shouting.

"'Course they do. Good-lookers too."

"Well, our Rose is good-looking enough. Aren't you, love?"

"She'll pass on a dark night," said Fred, in the true brotherly style. "Well, I fancy I could work it. Mind you, it'll have to be worked—an' I'll tell you for why—there's a lot after them jobs."

"All right, then. You try and get her in, lad. What do you say, love?"

"You needn't bother, Fred," said Rose, now sitting in a corner of the lumpy horsehair sofa. Everything in the house was old and nearly worn out because the Salters could think of a thousand more amusing things to do with their money than to spend it on furniture.

Fred was outraged by this indifference. To him the world revolved round the Track. If you didn't work there, it was simply because you couldn't. "Oh, all right, all right," he grumbled. "I'm just offering you a chance of a fine job, that's all. I don't even say I could get it for you, but I could try."

"Well, if she doesn't want it, she doesn't want it," Mrs. Salter shouted.

"Then she's barmy," Fred retorted, and returned upstairs to dress.

Rose helped her mother to set the table. The cloth had several holes in it and was stained. The knives and forks were of odd patterns and the worse for wear. All the plates were badly chipped. These things would stay on the table for at least two hours, for Nellie did not get home until half-past seven; and sometimes they would remain until bed-time. George and her father arrived together, noisily discussing something they had read in the evening paper.

"Our Rose has got sacked," Mrs. Salter told them.

They took it quite calmly. Mr. Salter had been working in the same warehouse for over thirty years; his association with his firm dated from the sane pre-war days; and so he did not think of his children's work as he did of his own; for he realised that they had grown up in this new senseless world and it seemed natural that they should flit from job to job, like birds finding a bit of seed here and there.

"You know what you ought to be, kid?" said George to Rose, not for the first time. "Manniekin. One o' them show girls in the big shops, same as you see on the pictures sometimes. Manniekin."

Rose smiled, shook her head.

"What's it to be this time, then?" roared her father. He was a squarely-built man with a large grey-black moustache and twinkling brown eyes. He could make more noise, and frequently did make more noise, than any of his family. "We can't keep you 'ere doing nothing, y'know."

"Who says we can't?" demanded his wife.

"I say so, and so does Stanley Baldwin," said Mr. Salter, suddenly guffawing.

"Never mind 'im. Go get washed and 'ave your teas."

There was nothing more said about Rose's future, for the male Salters had always plenty to talk about, and even when Nellie came home, it was not discussed. It might have been—for Nellie considered she worked harder than anybody else in the family, because her hours were longer—but it happened that that day, as it happened on many a day, something mysterious and exciting had occurred at the shop, and they all had to be told at length. Nellie, a rather tall and handsome brunette, not as pretty as Rose but much more dashing and stylish, very fond of dancing and being taken into Leeds, was one of those young women who live excitedly in a world of vast intrigue, where a certain thing said to a friend's friend about another friend has the most momentous consequences, where mysterious and vaguely amorous gentlemen friends, usually commercial travellers or motor salesmen, loom and soar and suddenly vanish, leaving behind them a babble of conjecture. On this particular day, a certain Mr. Ormby—or Ormsby—had actually called at the shop to ask Nellie right out if her friend Ruby Pearson were deliberately avoiding him, and Nellie could not make this Mr. Ormby-Ormsby out—nobody quite knew who he was, though he obviously had a good position, and he was quite old, forty if a day—and Ruby hadn't said anything to her, she hadn't seen Ruby for over a week, and of course she didn't want to say anything though she had her own ideas, and anyhow—this was the point—why should he come into the shop like that, and how did he know she, Nellie Salter, worked there at all? And so it went on. Rose slipped out and went to find her friend, Alice Hargreaves.

Wearing dresses and hats that matched (they even used the same kind of face powder, though it suited neither of them), moving along very close together, with an air not merely confidential but also suggesting, to any impudent staring boys who might be about, that there was something exquisitely delicate, infinitely precious, about this society of two, they walked slowly up into Ackroyd Park, which is the best place to walk in East Haliford on a summer evening, and is patronised largely by bowling enthusiasts, lovers trying to forget the world and not succeeding, and old pipe-sucking gentlemen talking about house property. Round-eyed, whispering urgently, squeezing one another's arms, the two girls discussed their future. As Rose had now taken the first decisive step—for her dismissal assumed that appearance in her description of it to Alice—it was up to Alice, the bolder one, to be more venturesome in her ideas than she had been before. So now she dismissed Leeds and Manchester, which she had seen, and was all for London, which she had never seen. (Many of the notions of it she had were taken from those of film scenario writers in Southern California.) Six years before this, an earnest and admirable elementary school teacher had given both girls some excellent lessons, taken from a textbook written by a second-class civil servant, who would have made a good thing out of the book if he had not signed a bad contract with the publisher, on "British Citizenship," but not one glimmer of it illuminated their minds now. The six years they had spent out of school had brought their own values, their own crazy little patchwork of ideas. Thus, Alice knew a girl who knew a girl—not very good-looking neither—who went to London to work in a café, had not been there more than six months—and what months!—before she had married the nicest boy, crazy about her, and something to do with tea, and now she lives in a flat at Bournemouth, with a car and everything. And not only that, but her brother Frank had met a man—it was when he went down to Leicester that time—who had something to do with cafés in London. What about that, eh? And there weren't only cafés in London, of course, there were the big shops and everything, dozens of chances for a girl. Films possibly, you never knew. Look at that girl from Bradford, a mill girl too. "Rose," she concluded, squeezing her arm really hard, "you don't know what might happen in London, do you? Haliford's no good. It's a wash-out. Isn't it a wash-out?"

Rose said it was, rather absently. At this moment, here in the Park, with the flowers so lovely, the trees shutting out the town, she was liking it in what seemed to her a special way of her own. It was all rather sad but nice. Alice never seemed to feel like that; it was the only thing wrong about her; she was always wanting to be doing something, to be going somewhere, and nothing seemed to happen inside her by herself. But Rose was back again in the dreaminess of the afternoon, when she forgot her machine. At the junction of two gravel paths, near a great bed of flowers, their colour fading now but very fragrant, she halted. Above the distant shouts of the men on the bowling greens, there came from far away the tiny silver sound of a piano. The sky had retreated before it finally began to darken, and was very remote, peaceful.

"What's the matter?" asked Alice, as if Rose must have a pain or have forgotten something.

"Nothing," said Rose dreamily, not stirring. She wished she was by herself now. She did not want to talk about London or anything, unless it was something, just some silly nice thing, that had happened to her years ago, when she was a little girl. But Alice never talked about things like that; she always talked about the future, where she wanted to go, what she wanted to do. Rose felt herself expanding, dissolving, all at peace, yet there was one bit of her that was expectant too, waiting for something wonderful to happen.

"Come on, dreamy," said Alice, tugging at her.

It was then, as she moved, that she noticed the boy who was on the seat, which he had to himself, only a few feet away. He was not wearing a hat, and he had untidy dark hair, a dark thin face, and when he looked up at her, in a startled sort of way, his eyes glittered. That was because there were tears in them.

"Did you notice that boy sitting there?" she began, when they had gone past.

"No," said Alice, interested at once. "Was he nice?"

Rose wished she had not spoken, though she did not know why she wished that. "He was crying or something," she muttered.

Alice turned round to have a look at him. She was a great turner-round, except where tactics definitely demanded that she should keep straight on, and more than once she had annoyed Rose by doing this. She had annoyed her now. "He's leaning forward and watching us," Alice announced triumphantly. "He couldn't have been crying."

"No," said Rose indifferently, though she felt curiously angry inside.

"Shall we turn round at the corner and have another look

at him?" Alice was all for adventure, her own or anybody else's.

"No, why should we? Of course not," said Rose, quite snappily. "Go on, about London."

Alice did go on, but not about London. Her thoughts had been turned to boys and as this was a subject about which she had always a good deal to say, she proceeded to say it. And in the middle of listening, even of adding an opinion and anecdote or two of her own, Rose suddenly had a quick inward vision of that boy with the dark untidy hair, the dark thin face, the eyes glittering with tears. She could not help wondering who he was.

II

HIS name was Edward Fielding. He was as much a product of Haliford as Rose herself; perhaps more so, for his family had been engaged in the local trade for the last four generations. Like many other families round there, they had come down in the world. Edward's grandfather, dead these last ten years, had been in his time a prosperous wool merchant. Edward's father had lost what the old man had made, and had latterly been only a clerk, and not even a good and respected clerk. There was a time when the wool trade could afford to support hundreds of men like Edward's father, who bought a few bales here, sold them there, and made a nice profit. Those were the days of the easy middlemen, who spent half the morning chatting on 'Change, took two good hours for lunch, then returned to smoke a few pipes over the letters and samples; and those days were gone. Edward's father could never properly understand why they had gone, and used to talk about luck. Edward's mother, who knew nothing about trade but a good deal about her husband, never believed they had gone, simply coming to the conclusion she had married a lazy fool. Edward himself, now twenty-three and a bit simpler than many young men of that age, had grown up with the slump, had seen the last of his grandfather's profits vanish, had watched his father shamble into a clerkship offered out of charity, and had been glad himself, at first, to find a miserable little job with a miserable little firm of noil and waste dealers. Thanks to his mother's insistence, his older brother, Herbert, a wooden chap who had always known exactly what he wanted to do, had been able to pay the necessary premium for a training, and was now a fully-fledged analytical chemist, working in the town laboratory. This last year or two, it had been Herbert, now thirty-two but still unmarried, who had been the chief prop and grand male of the house, which was one of a gloomy decaying row in Sutcliffe Place, once the home of comfortable merchants and manufacturers, stately chief cashiers, and the like, but nowadays given up to little insurance men, corset agents, widowed women and their lodgers. (Haliford had turned into a town without well-to-do people. The few who still made plenty of money out of it, did not live in it—a shabby trick that left Haliford even shabbier.) Edward and his father, both judged to be feckless, had been in the home only on sufferance. This ought to have brought them together, made them form a defensive alliance against the grand Herbert and his proud mother, but it had not done. And now it was too late.

Only half an hour ago, Edward had rushed out of the house, half-blind and choking, and had wandered into the Park without knowing where he was going. In the front bedroom, now so terrifyingly transformed, with the reek of a doctor's waiting-room or a hospital hanging about it, his father lay inert, glassy-eyed, visibly dying. It had been awful. Edward had been allowed to tiptoe in, just to look at his father. The doctor was not there, but the nurse was, a horrible woman with a long nose and button eyes. After Edward had taken a scared glance at the bed, he had looked up to see the nurse's button eyes fixed upon him. There was triumph in them; her whole horrible face was alight; and it said, quite plainly: "Now, you see, you silly young man! You thought I wasn't important, didn't you, ignored me when I tried to pass a few bright remarks about the weather? Now then, you silly baby—look—look!" And Edward, retreating from that evil face, had looked again. His father, a weak, shambling, boastful little man, given to sudden useless rages and then bouts of elaborate self-pity, had never been dignified in life, and even now, when he was so near to death, he had no dignity. His little turned-up nose was even smaller, sharper; his moustache drooped more than ever; his poor chin fell right away; one stubby hand, the hair on it still glinting in the evening sunlight, as if there alone life still went on, made mechanical little movements, clutching feebly at nothing. The nurse bent over her patient, making a little gesture with one hand that wiped the useless Edward out of the room. At the bottom of the stairs, he passed his mother, tall, dark, weary, tried to stop and speak, received no encouragement from her stony glance, then ran, choking, out of the house. He had often thought about death, of course, but he had seen it more or less in the likeness of his grandfather's end, that of a grim old man, making a fight of it at first and then giving in with a kind of contemptuous nobility. But his father was only in his fifties. He was not fit, not ready to die. There was a horrible meanness about it, as if some great brute had stolen up behind his father's chair, when the little man had come back from the club and several whiskies and was believing in himself again for a moment, and had struck him down, beyond recovery. As he sat on that seat in the Park, Edward's heart was moved by pity for his father and by terror of this life, which could give a man so little and take that little away so meanly, miserably. You struggled on, doing your pitiful best, and then you came home one day complaining about a pain in your side—with nobody listening to you—and then within a week you were there in bed, nothing to anybody except weary impatient Doctor Martin and that beast of a nurse. Edward had no religious convictions of any kind. He had been born too late to accept the stern Methodism of his mother, his grandfather, all the older members of his family, and too early for anything that may take the place of that Methodism in Haliford. He was not even a fighting materialist, deriving satisfaction from not accepting the consolations of religion. He still believed dimly that he had a soul, but that soul did not belong anywhere, had no destiny. His father, a chapel-goer in his youth, was in no better state, Edward knew. His father had developed a contempt for chapel-going since the War—the existence of the War had somehow given him a pretty smart argument against all religions—and had been in the habit of making remarks neither very witty nor shrewd against chapels, churches, and all parsons in general, much to the annoyance of Mrs. Fielding. Remembering these contemptuous remarks—and his father had had a trick of repeating them to him when they were alone—Edward wondered wretchedly now what was really happening to his father. Was he being simply squashed out of existence, like a beetle under a heavy foot? Or was he going somewhere, and, if so, where? (If his Heaven did not look like the North Haliford Constitutional Club, it would be useless.) Edward was miserably conscious of his ignorance, helplessness; he might just as well be a baby; and as he sat there, these feelings, mingled with a deep pity for that other ignorant, helpless, babyish creature, his father, so worked in him that the tears came swiftlv, not falling, but staying to blind him. He blinked several times, then looked up, involuntarily. Two girls were standing a few feet away from him.

"Come on, dreamy," he heard one of them say.

As they walked past, the nearer one looked at him. His heart bounded. Something in the very depths of the glance, which was gone in a second, remained with him for ever; but though afterwards he tried and tried to remember what this girl looked like, he could not remember. He had a vague impression of a golden face, warm and living gold. He stared after them, for the moment forgetting everything else. The other one, the one he had never noticed, looked back and caught him leaning forward. They disappeared. Oh, they were just two ordinary Haliford kids, strutting round the Park, trying to find a couple of boys as silly as themselves, to take them to the pictures. Huddling in his corner of the seat, he dismissed them, and began to smoke a tasteless cigarette. Two lovers—with that wistful homeless look of all their kind in this island—came to occupy the other end of the seat. He saw the girl's thin shoulder curve out, her hand fall easily into the young man's hand in her lap, and he rose, bleakly, disdainfully, feeling that he knew so much more than they did, with Death waiting for him at home. But as he went there, the evening hastily darkening, shrinking and turning suddenly cold round him, there returned to him, unlooked for, a vague remembrance of that girl. Some trace of her, perhaps the dusky golden heart of her glance at him, accompanied him home, and he felt ashamed because his misery would suddenly vanish for a moment. He told himself that there was nothing, could never be anything, to be glad about. The house, which smelt close, almost stifling, with dark hints of vaults and graveyards about it, seemed to agree with him.

There was a light in the kitchen, which was also the dining-room. He found Herbert in there, soberly examining through his spectacles (which were of light tortoiseshell, seemed to Edward bigger and rounder than anybody else's, and more Herbert even than Herbert himself, so that you would never dare to make a remark about him if they were in the room) the smudgy sheet of Haliford's one evening paper; a solid and thick-set but natty figure; the pink solemn face, with its tremendous chin, very vivid under the three white bulbs of the chandelier. Nearly as vivid, and hardly any more interesting to Edward at this moment, were some biscuits, cheese, half a plum pie, and a jug of milk.

"Mother's upstairs," said Herbert gravely, lifting his gaze from the *Haliford Argus* and fixing it steadily upon Edward. "Doctor Martin called again."

"What did he say?"

Herbert cleared his throat, rather importantly, put down the newspaper, and looked harder than ever at Edward, who was extremely irritated by this typical pompous Herbert business. "He told me," and here Herbert lowered his voice, "that it was only a matter of time. Nothing to be done, apparently. Might happen tomorrow, he said, or the next day."

Edward realised the horrible enormity of the thing all over again. Here they were, quietly talking as if waiting for their father to come in from the club, when all the time they were really discussing his final disappearance from their lives. "I say—isn't it—awful?" he stammered.

"Yes, Ted, it's bad."

This annoyed Edward. There was a faint shade of patronage in it; wrong at any time; insufferable now. Then again, he hated being called "Ted." And then again, Herbert was always annoying. He was so self-satisfied, wooden, and, though energetic enough, lifeless. On the surface his life was far more satisfactory than Edward's: he had an interesting, pretty well-paid job, whereas Edward's was a poor dull affair; he was the great man of the house; he had enough money to give himself all manner of little treats that were impossible to his brother; indeed, he appeared to have everything he wanted, whereas Edward had nothing he wanted, hardly began to know what he did want and only knew that, whatever it was, he had not got it. Yet Edward would no more have changed identities with Herbert than he would with a mummy. Looking across at him, Edward wondered for the five-hundredth time how Herbert lived at all, for Herbert seemed to him a kind of automaton, moving through a mechanical routine of tasks and mild pleasures without any inner spring of desire and feeling. Edward did not put it to himself in this way, but he felt it all obscurely, and a good deal of his irritation came from a deep bewilderment. There was a poet somewhere in Edward. He would never understand the solemn jog-trot prose of Herbert. The latter had made his great gesture when he had determined to be an analytical chemist and, in face of many obstacles, lack of money at home, his father's opposition, his own honest but not quick brain, had turned himself into an analytical chemist. Since then he had rested securely on life, constantly receiving a grave pleasure from the thought of himself, Herbert Fielding of Sutcliffe Place, as an analytical chemist. Such intelligence as he had, he kept for his work. Outside his work, he was solemnly silly, and dangerously so because his professional training and standing gave a certain solidity to the nonsense he repeated out of the newspapers, the ridiculous flimsy opinions he picked up anywhere, from anybody. In Britain, America, Germany, there are millions of Herberts; little technical men or minor professional men; fellows who used up all their wits and courage and resourcefulness in their teens or early twenties for their training and that precious first appointment; and are decent, kind citizens who never neglect an obvious duty, stout little pillars of their communities, who never mean any harm. But from them flows out a tide of stupidity and prejudice that goes rolling round the world and, when some wind of wickedness lashes it, goes spouting up until it falls in dreadful cataracts of blood.

The brothers, who had spent all their lives close together and yet would never understand each other, said no more, but began their supper, Edward indifferently, Herbert with more energy and enthusiasm. They had not finished before their mother came downstairs, looking very drawn. She sat down in a small rocking-chair, her favourite chair perhaps because it enabled her to relieve her feelings, by furious rockings, while sitting in silence. Except in her complete possession of Herbert, who seemed to her an ideal specimen of manhood, Mrs. Fielding was an unfortunate woman. If her husband had been wilder and worse (and lots of Haliford men, even now, when few of them go off on great drinking and womanising bouts as they used to do, are wilder and worse), she could have followed the practice of so many women who marry badly, could have carefully turned herself into an admired figure of sweet wifely resignation and goodness. But her husband was not bad enough for that; he was merely, and maddeningly, weak and unsatisfactory. So she had become an almost permanently angry woman. As the money vanished, as her husband's faults hardened, as the world became increasingly difficult to understand, she put more and more furious energy into her task of running the home; she cleaned and cooked and mended every day with a tormented despair, like the last commander on his feet in a starving beleaguered fortress; she did not pick up things but snatched at them; she never asked, she sharply commanded; even her attendance now at the rapidly emptying chapel of her youth had an aggressive quality; and it was only on very rare occasions, returning from chapel on a fine Sunday night, rocking herself quietly when the last bit of cleaning, cooking and mending had been done, and the others were out, that she achieved a moment's peace. Though Herbert was her joy, he was also the source of her chief terror, for sooner or later he might get married; and the thought that any one of these idle painted girls about the town might suddenly put an end to her world alternately filled her with terror and anger. She seemed to detect in Edward too many of his father's unsatisfactory traits to be very fond of him, so that he was only another of her responsibilities. For a long time, her husband had seemed one of the great nuisances of a woman's life, like the dirty rain that fell just after the front steps had been cleaned, but now that he could no longer walk about or even speak, had shrunk into the poor thing in the bed upstairs, she had recaptured some of the feeling she had had for him so many weary years ago. But as her natural expression had been for so long one of angry protest, even this feeling had to come out in that form. Fortunately, the nurse, whom she had disliked on sight and had not wanted in the house, gave her an excuse.

"That nurse," she began, rocking so hard that there seemed something oddly incongruous about her dark tragic face there, "that nurse is a lot more bother than she's worth, a lot more. Whatever Doctor Martin wanted to land her on us for, I don't know. She takes more waiting on—with her hot water and cups of tea and whatnot—than your poor father. Who does she fancy she is, I'd like to know."

"I hate her," Edward muttered.

It was Edward's turn now. "I'm not asking you," said his mother. "If you're so particular, you might have stopped and asked to-night if there was anything you could do, instead of running out of the house, first chance you had."

Herbert nodded, and his spectacles, as they turned upon Edward, looked deeply reproachful.

Edward knew that it was no use trying to explain what had happened to him. It is the tragedy of most family circles that it is precisely there, where they are supposed to know you to the last flicker of an eyelash, that it is no use trying to explain when anything important has happened to you. So Edward merely looked sulky, disliked himself for looking sulky, and was thoroughly annoyed with his mother and brother because they made him look sulky. And all the time—that was the awful thing—there was his father upstairs, getting ready to leave them all for ever.

"Doctor Martin spoke to me," said Herbert, gravely and importantly. "He said——"

But even Herbert was not to be allowed his moment. "Yes, I know what Doctor Martin's saying," his mother interrupted angrily. "But Doctor Martin doesn't know everything, none of them do, for all their big talk. I've seen people get better when they were a lot worse than your father. Look at Mrs. Grigson's husband. Gave him completely up, didn't they, said it was only a matter of time. So it was, before he was up again and back to work. Doctor Martin or any other doctor—and them specialists you pay so much for are just as bad—can make a mistake. They can all say what they like but," and here she dropped her voice, stopped rocking, and looked solemnly at her children, "we're all in God's hands, and that's the beginning and end of it; we're all in God's hands."

"Well, I don't think so much of them," Edward burst out. "Look at my father——"

"Yes, look at him," cried Mrs. Fielding angrily. "And look at you, sitting here, talking like that. You ought to be ashamed of yourself."

"I should think so," said Herbert sternly. He had no religion himself, but he had a decent respect for God, just as he had for the Board of Trade or any other properly constituted authority.

"Aw, shut up." This to Herbert, not to his mother.

But it was his mother who answered him. She even got up, tired as she was, to do it. "Now you go straight off to bed, go on. Big as you are and old as you are, you're not going to talk like that, specially at a time like this. Go on, off to bed. And see you get up in the morning. I've enough to do without bothering to see you off to your work at a reasonable time. And see you're in a better frame of mind in the morning, you big silly lad. Go on."

Edward lamely retreated, feeling a small boy again as his mother's angry cavernous eyes bored into him. He was sleeping in the tiny attic, among broken chairs, old trunks, and other lumber in the hot musty space just under the roof. He went tiptoeing past that sinister bedroom, which greeted him in passing with just a whiff of that doctor's smell, and once again he felt helpless, tearful. If only he could talk to his father again, just for five minutes. He felt like calling wildly to him: "Father! Dad! Daddy!"

going back in three cries to that childhood when his father had been a towering splendid being, capable of changing the whole world, all strength and fun and generosity. He climbed to his attic in an agony of impotent grief.

There was no electric light up there, and he did not bother to light the candle. Blindly, he threw off his rather dusty clothes and got into his neatly patched pyjamas, crawled into the makeshift bed, and closed his hot eyes, though feeling further from sleep than he had done at noon. The tough-minded have now time to condemn him for the poor weak young fool he appears to them to be. To the tender-minded, he may appear something of a tragic figure, one of millions, all busy putting their engines in and out of gear, turning on and off their miraculous wireless sets, watching their incredible moving talking pictures, taking out of sealed tins their food from the ends of the earth, all guests of Science and lords of Nature, but hopelessly bewildered by any major event in their lives. Their tragedy is that their emotional patterns and responses, their hopes and fears, have been inherited by them from generations of folk who lived in a reasonable secure world that was itself an important part of an ordered and not unfriendly universe; and that they themselves know that they do not live in such a world, such a universe, and have not even the pleasure, derived from intellectual conceit, of those philosophers who gleefully prove that we are merely a bit of scum on the face of a cooling cinder. They are no longer children of God, and are not yet contented and unwondering big bees and ants. Not having gone into these questions thoroughly, not having reached pure rationality, they still feel that there are mysteries, vast unfathomable gulfs in which birth, love, death are created out of darkness and inexplicable light, but now they are out of touch with any possible explanation of these mysteries, any explorations of these gulfs; the old accounts of these things they instinctively reject, the new have not arrived; and no sooner does anything of real importance happen, something that a dynamo or an internal combustion engine cannot work, than they are back in the wilderness with only the bleached bones of prophets to comfort them. So they climb to their attics, eyes pricking and burning, stare into the deeper darkness of their closed eyelids, and are tormented by vague moving shapes of fear and despair. As this youth was.

III

IT was Saturday evening, and the house in Slater Street fairly shook with noise. All the Salters were there except Nellie, still busy in the toyshop. And various friends of the Salters, who had called for them, were there too. Dad's pal and fellow bowling expert, Mr. Grimble, was there, sitting in the kitchen, smoking a calabash pipe, and talking so incessantly in that deep bass voice of his that it seemed as if a circular saw were cutting its way through the house. In the sitting-room, securely wedged between the piano and the fireplace, was Mrs. Salter's oldest and fattest friend, Mrs. Watson, and she was talking at the very top of her voice to Rose's friend, Alice. Mrs. Salter herself was shouting to everybody in the house. Fred was singing lustily and out of tune, as he washed and dressed for the noble ordeal of a night at the Greyhound Track. On the bedroom floor, Dad and George, squeezing their necks into tightish collars, bending purple-faced over their boots, were still continuing a loud argument about the county cricket team, yelling through open doors across the landing. The radio was giving the whole house, and several of its neighbours, some valuable agricultural advice, oddly mingled with the shrill music of a quintet. Only Rose, standing before the small and treacherous mirror (it had a trick of making you look yellow and rather blotchy) in her bedroom, was quiet. Indeed, she was grave, concentrated. This was a serious moment.

During this last week, Alice Hargreaves, who was given to this sort of thing, had met and at once fallen for a new young man, a most generous and dashing young man, who worked in a bank and lived in one of those semi-detached bungalows out on the Leeds road, and whose name was Gregory Porson. Now of course Gregory Porson had a special friend, also in the bank, and a chap you could not help liking, and Alice had a very special friend, Rose Salter, so what could be more convenient and friendly than that the whole four of them should meet and have a good time together this Saturday night? So here was Alice, calling for Rose, who after being out of work all this last week, perfunctorily appearing at the Labour Exchange (Haliford at its worst) and then feeling less hopeful about her future, and not seeing Alice for several nights, was eager for any possible entertainment. Alice had arrived early, and one glance at her told Rose that her friend, normally a rather sallow girl but now so liberally made-up that she looked as if she had a high temperature, regarded this as a very important occasion, when a girl must make the best of herself. They had exchanged only one look and half a dozen words—and no more was safe before the enormous Mrs. Watson, who missed nothing—but they were enough to compel Rose to run upstairs and concentrate upon that wavering image in the mirror. She had put on her best dress, best shoes and stockings, and was now busy with her face. Actually her face needed no attention whatever, for she was not naturally sallow like Alice but had all the fine colouring of healthy youth, a delicate tinting of lip and cheek beyond the craft of cosmetics. Because, years before, just after the War, men had returned to their homes all weary, spiritless, not easily ardent, because the youths who had grown up among women during those war years were hard to inflame, because women everywhere, without saying a single word on the subject to one another, had told themselves that now was the time to call to their aid every device formerly associated only with abandoned creatures of their sex, here was Rose Salter of Haliford working away at her face. By the time she looked several strenuous years older, and appeared to be suffering from nearly as high a fever as Alice, she was satisfied. She had run upstairs, all eager young arms and legs, but now she came down carefully, mincing a little, like a very elaborate, delicate, expensive young lady.

"My word!" cried fat Mrs. Watson, not too pleasantly. "Aren't we fine to-night? Out with the boys, eh? Where is it this time?"

Smiling, but with a touch of disdain, the two exquisite beings, who felt that no matter how long they lived they would never, never turn into such a vast sagging mass of flesh as Mrs. Watson, tripped out, and once free of the cramping atmosphere of home, with its cool stares and ironical comments, they began to talk properly.

"We can go where we like too," said Alice, "because they've got a car. I don't know whether it belongs to Greg's friend or to some other chap who's lent it to 'em, but I know they've got a car. And I know you'll like Greg's friend, Rosie, because he told me all about him the other night and I said then he was just your style, and when I told Greg about you, he said he would be too. And we're meeting them just by Borrowby's. Come on, we're late. I said seven. If we 'urry," she cried, very Halifordish in her excitement, "we can just catch tram."

The tram was full, but they pushed their way in. All East Haliford was descending upon the centre of the town, to shop, to go to the pictures or the music-hall, to drink beer or bottled stout, to walk about and stare. It had been a fine afternoon, but the evening was rapidly overclouding. (They get a lot of rain in Haliford.) By the time they had arrived at the terminus in Gladstone Lane, and Alice had finished describing all her adventures with the miraculous Greg, a few drops were falling, to the disgust of the girls, who had not even brought raincoats. They hurried across to Borrowby's corner, and found the young men standing beside a four-seater that was, with its raking lines and vermilion paint, almost a symbol of the dashing life. Gregory Porson was pink and rather plump, and bore no resemblance to the romantic being of Alice's description. His friend, one Eric Satterly, who displayed a great deal of yellow pullover, seemed to Rose most disappointing. He was rather tall and very thin, with a long knobbly neck and a head so narrow that there had been some difficulty about squeezing his little black eyes into it. He was—and Rose knew the type well—the funny man of the party, and Alice, out of loyalty to Greg and the whole evening, shrieked with laughter every time he made a remark.

"Well," said Eric Satterly, "what shall we do—or go fishing?"

After they had all recovered from this, it was agreed that

the evening was already too wet for that "run round in the car" which had been the first part of the night's programme. The pictures were proposed, and accepted; but the young men thought—and the girls agreed with them—that it would be altogether too tame merely to walk into a Haliford picture theatre, which any of them could visit at any time, without a car. Fifteen miles away, there was a new and super-gigantic Astoria (carefully planned for them by an elderly Polish Jew and a young German-American in an office thirty-five storeys high in New York City), and they would go there. The girls had heard about its wonders, but had never been, and instantly brightened at the suggestion, even though the films they would be shown there might be just the same films they could see here in Haliford. Eric Satterly, who had borrowed the car, was driving, and Rose, now beginning to enjoy herself, got into the seat beside him, leaving Alice to pick up her romance, with many little squeals and giggles and cries of: "You didn't," and, "I'll bet you weren't," and, "You never did?" where she had dropped it on Thursday night. So busy making fun of the other cars and their drivers that he disregarded most of the rules of the road, Eric Satterly piloted them along the fifteen miles of wet tramlines, closed warehouses, melancholy greengrocers' shops, crying children and irritable mothers. In a wonderfully short space of time, this new Astoria, designed to look like a compromise between a Babylonian temple and a gigantic wedding cake, shone and glittered at them. Its great golden mouth was slowly swallowing queues of wettish people. Above them, with melting blue eyes fully a yard in diameter, was the blonde and glamorous head of the latest blonde and glamorous film star. (She was the latest in Haliford, but already they were saying in Hollywood that she was "through".) By going into the select front half of the balcony, they were able to find seats, but had to split up the party, Rose going two rows further back with Eric Satterly, who sat very close to her, whispering his funny remarks into her right ear, and occasionally bringing his sharp bony self much too near.

When she was able to forget the presence of Eric Satterly, and especially his foot, shin and elbow, Rose enjoyed herself. She liked films, and this new theatre was very grand indeed. On and around the ceiling were models of Spanish villages, and clouds and twinkling stars. Floods of golden or mauve light were poured down upon a gentleman in evening dress, who rose from the darkness below to perform upon an elaborate shining keyboard, producing the most astonishing whimpers and thunderings from his vast instrument, which had been designed to do everything except give out one single honest note of music. Then there were the usual news pictures, which told you, with the assistance of a barking facetious gentleman, what was happening in the world, that is, military parades, a flood, a fire, a naval parade, an earthquake, an aeroplane parade, a motor race, a parade of cadets; clearly a world given up both to natural and to man-made violence, a world of disaster and sudden death, a nightmare planet, calmly accepted by Rose and Eric Satterly and two thousand of their fellow-citizens, probably because it never once occurred to them that they were actually living in it.

The big film, starring the blonde and glamorous one, showed them how this girl, who combined in herself the extremes of seductiveness and chastity, attracted the attention of a millionaire, one of those heavy bad-tempered American gentlemen who snarl into three telephones at once, how she allowed him to buy her beautiful clothes, a fine car, any number of theatre tickets, railway and steamer tickets, and how, on a voyage to Europe, he tried to take advantage of her innocence and was successfully repulsed by having his face slapped, and how, finally, she fell in love with a poor young man and made him rich simply by telling him something she had once heard the millionaire say, thereby enabling the poor young man to blackmail the rich old one and to marry her on the proceeds. This chronicle of feminine ingratitude and treachery was received without protest, and indeed with some approval, by the two thousand Yorkshire folk, to whose own lives and ethics it bore about as much resemblance as it did to those of the Man in the Moon, or, for that matter, to the lives and ethics of the people responsible for the film. The moment that the blonde and glamorous one had pursed up her lips for a kiss, the final one with musical honours from the organ, Eric Satterly gave Rose a peremptory nudge and stood up. Out they went then, blinking, into the three-dimensional world, which was darker than it had been but not quite so wet. Alice and Gregory Porson came out too, looking very warm, and reluctantly disentangling themselves, and announced at once that as it was still quite early, only nine o'clock, they might as well run on somewhere in the car. The point was, where?

The two young men loudly announced that they wanted a drink. Alice told them she wanted to dance, and did it as if she was always dancing. Rose said nothing, but tried to look bright and eager about everything, although she was quite ready to go home, as she usually did after the pictures. Then Eric Satterly knew the very place, and challenged his pal Greg to deny that it was the very place. That new roadhouse, "The Ten of Clubs," out on the Bradford–Haliford road. You could dance there, to the music of Jack Haley's Razzle-Dazzle Boys. You could not drink under the same roof, for the authorities in that part of the country like you to do one thing at a time and do not see why you should have everything at once. But "The Ten of Clubs" had been built next door to, only three yards from, that fully licensed tavern, the "White Horse" (the landlord's cousin was the proprietor of "The Ten of Clubs," and the pair of them were laughing at the local authorities), and there you could pop in for a drink. So what about it? Exchanging rather awed glances, the girls agreed. They had never been to "The Ten of Clubs," but of course they had heard of it, just as they had heard of everything new in or near Haliford, except the state of the local trade, the town's debt, the mounting municipal taxation, and other unimportant matters. As they got into the car again, they felt that this was seeing life. Even though she had the bony waggish Eric on her hands, Rose was compelled to admit to herself that she was doing very well. Here was an evening she could refer to for a long time whenever her sister Nellie or any other knock-about girl tried to tell her she had never seen anything. This evening would soon figure pretty freely as "that time we went to the Astoria and then on to 'The Ten of Clubs,' you remember?" As Eric, with a ferocious grinding of gears, hurled the Astoria away from them and then tore through the dusk to the Bradford–Haliford road, she felt more friendly towards him, did not protest when, merely to emphasise a remark perhaps, his left hand left the steering wheel to pat her knee; and she listened indulgently, without disgust or envy, to the heavy breathing and amorous gurgles of the pair in the back seat. It was really exciting when they arrived at the roadhouse, which not only had quite a large number of cars parked round it but had also decorated its exterior with at least twenty coloured lights. She could hear the fascinating throb-throb of the band, the fabulous Jack Haley boys. Here she was, Rose Salter, coolly getting out of a car, going into "The Ten of Clubs." This was almost like living in a film. As she and Alice, exultant though a trifle nervous, went to the ladies' cloak-room, wondering if you had to pay anything or just give a tip, they kept very close together and squeezed hands hard.

They were not allowed to go upstairs at once and dance, however, for having arranged for their admission to the dancing floor, the boys insisted upon first having a drink. So they all pushed their way into the neighbouring "White Horse," which was very crowded, very smoky, very noisy. In the large room, in which they managed to find a tiny table, a tubby fellow with a bald head and beery eyes was thumping away at a piano, a melancholy man, who looked like a dissipated undertaker, was tapping a drum, and a nasty woman, with dyed hair and a contemptible imitation of high-spirited girlhood, was trying to sing. These three were making noise enough, but they were occasionally drowned by the colossal drunken voice of a man in the far corner, who was telling somebody or everybody that he knew "jus' how things are, see?" His only rivals were two solid hard-faced women sitting with two solid hard-faced men; for these women, suddenly and simultaneously, would regularly go off into the most piercing shrieks of laughter. The large room at the "White Horse" was obviously in full swing.

"Well, people," said Eric in his best manner, "what's it to be? Malted milk and cough-drops?"

"This is on me, Eric," said his friend.

"No, old boy, I'll do this. Mother said I had to."

"You *are* a scream," cried Alice, who was very gay. "I'm going to have a cocktail. What about you, Rose?"

So Rose, who knew nothing about cocktails except that life at its gayest was apparently impossible without them, said that she would have one too. Nearly all the younger women in the room were drinking cocktails of a kind, not to help them to get an appetite, for they had had the principal meal of the day long ago, but simply as a stimulating drink. In London and other capital cities, they may drink cocktails only before dinner or supper, but in the provinces they now drink cocktails after their meals, instead of the bottled stout and small ports of yesterday. So the waiter, a leathery old man with a dirty shirt-front, brought two warmish little drinks for the girls, who looked hopefully at the cherries in them, and two tiny whiskies and sodas for the boys; and they all said "Cheerio!"

and "Chin-chin" and "Mud in your eye" (Eric), sat very close (there was no help for that), made fun of the singing woman with dyed hair, and were very jolly. And it was then that the fatal Major Beamish first claimed them. He was a fattish middle-aged man, with a very red face and an enormous ginger moustache that did not seem quite real. He was carrying several drinks, and was trying to push past them, when Eric Satterly looked up at him and said: "Good evening, Major Beamish. How's things?" The major, who was not very sober even then, blinked a little, stopped, and then recognised both young men.

"Well," said the major heartily and rather thickly, "if it isn't young Satterly and young Porson. Boys, I'll tell the bank." All three roared at this, while Alice and Rose listened in a dignified ladylike manner, occasionally sipping their cocktails. "Never knew you lads got out this way. Here, we must have a drink to celebrate this." And he dumped all the drinks he was carrying on their table, then put one hand on Eric's shoulder and one on Alice's, leaned over and beamed down on all four of them. "Nice girls, too. I like nice girls."

He was introduced to the nice girls, who looked—and felt—rather startled. Then he insisted upon their health being drunk at once, and the young men had to finish their miniature whiskies and start on the larger ones he had brought with him. The girls refused to join in this, and continued to sip their cocktails.

"I'll tell you what," he confided to them. "I've got couple o' fellas over there—don't amuse me, don't amuse me at all, at all—and when I've got rid of them, we'll all have a nice little party—what you say?"

The young men were clearly flattered by the suggestion, but one of them, nudged by Alice, told him that the girls wanted to dance first.

"Certainly, certainly," said the major gravely, as if he had now been appointed master of ceremonies for the evening. "Go and have a nice little dance. Couldn't do better. No objection at all. You dance while I get rid of these fellas. See you later, boys. See you later, girls." And off he went.

"Come on," said Alice. "We came here to dance."

"But d'you know who that was?" said Greg, as they pushed their way out. "That was Major Beamish—of Beamishes', y'know."

Although the major had seemed absurd and half tight, the two girls exchanged awed glances now, for the Beamish family had been manufacturers in a big way in Haliford for over fifty years, and counted among the local aristocracy. Mr. Salter would no more believe that his daughter had been asked to have a drink by a Beamish than he would believe she had been offered a civic reception by the Mayor and Council.

"Of course, the major—he's a lad, isn't he?—isn't one of the big pots of the family. He's Sir Henry's nephew. Comes into the bank sometimes," Greg concluded.

"And can't he shift it!" Eric added, not without respect, as one heavy drinking man of the world paying a tribute to another. "We'll have some fun with him when we go back. D'you remember that night we saw him down at the 'George,' Greg? Oh, what a night!"

The girls, though a trifle uneasy about this drinking in high life, feeling a little out of their depth, could not help regarding their escorts, now marching them up to the dancing floor, with increased respect; and the look that Alice gave Rose said plainly, "What did I tell you? I'm showing you something, eh?" and the look that Rose gave Alice replied, "Yes, you are, and we're going to have an awful lot to talk about afterwards, but I'm just a bit uneasy;" to which Alice's final glance said, "Don't be silly, Rose. We're having a grand time." Which brought them to the top of the stairs and on to the dancing floor.

The room itself was a fine medley of red-and-black beams, paper festoons, coloured lights, large outlines of Mickey Mouse, the bright dresses of girls, damp and crimson-faced youths, and the mixed smells of face powder and warm bodies. Jack Haley's boys, all in blue jerseys and white trousers, had been resting, but now, as if heartened by the sight of Rose's eager face, they hastily returned to their saxophones and drums, and at a languid yet masterly signal from Jack himself they swayed enchantingly into one of the tunes of the moment called "Kissing Your Hands." Somewhere inside Rose's head a rocket went up and burst: it was so lovely. Her life seemed to move to the rhythm and timbre, now perky, gay, now exquisitely slow and melancholy, of these little popular dance tunes; and so did the lives of millions of other young creatures, all over the world. If the future historian of our age does not devote a section of his work to the consideration of these tunes, he will not know his business. They are among the great social phenomena of our time. Like colossal butterflies, they go winging their idle frivolous way, past all national boundaries, past all the ranged battleships, tanks, bombing planes, successfully defying even the strongest dictators. Cunning little experts meet round a piano in Hollywood, Broadway, Charing Cross Road, play, listen, revise, bargain, sign contracts, and out from them, into picture theatres, radio stations, dance halls, restaurants, gramophone shops, go these easy strains, half-creating and half-expressing the mood of the moment, now in New York and London, now in San Francisco, Paris, Rome, Buenos Ayres, now in Shanghai, Melbourne, Rio, Stockholm, Madrid, Cape Town, and Calcutta. Strictly considered as pieces of music, they are contemptible; they cover the earth, but their lives are short; but while the dance bands of the world are strumming, moaning and whimpering away at them, their influence upon human destinies, catching and dominating as they do men and women in their easy amorous moods, must be so staggeringly vast that no contemporary mind could estimate it. Let the future historian tackle the job for us.

To the swimming enchantment of "Kissing Your Hands," followed by the livelier enchantment of "See Them Feet" and "Who's Your Goosy-Gander?" Rose did her best to dance with Eric Satterly, who like so many of your long thin fellows was much too springy and jerky and Jack-in-the-boxy to be even a tolerable partner. His bony arm dug into Rose's back. His knobbly knees kept knocking against her thighs. He had too many feet. His eyes seemed to be closer together than ever. It was difficult to forget he was there, but Rose did what she could about obliterating him, for she loved dancing, and though Jack Haley and his boys were by no means at the top of their profession, and may indeed be considered somewhere near the bottom of it, their dance music was so much better than anything she generally heard that it seemed to her as near perfection as one had a right to expect in this world. So when she could forget Eric Satterly, and all the people he bumped her into, and the dancing was something between her and the Haley boys, she was very happy indeed, closing her eyes and moving in a rhythmical trance, into which there came, now and again, a vague masculine figure most painfully unlike her present partner.

As soon as Jack Haley's boys left their platform and the floor cleared, the young men insisted that the four of them should return at once to the "White Horse," which would be closing very soon. Alice, anxious to please, made no objection, and quickly nudged Rose as she saw her hesitate. The nasty woman with dyed hair was no longer visible or audible, but the tubby pianist and his melancholy friend were still hard at it, with a great many empty beer glasses encircling their feet. The major, who appeared to have grown during their absence, moustache and all, was just inside the room, leaning over three people at once to talk to a fourth. He greeted them as if they were his oldest friends, practically took them all in his arms, breathed a good deal of whisky over them, and then, there being no vacant table, swept them out of the room altogether, made a way for them, by sheer charging bulk, through the crowd round the bar outside, and ended by pushing drinks of his own choosing into their hands. Rose found herself with a tumbler of gassy colourless liquid that looked harmless enough, and as she was thirsty after dancing in a hot room, she took a good drink. It had a rather bitter flavour and was stronger than it looked.

"That's right," shouted the major, patting her on the shoulder. "Gin and tonic. Good for li'l' gals. Where's my whisky?"

So this was gin and tonic, Rose reflected, having heard of it before. Well, she was living and learning.

"Nah, wait a minute, wait a minute," a man shouted in her ear. He wore a bowler hat too small for him and no collar and tie, and even when sober would have looked like a comedian. "I'm asking you, understan', you're not asking me. *I'm* asking *you*. Give me the name—that's all I ask, the *name*—of any county cricketer that ever took seven wickets in his first match. An' I'm not arguing—I'm asking."

"Charlie Chaplin," roared the major, without being invited to join in the discussion.

The earnest questioner resented this. He turned quickly, so that Rose now found herself within three inches of his bowler hat. "Nah, don't try to be clever, mister, don't try to be clever. I'm asking our friend 'ere a sensible question, see, and if you've got a sensible answer, all right. If not, put a sock in it."

The major retorted loudly that he never put a sock in it, and was at once involved in a tempestuous idiotic row. Rose, trying to get a few inches further away from it, went into somebody behind her, was the cause of some valuable liquor being spilt, and received some of it on the back of her dress. She was now separated from Alice and the two young men, whom she could see a few yards away, apparently all talking at once. But everything was rather unreal, as if either she or everybody and everything around were not properly there at all. She felt a finger rubbing along her arm and looked down upon a little old man, whose veins stood out from his yellow face and whose sharp nose and chin seemed to be dripping with drink. Having attracted her attention, he wagged his head at her.

"Nay, lass," he said sadly. "Nay, lass. Ye're young an' ye're bonny, so get along home wi' yer afore ye're sorry for yerself. Ah've known a deal o' queer things happen to a young lass like yerself when she's ta'en a drop or two in suchlike places as this. By Gow, Ah have! Hee hee hee hee!" And, cackling away, he put his shrivelled dirty hand over her wrist, and came closer. She shook him off violently, as if he were a spider; and, indeed, he was not unlike one. At that moment, several voices from behind the bar called: "Time, gentlemen, please!" and kept on calling variations of this theme, while a loud protesting party on this side of the bar, led by the major, demanded further drinks. She pushed her way through to Alice and the others, arriving at the same time as the major, who could not get his drinks and was disgusted with the whole "White Horse" establishment. It was he who shepherded them outside.

"Now, boys! Now, girls!" he began, forcefully and yet with an undertone of melancholy appeal. "You're coming with me. Yes, you are—with me. Where? To my house—

jus' down the road. Wha' for? To have a las' li'l' drink together. I'm all alone there. All alone," he repeated, with an effect of great pathos. "Come on, boys and girls, don' let the ol' major down."

"Thanks, major," said Gregory Porson, who obviously wanted to go. "Shall we?"

"Let's," replied Eric Satterly.

"What do you say, Rose?" asked Alice.

"No—thanks—I'd rather not, if you don't mind," Rose stammered, feeling very uncomfortable.

"Wha', wha'!" cried the major, astonished and pained. "A beautiful li'l' gal like you, an'—an'—refuse my invitation—jus' for one las' li'l' drink—to cheer us up—oh, come now, Rose, Rosie, li'l' Rosie-posie—don' spoil it——"

"No, come on, Rose," said Alice. "Don't spoil it. If you won't go, I can't——"

"Oh, all right, Alice."

The major had a car (and nobody told him he was in no fit condition to drive it) and they arranged that he should take Alice and Greg with him, and that Eric Satterly, who knew where the house was, should follow in the other car with Rose. Eric had parked his car in a rather dark corner, and when he and Rose arrived there, he promptly wound his long thin arms round her and began kissing her. He did not reach her lips because she managed to keep them away from him.

"What's the idea?" said Eric, annoyed by this lack of enthusiasm. "Don't you like kissing?"

This was a difficult question to answer. If she had been

determined to be truthful at all costs, she could only have replied: "Yes, I like kissing, but not with you." As this would have been rude, she could only mutter that she supposed she didn't like kissing, thereby giving him the impression that she was a prudish little creature. It was all very difficult and irritating, as this kissing business so often was. Rose and her friends had no exact code of behaviour in these affairs, but it was understood among them that if a youth took you out for the evening, spending good money on you, he should be allowed a reasonable amount of hugging and kissing, so long as he was not absolutely repugnant. (And unfortunately one's friends' friends' friends were apt to be.) The length he could go was, of course, determined by his own charm and your own mood. With Rose, who was much cooler and less awakened than she looked, they did not get very far, but were rarely repulsed right at the beginning, if only because she was both conscientious and good-humoured and liked to do what was right and reasonably pleasing in this as in other matters. Eric seemed to her a very unattractive young man; she did not want any physical contact with him whatever; but he was her host for the evening, she did not want to see him sulking, and so she suffered his bony grasp and dabbings and peckings without protest.

But after a minute or two more of it, she pushed away and said: "Come on. They'll wonder where we are."

"Oh, all right." He was sulky now, of course. It was queer how soon they turned sulky. One minute they talked as if they wanted to give you the earth; the next minute, they were sulky. Well, let him sulk.

"Strikes me," he grumbled, on their way to the major's house, "you've a lot to learn, Miss Rose What's-it. You look all right. Matter of fact, you're a pretty kid, a very pretty kid. But you're no sport."

Rose did not reply. She was rather cross and a bit sad, for she did not like to be told, even by this chap, that she was no sport. She was anxious to be a sport, within reason. Perhaps some day she would be. But he must not be so long and bony and have beady little eyes so close to the top of his nose. And, although the evening had had its splendours, she felt slightly annoyed with Alice for landing her with this chap. They arrived at the short curved drive of a detached house, no bigger than most of the houses in this part of the country, but definitely bigger than any house occupied by Rose's friends and relations. The major was standing in the open doorway, roaring a welcome. They followed him into a grand lighted hall, with several doors and a fine staircase leading out of it. On one side were a lot of sticks and golf clubs, and on the other a barometer and a stag's head. All very posh.

"In there," said the major, who had already given himself another whisky and soda, for he was holding it, "is the dining-room, with drinks. Anything you like—any dam' thing. Your friends are in there, boy. Go in an' help 'self." He gave Eric a slap that somehow turned into a push, which sent him towards the open dining-room door. Then he turned to Rose, and with the immense gravity of the man who thinks he can carry his liquor, he goggled solemnly at her and said: "My dear, want to show you something. Very in'er'es'ing for you, this. Picture in drawing-room. Ex'rornary resemblance. Puzzling me all night."

Then he took her firmly by the arm and saying no more led her down the hall, past the bottom of the stairs, into a dimness beyond, where he marched into a mysterious large room only illuminated by the distant ruin of a fire. He left her alone, wondering and breathing rather hard, and then went to fall over one or two small pieces of furniture and to damn and blast them in a loud whisper, until at last he turned on a shaded electric light in a standard lamp in the far corner. The room looked very nice. It had a grand piano, some very large easy chairs, lots of pictures, and a very thick carpet. There was neither time nor light enough to see what else it had, for now the major returned, impressively silent, and led her forward by the arm again, as solemnly as if she were a bride being led to some invisible altar. "There y'are," he cried triumphantly, showing her an oil painting that was hanging quite near the solitary light. It was a painting of an Italian-looking girl staring over a kind of marble balcony, with a lot of very blue sea behind it. Quite a pretty picture, Rose thought, but could not understand what it had to do with her, though she was flattered—and relieved too after these mysterious movements about the strange house—to think she had been specially chosen in this manner.

"Don' you see?" cried the major, grasping her arm with one hand and indicating the picture with his whisky glass. "Don' you see?"

"It's—very pretty," she stammered.

"Yes, yes, yes. But who is it? Tha's point. Who is it?"

Conscious of her deficiencies as an art critic, she murmured that she didn't know.

The major, who had sounded almost angry a moment ago, now chuckled, and as if out of pure amusement and a happy absence of mind, released her arm only to put his own very heavy arm round her shoulders. "You," he cried triumphantly. "No doubt about it. Abs'lutely you, my dear. Saw it at a glance. Living image. Marv'lous!"

Rose could see no resemblance, but did not like to say so. The major, begging her to examine it more closely, brought his face nearer to hers, so that she could feel his enormous moustache tickling her cheek and was drowned in a reek of whisky and stale cigar smoke. And the arm about her shoulders was very heavy indeed, and would take some removing. "When I saw you," said the major, rather sadly now, "I said, 'Now where have I seen tha' beau'iful li'l' gal before?' I said. An' then I said, 'Why, tha's same beau'iful li'l' gal I have in tha' picture at home,' I said. An' there y'are. Jus' the same. Marv'lous!"

And now he did take his arm away, but only to lurch forward and drop into the nearest big chair, into which he collapsed and then took a reviving draught from his tumbler. The next moment, he had somehow contrived to reach out and take Rose's hand and to pull her nearer to his chair. She suffered this and said nothing, but kept on wondering hard, and was nervous, taut. He squeezed her hand, and pulled her nearer still, so that now she was standing, rigid, by the arm of his chair. She murmured something about going to see what the others were doing.

The major dismissed this. "Le' 'em alone. They're

enjoying themselves—in *their* way. We'll enjoy ourselves—in *our* way. Jus' sit here," giving her a little tug. "An' don' worry. You're all right, li'l' gal, quite all right. There, si' down."

Wondering what would happen next and how to get out of this without a fuss, Rose did sit down on the very edge of the chair arm. The major still held her hand; his own was very large and hot; and she wished he would take it away.

"D'you like Haliford?" the major suddenly demanded.

This was better. "Well, no—not very much," she replied, hesitating a little, because after all the major was a Beamish and might be offended by any slur upon a town so closely connected with his family.

"You're abs'lu'ly right. Very sensible li'l' gal as well as beau'iful li'l' gal. Haliford's in my opinion—for wha' it's worth—a hell-hole." This seemed to depress him and he sank lower into his chair and comforted himself by playing clumsily with Rose's shrinking fingers. He muttered something about the place being full of dirty little money-grubbers, and then, feeling the need for a further revival, swallowed the rest of his drink. This made him suddenly sit up, and he released her hand and, before she could move, put his arm behind her and crushed her against his shoulder.

"I say—please—don't," cried Rose, dreadfully embarrassed. If he had been one of her own set of youths, she would have known more or less how to deal with him, but his age, social prestige, and present condition all made it difficult for her.

"Don't! Don't! Don't!" The major repeated these with a kind of fierce contempt. "Y'oughtn't to talk like that, li'l' gal, not here—to me." He was sad again now. "Poor ol' Bob Beamish, tha's all. Wouldn't you like to make poor ol' Bob a happy man? I'm not a happy man, y'know, my dear," he added earnestly. "Probably you think I'm happy man. Well, I'll tell you a secret—jus' between ourselves—now. I've been very—ve-er-y unhappy mis'rable devil. Until—when? Till I saw you to-ni'. Then I said to myself, 'There's beau'iful gal in picture at home come to life.' An' I'll bet—I'll bet any mortal thing—you'd like to kiss me for saying that, wouldn't you?"

Rose said she wouldn't, in as nice a way as possible. She did not want to hurt his feelings, and apparently he was very easily hurt. Idiotic as he was, she could not help feeling rather sorry for him, and would have felt even more sorry for him if he had not kept her pinned to his shoulder, sprawling ridiculously over the arm of the chair. He burst into a loud protest.

"No, listen," she said, trying to free herself. Something seemed to be happening outside. It was happening a long way from them, in this far corner of the house; and the major himself was so noisy, it was hard to hear anything but him; but she was certain she had heard angry voices, doors being slammed. She told the major so.

"Wha'? Nonshense!"

"I must be going."

"No, no, no. Your frien's having li'l' argument. I'll see."

He let her go so quickly that she had hardly time to

recover herself before he had gone blundering out of the room. She drew several deep breaths, stood up, then sat down again on the arm of the chair out of sheer indecision. She did not know what to do. What was happening? The major had closed the door behind him. She was a very small forlorn object in this large dim-lit room. There were sounds of voices, angry voices, again. All she wanted to do now was to run away, but she did not like the idea of wandering about this strange house by herself, and also she was afraid of walking straight into some nasty piece of business—she did not know what—somewhere beyond that door.

That door was now flung open. But not by the major. The figure standing there was that of a woman. The next moment, Rose saw her quite plainly, for the woman had switched all the lights on and had produced an almost indecent glare in the place. It was nothing, however, to the glare she produced for Rose's benefit. She was a thin, smart-looking woman in her forties, and she had been angry when she had switched on the lights and now that she had clearly seen Rose, she was angrier still, a fury of a woman.

"Of all the——" she began.

Rose tried to stammer something.

"Get out," the woman screamed. "Go on, get out. I don't know who you are and I don't care. Just get out, that's all. If you don't, I'll send for the police."

Trembling all over, Rose shakily walked to the door, where the woman drew back to let her pass, and very ostentatiously drew back as if Rose might have the smallpox or something. As Rose turned to go up the hall, she heard the woman behind her damning all impudent little hussies, but did not attempt to reply. There was no sign of the major. At the door of the dining-room, where Alice and the two young men had been, involuntarily she slowed up, but something told her at once that they had gone and it did not need another screaming: "Get out, go on" from the woman behind to make her hurry to the front door, which was immediately and noisily locked and bolted behind her. She remained a few moments in the shelter of the porch, for it was raining again, and very dark outside. Tears of humiliation and vexation came now. She felt lost and hopeless. All the people who had insisted upon her coming to this miserable house had vanished. It was late—midnight at least—and she was miles and miles from home, with nothing but a thin dress on (her best too), and of course it was dark and pouring with rain. She took a step or two forward, and was instantly rewarded by having a few cold drops find their way down her neck. This changed her humiliation and self-pity into anger. She was angry with that woman (and for two pins would have rung the bell and told her so), with the sloppy whisky-sodden major, with Gregory Porson and Eric Satterly and Alice, who had run away and left her in the lurch. She could have brained the lot of them.

So angry now that she was careless of the rain, she set out to walk more or less in the direction of Haliford, ten miles away. Sooner or later on this road, she would find a late bus, that is, if it did not simply go splashing past her in the dark. She had not gone more than a few hundred yards, however, though they were a particularly dreary wet few hundred yards, when she noticed the lights of a car behaving curiously a little way ahead. They were indecisive lights, these; now they shone this way, now that, until finally they turned and came slowly towards her. She hurried towards them, furiously hoping. Yes, the car stopped when she was in the full glare of the lights. The next moment, she was being pulled into the back seat by Alice, who was as angry as she was.

"I thought you'd all gone for good," Rose began, breathlessly.

"Well, we didn't know what to do," Gregory began explaining. He sounded sulky.

He was cut short by Alice, clearly out of temper with him. "You just drive us home as quick as you can," she commanded. "And never mind any more talking."

"All right," he grumbled, "but it wasn't our fault. How did we know——?"

"Oh, shut up, and get on with it," said Alice. The car was turned and went roaring towards Haliford. Alice came closer to Rose. "Oo, you are wet, aren't you?"

"Of course I'm wet," replied Rose shortly. "You'd be wet if you'd been walking out there. Why did you leave me?"

"Well, you see, we were in that dining-room, waiting for you and that major to come back, and then suddenly that woman came in—I suppose she was his wife—and turned us straight out, and we didn't know where you were, and she just marched us out. Where were you, anyhow?"

"He was showing me a picture, and then—being silly."

"You didn't like him, did you?" asked Alice.

"Like him! Of course I didn't like him. I didn't want to go there, did I? Silly old drunk, like that! And then—to be turned out—just as if——!"

"I know, Rose. I'm sorry."

"I should think you are."

"It's their fault," said Alice, indicating the two young men in front, "for introducing us to him at all, and then making us go there. Major Beamish!"

Eric Satterly turned round. "Well, how did we know——?"

"I'm not talking to you," said Alice sharply. "You get us home. That's all you've got to do. And go to Slater Street first. Rose is nearly wet through."

No more was said. They were all tired and cross. Rose did not thank either Alice or the young men for her evening, but said a quick "Good night," then ran in. Fortunately, the Salters were never in any hurry to get to bed on Saturday night, and she found her father, mother, Nellie and Fred (George was still out somewhere) all drinking tea and eating jam pasty over the kitchen fire.

"And this is a nice time to be coming home," cried Mrs. Salter. "And look at your dress, you silly monkey!"

"Where've you been?" asked Nellie, with the patronising interest of the older sister, who had been everywhere in her time.

"We went with two boys to the Astoria, and then to 'The Ten of Clubs.'" Rose was offhand about it, not deliberately but because by this time she felt offhand about it.

Nellie was impressed. "You're not doing so bad, are you?" Normally Rose would have been pleased, but now she did not care. She accepted a cup of tea and found a slice of bread and butter, got near the fire to warm and dry herself, but in spirit did not join the family group.

"I've made a few enquiries," Fred began solemnly, "and it's my belief that if you'll just wait a week or two, I can get you a job on that Tote up at the Track."

"And I've told you already, Fred," said Rose, trying not to sound too ungrateful, "I don't want it."

"Well, my little madam," said her father, not without affection, for he was proud and fond of Rose, "what do yer want, eh?"

Rose hesitated a moment. "If Alice Hargreaves goes to London and she can get me a job there, I shall go," she finally announced. "I've had enough of Haliford. And now I'm going to bed. Good night, mother. Good night, father. Good night, you two." She included Nellie in her good nights, although Nellie shared the same bedroom, because she was determined to hurry through her undressing and to pretend to be asleep when her sister came in. She did not feel like answering any of Nellie's searching questions to-night. She still burned at the thought of that woman who turned her out. So—"Good night, all. Good night."

IV

A FEW days later, about eleven o'clock on a fine morning, four Daimler cars, oldish but still quiet and serviceable, moved slowly out of Sutcliffe Place, Haliford, and out of the view of several dozen watching eyes there. The first car had unusually large windows and a good deal of silvery metalwork inside, and it contained a number of flowers that had been securely wired together, an expensive, highly polished elm casket with a shining brass plate on it and shining brass handles, and a human body, already in a state of rapid decomposition. In the first of the three cars that followed were Edward Fielding, his mother, and his brother Herbert, looking pale but red about the eyelids. In the next car were five relatives, who looked sad but only pinkish about the eyelids. And in the last car of all, rather crowded, were more relatives, who looked solemn but comparatively cheerful, with eyelids the usual colour. They were all on their way to the enormous Haygarth Cemetery, where thousands upon thousands of Haliford citizens lie buried, under various tokens of affection and esteem in marble, granite, gilt and metal, resting—as we are assured there on every side—in peace, but nevertheless silently menacing the health and happiness of their survivors as year after year of Haliford's heavy rainfall seeps through their rotting remains. Mrs. Fielding had called in one of the town's best undertakers, Mr.

Verrey, who was now sitting with the driver at the front of the hearse and exchanging remarks with him in a sort of ventriloquial fashion, each man freely expressing himself, and perhaps telling a good story, while keeping a straight and professionally woeful face. Mrs. Fielding and Mr. Verrey between them had spared neither expense nor trouble to make the late Mr. Fielding's final passing as hideously impressive as possible, and if they had been a couple of mad tragic Elizabethan dramatists, a Webster and Tourneur, they could hardly have worked more cunningly. Only Death, with his dreadful raven-black trappings, his coffins, his tributes of sickly-smelling lilies, his yawning graves, his massive marble or granite tombstones, is welcomed with such pageantry and poetic symbolism in places like Haliford, where all the rites and ceremonies that belong to Life are merely shuffled through and have drearily dwindled. But Death still commands and receives his due of costume and ritual. The very poor save their shillings and pence, freely denying themselves, against his coming. It is the only poetry left them.

Sitting with his back to the coffin, Edward watched the familiar streets glide by, a little like the scenery of a dream. He had passed the peak of his sorrow some days ago. His father had gone now. This was only a dreadful sort of tidying up. Since the actual death, he had been halted on a plateau somewhere between the agony of final separation and the plain below of normal life. This day of the funeral was very queer, half a holiday and half a nightmare. It was like having a temperature. Everything done and said was further away, not quite real. He felt very lonely. He had plenty of acquaintances, chaps he could walk up the road or go to the pictures with, but no close friend, to whom he could talk freely. (His best friend, Albert Marsden, had recently gone out to India as a wireless operator, and this had left him lonelier and more dissatisfied than usual.) He felt further away from his mother and Herbert than ever. Since his father had disappeared into that bedroom for good, these two had been closer than before, and he felt that they excluded him. Only this morning, when he had grumbled about something, they had both accused him of having no proper feelings, whereas it seemed to him that he had the proper feelings and they had none, for they were only being smug and were, in a way, enjoying all this horrible business. The very sight of Herbert in his new neat black suit, the complete mourner, irritated him. Nobody spoke in the car. It is a good four miles from Sutcliffe Place to Haygarth Cemetery, and they travelled at the regulation funeral pace: he had plenty of time to think. Also, to watch the men they passed solemnly raising their hats. How pleased his father would have been if a few of them had raised their hats so respectfully to him when he was alive!

At the main building in the cemetery—which seemed a pleasant spot this fine morning, with birds singing everywhere, and a richer green, fed by the bones below, on all sides—they got out of their car, and stood apart from the group of further relatives and friends of the family who had not gone to the house. Mr. Verrey and his assistant came and beckoned, and then they headed a slow procession to the open grave, where the assistant, apparently afraid of their missing the least sensation, almost pushed them to the very edge. The minister from Mrs. Fielding's chapel, a broad gloomy Scotsman much more at home now than he was when trying to preside gaily over a tea and concert, conducted the service, pronouncing the beautiful words of our despair and hope very slowly and distinctly, as if for the benefit of the unbelievers present. One of them, Edward, was now clenching his hands until his nails hurt him, though he did not realise until afterwards, when there was no longer a coffin to stare at, down there in the clay, how deep they had gone into his flesh. They returned to the main building again, and now people began talking, as if they felt life flowing back into them once more. It was queer looking at the people. There were relatives he had not seen for years and years; strange figures out of the dimming epic of his childhood, figures from half-forgotten Christmases, fantastic and incredibly old great-aunts and uncles that had once seemed like giants, looming in corners during old Boxing Day family parties, and now almost shrunk into dwarfs. One or two of them spoke to him, but only until they could command the attention of his mother, who was much in demand as the chief character of the funeral. The only person who really talked to him was not a relation at all, but an old friend of his grandfather's, Jonathan Crabtree, the owner of a small woolcombing mill just outside Haliford. Edward was surprised to see him there. He did not appear to know anybody or want to know anybody, and, in defiance of all possible conventions, he had lit his pipe, which, like himself, was old, short, gnarled and tough. He was one of those West

Riding men of the old school who know very well that they are characters, and enjoy—more and more as they get older—playing the character parts allotted to them.

"An' you'll be Edward, Ah'm thinking," he said, after giving Edward a sharp poke on the shoulder, coming very close and puffing very strong smoke in his face. "Ah well, yer father's not lived so long after *his* father, yer grandfather, lad, has he? Ah said to me-sen, nobbut a few weeks sin', when Ah saw him at t'club, that he wor looking poorly then, but Ah nivver thought it 'ud finish him so quick. But he nivver had staying power, yer father hadn't. He worn't man yer grandad wor, nowt like, though Ah'm saying nowt agen him 'cos Ah liked him a lot better nor a lot o' fowk did."

"Yes, I know, Mr. Crabtree," said Edward, for something of the kind was obviously expected of him. His gaze wandered from Mr. Crabtree's nose, which might have been made of crinkled brownish-red leather, to Mr. Crabtree's tie, black and nearly as thin as a shoelace, and not tied at all but simply held by a metal ring.

"An' that'll be yer brother 'Erbert, eh?" Mr. Crabtree continued, looking about him with sharp little eyes. "Not in t'wool trade, is he? Oh—analytical chemist, eh? Well, he seems a smoothish soart o' chap and fairly pleased wi' his-sen, though what for, Ah don't know. But then Ah know nowt, these days. Ah expect tha's pleased wi' thi-sen an' all, lad, eh? Tha's a fairly well-set-up lad, and fairish looking."

Edward said definitely that he was not pleased with himself, and the old man gave him a shrewd look.

"Ay, well, tha knows best. Nah where is it tha's working? Ah did hear."

"Clewes and Tirril, y'know, noil and waste merchants in Pooley Road," Edward told him, indifferently. His voice always took on an indifferent tone when he mentioned his work, for it bored him and his position there was a poor one, and his prospects were worse.

"Oh ay, Ah know 'em. They're no great shakes, lad. Tommy Clewes's been dead this last ten year, an' Tirril's nowt; he'll nivver carry corn. Ah don't have no truck wi' em me-sen, but Ah did 'ear 'at Frank Tirril wor finding his-sen i' queer street. Tha'll nivver mak' much aht o' yon' lot, lad."

Edward was not slow to admit it. The old man gave him another shrewd look.

"Doesn't look to me as if Fieldings 'll 'ave another wool merchant i' thee, lad. Well, Ah don't know as Ah blame yer. Trade's gone ter nowt, like all good owd trades. Looks to me as if we'll ha' to get our brass i' this country now by makking bits an' bats o' things—wireless sets an' bathing drawers an' tuppenny toys an' suchlike—that yer get bits o' lasses makking during time they're not drinking cups o' tea or pahdering their noses. Laking, Ah call it, not working. Well, Ah mun do a bit, and see after that mill o' mine. Glad to ha' paid me respects, for Ah've known Fieldings a long time and yer grandad wor a right old friend o' mine. An' sitha, lad. You 'old yer head a bit higher. If yer don't do it yer-sen, nobody 'll do it for yer, not even i' these days, when ivverybody tries to pretend they're doing ivverything for ivverybody. Just show a few folk that if they don't like it, they can bloody well lump it. I mun be off."

Edward remembered this conversation next day, when he was back at work. Messrs. Clewes and Tirril, noil and waste merchants, occupied the second floor of a tumbledown, greasy building in that tumbledown, greasy little street, Pooley Road. It was one of those small firms of middlemen that are rapidly being eliminated from the trade. Its personnel consisted of Mr. Tirril himself, who did the buying and selling; Mr. Clark, who did the books and also bought and sold a little; Edward, who helped Mr. Clark and looked after the samples; two underpaid warehousemen, and an office boy who could hardly be said to be paid at all. Edward spent a good part of his day in ticketing samples of noils and waste and then in wrapping up these samples in blue paper and labelling them for the post. He had no expert knowledge of wool, though he had picked up a little loose information about it during the last few years. (And men had made fortunes in Haliford without knowing much more than he did, the lucky gamblers of the old days.) He had no interest in wool, whether in the form of raw wool or tops, noils and waste, and he was heartily sick of standing in front of that long greasy smelly counter of theirs, wearing his check overall (known locally as a "brat"), wrapping up the stuff in that eternal blue paper. The miserable little firm, clinging to the very edge of the solvent trade, had a depressing atmosphere about it. Not a penny had been spent on the office and the warehouse for years; they were stifling in summer and arctic in winter; they had holes in the floor and cracks in the ceiling; everything would have rotted away if it had not been covered with a thick film of grease, not from the noils and the waste, which were comparatively clean, but from the samples of raw wool, and occasional bales of it that found their way into the warehouse and seemed to stay there for ever. It was Mr. Tirril's dream that he could do a trade in raw wool. It was probably his only dream. Mr. Tirril was a sagging middle-aged man who had lost most of his hair and teeth and nearly all hope. He had a wife who was nearly always ill, one not very satisfactory daughter, and a declining business. Edward ought to have been sorry for him and probably would have been if he had not been brought into contact with him all day long. The trouble was that Mr. Tirril was an incessant nagger and grumbler in the office. No doubt he grumbled on 'Change, but at least there were times when he had to pretend to be bright and alert there; probably at home, with an ailing wife on his hands, he had to do his best to appear cheerful; but in his own office he could let himself go, which he did in one of those dolefully flat West Riding voices. There were times when Edward felt that this voice, going on and on and on, a vocal Trans-Siberian slow train, would drive him crazy, that sooner or later he would scream a few oaths and then bring down the heaviest ledger on that uneven bald scalp. He was not even free of Mr. Tirril when the last bundle of samples had been given to the office boy to post and work was over, for if he had a poor night's sleep, he would find himself staring at Mr. Tirril's protruding pebbly eyes and listening overtime to that hopeless nagging drone. No, Edward could not be sorry for him. If there was a God, you could not blame Him for turning Frank Tirril into a dismal failure; indeed, there was no need for any turning, for he had been created for the part. He always expected to fail, and probably would have been disappointed—except in this matter of raw wool—if success had suddenly been thrust upon him.

This very afternoon, he was in one of his most irritating moods. He came back from a round of calls about a quarter to five, and at once fastened upon Edward. "I suppose it's no use me talking, seeing that I only pay your wages, but have them samples gone to Logan's?"

"Yes," said Edward, going on with his work.

"Well, what for?" he demanded, his voice rising for once.

"Because," said Edward, with the tone of a man addressing an idiot child, "you told me to send them, this morning."

"Just listen to me a minute, Fielding, and don't try to be so smart when nobody wants you to be smart—and if you'd be a bit smarter when somebody *does* want you to be smart, you'd do a lot better, though I've just about given up hope. I said—and just remember I'm giving orders here, if you *don't* mind, lad—that we'd get off them samples to Logan's before the day was out, that's what I said and not a word more, and now you've gone and sent 'em off when I want to send 'em some of our new Fifty-Sixes. Well, you can just get on and make a range o' them Fifty-Sixes, and let me see your tickets before you wrap 'em up so that there's no mistake, and if you'd just pay a bit more attention when I'm talking——"

"I did pay attention," Edward shouted at him, maddened by the horrible voice.

Mr. Tirril came so close that Edward could see a strand or two of cigarette tobacco that had lodged itself in his rather long, tow-coloured moustache. "And who," said Mr. Tirril, trying to do a bit of bullying now, "are you shouting at, eh?" Then he dropped back at once into the familiar strain, like a well-worn gramophone record. "Not me, I hope, because let me tell you, I won't have it. You're paid to come here and do as I tell you—and you seem to find that hard enough—and not to start shouting as if you owned the place."

"I did do as you told me," Edward protested, not shouting but still raising his voice a little. "I'm not a thought-reader. You told me to send the samples of the Forty-Eights to Logan's and I sent them. How do I know if you——"

"Now for the last time," said Mr. Tirril, almost passionate, "will you make up that range o' Fifty-Sixes without any more of your lip? Any more of it and you know where to go. Finding money to pay impudent young devils who won't even try to listen," he grumbled away, as he went to the other end of the office, "you'd think there was a boom on 'stead of a slump. Had just about enough of it, yes, and more than enough of it. Some people 'ud have shown you the door a long time since. Here, Clark, what's this about Wetherby's?"

It was a mutinous and sullen Edward who wrapped up those samples, tidied up, asked if there was anything more, grabbed his hat and hurried out into narrow, cobbled Pooley Road, where even now, early on a fine summer's night, there was more than a hint of winter gloom, of mud and sleet and darkness to come. All the people he passed annoyed him: if they looked as sulky as he did, they reminded him of the cheerless life they were all living; if they hurried along, eager to get home, to clip the grass or the privet, to smoke a pipe over the garden gate, to turn on the wireless, to listen to the military band in the Park, they only threw into relief his own bleak prospects, at home or anywhere else. At the corner, turning into Beckgate, a large blue motor-coach passed him, filled with idiots going to Morecambe. At Jobling's shop—the biggest of its kind in Haliford—the fish that remained on the long slab at the open window flung out strong odours of the seaside, and for a moment he almost tasted the brine and wished he were somewhere by the sea, even at Morecambe. Just past Foxley's, who sold raincoats and were now passionately imploring you to buy one for your holidays, he caught the bus that would take him to the end of Sutcliffe Place. (On a monthly season ticket, it was very little more expensive than the tram, and Edward hated trams, which mysteriously combined in themselves nearly all the things he disliked about Haliford. When you were in a tram, you were really in and of Haliford: it had got you.) The bus was full of middle-aged men staring at the *Argus*, middle-aged women staring at nothing, and a few younger people. Edward gloomily looked them over, so far as that was possible down the length of a bus. There was only one pretty girl, and he knew her by name and sight, and knew that she was deeply and busily engaged to a bow-legged chap at the

Post Office. What she could see in him, Edward could not imagine. The complacent look on her fair face was irritating. Very soon, she and the bow-legged chap would be pushing a pram up the road and into Ackroyd Park, and that, in Edward's present view, would be the end of them. There was nobody else worth looking at. There hardly ever was. Why shouldn't that girl who looked at him that night in the Park be riding in this bus? Why, for that matter, didn't she come back to the Park? Probably too busy walking out with some other bow-legged blighter from the Post Office. Hopeless!

It was a pity that Herbert chose that evening to try—as he expressed it to their mother—and "make some sense out of Edward." The occasion was after supper. Mrs. Fielding had gone to bed early. Edward had been a meaningless and unprofitable stroll, chiefly through places frequented by lovers, who regarded him as an intruder. He returned in the mood in which he had been when he left the office. Herbert, now without question the head of the household, presided over the supper table without saying much, and Edward glanced at the evening paper; but as soon as they had both done, Herbert looked solemnly across at his brother, cleared his throat, and said: "I don't suppose you read that article in the *Post* this morning, did you, Ted? It was saying that it's all nonsense about there being no openings for young men these days. Plenty, it said, for properly trained men. But you've got to have training—oh yes."

Edward grunted and tried to look as if the *Argus* were taking all his attention.

This would not do for Herbert. "Just put that paper down a minute, Ted," he continued, in a kind but firm tone. "I'd like to have a talk to you."

"What about?" Edward's tone suggested that there was no possible topic—or at least none that had ever entered Herbert's mind—that could interest him even for a minute.

"About you—and what you're going to do."

This made Edward wriggle uncomfortably. But he put the paper down, ostensibly to make a better job of lighting a cigarette.

"And that's another thing," Herbert went on, kindly but firmly. "Mother was mentioning it to me, only the other day. You smoke too many cigarettes. Now"—he hurried on, fearing an interruption—"you know I don't mind smoking—smoke myself, in fact——"

"Yes," said Edward bitterly, "we know. Two cigarettes a day, and four on Bank Holidays. That's neither smoking nor letting it alone——"

"It wouldn't do you any harm to let it alone. But that's not what I wanted to talk about. Mother's worried—and so am I—about you."

"Well, you needn't bother," said Edward sulkily.

"It's not a question of bothering," replied Herbert firmly, shaking his head a little, so that his glasses flashed and seemed about to join in the conversation themselves. "We've got to think about your future. After all, you're twenty-three, Ted. And what are you getting at Clewes and Tirril's? Two pounds ten, isn't it? And what are your prospects there?"

Edward managed a small, bitter laugh. "Nix, Herbert, just nix."

Herbert looked business-like, the solid practical man. "All right then—nix. What are you going to do? I know the wool trade isn't flourishing just now—though they tell me it's definitely on the mend—but if you'd done what I wanted you to do, gone to the Technical College at nights to the textile classes, and then gone to night school and learned a few languages——"

"Go on, go on," said Edward wearily. They had fought about this several years ago.

"Well, you'd have had a proper training and by this time you could have left Clewes and Tirril's and perhaps found a good job."

"And perhaps not."

"Other chaps have done it, not much older than you. Look at young Anderson——"

"I don't want to look at young Anderson. Gives me a pain, always did."

Herbert breathed heavily. He did not want to lose his temper. Edward was always at his silliest and worst during these attempts at serious discussion. Herbert knew that his brother was by no means without intelligence, and had actually done very well at his secondary school; but now, after several half-hearted attempts to do something for himself, mostly idiotic things like trying to learn to play the saxophone ("Big Money In Jazz, You Fellows!" said the advertisement), messing about with home wireless sets, even applying for a job as a forester, Edward seemed to him to have drifted into a planless and mindless state of slackness and mere grousing. He only needed to start drinking, as he would inevitably do in a few years at this rate, to make an even bigger hash of his life than his father had done. To Herbert it was all incomprehensible and sickening; he saw his young brother as a foolish child meandering slowly but almost wilfully into disaster; and, like the decent fellow he was, he would rather have made monetary sacrifices himself, month after month, year after year if need be, to give him a proper training for life (like that of an analytical chemist, for instance) than see him mooning and grumbling his precious time away. And now the two brothers looked at one another with the irritable bewilderment of two opposing types, of all the stable and the unstable folk of this world.

"Now, Ted," he began, slowly, impressively, "you've got to be serious for a minute. You're still almost a kid, but soon you'll be wanting to settle down, and then you might realise it's too late. People aren't going to pay you good money unless you can do something that a lot of other people can't do, unless you've had a training."

"I wonder," said Edward, belligerently rather than thoughtfully.

"Don't be silly, Ted."

"I'm not being silly." Nor was he, for even in his short life he had noticed that people did not seem to be rewarded in this careful fashion, that the richest men in Haliford, for example, were not those who had trained hardest to serve their fellow-citizens.

"Well, never mind. The point is, what do you want to do with yourself? You've got no future where you are.

It's not likely you'd do much better for yourself anywhere else in the local trade——"

"Damn the local trade!"

"All right." Herbert was still keeping his temper. He would not be provoked into losing it. "I didn't want to go into the wool trade myself. But I did know what I wanted to do, didn't I?"

"Oh yes," said Edward wearily. "You're a wonder, aren't you, Herbert?"

This was too much. "I'm not pretending to be a wonder," Herbert shouted. "But I knew what I wanted to do, and I did it. And let me tell you that it's been a good thing for this family that I did."

"Well, let me tell you something," Edward shouted, getting up and glaring down at his brother. "And it may surprise you. I know what you think. You think you have a grand time, don't you? You think I'd be lucky if I could find anything half as good, don't you? Well, I wouldn't have your life given, not if it was handed me on a plate, I wouldn't. You don't live, you just exist. I'd just as soon be one of those dummies in pants in Borrowby's window as you. And if I thought I couldn't get anything more out of life than you seem to get, I'd rather pack up and peg out and have done with it. So there!" And out he went.

Herbert stared after him, with deepening lines of horror in his large, pink face. The kid must be mad. He couldn't know what he was saying. What did he want—the earth? An unbalanced type, that's what he was. One part of Herbert kept on repeating that Edward was an unbalanced type, while another part, somewhere behind, rapidly examined the fine, decent, comfortable life of Herbert to discover any possible cracks or flaws in it.

The door opened quietly. Edward came in, but not very far in, a wavering irresolute figure. Herbert looked sternly at him. "Well?" he enquired, sharply.

"I say, Herbert," said Edward in a muffled tone. "I'm sorry I spoke like that."

"I should think so."

Edward shuffled nearer, his hands deep in his pockets, a twisted troubled look on his thin, dark face. When he spoke, he mumbled badly. "I know I must seem a fool to you, Herbert. I expect I am. And I know I must be a nuisance, though I don't want to be——"

Herbert was softened by this appeal. The kid looked so miserable, and after all, even for his age, he *was* a kid. Memories of their childhood, when he was so tremendously the big brother, returned now to Herbert. "That's all right, Ted. No good losing our tempers. And, y'know, I was only talking to you for your own good—or trying to, anyhow. Haven't you any idea what you want to do with yourself?"

"No—not now, I haven't," Edward replied slowly. He looked across at his brother very earnestly. "I can't explain. I would if I could, but I can't—it's all so muddled."

"What is?"

"Oh—everything. And with father—just dying like that—it's only made it worse. Perhaps—I dunno—I want to go away—somewhere." His voice went away, somewhere, just trailed off.

Herbert frowned. "But where? What to do?"

"I dunno." He sounded despondent. "You see, just now I know what I don't want, but I don't know what I do want. There's—it's hard to explain—but there's nothing happening—here, inside me, so nothing's worth the trouble. Don't you understand?"

Herbert shook his head. He didn't. An unbalanced type, that was the only explanation he could offer himself.

"I'll tell you what it is." And Edward suddenly lit up. He had the kind of face that can suddenly light up. "It's just as if I was waiting for something to happen. D'you see?"

Herbert gave this his most serious consideration. Then he shook his head again. "We'd better leave this, for the time being," he said finally. "You're probably still upset, what with one thing and another. But if you ask me, it's a bad thing to wait for something to happen. You've got to do it yourself."

"Yes, I know," and this came almost triumphantly, "but don't you see—until something does happen, something real, I can't even bother doing anything for myself? Listen, Herbert, it'll be all right. Don't worry. And tell mother not to worry too. I'll look after myself, and I won't be a nuisance. Honestly!" And as he said good night, he produced a smile, to which, after an effort, Herbert suitably responded. But they could make nothing of one another.

So Edward waited for something to happen. Every morning, about half-past eight, he caught the bus, plunged into Pooley Road and mechanically did what was required of him at Clewes and Tirril's, ticketing and wrapping up samples, telephoning customers and railway goods offices and road transport companies, helping Mr. Clark with the invoices, and enduring the unending flat whine of Mr. Tirril. In the evenings he wandered about Ackroyd Park or round the edge of the town, saw a film or two at the nearest picture theatre, the Bijou Palace, or lolled at home negligently reading books from the local Free Library, where he was well known to the two overworked women assistants as a young man who did not seem to know what he wanted to read, an indecisive, sulky, maddening young man. Most of the books that Edward took out, books all bound alike in a strong, serviceable and hideous stuff that looked as if it had been made out of the hides of blackened and festering alligators, were works of fiction, and from them Edward learned about other people's lives and discovered how difficult everything was. There were old-fashioned kinds of novels, in which noble young men came into family estates only to find them terribly encumbered with debts and unpaid taxes. Then there were much more up-to-date novels, written in a queer jerky style, in which very clever young men, so sensitive that they could only write or paint or compose music in one particular remote spot in the Balearic Isles, fell in love with three women at once and realised that life was hell. These were the heavies. The others described how superbly fit fellows, with lean bronzed faces, dashed from country houses in Hereford to Geneva, from clubs in Pall Mall to mysterious cafés in Budapest, on the trail of either Bolshevik spies or dope-dealers, or produced a battered corpse or two in the first chapter, made a lot of jokes about the missing head or pulped face, and did not find the criminal until the cleverest detective had demanded the presence of everybody concerned at nine-thirty in the library. To all these masterpieces of thrilling narration, sound characterisation, brilliant description, profound observation, Edward gave the same degree of rather absent-minded attention, just as the Haliford Town Council gave them all the same crinkly black binding, possibly to try and knock the silly nonsense out of them. He could not make up his mind whether life was really like the descriptions of it in these books (which meant that he himself had not begun to live at all), or whether the authors just made up a lot of stuff that had no relation to anything he himself had ever observed, suffered, enjoyed and thought. But it did not much matter. They helped to pass the time. And whatever he was outwardly doing, whether ticketing samples of Mr. Tirril's Fifty-Sixes or going home on the bus, whether reading at home or lounging in Ackroyd Park, this unsatisfactory youth was busy day-dreaming in the most contemptible fashion. Suddenly, it seemed, he invented something—and it was always a very vague something—that brought him two hundred and fifty thousand pounds at least, put his photograph into all the newspapers, gave him a big house on the moors and a flat in London, and enabled him to go on luxury cruises (he knew the advertisements well) round and round the world. Or again, a very beautiful and possibly famous girl—a film star or something—not only came to Haliford, not only wandered into Ackroyd Park, but actually shared his seat there, and forthwith told him all her troubles and allowed him to settle them for her, and then took him away with her into some terrific amorous adventure, all shaded lights and silk cushions and twining white arms and starry eyes. These vague epics went on and on at the back of his mind, like a very shadowy but delightful moving-picture show. And they made the reality of Haliford, the miserable descent into Pooley Road, the wretched transactions with noils and wastes, the bits of cold mutton and tinned apricots and lumpy custard at home, the silly, giggly girls who walked provocatively in pairs round the Park, the very bagginess of his trousers and dustiness of his shoes, seem by comparison a pitiful parody of life, not worth bothering about at all. Something worthy of that inner show would have to happen.

On the second Sunday after the funeral, a fine day with a hint of autumn about it, Edward decided to have a good long walk in the country, setting out immediately after the heavy midday meal, taking a bus as far as the edge of the moors, walking over to some place where he could get tea, then walking back to the terminus again. Living in an area in which all trace of the country has been savagely destroyed, the Haliford folk have a passion for returning as often as they reasonably can to the real countryside, to see if it is still there. By motor-car, by coach and bus, by tram, or bent by dozens over bicycle handlebars, off they go every week-end, every holiday, up into the neighbouring hills, and fortunately—it is the supreme consolation of life there—those hills, being high moorland and of no use to anybody except ordinary human beings in search of happiness, are just as they have always been, enormous tracts of heather, ling, moorland grass, with larks springing up from them and curlews crying over them, naked to the sun and the salty winds, hummocks out of a wild Eden. No sooner are you climbing up to them than Haliford and all its neighbouring towns sink into a mere haze of smoke in the valleys, and it is not long before the towns are clean out of sight and mind. This is probably why Haliford men and women can endure so much and yet still regard you—and the rest of life—with such clear eyes: they have not been living all the time in those black mills, in those tilted rows of little houses that seem to have grown out of the grey rock, in those dark cobbled streets noisy with trams and lorries; but were only yesterday wandering a thousand feet above the town, up on the moors, which have known no slump but have paid a steady dividend of ten thousand per cent for generations. So Edward did the only wise thing we have seen him do yet: he went up on the moors.

There were hundreds of others going that way too, but once he had managed to scramble into a bus and had gone a mile or so afoot beyond its terminus, he could forget about them. From the main road over the moors, where cars and cycles were thick, scores of paths went wandering up and up, and he took one of these and was soon alone. He did not want to be alone, but there was nobody he knew, and nobody he had seen on the way, whose company he preferred to his own; and so he was fairly content. It was a grand afternoon, not too warm to be walking but sufficiently warm to make resting a pleasure. The little moorland path, so clean that it might just have been unpacked from cardboard and cellophane, glittered before him in the sunlight. Above, the heather and ling were in bloom, and were miraculous heights of purple. A breeze continually rasped the bracken and brought sharp scents with it. There was a trilling in the blue air. Alongside the path, a tiny stream gurgled and shone, flashing tiny cascades at him. All his senses, starved by the meagre and all-too-familiar provender of the streets and houses, were handsomely fed, and at once repaid him by allowing his whole being to expand, so that he felt twice the chap who had left that bus below. Now he kicked a stone a few yards with him up the hill; now he hurried along as if the purple summit might burst if he did not reach it soon; now he loitered, looking dreamily at the stream, wiping his moist forehead, taking in enormous deep breaths of that slightly intoxicating air. He sang bits of tunes over and over again, repeated ridiculous little phrases that came unbidden to his mind, and had a dim vision of himself leaving towns for ever, becoming a fine stalking figure of a moorland man, engaged in some easy and not yet defined occupation. It was a grand afternoon.

Once he had passed the first crest, he was fairly on the moors, which shimmered and blazed round him for miles. Haliford might have been at the bottom of the sea. Not a single mill chimney in sight. He might have just walked into an older century. The only buildings still in view were a few distant farmhouses or taverns-cum-tearooms, not to be missed because of their whitewashed walls. There were a few coloured specks of people here and there, and he could still hear the cars groaning and hooting

despairingly away on the main road. His path came int
a broader one, which set out bravely across the bare table
land, as if it knew exactly where it wanted to go. He wen
with it. He had been this way several times before. Quarte
of an hour's walking, this way, would bring him to
sharp dip in the moorland, a valley with a good strea
dashing through it and plenty of rocks, and a tea-room o
two, known as Bilberry Glen. (You could pick bilberrie
there, dye your mouth dark purple with them, or hurr
them home by the basketful to make pies. It was lik
eating a fine day on the moors when you had bilberries.
There would be people, of course, lots of them, but afte
a full hour's solitude, he felt ready for people again
Besides, the Glen was a fine place to lounge about in, an
you could be certain of some tea there. Very soon, th
path began descending, past huddles of grey rock, where
in the shade, young couples were sprawling, half-aslee
or negligently fondling one another or taking stick
chocolate out of silver paper. He turned right where th
path divided, taking the one that led to the bottom of th
Glen, so that he could follow the stream up towards th
tea-rooms at the top. The water, now broadening int
pools, now rippling over toothy little rocks, had attracte
most of the people in the Glen to its side, and they an
their children, who were paddling and screaming to on
another and pretending to fish, were thick around it a
the bottom. Two fattish men, their trousers well rolle
up above their mottled legs, were amusing a large grou
of their friends, well provided with paper bags and bee
bottles, by jumping and splashing. Three young men,

higher up, were throwing stones at a tin can, and not hitting it, perhaps because they were keeping an eye on three young women, who said things to one another in low voices, laughed a lot, and rolled about and showed a great deal of stocking. Their neighbours were four middle-aged women, very carefully dressed in dark clothes, perched on the edge of a dumpy rock, passing a small paper bag of boiled sweets to one another and talking in lugubrious flat voices. Wherever Haliford people are enjoying themselves, there are always these sad middle-aged women, even gloomier than they are at home, and Edward, who did not even try to understand what life might possibly look like to a middle-aged woman, was always puzzled by them. There were other people, too, scolding their children, snoring in the shade of a rock, throwing stones into the water, holding warm hands or snatching sticky kisses, talking about illnesses or house rents, yawning and wondering what time it was. Their presence did not improve the Glen, but it did not spoil it, for there was room under the wide sky for them all; and the sunlight, the glint and blue shadow of the rocks, the flashing stream, the patches of smooth grass that lay about like vivid green rugs, all remained to soften and mellow the most raucous voices and the most idiotic antics. Edward walked among them, the lonely one, always hoping that they would notice that he was an unusually interesting young man, aloof and rather melancholy to the lively people, a gay young spark perhaps to the sad middle-aged women. Actually, he did not seem to be anything to anybody, though one girl (very hot and flushed, with a wide grin and poor teeth) did pass some remark about him to three other girls, and whatever it was, unfortunately they all laughed (silly chumps!), and laughed so heartily that their voices seemed to pursue him up the Glen, so that he wondered, for one horrible moment, if there was something dreadfully wrong with him, something that nobody had ever dared tell him.

It was quieter higher up, where the stream came down through narrow little gorges and there were no pools to play in, and where the path climbed round rocks and left the water to look after itself. He had not once sat down since he had left the bus, and was rather tired. He decided to sit down for half an hour or so, then stroll up to one of the tea-rooms at the top. Looking about for a likely place, he noticed a spot of colour among the rocks still higher, and, moving on, soon saw that it was the dress of a girl sitting there by herself. She had climbed to a sort of natural seat about fifty feet above the stream, a very good place to sit. When he drew nearer, he saw that she was looking down the valley, her head in her hands and her elbows supported by her knees. Apparently he did not exist for her. He was determined that he should, for here was a girl, all by herself, just as he was all by himself, and it was only right that they should have at least one good look at one another. Though he had to leave the path to get anywhere near where she was sitting, there was something of a track, a flattening and whitening of the grey stone, going that way, and so with an elaborately abstracted air, more like a botanist or a geologist than a young man going to look at a girl's face, he moved slowly up this track. It took him finally along a large flat rock a few feet below her. He arrived here at a snail's pace, and more abstracted, more the student of Nature, than ever. At first, he did not even look her way at all, but looked sternly at the opposite slope of the valley. Then, having given Nature her due, he glanced quickly round and up at the girl. And if somebody had just thrown him into the deepest pool of the Glen, he could not have caught his breath so sharply, could not have felt nearer choking.

Her eyes, narrowed to gaze dreamily down the valley, met his look and suddenly widened, were gold in the sunlight. Immediately then, she frowned and looked away again. What was he to do now? He was no girl-chaser, but he had not lived to be twenty-three in Haliford without introducing himself to quite a few of them in his time, and prided himself upon doing it very neatly. But this was different; this was terribly yet entrancingly different. One false move, one severe snub, and he was lost. Yet he felt that if he did not get to know this girl now, he would never get to know her. This was his chance—and, oh, what a chance!—and if he let it go, he was done for. He looked away again, hastily, fearfully, as if she might disappear. He could hear his voice inside, practising opening remarks, silly remarks, a silly voice. Perhaps she was already getting up, preparing to disappear, to vanish for ever. Oh please, please don't go! His head shot round, just in time to see her vaguely smiling in his direction. He kept his head but not his feet. Down he went, sliding and bumping painfully for several yards.

When he got up again, he had two bruised knees, hands scratched and dented with sharp granite particles, and torn trousers. But there she was, not going away, not laughing at him, but looking down with evident concern darkening her eyes. As he brushed the pricking bits of stone off his hands, he looked up and smiled at her. She smiled back at him, a tiny shy smile, but as decisive as a telegram of victory.

Talking was easy now. "That was silly, wasn't it?" But his voice trembled a little.

"Did you hurt yourself?"

"A bit. Not much. I'm not sure." And he laughed, and she laughed, and it was all very easy and friendly. He climbed up and sat beside her, and pretended to examine very carefully his torn trouser-knee. She looked at it, too.

"What can I do with that?" he asked her.

She took the question quite seriously. "You could pin it, perhaps."

"I haven't a pin."

She had several. She gave them to him, but he made such a hash of the job that in the end she had to do it herself, very neatly, too. After that, he lit a cigarette and they sat quietly together, looking dreamily down the Glen. When he had first climbed up there, he had felt exultant, all swelling heart, but now that emotion had gone and in its place was a feeling of deep peace. At last he was so placed that there was nowhere else in the world he wanted to be. Here and now were perfect.

But he had to tell her. "Y'know, I've seen you before. Not very long since."

"Have you?" She was cautious.

"Yes, and I'll tell you where it was. In Ackroyd Park, one night, and I was sitting on a seat and you passed, with another girl. And I've been in the Park lots of times since, but I've never seen you there."

"No," she said, rather carefully, "I haven't been there much lately."

"I thought I wasn't ever going to see you again."

She did not reply to this and did not even look at him. After a moment, he looked at her. She was even prettier now that he was close to her, astonishingly good-looking. Her eyebrows and thick eyelashes were darker than her hair, which was goldeny-brown with strands of bronze in it. Her eyes, very full and soft, were brown, but seemed to have flecks of gold in their depths. Along the curve of her arm and the curve of her cheek above, he could see the faint down catching the light. She was the prettiest girl he had ever seen, he decided, and it was incredible that she should have been there in Haliford all the time without his knowing it. But perhaps she hadn't. He must find out at once. "I say, do you live in Haliford?"

"Yes," she replied shyly, not looking at him.

"Then why haven't I been always seeing you?"

She laughed now. "I don't know. I'm always about. Perhaps you aren't."

"Yes, I am. I live in Haliford too. Always have done. Sutcliffe Place. Know it?"

"Yes." She looked at him, smiled faintly, coloured a little.

"Where do you live?" he demanded, almost sternly.

She hesitated a tiny moment. "Slater Street," she replied softly.

He was rather surprised. He knew Slater Street and she did not look at all like Slater Street. But now, of course, Slater Street was quite different. Even at this moment, far away, its dingy monotonous length was brightening in his imagination, rapidly taking on colour, drama, glamour. No, nothing was wrong with Slater Street.

It was time to learn names now. This is always an ordeal. Only the really insensitive can pronounce their own names quite brazenly, and these two were not insensitive at any time, and at this moment were sitting there without a usual skin or two, almost all quivering nerve-ends. "My name," Edward began, with brave deliberation, "is Edward Fielding. What's yours, please?"

But this was a girl. "Why do you want to know?"

"Well," he blustered, "well—of course I want to know. I want to know all about you. I've—been thinking about—oh, a lot—ever since that night."

"You haven't?" she cried, and suddenly turned on him a face radiant with delight.

"I have—really," he said, almost overwhelmed.

"I don't believe it. You're just—saying it——"

"What d'you mean, I'm just saying it?" he demanded, quite fiercely.

Perhaps it was his tone of voice, or perhaps it was the look in his eyes, that confused her. "Oh, I don't know. Just—for something to say." And then, just when things were in this sad mess, she took her own brave feminine leap out of them. "My name's Rose Salter," she announced.

"Rose Salter," he repeated slowly, as if it were a password into a camp of refuge, which indeed he felt it was. Then he gabbled: "Well, there we are. Rose Salter and Edward Fielding, and we both live in Haliford and we've never met till now and I think it's a rotten shame, don't you? But here we are, and it's a grand day, isn't it? Do you often come here by yourself?"

Now this was what she had been wanting to explain for the last five minutes. A true Haliford girl does not sit alone in Bilberry Glen without some very special reason. Rose was very anxious not to be mistaken for an eccentric or a social failure. So she rushed at once into her explanation, a breathless affair. "No, I've never come here by myself, wouldn't think of it. Only, you see, what happened was I came here with two girl friends and then we met two boys, and they wanted to go with them, and I didn't, because I didn't care for these boys, and so I said to Alice—she's my special friend—'You two go, Alice, I don't want to, I don't like these boys, you know I don't, and honestly I'd rather be by myself, I don't mind a bit being my myself.' And so they all went off—and I was really glad they did too, I didn't mind a bit, it's nice sometimes just being by yourself. And that's how it happened, you see."

To all of which Edward listened solemnly, not missing a single precious word. He knew already that there was nothing that happened to this girl, Rose Salter, nothing that happened in her home, practically nothing that happened in the whole of Slater Street, that would not be important to him from now on. His life was suddenly, enormously enlarged. He had a quick vision of glittering new territories.

"Well, I'm glad those chaps were no good. And I'll bet they weren't either."

"I don't like them. They work in a bank."

"I hate chaps who work in banks," said Edward, who knew very little about them.

"One was called Eric Satterly," Rose went on. "Awful long streak of nothing, he is. A mess, I think."

"I'll bet he is," he said heartily. "Too many of those chaps about," he added, as if the whole place were menaced by long streaks of nothing and messes and sooner or later he would have to do something about it. Then he became a trifle wistful. "But I wish you'd remembered seeing me that night in the Park."

"Oh, but I do," she replied calmly, surprising him for the first of many, many thousand times. "I remember—because you looked——"

"You needn't tell me," said Edward quietly. "I know how I must have looked. Shall I tell you what was the matter?"

"Yes," she said, meeting his seriousness with complete frankness. "I've often wondered."

So he told her about his father, trying hard to put all his complicated feelings into words and glad at last to be able to tell somebody, and whether she understood it all or not, she seemed to understand and sympathise, and it was wonderful talking to that expressive face, seeing those glorious eyes darken and brighten with horror, pity and friendly laughter. By the time the last word had been said, the sun had wandered down the sky, now a very pale pure blue, the rocks were throwing strange shadows, and the lower reaches of the stream below went quivering through golden light. The afternoon had slipped away. No matter how big your Sunday dinner had been, it was now time for tea.

Yes, she was ready for tea too, quite hungry, in fact. It had been a joy to sit talking to her, and now here was joy in a new shape, walking with her up to the tea-room, almost taking charge of her, as if she belonged to you. Edward felt twice his usual size. There were three tea establishments at the top there, one belonging to the inn, and the other two owned respectively by T. Birch and M. Sowden. Edward left the choice to Rose, and Rose, who had tried all three in her time, plumped for Mrs. Sowden. At the back of her cottage was a long white-washed room containing a great many deal tables and chairs, an old piano with a torn comic song on it, three spotted china dogs with immense necks and a severe expression, several coloured texts, and a large photograph of the Haliford Clarion Cycling Club of 1901. There was also a fine confused country smell compounded of white-wash, cows, ham and eggs, and the flower-beds outside the windows. A lot of people had been feeding in that room, which was thick with their used cups and jammy plates, but only a few of them, looking very fat and sleepy, were left, and Edward and Rose had a whole big corner and a window, gay with sunflowers and delphiniums, to themselves. You would have thought that by this time Mrs. Sowden and the plump scarlet girl who helped her would have been tired of feeding people; but no, for when Rose, who believed it to be the woman's duty to put these enquiries, asked if they could have tea, Mrs. Sowden cried heartily: "An' that yer can, love! Whativver yer like!" And she and the plump scarlet girl, who might have been a pair of conjurers, produced plate after plate of white bread and butter, teacakes, buns, pasty, lemon cheese tarts, sandwich cake, and strawberry jam. There were white cups ready to hold a good half-pint of tea, and a teapot big enough for six. What happiness to stare across this richly loaded table and see Rose, pink and bright-eyed, lifting the gigantic teapot! What a magical transformation of life! Young as he was, even Edward knew that here was happiness, that out of the leaden flow of time had miraculously come an hour of pure gold, and now and then, as they ate and drank and passed one another things and made rude remarks about each other's appetite and laughed together and found their bright glances for ever getting entangled, one bit of him would retreat quickly from the scene, almost see the rest of him sitting there so deep in happiness, and would be suddenly sad, as if there came then a glimpse of a future from which this would look like an hour in a lost life.

When they came out again, the moors were nearly black under a sky of flame and wonder. They decided to return the way Edward had come, up the opposite slope, across the ridge, then down to the bus stop. They scrambled over rocks, ran crazily down steep paths, lingered for a while near the stream, which was already murmuring in a little night of its own, manfully strode up the slope together, and then found themselves on the ridge just as the last glow had paled in the west and the stars were beginning to shine through and a cool breeze was springing up and every hollow was filled with blue dusk. They were walking on the top of the world together. Very soon nothing was left in the whole universe but Rose and Edward and a black shoulder of moorland and a glitter of stars. They hardly ever stopped talking all the way, but their talk was only so many ripples and eddies on the surface of their being. Edward told Rose about Clewes and Tirril's, and Rose told Edward about the Keep-Yu-Kozee place (but said nothing of any plan to find a job in London), and they talked about Haliford and Leeds and Bradford, films and band concerts in Ackroyd Park and stories they had read, Morecambe and Blackpool and Scarborough and the Dales, food and shops and clothes and relations, Christmas and Easter and summer holidays, and sometimes they agreed, very eagerly, as if assisting at a miracle, and sometimes they disagreed and were very solemn about it. Even when they were in the bus, which was very crowded and compelled them to stand up all the way, very close to one another, they did not stop talking. By the time they were back in East Haliford, it was quite late, and everything had that shuttered, echoing, rather weary look peculiar to the last hour of Sunday night. They stood at the end of Slater Street, looking into one another's faces with great seriousness, as if intimate messages in letters of fire might suddenly appear across their dim ovals.

"Are you tired?" asked Edward.

"Yes, I am a bit. Are you?"

Yes, he was a bit too. "But by gosh!—I've enjoyed it, haven't you? I haven't enjoyed myself so much—oh!—for years and years."

She had enjoyed it too. It had been nice. Those were her words, but her eyes, in that dimness, were two gigantic mysteries.

"Listen," said Edward eagerly, as if she had been paying no attention to him for the last ten minutes, instead of steadily drinking him in, "listen, Rose. When can I see you again? To-morrow night?"

Rose shook her head. No, she was afraid he could not see her to-morrow night. She did not explain why, for she was not a good quick liar and knew very well that there was no real reason why she should not see him the next night, except the time-old feminine one of not letting the male have all his own way at once.

"Oh!" he was disappointed. For a second he was tormented by a vision of her with some other fellow, probably one of those terrible blighters who worked in banks, joined tennis clubs, and even ran to cars. But then he comforted himself by remembering that girls often insisted upon staying in some nights, fantastically pledging themselves to sew or wash their hair or some such nonsense.

"Tuesday, then?"

This time she nodded. "All right. Tuesday."

"Oh—grand!" In his excitement he grabbed both her hands and held them. They were cool, and splendid to hold. "Where? What time? Half-past seven?"

"Yes, half-past seven, if you like," she said quietly, not trying to take her hands away.

"Where? Here?"

"No. Let's see. The bottom gate of the Park, eh?"

"The main gate, you mean? All right. Grand! Half-past seven at the main gate of the Park on Tuesday. You will be there, won't you?"

"Of course!" She was rather severe about this. "I wouldn't think of making an appointment and not turning up. I know some girls do, but I wouldn't do it for anything. And if anybody did it to me, I'd never forgive them."

"I should think not," cried Edward. "But then nobody would miss one with you."

She smiled at him. "All right then, Tuesday. I must be going now." And she gave her hands just a tiny little tug.

"Oh! But I suppose you must. I wish—oh!—I dunno—millions of things." He gave a little tug too, and then she was close to him and he put his arms behind her shoulders, lightly, not pressing her to him but just holding her where she was, near enough for him to feel her soft warmth through the thin dress she was wearing. She drooped a little, and then, as heavy foot-falls sounded on the pavement not far away, she tilted her face, perhaps only to wish him good night, and hastily, not very neatly, he kissed her; and though it was all very scrambling and did not last more than a second, he knew at once that this was the best girl to kiss in the world. He had not quite recovered from the confused splendour of all this before she was walking quickly, with little echoing footsteps, down Slater Street, now so rapidly taking on glamour. He did not wait to see her go in, partly because Slater Street is a long street and poorly lit, and partly because the heavy footfalls were those of a policeman and probably one given to making facetious remarks to youths in Edward's position. So off he marched towards Sutcliffe Place, a spring-heeled giant, quite unlike the young man who had left there nine or ten hours before. He had been a miserable nobody. This new Edward—and had he not evidence enough ringing in his memory to prove it?—was not only a sharp, humorous fellow (she had laughed a lot at his jokes), an extremely sensible chap (she had practically told him so), a stalwart protector of tender beauty (look at them coming down those rocks and then when that chap tried to push past in the bus), the lad who calmly collected for himself the prettiest girl in Haliford or anywhere else, but he was the Edward to whom something—and, by gosh, something indeed!—had happened. Think of old Herbert at home! Think of practically anybody, for that matter! He felt contemptuously sorry for the whole miserable lot of them. As for himself, he reflected, as he went almost floating home under the stars, with bedroom windows suddenly going into darkness down street after street and late cars roaring and honking in the distance and occasional privet hedges and railings etching their dusty edges in the yellow light of the street lamps, and all Haliford sinking into unconsciousness before answering he bleak queries of Monday morning, he had only one reat immediate problem. How was he to live, to shovel way and burn the rubbishy hours, until half-past seven on Tuesday night?

V

NELLIE, splendid in purple knickers, had said good
bye to her Sunday face and was now rubbing cold
cream into it to prepare it for a long dreary day to-morrow
at the toyshop. The jar into which she was dipping her
fingers for the cream was a magnificent affair and it had
cost Nellie a horribly big slice of a week's wages. But
then, as she always said, she did believe in having the best
and, because the firm that made the cream also believed
in having the best possible testimonials that money can
buy (they had paid a duchess £750 for hers), Nellie was
quite happy paying ten shillings for ninepennyworth of
lanolin, beeswax, borax and a drop of almond oil. And
Rose, who paid sixpence for exactly the same preparation
under another and more plebeian name, envied her sister
this and other luxurious aids to beauty. She was not
envying her at this moment, however, being busy with a
tooth-brush rubbing potassium chlorate (a poison) into her
dental cavities, happily convinced, for she had often read
the advertisements of this tooth-paste, that she was protecting herself against pyorrhœa. The advertisers had
warned her solemnly against this disease, but had not seen
fit to add that neither their tooth-paste nor anybody else's
could prevent or cure it. Both these girls spent a good
deal of their money on rubbish that clever advertisement
copy-writers either cajoled or frightened them into buying,

and perhaps they were fortunate in not having more money to spend, otherwise even their powerful constitutions—and they were both as strong as horses—might soon have been wrecked by this search for health and beauty. They never dreamt that a small army of extremely clever and quite unscrupulous persons, trained to lie with enthusiasm, steadily took the field against them, and that they were as simple and unprotected as rabbits. All that they were afraid of, in their heart of hearts, were dark sinister foreigners who would lure them into luxurious flats, give them dope, and then in some mysterious fashion ship them off to South America. The Sunday papers and the twopenny weeklies had told them all about these sinister foreigners. But they had never had a word of warning about those bright columns of advertisements.

As usual, Nellie, busy as she was, was talking, and Rose was listening or pretending to. There had been yet another crisis in Nellie's set. "So when this chap had gone, Charlie Sugden—would you believe it?—turned round, calm as you please, and says, 'You know he's got a wife in Manchester, eh?' And I says—and Gladys joins in, of course, 'Well, you fathead, how did we know he'd got a wife in Manchester or anywhere else? And if he has, what's he come here for pretending to be single? You introduced him—he's your friend—we didn't want him.' And we didn't neither, because as soon as we set eyes on him, Gladys says to me, 'Well, if this is their Mr. Appleyard, they can 'ave him. Look at his eyes.' And I said, 'He'll want watching'—right off. Well, then, of course the wonderful Miss Belmont—*Violet*—an' I'll bet she's thirty-two if she's a day—and why Charlie Sugden ever brought her, God knows, I don't—must say something, just to curry favour. *She's* broad-minded, she says—an' I'll bet she is too—manageress of a shop in Sheffield!—I'd like to know just what it was she *did* manage in Sheffield—anyhow, of course she has to say something—and what she says—oh, very sweet, as usual—is that we mustn't judge before we know everything, they may have separated and it may not be his fault, and that he seems a very nice man. And of course the boys are on her side at once, they would be. She wouldn't have said it if she hadn't known that. And Gladys—you know how she goes on—says 'Oh yeah?' And then it really started."

There was a lot more of it, but to Rose, in her present mood, it was all very far away, an affair of shadowy silly figures. She made the usual polite sounds of the listener from time to time, but as she climbed into the large but rather lumpy double bed and occupied her neat little corner of it (Nellie was the sprawler, and before morning seemed all gigantic hot legs), her mind was working steadily back through the evening and the afternoon. As soon as the light was out and there was only the darkness and herself together, she would start properly, going back to herself sitting on that rock and the boy first coming along, pretending not to notice her, and giving her the surprise of her life. And she silently commanded Nellie to hurry up and turn out the light.

But it was not to be as easy as that. Nellie, with her hair pulled back and her face shining with cold cream, looking rather like a young clown, sat on the edge of the bed, rubbed a bare knee with the palm of one hand, then suddenly turned and stared down at her young sister, whose round eyes gleamed above the sheet. "And what," she began coolly, "is the matter with you, Rose?"

"Nothing," said Rose, rather hastily. "Tired a bit, that's all. Hurry up."

"I won't." She continued to look down, speculatively. "Where've you been?"

"I told you. I went with Alice and another girl—Doris Ireton—on to Bilberry Glen."

"An' then what?" Nellie was relentless. "Come on, it's no good shutting your eyes. I know you're not sleepy. Something's up. What is it? What happened?" Still there was no reply. This would not do for Nellie. "I suppose you went off with one of your little boy friends—like those nasty knock-kneed kids I saw you and Alice with that night in the Park, eh?"

Rose opened her eyes, looked annoyed, and shook her head.

"Well, come on, tell me. I know something's up. And don't forget what I've told you," Nellie continued, more serious now. She was one of those girls who, not without reason, see the relations of the sexes as a series of strategic moves, with the male plotting to get as much as he can and to give as little, and the female checking and counter-checking him at every turn. "You didn't get landed with some older chap, did you? Because you know what I've told you about them, don't you? And you're just the kind of simple pretty kid they're always after."

Rose could not stand any more of this nasty stuff.

"Oh—shut up—please, Nellie. It wasn't a bit like any of that. He's quite different."

"I knew it was a chap," cried her sister triumphantly. "I could see it written all over you. And you're sweet on him already, aren't you?"

"No, I'm not." Rose looked indignant.

Nellie winked at her, and looked more like a young clown than ever. "What's he like? Is he knock-kneed, with specs and pimples? I'll bet he is. And he's going to take you to the ninepenny seats at the Bijou."

This was too much for Rose, who did exactly what Nellie had calculated she would do. "He's not a bit like that. He's twenty-three, and he's very dark and quite good-looking, and his father's just died, and he's fed up about everything—and—oh—he's nice——"

"And when are you seeing him again?" asked Nellie softly, without further comment.

"Tuesday," replied Rose, cosily, happily, snuggling down.

Nellie got up and turned off the light. It was not until she was in bed that she spoke again. "If that's how you're feeling," she said quietly, over her shoulder, "you might have a try for that job I told you about—y'know, that cut-price shop three doors down from our place. Because—you don't still want to go to London, do you?"

Rose murmured sleepily that she didn't.

"All right then, Rosie, you come down with me in the morning. Goo'night."

But when Rose woke up the next morning—and she did it with the conviction that something very nice was about to happen, and then remembered that it was that boy, Edward Fielding—she found that Nellie had gone, leaving behind a message to say that if Rose wanted that job, she must be sure to go down that morning. Nellie was anxious to get her sister into a shop, though she herself was always grumbling about the hours and the people you had to put up with in shops. She considered shop assistants, however, to be on a higher social level than factory or warehouse girls. And this was important to Nellie. She was the only one of the Salters who cared very much about these social distinctions. Mr. and Mrs. Salter, of course, never bothered their heads about such things, just as they never bothered their heads about a great many other things that troubled their neighbours. George and Fred had their own small snobberies, but they were not of a kind easily recognised by people outside their particular world of greyhound tracks, cheap race-courses, second-rate boxing matches, and public-house singing rooms. And Rose herself was quite different from Nellie. There were not so many years between them, but they were important years; and Rose had grown up to look at a job as so many hours of work of a certain kind for so much money, without much thought as to its gentility, its place in the elaborate social hierarchy, to which Nellie and her like were still very sensitive. In the same way, it would not have mattered much to Rose what a young man did for a living, whereas Nellie's gentleman friends were ranked according to the social status of their various occupations. Temperament would account for some of this difference, but not for all. Rose did not belong to quite the same

England that Nellie did. We all know Nellie's England, but we have a lot to learn yet about Rose's.

Departing with her mother's soapy blessing—and it says much for Mrs. Salter that she could still be loudly good-humoured even on Monday morning, elbow-deep in her washing—Rose set out to walk into the centre of Haliford. It was a pleasant morning, with plenty of sunshine finding its way through the smoke, and indeed combining with it to make a mixed atmosphere, a kind of heavier sunlight, not unlike that of a big railway station on a very fine day, which has quite an attraction of its own. Haliford seemed very friendly to Rose this morning. It had something about it not visible the week before. Perhaps this could be described as a vague Edward Fielding quality. He might be—indeed, he was—just round the corner, you see. She did not think about him a lot, but she kept him, smiling eagerly, his dark eyes fixed upon her, somewhere at the back of her mind. And she felt very special, which is always a nice thing for a girl to feel. And of course the result was that she looked—and knew she looked—very special too. And if she got this job, well that would be something new and amusing. And if she didn't get it, well, it didn't matter much. And as there are few better states of mind to be in than this, everything was all right, and she enjoyed her walk.

She called first on Nellie in the toyshop, which had no customers and was passing the time leisurely moving things from one part of itself to another. Nellie in the shop, even to her sister, was different from Nellie at home, much grander and more distant, but she went to the door with Rose, pointed out the new establishment that needed at least one more assistant, and told her the current gossip about its owner. "He's a sheeny from Leeds, but he's all right, they say—one of our girls knows a girl who's been started there—and you oughtn't to have any trouble with him. Only don't be shy, Rosie, 'cos he'll think you won't know how to sell properly if you seem shy. And don't take a penny less than two pounds to start with, whatever he says. Now go on, and show him—Mr. Levison's his name—what you're made of."

Mr. Levison's shop was still sticky with fresh vermilion paint, like a cheap new toy. Its two windows were heaped up with packets of chocolate, cigarettes, slightly fuzzy cigars, shaving soap, razor blades, tooth-pastes, face powder, bottles of scent, and tins of toffee; and there were dozens and dozens of little notices, bristling with exclamation marks, telling you that Mr. Levison was cutting prices, and not only cutting them but slicing, slashing, hacking, butchering, slaughtering them. There was enough red ink and red paint about to suggest that this was a battlefield, from which the manufacturers of proprietary articles and their wholesalers, who insisted upon an honest retailer like Mr. Levison obtaining more profit than he wanted, had retreated, broken and bleeding. Inside, there were so many newly opened packing cases, so many half-rifled cardboard containers, spilling goods all over the place, that it looked as if a volcano of chocolate and cigarettes and razor blades had just erupted in the back premises. But there was no Mr. Levison. There were only two young women: one of them, older than Rose, a thin anxious-looking creature, obviously was working there; but the other was wearing her hat and looked as if she might have called on the same errand as Rose.

"Is Mr. Levison in, please?" asked Rose.

"He won't be in this morning," said the anxious-looking young woman. "Is there anything I can do?"

Rose explained that she had heard there was a job going. Instantly, the two young women exchanged glances of despair. Rose had time now to examine the other caller. She was a girl with a pinched face, a sharp nose, and very thick glasses through which she blinked hopelessly at a world that refused to take any interest in her.

The assistant hesitated after this exchange of glances. "No, I'm sorry," she began, stammering a little, "but I'm afraid there isn't. The position——"

"No, Aggie," said the one with thick glasses, with a kind of sad despairing honesty. "You can't say that. It wouldn't be true."

Aggie nodded rapidly, and her eyes snapped furiously, not because she was angry but apparently because she could easily cry. Both girls now looked at Rose, who could not make anything of them. "What's the matter?" she asked, looking from one to the other.

"It's like this," Aggie explained, miserably. "Mr. Levison had to go to Leeds this morning, but he wants somebody—besides me—quick, and told me I could start a girl if she seemed all right. Well, you see——"

The one with the thick glasses took up the tale. "I'm her sister, and I could do with some work very badly, you see. My father can't move for arthritis, and we don't know what to do. And I'm not very strong either, you see, and there are a lot of jobs I couldn't do. I know 'cos I've tried, haven't I, Aggie? And I'm sure if Mr. Levison saw you, I wouldn't have an earthly, would I, Aggie?"

Aggie shook her head, looking hopelessly, first at her sister and then at Rose. "Do you want it badly?" she asked. "Because, you see, we do."

"You do see what we mean, don't you?" said the other one, coming closer, so that Rose saw a little reflection of herself in one of the thick lenses. And what she saw made her still sorrier for this girl.

"All right," she said cheerfully. "It doesn't matter. I don't care very much."

The other two brightened up at once and both together told Rose what a nice girl she was and how easy it would be for her, with those looks, to get anything she wanted. She left them plotting eagerly over the counter. But when she popped into the toyshop again to see Nellie, she did not tell her what had happened, but merely said that there was no vacancy at Mr. Levison's. She spent the next hour strolling in a fine luxurious fashion round the two or three chief shopping streets of the town, mentally accepting or rejecting the hats, dresses, stockings, shoes, in the windows there, and occasionally disturbing the complacency of the young men in their shirt-sleeves who were beginning to decorate some of those windows for the autumn season. But the young man whose complacency was most disturbed was a plumpish, pink, spectacled fellow into whose arms she walked dreamily as she turned into Gladstone Lane. "Oo, I'm sorry!" she cried, extricating herself, blushingly.

"Not at all. Quite all right," he said, regarding her with owlish admiration. She rewarded him with a smile, and went on, and did not know that this was Herbert Fielding, older brother of Edward. (It was this tiny encounter that started new trains of thought in Herbert's mind, trains that eventually took him into the vestry of the East Haliford Wesleyan Methodist Chapel with one Bertha Lawson, and finally, with his bride and his mother, into a new semi-detached villa off the Leeds road, where the two Mrs. Fieldings quarrelled continually and between them more than revenged Edward for any slights that his brother may have put upon him.) Rose returned home and spent the afternoon helping her mother with the family washing. And if it should be thought that for a working girl, in a neighbourhood where there was a good deal of unemployment and real suffering, she was taking her present condition of being out of work very lightly, it must be pointed out that she had been working on full time at the underclothing factory for nearly two years, that the other Salters were all earning money, that she was for various reasons an employable type, and that she was a very feminine, handsome young girl whose private dreams had little to do with the Ministry of Labour's statistics. And at this time she was deeply immersed in those dreams, though even if she had wanted to, she could not have said what they were all about. Most of her personality moved idly below the surface of ordinary expression, as little concerned with what went on above as a fish in a tank is concerned with the variations of wind and weather.

It was this passivity, this dreaminess, that annoyed her

friend Alice, that very night. Alice came round in a state of what was, even for her, unusual excitement, looked as if she were bursting with news, and insisted upon Rose coming out at once, so that they could talk properly. They went into the Park again (it looked to Rose almost like Edward Fielding's private property now), and once there, Alice never stopped talking. To begin with, yesterday's meeting had definitely established the fact that Gregory Porson was no good, a blighter, a mess, a worm, a wash-out. "I gave him his chance," cried Alice breathlessly, though exactly what this meant she did not explain, "and nobody could have given him a better chance. I told him he needn't think I had to stop here in Haliford, even if he had—for all his bank and whatnot—and that I was one to please myself whatever anybody said, nobody could say I ever went chasing fellows round, and he ought to know it. Silly swank-pot! And that Eric! Did you ever see such a mess? I told him right out he could keep his Eric. I told him a lot of other things as well before I'd finished. You ought to have seen his face. Talk about taking him down a peg or two! Then he tried to come the swanky bank clerk over me. I let him have it then, Rose, I can tell you. Anyhow, I've finished, honest I have. I was silly ever to start with him. Fat fool! I called him fat fool too. Oo, you ought to have seen his face!"

There was a great deal more of this, none of it very new to Rose, for Alice had a trick of falling out with boys as fast as she fell in with them, and to Rose, who kept on a steadier course, the end was always nearly as mysterious as the beginning of these affairs. The great point was however, that Alice felt that her last link with Haliford—that ring of base metal, Gregory Porson—had snapped now, and that there was no reason why she and Rose (for she assumed, as one's friends so often do, that Rose had no changing moods of her own) should not leave as soon as possible. But that was not all; only half of it. And here they sat down by the side of the Park lake, which had some boats, some swans, and a great many dead leaves and crumpled paper bags floating on it. Alice then contrived to find enough breath to continue: her elder brother, Frank—and doesn't it just show you! Really, chaps are the limit!—had calmly told her, without a word of preparation and warning, that very tea-time, that he had gone to the length of writing to this man who helped to run the cafés in London, and had not only explained to him about Alice and Rose but had actually sent him a snapshot of them both, one of the "snaps" that he himself had taken of them early in the summer. And when Alice, flabbergasted, had said she liked his cheek, he had replied calmly, quite calmly: "Well, that's what you wanted, isn't it, kid?" Wasn't that just like Frank? And when she had first asked him about it, suggesting that he might do something, he had done nothing but raise his eyebrows and whistle. But wasn't it exciting? They might get a reply from that man in London any time, perhaps to-morrow.

"Well?" cried Alice impatiently. Really Rose was very sweet and all that, but sometimes she was terribly aggravating. This was one of the times. Instead of being all interested and excited, here she was, staring at the water, not saying a word. Did she want to go to London or didn't she?

Rose had heard everything that Alice had said, but it had meant little or nothing to her. As she watched the long golden ripples of the water, in which the sunset was reflected, she was thinking in a pleasant dim sort of way about that boy Edward Fielding, where he was now and whether he was thinking about her, and the golden ripples, the birds that flashed over them, and her dreamy thoughts, all got nicely mixed up. So it was impossible for her to work up any excitement about Frank and cafés and London. She looked apologetically at her friend.

"I must say," Alice grumbled, "you don't seem to be taking much notice. Last time we talked you were all for going, didn't want to stay here another week if you could help it, and now you can't take any interest in it. Here, Rose Salter, what happened to you yesterday—y'know, after we left you?"

Rose hesitated—and was lost. Alice had it all out of her—all, that is, except any suggestion of deeper feelings being involved—within the next five minutes. "So that's why you're not bothering," said Alice. "Doesn't seem much of reason to me."

"Well, what about you? Didn't you change your mind when you started on with your Gregory Porson?"

"No, not really," said Alice, snorting. "That was different. Besides, I'd seen a bit more of him. When are you meeting this boy again?"

"To-morrow night."

"Humph! Let's hope he turns up."

This annoyed Rose. "Don't be silly, Alice Why shouldn't he turn up?"

"Well, you never know. If you ask me, these sort of serious, mystery chaps are worse than the other kind for not turning up. They're all for you, just for one night or two, when they're in that mood like, and then they wish they hadn't bothered with you and so they don't turn up. Look at that boy I met that time at Bridlington, and yours sounds just like him. Lovely boy he was," Alice sighed, "serious and good-looking and no messing you about all the time. But he didn't turn up. They go and read books or something. Changeable, that's what they are. And you needn't look mad, Rose, 'cos you know it's true."

"I don't know it's true and I think you're talking silly." She got up and moved off so quickly that Alice had to hurry after her, which she did good-humouredly enough, catching her friend by the arm.

"I expect it'll be all right," said Alice apologetically. "They're not all like that. And you're sure to be the lucky one."

"Well," said Rose with decision, "nobody's ever done that to me yet, and if they did I'd never forgive 'em, whoever they were. What are you going to do to-morrow?"

"Mess about, I expect. Anyhow, no more boys for me—not Haliford ones, anyhow. And I'm going to get out of here if I've to go by myself and walk it. Come on, let's go home. Our Frank's got a new wireless set, and he lets me work it."

For the next twenty-two hours, except for the period when she was drowned in sleep, Rose pretended hard that the fact that she was to meet this boy, Edward Fielding, at half-past seven at the main gate of Ackroyd Park, was of no particular importance. She avoided sitting about and thinking of it; she tried to make everything that came along, some washing up, a bit of sewing, shopping for her mother, seem so important that it filled the whole horizon; she clung hold of every passing minute. This worked fairly well until about half-past six, when she suddenly found herself quite unreasonably and ridiculously excited, and wanting to make the most elaborate preparations for the evening. Determined to keep her sillier self in check, she did nothing at all, simply wasted time, for the next forty minutes, and then spent the next ten minutes in a frenzy of washing, changing, hair-brushing, nose-powdering, snapping the head off anybody who came near her. At seven-twenty exactly she left the house, rather pink and breathless, hurried along Slater Street, wilfully slowed down up Elm Road, and came within sight of the main gate of Ackroyd Park within half a minute of the appointed time. It was a cool evening, and the sun was setting behind heavy dark clouds. There were not many people making for the Park.

The main gate of Ackroyd Park is an imitation Norman arch, and was presented to the town by its distinguished former citizen, Sir Thomas Cuddilip, Bart., probably in consideration of his having swindled one of his fellow-citizens out of the proceeds of a notable invention in textile machinery, and having, for a great many lucrative years, underpaid and overworked a great many other of his fellow-citizens, who had seen the last of Sir Thomas just after the War, when he had retired to found a county family in Gloucestershire. At two minutes past the half-hour,

Rose arrived under this arch, which has a portcullis as abbreviated and bogus as Sir Thomas's county family. Edward had not arrived. The only persons there were two middle-aged men who were bending earnestly over a bull-terrier and puffing smoke at him. Rose went a little way into the Park, and looked at a bed of dahlias that ought to have had their faces washed. She felt that if she did this long enough, she would finally be able to turn round and find Edward hurrying towards her. But after keeping it up for what seemed a weary length of time, she turned round only to discover that the two men with the dog were moving off, and that a nasty-looking fellow in a tweed suit and a bowler was staring across at her with marked interest. No Edward in sight. This was annoying, especially as the nasty-looking fellow was moving in her direction. Well, he was late, and he must wait for her now. She would walk as far as the lake and then come back, to hope she had not kept him waiting. Off she went briskly, but only to stop suddenly, in a panic, about a hundred yards further on, because it occurred to her that there might be a mistake about the gate. Desperately she searched her memory. She had said "the bottom gate." This was the bottom gate. He had said: "You mean the main gate." This was also the main gate. There couldn't be a mistake. And yet—there might be. There was the top entrance, of course, but obviously he knew she did not mean that. But then there was also a smaller entrance, a single gate, which was also at the bottom of the Park. He might be waiting there. She turned and hurried across the grass, to the evident pleasure and encouragement of the nasty-looking man, who was still hanging about. She had to pass close to him now, so she showed him how much he was wanted and also saved time by breaking into a run. This smaller gate was less than quarter of a mile away. She was within sight of it in no time, and she did not need to go right up to see that no Edward was there. Stupid of her to have bothered even looking! He would be there, back at the main gate, waiting for her, and as she hurried back, she could almost see the anxious look on his dark face. Yes, he was! No, he wasn't! It was another young man, not unlike him, who had just been joined by a girl in a red hat. Perhaps he was in the road outside the Park, looking for her there. As she went under the arch, she heard a clock striking eight. No Edward outside. No Edward at all. And then something bright and happy inside that had been coiled like a spring suddenly ran down, letting a weight of misery fall upon her. For a few more moments, she lingered on, a miserable little creature.

He had not turned up. Alice had known more about him and his kind than she had done. Bitterly she remembered her bright confidence. Probably, once he had left her on Sunday night, he had never even intended to keep the engagement. She had amused him for a few hours when he had had nothing to do, and that was that. As she walked quickly away, her eyes were smarting with tears of humiliation. It was not so much what had happened between them on Sunday—for that was little enough—that returned to her memory now to make her feel humiliated and angry, but the thought of what she had been so busy building on her recollection of him that hurt. He had made her appear a silly little fool to herself, after first encouraging her to see herself as somebody very special, and that was unbearable. Damn him! Damn everything! She wanted to go miles and miles away, lose herself, start a quite new kind of life, and a life in which undependable dark young men were treated like dirt. While her mind was racing away, her feet were carrying her in the direction of Alice Hargreaves' home. She arrived there just as it began raining, and no sooner had Alice herself let her in than she realised what a fool she had been to call and not go straight home, when Alice would most certainly discover that the boy had not turned up, after all.

If Alice had made her confess what had happened and had then crowed over her, there can be no doubt that Alice would have had to have gone to London alone. But Alice did nothing of the kind, not because she was tactful or magnanimous, but because she was too excited to care. She rushed Rose into the empty sitting-room, turned on the light, and pushed a letter at her. "Frank got it to-day," she explained. "Gave it to me to-night. Look! Read it. From that chap who helps to run the cafés, see? They're opening a new place next week, and he'll give us both a trial. What d'you have to do in a café, d'you know? I don't. Serving and washing up and all that, I suppose? Or perhaps you start washing up, then get on to serving. Or perhaps if you look all right, you start serving right away and get tips and everything. Fancy uniforms too! An' I'll bet you've got to look smart. Well, that'll suit us, won't it, specially you, though I'll look all right if they're my colour." And Alice went on and on.

Rose looked up from the letter, which she had read very carefully. It was typewritten, had a London address, and altogether was very metropolitan and grand, a sort of sign post to a richer life. Her eyes were big and dark with speculation.

"Well, girl, come on, talk," Alice commanded, seizing her by the arm and squeezing it hard. "It's a great chance, isn't it? Are we going or aren't we? Speak up, kid."

"Alice," said Rose, looking at her earnestly. "We're going."

VI

THESE two days Edward had been living in a new Haliford. This was not the town, these were not the streets, houses, shops, trams, he had known before. Everything was transformed. It had a golden, Rose Salter look about it, this new Haliford. You wouldn't be living anywhere else, for the world. The travellers going down to the railway station, the cars hastening along the main roads, were all going into an outer darkness, a bleak parody of life. Here in Haliford was the radiant heart of things. Even Pooley Road had not missed this transformation; it had a quaint friendly look, like a gnarled old Mr. Crabtree among streets. Even Clewes and Tirril's office and warehouse might have been worse. There was some fun in taking a handful of white noils and turning it into a neat blue-wrapped package. There was romance in one's dealings with the railway, canal, and road transport companies, in those enquiries for delayed or lost bales, in the passionate arguments about them over the telephone. This stuff in paper bags in the office and in great sacks in the warehouse had a strange and exciting life of its own; here in Pooley Road to-day, gone all over the place to-morrow; and some of it would eventually return to the outer air, after various conjuring tricks had been performed with it, in the shape of green and brown and black felt hats, to have all manner of adventures. Even in this mood, it was impossible for him to discover any romantic appeal in his employer, Mr. Tirril, but he could at least be sorry for him, pretend to listen earnestly to his complaints, and work away without a murmur. And when he took the bus home, was he not possibly surrounded by people who might be connected in some way—they might be relations for all he knew—with Rose Salter? Slater Street was always just round the corner. Thus, threads of gold—the magical skeins of the fairy tales—linked every road; the whole place was glitteringly cobwebbed with them.

Now and again, usually when Mr. Tirril in his despair suddenly decided to send samples of everything to everybody, Edward had to work late. (He received a shilling for "tea money" if he stayed after seven o'clock.) On Tuesday afternoon, Mr. Tirril returned about quarter to five from one of his useless rounds, and for a few horrible moments it looked as if he were about to scatter samples of noils and wastes over the whole West Riding. As he came and stood, looking down at the sample counter, not three feet away from the anxious Edward, the thought was written on his foolish face. His mouth was already open, to issue the fatal command. Watching him, Edward summoned all his will-power to command him silently to shut up and go home. "What's the good?" Edward asked him with his eyes. "Just wasting time and samples and postage," said Edward's mind. "Now, isn't it, Mr. Tirril? Don't be silly. Go home. Your wife wants you. *Now don't do it. Let's all go home.*"

It worked. "Well," said Mr. Tirril, "I don't know. We must have a big sampling afore so long. Trade's up a bit in Bradford, they tell me. But we'd better leave it a day or two. We haven't got them Forties in yet."

"That's right, sir," said Edward briskly, the keen young wool man. "Shall I see if I can get some in the morning?"

"You can see about it when I tell you to see about it, and not before," said Mr. Tirril, slouching away to his own end of the office.

"Come on, kid," cried Edward softly to the boy. "Look slippy with those copies. We don't want to be here all night." And what a model of neat industry he was for the next quarter of an hour or so! "Anything more, sir? Good night." His overall was off, his hat was on the back of his head, he was racing down the steps, he was out in Pooley Road, hurrying for his bus, before the others had begun to think about going home. Not quite six o'clock and free as air! An hour and a half before he met her! And Edward, too young yet to be aware of the deep malice of things in this world, brazenly congratulated himself.

"And what," said his mother across the tea-table, "have you got on?" And she gave him a penetrating look, which Edward tried to avoid meeting. The hardest people to live with are those who have been given insight into your nature without any deep affection for that nature. They read you like a book, but it is a book by an author they do not admire. Mrs. Fielding was one of these people, in her relations with Edward, and this was one reason why he was not happy or even comfortable with her.

"Nothing," he mumbled, pretending to be busy with his fruit and custard and brown bread. Herbert had not arrived home yet. So there was no escape.

"Some piece o' silliness, I'll be bound," his mother continued, not taking her eyes off him. "And I wouldn't be hard put to it to give it a name. Bits of lads and bits of girls! Mind you don't get yourself into trouble, one o' these days. I don't know when you're going to find some sense."

Edward did not even look up, but he was very angry inside, and though he did not make a sound, he was shouting: "Oh, shut up! I've got plenty of sense. More than you and your precious Herbert. What do you know about anything? For God's sake, leave me alone."

"Yes, an' I know what you're thinking." His mother was fond of saying this, and unfortunately she was nearly always right. Ironically enough, she could not do this with Herbert, whom she really loved: he was a splendid mystery; not the miserable open book that Edward was. Mrs. Fielding did not enjoy this irony, she resented it, and this resentment encouraged a certain cruel gusto in her penetrative handling of her younger son. This was an example of it. Ever since the morning before, she had noticed that he was excited and happy—"above himself," as she described it—and she was bent on flattening him. She told herself that she did this for his own good. "One day perhaps you'll learn, though you're a long time starting. And there's lads round here—I could name a few—who'll be men when you're still a monkey."

"All right then," said Edward sulkily, "I'll be a monkey."

"Yes, that's what you say now," said his mother grimly. "I've heard them tales before."

Edward stopped eating and looked up at her now. He did not want to be sulky. He wanted to be right with everybody in the world. It was more difficult to start with his mother than with almost anybody else, for he felt it hard to be more than a shadow of his real self, not the self who ate and drank and wore clothes and went to bed and was given ammoniated tincture of quinine for a cold, but the Edward Fielding inside, the one who had gone on the moors last Sunday and was going to meet Rose Salter at half-past seven, here at home, with this mother who knew so much about him and yet understood so little. "Mother, I'm sorry if I seem such a nuisance to you, honestly I am. I'll be all right. You needn't worry. And I wish—I wish——"

"Go on." But she was not looking at him now. She was doing something—or pretending to do something—at the gas stove. And her voice gave him no encouragement.

"Well," he hurried on, "I wish you wouldn't keep on at me like this——" No good. He knew it the moment he had spoken. Somehow the appeal had gone wrong.

She straightened herself and turned on him. "Keep on at you! Now I like that, Edward, I do! Here am I, washing and baking and cleaning for you from morning till night—and a lot o' thanks I get for it—and when I try and talk to you for your own good, try to make something of you, you start sulking and grumbling and behaving like a big silly baby——"

"Oh, all right, all right," he said wearily, getting up.

"It isn't all right. I've got to go down the road. Just

tell Herbert his tea's all ready for him. There's a bit of fish in the oven. All he's got to do is to mash the tea."

"Then let him do it, without me telling him," said Edward to himself as he went upstairs. Long before he had reached his bedroom, his failure to come to easy terms with his mother had passed out of his mind and he was as jubilant as ever. It was the victor below who, lacking this elasticity of youth, was now miserable, and as she slowly left the house she wondered sadly why she could not feel more kindly disposed towards her younger son, who was not really a bad boy. Meanwhile, Edward in his bedroom was feeling a mounting excitement. It was quarter to seven. Just right! Everything was just right. Down he went to the bathroom, whistling away. He had heard the front door bang. His mother had gone, Herbert had not yet arrived. He had the house to himself, and there was something very pleasant about that.

He did not know yet that once man feels so secure in his happiness, he challenges the very stars and is immediately marked down as the next victim of their cold malice, and that the workings of this malice are so contrived that even the humblest inanimate object at our elbow can enter its service. This is the moment when machine-belts snap, bolts are shorn off, screws unwind themselves, nails fly out, and watches stop. On this occasion, the chosen instrument was a bathroom key. There was no sound reason why Edward should have locked the bathroom door at all, for he was alone in the house, and the only possible intruder would have been Herbert. There was an excellent reason why he should have left it alone, for the bathroom door had no bolt inside, only a lock and this old, slightly bent key, which could be turned only with some difficulty. Habit prevailed, however, and he locked himself in. As he did so, the key gave a little squeak, probably of satisfaction. It was an old typical Sutcliffe Place bathroom, with a long narrow bath, rusty under the taps and along the bottom, enclosed in bleached woodwork and raised very high above the floor. At the foot of it was a lavatory, also raised high, rather like a yellow-ochre throne. At the other side of the room were a wash-hand basin with two cracks in it, a cupboard containing so many of Herbert's toilet bottles that you might have thought he was going to set up as an analyst in there, and a cistern inadequately covered with varnished boards, an old rumbling grumbling cistern that seemed to threaten to smash its way through the boards and walk out of the house altogether. The solitary window, which looked out to the back of Sutcliffe Place on to a number of wireless aerials, clothes-lines, bassinette and bicycle sheds, and decaying asters and wallflowers, was decorated with small leaded panes of coloured glass, as if the Victorian builder had felt that the toilet was best performed in a dim religious light. When Edward was younger, he had enjoyed this window and its coloured glass, through which the Robinsons opposite, their back door caught between the blue and green sections, became all fantastic, creatures from the moon. But the Edward who whistled in there now had no time for lunar Robinsons; he was preparing himself to meet a golden girl from the sun; and very thoroughly preparing himself too.

He had taken care to bring his watch—gun-metal,

battered, but reliable—in with him, and it had needed great self-control to prevent himself from looking at it every minute or two. Coming to the conclusion that the best way to make the time pass was to ignore it, he had worked away at himself with soap, brush, razor, sponge, towel, without so much as a glance towards his watch, and now, when he was dressed again (for he had taken his best suit in with him), he pounced upon it and found to his delighted surprise that it was quarter-past seven. He would have to hurry, but then he wanted to hurry, did not mind if he ran all the way. He rushed to the door and tried to turn the key. It stuck, as it often did. Not the fellow to stand any nonsense from old keys, he put both hands to it and used all his strength, quickly, savagely. It snapped off, close to the lock. There he was holding a useless bit of bent metal. For a moment or two, it did not seem serious. What were keys and locks?

Very soon, however, he realised that there was no doing anything with the fragment of key that remained in the door and that was keeping that door firmly locked. There was not half an inch protruding, not nearly enough to grasp securely and turn. He poked about the lock with his penknife, but nothing happened. Then he grew angry and after first rattling the door hard, as if to recall it to its senses, he tried battering at it with his shoulder, hoping to burst the lock. But both the woodwork and metalwork were a solid Victorian job. They did not budge. It was his shoulder that suffered. He retreated, rubbing it, and cursing the door, the bathroom, the whole damned house. He could have cried with vexation. What was the time now? After twenty-five past, by thunder! At any minute now she would be waiting there at the Park gate, and here he was, blasted well locked in this blasted bathroom! The window! It was his only chance. Only the top half opened, and he pulled it down violently, knelt on the narrow sill, and looked out. He could not see enough, so laboriously he hoisted himself up, stood on the sill (his foot slipped once and he hurt his shin), and managed to look down. The kitchen window was below, and below that the back yard, all solid concrete. It looked a good drop down there. He had often read about fellows shinning down water-pipes, but he had never tried it himself, and from the look of the water-pipe there, a few feet away, he did not feel like trying it now. To begin with, it would not be easy to get hold of the pipe at all. And then again, that pipe did not look at all safe. One of its staples was obviously loose already, and might fly out of the wall altogether the moment the pipe felt his weight. The only thing to do, he concluded, was to chance it and drop. He would have to climb out, let himself down somehow outside, cling to the stone window-sill there, hanging down as far as possible, and then drop. And all that would not be easy. Even the climbing out would be no joke, for the lower and rigid half of the window was fully three feet high. But if that was his only way out, then that way he would have to go. And he had just raised a leg over the sash, and was balanced perilously, when there came a loud knocking on the bathroom door. It was Herbert. He heard his voice. He jumped back into the room.

"Can't get out," he bellowed through the door. "Key's broken in the lock."

"But I want to get in," Herbert shouted idiotically.

"And I want to get out, you blasted fathead," roared Edward. "Can't you do something? Here, what about taking the lock out? Get a screwdriver, quick!"

Herbert seemed so long getting the screwdriver that Edward, jumping with impatience, nearly went to the window again. He dare not look at his watch. "Come on, come on," he yelled uselessly. And even when Herbert came back and began unscrewing his side of the lock, the whole thing seemed to be in maddening slow motion. There was no kind of bad language that Edward had ever used before or heard that he did not repeat now, over and over again. At last Herbert did something useful. Quite suddenly, the door flew open.

"What happened?" asked Herbert.

But Edward rushed past him, shouting incoherently, and charged straight downstairs and out of the house, without stopping to find his hat. No better time was ever made between Sutcliffe Place and the main gate of Ackroyd Park. Old people stared, small boys whistled after him. Damp with sweat, panting like a dog, he arrived at the gate at exactly ten minutes past eight. And no Rose Salter. He looked this way and that. Had she been and gone? Or had she simply not kept the engagement? He didn't even know that. He knew nothing. There was a man standing near the gate, a solid man smoking a pipe who looked as if he had been solidly there for hours. He might know.

"I say," said Edward, still out of breath, "have you seen a girl here?"

The man took his pipe out of his mouth, looked solemnly at Edward, then winked. "I've seen lots o' girls, lad. Some of 'em nice-looking, and some of 'em not. Mostly not."

"This girl's very nice-looking. She was waiting for me here. Did you notice her?"

"Nay, lad, what did yer want to keep her waiting for? They keep *you* waiting, but yer mustn't start keeping *them* waiting, 'cos the only ones that'll stand for that are just ones yer don't want, d'you see, lad?" And the old fathead chuckled away.

"Have you seen her?" asked Edward desperately.

"Nay, I don't know as I have," was the final idiotic reply. Edward walked away in disgust. But what next? Should he stay in the Park? Perhaps she had waited at the wrong gate. He set off, still hopeful, to walk round the edge of the Park, from gate to gate. And of course it had to rain. He had no raincoat, no hat, and this was no shower but the beginning of a wet night. But he was past caring for such trifles as sodden clothes. Let it rain. Having got half-way round the Park, however, he decided that she might have gone home. So now he started out for Slater Street. He did not know where she lived in Slater Street, but perhaps she would be looking out of the front window there, and, if he walked up and down the street several times, she would see him. All the luck had suddenly gone against him, surely it might change now? So he argued, still refusing to give up hope, all the way there. Meanwhile, it was raining hard and getting dark. Slater Street is a long street, and consists of two rows of squat houses all built exactly alike, as if they had been meant for insects and not for fantastically varied human beings. By the time Edward had taken his squelching shoes twice up and down its dreary length, and had seen more and more blinds drawn and front rooms lit up, he knew it was hopeless. Three times he had hurried up to vague figures that might have been but never were Rose Salter. He stopped a man and asked him where the Salters lived, but the man did not know and seemed to think it a silly question to ask on a wet night. At ten o'clock, the wettest and most miserable young man in Haliford went home, to face his mother and Herbert. "Go and break bathroom door, and then must go out and get your best suit all sopping!" cried his mother, as if in triumphant confirmation. Oh misery! Oh hell! He dragged himself and a heartache wearily up to bed.

If, during the next few days, Mrs. Fielding and Mr. Tirril could have met and talked about Edward, they would have had a very long and pleasant session indeed, for that youth was equally heedless, sulky, and unsatisfactory at home and at work. He could only think seriously of one thing, and that was—how to find Rose Salter? He inclined on the whole to the view that she had turned up that night, got tired of waiting, and gone away and condemned him as a fellow who did not keep his word. This was bad enough, but it was better than the alternative—that she had lost interest in him after Sunday night and probably found somebody more amusing for Tuesday. But whatever had happened, she must be found. So he divided his evenings between combing Ackroyd Park, which appeared to be full of girls who looked like Rose at a distance and painfully unlike her as soon as he hurried up to them; and hanging about the neighbourhood of Slater Street, where he soon became a familiar figure to certain residents, including a thin red-haired girl who kept hopefully popping in and out of the third house on the right, and three children in the end house who flattened their noses against the window and grinned at him. Rose herself had shed no glamour in his mind, had even acquired still more now that she was so mysteriously lost and unattainable; but any visionary light that had once illuminated the length of Slater Street had now faded. He came to dislike all the houses in it but one, all the people in it but one, but unfortunately he did not know which house was the exception and could not find the one exceptional person. He brought the name of Salter into his talk with all manner of folk, indeed he often began talking to them in the hope of getting some information, but he had no luck. But in these first days, he was hopeful of running across her, as one seemed to run across everybody in Haliford. He might have found her exact address in a directory. A letter to Miss Rose Salter, Slater Street, without a number on it, would not have baffled the Haliford postal service. He knew that the Salters had lived in that street a long time, and if he had called at every fifth house on either side, he would soon have discovered where she lived, and might then have called there, boldly demanding to see her. He did not do any of these sensible things because as yet it did not occur to him, just as it would not have occurred to most youths of his class, to do any of them: the hopeful hanging-about method, with a few cautious enquiries here and there to assist it, was to him the first obvious method. And nothing came of it.

This barren period of search, during which he never stopped cursing his luck, came to an end with the arrival of a most surprising, totally unexpected, piece of good fortune. It was exactly a week after he had missed meeting Rose that he was called to the telephone at the office. It was the old woolcomber he had talked with at his father's funeral, Mr. Crabtree.

"Is that young Edward Fielding? Ay, well, Ah'd like to have a word wi' you, lad. Ah've got summat 'at might surprise yer. When? Well, ther's no time like present, specially when yer my age. It's Toosda to-day, isn't it? Ah mak' a practice o' dropping into 'Fox an' Geese' hotel o' Toosda's, an it's nobbut a nice evening's walk for a lad like yer-sen, so if yer'll come ower t'hill an' look for me in t'private bar, yer'll happen hear summat yer won't expect."

So Edward agreed to be there that night about half-past eight. He could not imagine what the old man wanted with him, and could not make up his mind whether he was glad or sorry to be called away like this, for one night at least, from his search for Rose Salter. On the whole, he concluded, he was glad. He was beginning to feel foolish, not quite real, a shadow of a chap. That ridiculous red-haired girl and those three kids in Slater Street could all amuse themselves to-night. He did not tell his mother or Herbert where he was going. He never told them anything, these days. The "Fox and Geese," an old-fashioned public-house, was just below the bleak industrial village where Mr. Crabtree had his mill and his house, and was about five miles north-west of Haliford, not far from the edge of those grim moors that form a barrier between Yorkshire and Lancashire. Edward took a bus for the first two miles, then walked briskly up the steep road. A coldish wind was roaring over the top, blowing away the last shreds of summer. All along the road they were building dapper little red-roofed bungalows, which looked as much out of place on that stony height as thatched cottages would have done. Higher up, there were still a few farms left, grey huddles of weather-beaten stone. There were also a few little old mills, like Mr. Crabtree's, which nowadays look nearly as rural and old-fashioned as the farms. But even up here, mixed oddly with the farms and little mills, were signs of the new Haliford that lives in red-roofed bungalows, shops at Americanised stores, eats in cafés, and amuses itself in picture theatres and dance halls. The stone walls began here, those walls that run and twist and turn for miles and miles over the moors, carefully parcelling out wild tracts of land lost in the clouds; but above them now were large gaudy posters advertising bottled cocktails, hair shampoos, breakfast foods from Ohio, tinned salmon from British Columbia, blonde beauties from California. The walls had been there for generations, whereas the posters were already flapping in the wind; but the posters now would outlast the walls; they would win. Did Edward notice these things? He did, and a great many more, but his thoughts about them were all confused. No sooner did a thought arrive than the wind seemed to blow it away. But he enjoyed his walk, and felt better than he had done for days.

The "Fox and Geese," like the sensible old-fashioned place it was, looked cosy. The lights had been turned on, the red blinds pulled down, the fires well stoked and poked. Mr. Crabtree was sitting over a whisky in a corner of the private bar, where a bright fire was toasting his left leg and winking at him from the polished woodwork all round the snug little room. He was also conducting a loud argument with an old farmer-like fellow, who was standing near the door, holding a pint glass. "Well, Jonas," he was shouting, "tha'll nivver learn so it's no good me telling thee. Tha's bin asking for Tariff Reform all thi life, an' nah tha's gotten it, tha sees it's nowt only tha's too pig-headed to say so." Now he noticed Edward. "Come in, lad, an' shut door. Tha can leave me nah, Jonas, 'cos Ah cannot be bothered tryin' to put any more sense into thee."

Jonas, grinning, said: "Nay, nay, Mr. Crabtree!" and then vanished, leaving the other two with the room to themselves.

"Nah, lad," Mr. Crabtree began hospitably, not quite as broad in his accent now as he had been with Jonas, "yer can tak' a sup o' beer, eh? Ring that bell."

Edward could drink beer, though he rarely did, for his generation had somehow lost the old habit of sitting about and drinking beer all the evening. But the walk and the wind had made him thirsty, so that the pint of bitter—and Mr. Crabtree insisted upon a pint for him, "reckoning nowt," he said, of anything less—was very welcome. And

Mr. Crabtree let him take a good pull at it and then light a cigarette before he began to explain why he had asked him there.

"Nah Ah'm not going to tell yer a long tale, lad," Mr. Crabtree began, " 'cos yer'll nobbut think Ah'm getting old an' daft. But as yer knaw, me and your grandfather were old friends. We did business together for forty year. Ay, an' what's more, we had a lot o' sport together an' all—a dam' sight more nor you'll ever have, lad. Them were days when you could do business an' you could have some fun. Not like these days, wi' ivverybody scrattin' about, neither workin' nor playin'. But to cut a long story short Ah owed your grandfather a bit o' money. It wor nowt to do wi' business, o' course, or it'ud ha' been paid long sin'. It wor a private job. In fact, it wor a bet. Nah your grandfather wor keen enough i' business but he wor a fair man, an' he would have it Ah didn't owe him this bit o' money. Ah said Ah did, an' then it went clean out o' my mind, an' Ah did nowt about it. Nah, t'other day, at your poor father's funeral, it came back to me right sharp. An' Ah said to me-sen, 'Ah'll pay up, ay, an' Ah'll give it to t'lad. He could do wi' it.' So that's how it is, see, lad?"

Yes, Edward saw, but stammered something about his mother being entitled to it.

"Nah listen to me, lad," said Mr. Crabtree firmly. "Ah've a fancy for givin' it to thee, partly 'cos tha reminds a bit o' thi grandfather, an' he talked a lot about yer when yer were a little lad. So tak' it and don't be soft. Think of it as a present from a silly old man, if yer like. An' don't go thinkin' yer coming into a fortune or owt like that, or that

Ah'm Father Christmas. It's nowt very grand, but it'll be bit o' spending brass for yer, an' it'll be off my mind."

Edward thanked him, not very coherently. It was all very bewildering.

The old man brought out a piece of paper and laid it on the table. Edward saw that it was a cheque. "This is it, lad. Tak' it to t'Haliford an' District Bank an' they'll cash it for yer. Sixty-five pound. An' if yer've a bit o' sense, yer'll say nowt to nobody about this. That big brother o' yours—he's nowt i' my line, yon chap isn't—so don't let him have handlin' of it. Keep it yer-sen, lad. Are yer courtin' yet?"

Was he courting? He felt that he was, but one afternoon and evening on the moors, and then not a glimpse of her since? That could hardly be called courting. "Well," he admitted bashfully, "I don't really know. There's a girl—her name's Rose Salter," he added, suddenly hoping that old Mr. Crabtree might somehow know something about her.

"Salter, eh? Ay, well it's a good old Haliford name, that is. Ah've known a few Salters i' me time. Let's see? Yer did tell me where yer workin'? Ay, o' course, Ah remember. Ah telephoned. Frank Tirril's. Are yer makking owt out o' Frank these days, lad?"

Edward had to confess that he wasn't making much out of Frank, that he did not like Mr. Tirril, and saw no future for himself in the noil and waste trade in Pooley Road.

"Ah see," said Mr. Crabtree slowly. He finished his whisky carefully, smacking his lips once or twice. Then he looked shrewdly across at Edward, his eyes very bright in his leathery old face. "Ah fancy Ah gave yer a bit o' good advice at funeral, didn't Ah? Ay, well, a piece more'll hurt nobody. Nah Ah don't talk like a lot o' old folk. They've forgotten they ivver wor young. In fact, some on 'em nivver wor young—they wor born wi' one foot i' t'grave. Tak' no notice o' such folk. Just listen to me. Stick up for yer-sen, lad. Nivver mind what they say. Do whativver yer've a fancy for doing, see? It's yer own life yer laking about with, nobody else's. An' yer can only live it once, an' nobody else can live it for yer, see? If yer mak' mistakes, all right, mak' mistakes. So long as they're yer own mistakes. If yer want to court a lass, go in an' court her. Ah wor thowt a bit of a wild beggar when Ah wor a lad your age, an' my missis i' them days were the prize good lass round here—queen o' the Sunday School an' whatnot—and they laughed at me when Ah went courtin' her, but by gow!—within a month or two, Ah had her waitin' up here for me i' blizzards an' lying like fury to get there. An' if yer see nowt for yer-sen in Haliford or in t'Haliford trade, then to 'ell wi' em both, Ah say, lad. It's a wide world, an' there's still summat to be picked up in it, whativver they may say. An' as Ah think Ah said to yer afore—go yer own way, lad, an' them as doesn't like it, let 'em bloody well lump it. Nah, put that bit o' paper i' thi pocket—nay, nay, don't start on thankyou-ing me—and use it for spendin' brass. An' if tha wants to get drunk on it, well get drunk on it. Only don't ask me to bail thee aht. Ah mun be goin' home, Edward lad. Ah can hear me old bones crackin' like rotten firewood."

Outside, the old man shook Edward's hand, banged him

on the shoulder, then went off without another word. Edward set off briskly down the hill, with the wind assisting him and blurring the lights of Haliford below. Sixty-five pounds! What could you do with sixty-five pounds? Nearly everything, it seemed, at the moment. Never in his life had he felt so bold and free. It was not only the money that made him feel like that. The old man's heartening words had had their effect too. Edward was so used to hearing his elders preach caution that this bold advice was almost intoxicating. He made no plans. He could not think yet what difference the possession of sixty-five pounds could make to any plan he had ever had or might have. Indeed, his one immediate desire was to spend some of the money lavishly entertaining Rose Salter. But he was a bigger and bolder Edward Fielding than the one Haliford had known so far, and he descended upon it like a conqueror.

The Edward who two nights later rang the bell at Number Forty-four Slater Street had lost all resemblance to a conqueror. He looked apprehensive. But there he was, ringing the bell, and then rather shakily standing his ground, not too near the door.

A tallish, dark girl, whom he recognised at once as a girl he had seen several times while he had been hanging about the end of the street, raised her eyebrows at him. "Yes?"

"Does—er—Miss Salter live here, please?" He swallowed hard.

"Yes, she does," said the girl brightly.

"Oh!—er—is she in, please?"

"Yes." Brighter than ever.

"Could I speak to her, please?"

"You are speaking to her," said the girl coolly. She looked at poor Edward's face, then laughed in a friendly fashion. "Here, you don't want me, do you?"

"No, it's Miss Rose Salter——"

"I know. Come in a minute." And she led the way into the sitting-room, turned on the light, drew the curtains, put Edward into one slippery armchair and herself into another and then stared at him. He glanced uneasily round the shabby, congested little room, and then it came to him at once, with heart-breaking certainty, that though this was Rose's house, she herself was not here. He was so instantly positive about it and so miserable that he lost his shyness. "She's not here, is she?"

"Well, if you know that, why did you come asking for her?" said Miss Salter.

"I didn't know it when I asked, but as soon as I walked in here I knew."

"Well, would you believe it!" cried the girl, half-amused, half-impressed. "We'd better get on a proper footing. I'm Nellie, her sister. And if I'm not mistaken, I've seen you once or twice lately at the end there, haven't I? Thought so. Here, are you the boy she was out with on the moors, the other Sunday—week last Sunday, wasn't it?"

"Yes. My name's Edward Fielding."

"That's right. Y'know, Rose was a bit gone on you. Yes, she was. What happened? Did you have a row?"

"We arranged to meet," said Edward unhappily. "And I—had an accident and was very late, and she wasn't there——"

"Can't expect her to wait all night for you," said Nellie briskly. "Go on."

"Well—you see—I've never seen her since. I didn't know exactly where she lived or anything, and I've been looking for her ever since."

"What a pair of pie-cans!" And Nellie laughed, though not maliciously. "I'll bet anything that's why she decided to go to London."

Edward's heart jumped and then fell several thousand feet. "London?" he faltered.

"Yes, London. She and her friend, Alice Hargreaves, went off to London last week—Thursday, it was—they've been there a week now, haven't they?"

"But—but—she's not *staying* in London, is she?" he enquired miserably.

"'Course she is. Got a job there—in a café. Don't know how long it'll last or whether she'll like it, but if I know Rose, she won't come back in a hurry. She'll stick it. She's that sort of kid. Well, cheer up!"

"I'm sorry, but I don't feel like cheering up," replied Edward bluntly. "Everything's spoilt now. I don't know what to do."

Nellie regarded him sympathetically. "You're absolutely gone on her, aren't you? I can see that. Well, I can tell you this—though she is my own sister—there's not a nicer kid in this town than young Rose. She's very good-looking——"

"I know," Edward groaned.

"And what's more, she's got a lovely disposition, she really has——"

"Who has?" asked a voice, making Edward jump. A plump, rather untidy woman, with a merry face, had just entered.

"Rose has," said Nellie. "Mother, this young fellow's a friend of hers——"

"Well, I don't know!" cried Mrs. Salter, quite good-humouredly. "Wonders never cease!" She descended upon and obliterated a small stool, folded her arms, and took stock of Edward. After a moment of this, she nodded and smiled at Nellie, as if to say "Yes, he'll do. Looks a very nice young fellow."

"He didn't know she'd gone to London," Nellie explained, "and he's a bit upset about it. They arranged to meet, and he had an accident——"

"Fancy! Tut-t-t-t!" went Mrs. Salter.

"And so he was late and she'd gone. When was that?" she asked Edward.

"A week last Tuesday."

"That's it," cried Nellie in triumph. "You see, mother, that was the very night she came back from Alice Hargreaves' and said she was going to London."

"You're right, love, it was," cried Mrs. Salter, equally triumphant. "And that might have started her off on this London business."

"I'm sure it did," said Nellie.

"So, you see, young man, happen it's your fault she went away from home."

"But, Mrs. Salter, I couldn't help it," cried the unhappy Edward. "I don't want her to be in London. How can I see her if she's in London?"

"I believe," said Mrs. Salter, looking him straight in the eye and speaking with the most tremendous deliberation, "you're in love with our Rose."

Such words sound almost indecent to Haliford ears, but Edward was not afraid of them now. "I am, Mrs. Salter. Yes, I know I am."

"Of course he is," said Nellie, with relish.

"Well, well, well," and Mrs. Salter chuckled fatly, "I don't blame you, young man. If I were a young chap, I'd be in love with our Rose. You couldn't do better—if she'd have you. And mind you, she's particular and a bit serious, Rose is, not like our Nellie here."

"Mother!" It was the great Nellie's turn to be embarrassed, rather to Edward's relief.

Mrs. Salter looked solemnly at him, and, startled, he felt he was about to be called on to answer some terribly intimate question. "Before we go any further," she began slowly, "will you take a glass of beer or 'ave a cup o' tea?"

"Oh—I don't know—thanks very much——" he stammered.

"We'll all have a drink o' tea." She rose with surprising ease. "Kettle's on. Shan't be a minute." And out she waddled. Nellie now began firing questions at him. Where did he live? How old was he? Where did he work? What did he want to do? Did he like Haliford? And so on. This kept them busy until Mrs. Salter returned with the tea, some rock buns and half a jam pasty.

"Yes," said Mrs. Salter, with her mouth full, "chap that gets our Rose will be lucky. And I 'ope it's not going to be a Londoner now, 'cos I think nothing o' them. All lahdidah and show, and nothing at back of it."

"You don't know anything about Londoners, mother," Nellie protested.

"No, not I," said Mrs. Salter heartily. "But that isn't going to stop me not liking 'em. Why should it? But our Rose has got plenty o' sense."

"More than that Alice Hargreaves has," said Nellie.

"Oh, 'er! I never could understand why our Rose ever took up with 'er at all. First time she brought 'er here, I said to myself, 'You're a flighty little piece, you are. Bet you can't keep your eyes to yourself two minutes.' One o' these blondes you read about, she is."

"She isn't, mother. Alice is quite dark."

"It's all the same, dark or fair's immaterial. All depends on your disposition," said Mrs. Salter in a deep philosophical manner. "And though I'd trust our Rose anywhere, I'd just as soon she'd gone to London with anybody else. But there—what's to be *is* to be, I always say. So why worry? Be 'appy while you can. That is so, isn't it?" she asked Edward. "You're not trying my pasty. It's good. Won't do you any harm at all."

"No, thank you."

"He doesn't want to eat, mother. And you wouldn't," said Nellie.

"I would," her mother replied promptly. She chuckled, then suddenly looked grave, and both she and Nellie stared at Edward as if he were an interesting invalid. He felt a fool, but that did not prevent him from asking the question that had been trembling on his lips for the last five minutes.

"Could I have her address, please?"

"She has two addresses," said Mrs. Salter with pride. "One where she lodges, one where she works. We have 'em both."

"Perhaps I'd better have them both too," Edward suggested.

Mrs. Salter looked at Nellie, who nodded, as if to say that it was only right that Edward should have both addresses. "You write 'em down for him then, Nellie," said her mother. "Though what good they'll do you, I don't know."

"He can write to her, can't he?" said Nellie, as she went out.

"He can, but I reckon nothing o' writing. If I'd had to do my courting on paper, I'd have been working at Sligsby's to this day." She turned to Edward. "Our Rose has written twice. She's liking it, so far. She has to wear a fancy dress, she says, green with orange collar and cuffs, and a little apron. She'll look nice in it too. And she's been to the Tower of London and St. Paulses' and somewhere else, I forget. Have you ever been to London?"

"Yes, a long time ago, when I was a kid," Edward replied. "I went with my father—for three days. I don't remember much about it."

"Me and my husband went once. Two days. And what they charged, when you asked for bit of tongue or boiled ham with your tea, I'll never forget. Robbery! And all them buses and underground tubes and whatnot! And folks! I says, 'Well, wherever are they all going to?' And my husband says, 'They're not going anywhere.' And I says, 'Nay, they must be going somewhere, you fathead.' And then he gets a bit short with me. His boots were too tight for one thing, and I told him before we set off they would be——"

"Here you are." Nellie was handing him a sheet of note-paper. It had a design of pink roses at the top, and a buttery smear at the bottom. But it also had the two addresses, the two life-lines thrown to him in his desolating sea. *Miss Rose Salter, Copper Kettle Café, Halberd Street, London, W.C. 2.* And then again—*c/o Mrs. Burlow,* 18, *Pitt Square, Islington, N.*1. Very carefully, he folded up this precious document and put it in his pocket-book.

"Thanks very much," he said earnestly to them both. "I think—I ought to be going now."

"Very glad to have seen you," said Mrs. Salter, brushing crumbs off herself and then rising.

"When I write to Rose," said Nellie, smiling at him, "I'll tell her you called and said you had an accident that night and everything." She went to the door with him, let him out, and looked hard at him as he stood there, lingering rather miserably. "And cheer up!"

"Yes," said Edward mournfully.

She laughed. "Here," and she stepped forward into the dusk of the street, put a hand on each arm, and then, to his astonishment, leaned forward and kissed him neatly and warmly on the left cheek, "that'll do to be going on with. You're a nice kid. I'll tell her that too. Good night."

As the door banged behind him and he walked slowly away, his spirits sank lower than ever. There had been a certain interest and even excitement in talking in there to her sister and her mother, but now even they had left him. This Haliford was a desert of paving stones, railings and lamp-posts. Rose was two hundred miles away, lighting up some other place, glorious by day, in green with orange collar and cuffs, at the hallowed Copper Kettle Café in Halberd Street, and remote as a star, at night, in the mysterious Pitt Square, Islington. Miles and miles and miles away! And had been this past week. He saw himself idiotically looking for her, hanging about this street, night after night, when he ought to have known, when something ought to have told him at once, she was no longer there. It gave him a fierce contempt for himself. Somehow it made any and every chap who so much as looked at her in Halberd Street or Islington his superior. It was obvious that life could no longer be lived, only endured, here in Haliford, this empty shell of a town. Wearily, through dust and ashes, he trudged home.

"Herbert," he began, later that night, when they had both had supper and their mother had gone to bed, "you've been to London once or twice lately, haven't you?"

Herbert might be the great man of the house, but he was only human, and this sudden interest in his travels on the part of his sulky and vaguely scornful young brother was not unflattering. He brightened up, with a flash of spectacles, at once. "I've been twice during these last eighteen months," he replied, rather pompously. "Once to take that analysis——"

"I know," said Edward, who didn't. "Well, what did you make of it? I mean," he added hastily, "about jobs and that sort of thing."

Herbert looked bewildered. "I don't quite follow you, Ted."

"There aren't as many people out of work there as they're here, eh? Isn't that so? Aren't there more jobs going in London?"

"So far as I know," said Herbert slowly, "there aren't many jobs going anywhere, particularly for untrained——"

"Never mind about that," Edward interrupted sharply. He was not going to let this talk turn into the old dreary channel. "The point is, business is better there than it is here, isn't it? I'm sure I've seen that in the papers."

"Yes, you have." Herbert had now the air of the consultant. "They're not as badly off in London as we are in the north. In fact, a lot of new factories have been built down there. We've just had an interesting little case——"

"Yes, yes, Herbert, but just a minute. D'you think if I went there, and if I had enough to live on for a month or two while I was looking round, I'd pick something up?"

"You? What's the idea, Ted?"

"Never mind the idea. Would I?"

Herbert shook his head, solemnly, irritatingly. "I doubt it. You can put that idea out of your head. It's as bad as all the others you've had. To begin with, how are you going to live there while you're doing nothing? Costs money, y'know, Ted. We can't afford to keep you——"

"I don't want you or anybody else to keep me. I can keep myself."

"You can't. How?"

What was he to say? He hesitated for a moment, and perhaps it was the look of mournful triumph on Herbert's face, a look that told him plainly he was a baby who did not understand the world, that decided him. He plunged in. "Herbert, I've got some money. It's just been given to me. I can't explain. I promised not to."

"Ted, I don't like the sound of this. You've got to explain."

"I tell you I can't, because I promised not to. But you needn't worry. I didn't steal it, or didn't win it in a sweepstake or anything like that. It was given to me—if you must know—by a friend of grandfather's. It isn't much. But with that and the bit I have in the post office, I could manage until I found something. And I'd do anything, at first. Herbert," he continued in growing excitement, "you and mother don't need me here. I know that. You've told me often enough--no, I'm not complaining, honestly I'm not, I'm just telling you the truth—and if, as you say, I'm not doing any good here, I just might as well try there."

"But what do you know about London?" said Herbert, struggling out of his deep amazement. "I mean to say, you don't know anybody there, wouldn't know where to go or anything."

"What does that matter? Thousands of chaps like me go there without knowing anything. You know they do. Listen, Herbert, I'm going. I must go. I tell you—I must. And Clewes and Tirril's are no good. Mr. Cr—— somebody—told me only the other day they wouldn't last much longer. That's a fact, Herbert. I just might as well go now. You say yourself I'm doing no good here."

"Yes, but what good are you going to do there?"

"I don't know, but I can try. Herbert," and he stopped, then went closer to his brother, and when he spoke again, lowered his voice, "will you explain it to my mother? It's no good me trying to. She won't understand, and there'll only be a row. And I don't want a row, if I'm going. Will you, Herbert?"

Herbert, who clearly felt that he was being stampeded, said that he would see. Edward began asking him questions about London, and this time proved a good listener, so that it was very late indeed when they went up to bed. It was late, too, when Edward rose next morning, so that even if he had wanted to talk to his mother, there would not have been time for any proper explanation. But he did not want to talk to her, not before Herbert had said something. He was afraid of that dark penetrating glance of hers, afraid that she would discover all his secrets at once and make him look silly even to himself. Immediately after tea, the next night, Friday, he went up to his bedroom and turned the pages of a book, dreamily, for more than an hour and a half. When finally he descended into the dining-room again, Herbert had been and gone. And Herbert had said something to his mother. One glance at her told him that. And he felt frightened.

"Herbert's just been telling me a queer tale," she began, in an unusually flat tone of voice. "He says somebody gave you some money, and now you want to go off to London with it."

"Yes, mother," in a shaky little voice.

"How much is it?"

"Sixty-five pounds."

"Sixty-five pound indeed! It's a funny thing nobody takes it into his head to give me or Herbert sixty-five pound. What have you supposed to have done for it, eh?"

"Nothing. It was—because of my grandfather."

She came up to him, still carrying the cup she had been drying, and looked him full in the face. "Are you telling the truth, Edward?" she demanded.

He could feel his temper rising now as he stared straight back at her. "Yes, I am, mother. And don't ask me any more questions about it, because I'm not going to answer them."

"I see. And what are you going to do when you get to London, pray?"

"Look for a job. Like thousands of other chaps have done. You say I'm doing no good here. All right then, I'll try there."

"And then when your money's gone and nobody wants you there, I suppose you'll come back here and ask our Herbert to keep you, eh?"

"No, I shan't," Edward found himself shouting angrily. "Don't you worry. You'll be rid of me."

"There's no need to shout, Edward."

"And there's no need to tell me I'll be sponging on Herbert either," said Edward sulkily. "I haven't started yet, and I don't mean to. I can look after myself."

"That you can't," said his mother. But her tone had changed, softened a little. "You're nothing but a big baby.

Well, I suppose you'll have to learn some time." She regarded him speculatively. "There's a girl at the bottom of this business, isn't there? You've had her on your mind this last week or two, haven't you? Does she live in London—or what?"

He did not reply. He must either tell her everything or keep it all to himself. She would not understand, so he would keep it to himself. Perhaps she read this thought too in his mind, for she did not press her questions. Instead, to his astonishment and delight, she said: "When do you want to go?"

"Monday," he found himself replying. He had not thought about it until this moment.

"Well, you'll want some clean clothes to take with you. Don't see why you should leave this house—even if you're only going to make a fool of yourself—looking like a rag-bag." She thought for a moment. "I suppose you know you've got some relations in London. Your father's cousin, Alfred Fielding, lives there. I've got the address somewhere. Willesden, I think it is, unless they've moved, because it's years since we had anything to do with 'em. Alfred Fielding was never any great shakes, and his wife—a Londoner—is worse. Still, they're relations. You'd better go and see 'em. And I'll write and say you're going. And remind me to give you the address."

And that was all. No real shindy. So immensely relieved that he felt a sudden glow of affection for her, he wanted to say something that would express this feeling, but could not think of anything and was so afraid that her mood might change and plunge them into a terrific row, he did nothing but nod at her in a serious responsible sort of way, then hurry upstairs again. But this time he was not going to dream over a book. Now he could write to Rose (with a choice of two addresses), explain how he had missed her that night, tell her how he had tried to find her, then stagger her with the tremendous news. Should he admit at once, in this letter, that he was deliberately following her to London? Or should he keep that until later, and simply say now that he, too, had had enough of Haliford and was trying London? Before he had written a letter that did not appear to be the work of a blot-scattering lunatic, he had tried both versions and even a mysterious mixture of them, and by the time he ran to the end of Sutcliffe Place to make sure of the eleven o'clock post, he had had his fill of literary composition. The actual letter he dropped into the pillar-box began rather stiffly with a "Dear Miss Salter" and ended correctly enough with a "Yours sincerely, Edward Fielding," but in between it slackened and softened and warmed up a good deal, was downright steaming mush in places, and Edward, cooling down now that the letter had gone, remembered some of these passages with misgiving and saw a haughty young beauty in green with orange collar and cuffs (he had addressed it, after much consideration, to the café) turning her nose up at them and finally tossing them into the fire. True, the Rose Salter he remembered from that Sunday did not seem that kind of a girl. But somehow this actual Rose Salter was very dim in his memory. He could not even remember exactly what she looked like, could not summon a proper image of her face at all, unlike the lovers in popular songs, who were for ever being haunted by faces. In bed that night, he tried hard to see her face again, but it eluded him. Instead, all manner of ridiculous and disgusting faces came floating up out of the dark.

He saw her for a moment, however, and as clear as she was in the sunlight of the Glen, and this was in a dream he had just before waking the next morning. It was one of those rare dreams that you remember and that make no sense and yet seem more significant than most of the things that happen to you when you are awake and in your senses. He was back in a farmhouse where he had stayed as a child, not far from Pately Bridge in the Dales. There again were the white-washed walls inside, the long settle, the grandfather clock with the moon face, the case of stuffed birds, and other things he remembered. But of course the room was not quite the same. It was bigger, had a long desk in the middle, and all round the walls were piles of ledgers, old papers, and the like. He had to do something—some fantastic job or other—in this room that he knew he could not do. Yet if he did not do it, he could not get out, and he wanted to get out. Two men were there, one of them small and thin and sneering, the other a big fat fellow in black, with a pitted purple nose, who was roaring at him: "You miserable little lout. What d'you mean, you can't do it? Haven't I told you how? Hasn't *he* told you?" And then there, looking in at the window, from the bright terrorless world outside, was Rose, clear and complete to the least shimmer of down on her cheek, and their eyes met, and her eyes widened and widened, and there was horror in them. For another second he was still in that room, rooted in cold terror. And then he was awake, with a fading fringe of ghostly menace round him, safe in his bed in Haliford. Saturday morning. With something very important and very pleasant to do. Yes. To tell Mr. Tirril he had done with him.

And if Mr. Tirril had been coached in his part all through the night, he could not have performed it better. "Now I'll tell you what it is, Fielding," he began at once, after arriving late, "I'm just sick and tired of telling you to do things when you don't do 'em." The old dreary nagging.

"Such as what?" enquired Edward coolly.

"Don't *such-as-what* me," he cried, coming nearer. "I'll have none of that talk. Now did I or did I not tell you, last Wednesday, to send Wilsons samples of all our Fifties?"

"You did." Edward was enjoying this.

"Oh, I did, did I? Well that's something. I thought you were going to have the face to tell me I didn't. Well, if I told you to send 'em, then why didn't you send 'em? What am I here for? What are you here for? What," he pursued, in a passion now, "are we all here for? Is this an office or what?"

"Don't ask me," said Edward. "It's yours. You ought to know."

This, combined with bad trade, grumbling customers, an ailing wife, a poor digestion, a disagreeable bank manager, was too much for Mr. Tirril. He gave a sort of yelp, almost jumped off his feet, then to relieve his feelings swept an arm along the counter and with it a confused mass of noils, wastes, blue paper, sample tickets, thus destroying Edward's labour of the last half-hour. "I'd like to give you a clout on the lug for answering back like that," Mr. Tirril shouted. "Why didn't you send them samples?"

"I did," Edward shouted back at him.

"Then why haven't they got 'em?"

"They have got 'em. They owned receipt of 'em yesterday. I can't help it if you won't bother to read your own letters."

"That's enough. Get on with that sampling." And he looked at the mess of noils, waste, paper, and tickets, facing Edward on the counter. He even made it a bigger mess by throwing a half-wrapped sample into it.

This was enough for Edward. "Get on with it yourself."

"What!"

"I said, 'Get on with it yourself,'" shouted Edward, and swept the whole mess back along the counter. "And don't think you're going to sack me, because I've sacked myself."

"Clark, give him his money," said Mr. Tirril, white with temper. "And don't come asking me for a reference, Fielding, because you won't get one. I'm in the warehouse, Clark, if I'm wanted."

Half an hour later, when the head-shaking Clark had given him his week's money and his insurance card, Edward was sorry that he had behaved so badly, for after all he had been some time in this office and poor, nagging, unlucky Mr. Tirril was not really a bad sort. (And a good reference might have been useful.) But the mischief was done now. He said good-bye to the boy, and shook hands with Mr. Clark, who whispered that he might cook up a reference himself if it was urgently necessary. And when he learnt that Edward was going to London, he became excited, disclosed the fact that he had a sister there, married to a jobbing builder in West Kensington, and insisted upon giving Edward her address, all written out in that neat hand of his, even to a telephone number added in red ink. "You might do worse," he whispered impressively. "Her husband's a smartish chap, with a lot of irons in the fire, a lot of irons. One of these regular London chaps, he is, talks fourteen to the dozen. You might do a lot worse than ask him about things." So Edward, feeling something of a desperado, walked down the greasy stairs into Pooley Road for the last time.

His mother did not go with Edward to the station on Monday morning. After working hard all the week-end to make sure that all his shirts and underclothes and socks were clean and darned, and helping him to pack them and his second-best suit into the one big suitcase, all as willingly as if this had been her plan and not his, she suddenly drew away from it and him, as if ashamed of some weakness and lack of sense, and was dry and ironical with him at the very last. But Herbert contrived to get away from his analysing for quarter of an hour, to see his brother off on the ten o'clock train. Both of them knew all about the ten o'clock train. It took Haliford men to the wool sales in London. It took them to buy wool in Australia and South America. It took them to sell Haliford fabrics all over the world, from Paris to Shanghai. Some of these fellows, with bags fantastically labelled, were already settling into their corners of first-class smokers, frowning over their pipes at copies of the *Yorkshire Post* and *Manchester Guardian*. Wearing his best suit and shoes, with two newspapers under his arm, Edward was enjoying an adventurous holiday feeling. In a new notecase in his inside pocket, he had fifteen equally new pound notes, an immensely important cheque book from the Haliford and District Bank, and also a letter to a London bank, so that he might have been a financier. In his right-hand waistcoat pocket was a ticket to King's Cross, London, to say nothing of Beauty, Romance, Riches, Glory, Love. Both he and Herbert looked anxiously at the train, as if to see that it was all there, had no necessary parts missing. The station itself, with its glass-covered altitudes of quiet and indifference, its sudden snortings and red glares, its high echoing voices, its fascinating suggestion of only being half in Haliford, the other half being anywhere you would like it to be, diminished and engulfed them both in a not unfriendly fashion, so that they were a pair of bustling anxious midgets. Until, that is, Edward took his seat at the window of a third-class carriage, in which the only other occupants were two middle-aged women (the sad, whispering kind, the perpetual travelling mourners) even more anxious than himself. Then he became part of the train, and Herbert, standing outside near the open window, was gripped firmly by Haliford.

"It only stops at Doncaster, Grantham and Peterborough," said Herbert solemnly.

"That's right," said Edward, almost answering for the train now.

There is one word, waiting like a verbal man-trap, that all people who see other people off by train are compelled to use over and over again. Herbert began his session with it now. "Well," he said, and stopped, wondering what to say. "You know where to find a good cheap hotel just for to-night, don't you?"

As this question had been discussed at length the night before, Edward did. But this was not the time for saying so, shortly, rudely. "Yes," he replied earnestly. "Not far from the station, is it? Bloomsbury."

"That's it. Not far from the station." Herbert turned to watch a few late-comers, old hands, come strolling up. He recognised one as an important fellow-townsman and nodded to him. Then he gave his attention, with that reluctant conscientiousness with which one turns again to an invalid in bed, to Edward again. "Well," he began once more, "you'll let us know how you go on, of course?"

With the momentary aspect of the most dutiful son of a house, Edward said gravely that he would.

The whole platform was whistled at, severely.

"Well," said Herbert, "I think you're off now. Good-bye, Ted."

" 'Bye, Herbert!"

Clouds of steam, brightening for a moment in the sunlight, then the darkness of a tunnel, then black wet walls, then backs of little houses, washing on the line, hen-runs, children playing on cindered waste land, a mill or two, a brownish-grey scribble of houses changing into a green scribble of fields; and Haliford was gone. And the

Edward who had done with it, who was being carried due south at a mile a minute, no longer felt the elated impulsive adventurer, who slashed away his past at one stroke, but felt small, solemn, a little frightened to discover how actual events can shape themselves quite ruthlessly, and with an air of terrific finality, to a plan once put into operation. And here, in this carriage hurling itself down the long straight track, his plan stopped. What, then, would happen next?

VII

IN Greater London, a stone and brick forest nearly thirty miles long, thirty miles broad, eight million people eat and drink and sleep, wander among seven thousand miles of streets, pay their insurance money, send for the doctor, and die. Through the centre of this vast area of asphalt hills and paved valleys, these orchards of lamp-posts and traffic lights, the River Thames goes winding, looking from above no more than a silvered thread lying across an arterial road. Yet the river made all this. The river brought the old Roman galleys (one of them could be floated on the weekly milk supply of the modern city) from Ostia to the port of Londinium, for those cargoes of wheat and lead that might be taken as symbolic of the later national character of these island people. The river carefully laid along its terraces a nice mixture of clay and sand, that brick-earth out of which this forest grew. The inhabitants drink the river, run it through their wash-basins and bath-tubs, two hundred million gallons a day. Do they think about the river? Some do, even apart from those who still work on its greasy dimpled flood. Everything that man has thought about is considered here by somebody, from the diameter of Betelgeuse to the smaller parasites of the flea. Not since the City of the Golden Gates sank with all Atlantis has there been, in any one area of the world, so much thinking about everything, as well as so much stupidity about everything, as there is here. Eight million human creatures. The commercial capital of the globe. But there is commerce here unknown to the Port of London Authority, the Stock Exchange, the Board of Trade. The thoughts, the dreams, the old shuddering fears of these eight millions depart along fantastic wave-lengths, leaving our own familiar space-time continuum, to build little heavens and hells in new time and strange dimensions of space. In exchange, radiations from distant stars penetrate the haze and perhaps bring to the pavements below obscure news that cannot be found in the evening papers. As we know, there are eight million private dramas being acted in this jungle of brickwork and cement, where steel-clawed ravenous monsters like bankruptcy and unemployment and angina pectoris and starvation and cancer come crashing through the thickets, where a favourable bank balance and a good digestion and an easy mind and love-found-and-fulfilled occasionally light the jungle ways with a flash of blue wings. But there are also eight million parts being acted here in a gigantic Mystery, with green globes and moons and suns and black space as scenic sets, a few tattered pages as a prompt book, and two famous illusionists, Here and Now, as stage managers. And what this is all about, nobody knows. The youngest of six half-starved children, listening to the rats in the darkness of a back room in Hoxton, does not know. The expensively educated and comfortably maintained elderly clerical gentleman who writes for the papers telling us all is well (or as well as is deserved) with this youngest of six in

Hoxton, does not know. The gaunt young man hard at it in the Reading Room of the British Museum, preparing to denounce the elderly cleric and all his kind, does not know. Eight million, with all their houses, furniture, knick-knacks, mortgages, insurance policies, bills of sale, prescriptions and love letters, rolling on in one gigantic Mystery. And eight million busy with their own private dramas, making the whole stone forest steam and hum. And there among them, toiling away with a thousand other organisations to victual them, is the Copper Kettle Café Company, Ltd.

Strange as it may seem, this company owed its success to the fact that most of the eight million are still poetically and not scientifically minded. Sometimes in happy ignorance, sometimes perhaps not, it fed its customers with increasing quantities of citric and tartaric acid and cotton-seed oil, sulphur dioxide and sodium sulphate and potassium bromate, manganese and copper, lead and arsenic. But these chemicals and metallic poisons were consumed in an atmosphere, specially created by the company, that lured the vague poetical mind of the customer away from all consideration of scientific matters. It reminded the customer of the time when meat and fish were not taken out of a tin, when there was real yeast and honest flour in bread, when fruit came straight from the tree and not from sulphur dioxide gas chambers. It belonged to some Arcadian ideal of English life, in which buxom, apple-cheeked landladies and sweet demure serving-maids waited behind chintz curtains upon the traveller with all that was fresh, pure, delicious in food and drink. Once inside a Copper Kettle café, which had a large imitation copper kettle hanging above its entrance, you forgot the roaring and stinking petrol engines outside, the smoke and the fog and the mud, the miles and miles of brick and stone and steel concrete, the whole metropolitan madness. You were back where actually you never belonged. You were a child again with a picture book. That was the trick, and it worked well. Every branch had the same features: the copper kettle as a sign, the countrified patterned curtains, the imitation brick floor, the painted tables and chairs and settles, the picture-book crockery, the young waitresses in green and orange uniforms. The original café had been established in the City, not for the employers, with their passion for large authentic juicy pieces of meat and grilled soles and the like, things that cannot be faked and that cost money, but for the minor cashiers, the clerks, the typists. Now there were three more cafés in the City, and four other branches within three or four miles of the parent establishment. The latest to be opened was in Halberd Street, W.C.2, which is a short street just east of St. Martin's Lane and north of the Strand. It is a very mixed sort of neighbourhood this, a huddle and muddle of small taverns, unambitious business premises, shops that sell cigarettes, racing papers and Balzac's *Droll Tales*, publishing offices, Stage Doors, and obscure agencies. The Copper Kettle was the only light-lunch-and-tea place of the semi-genteel kind—for there were several small shops that catered for taximen and porters and door-keepers within two minutes' walk—and there was a fair chance of its doing a reasonably good trade, even though it could never have the turnover of the City branches. Mr. Isaacson, the managing director, who had once held high office with a famous firm of popular caterers, had been strongly in favour of the venture, and as Mr. Isaacson seemed to know everything there was to know about people with a shilling or two to spend on refreshment, he had been allowed to have his way. If he had not (and it was touch-and-go with Colonel Brandley at the board meeting), probably Rose Salter would not have left Haliford for London.

She and Alice had not seen Mr. Isaacson, and never did see him to their knowledge. They had seen Frank's acquaintance and a Mr. Smalley, and it was Mr. Smalley who had decided to give them a trial. It may seem odd that two inexperienced girls from the provinces, backed by nothing more than an unimportant introduction, should have succeeded so easily when there were hundreds of London girls, many with previous experience, in search of work. They themselves imagined that Frank's introduction had done the trick. Actually, Mr. Isaacson had recently told his subordinates that, so long as there were two or three steady old hands in every café, the Copper Kettle waitresses must be attractive and lively, for people were tired of being waited upon by weary-looking girls. Mr. Smalley saw at once that both these girls had a certain North-country freshness and vitality about them, that Rose was attractive, unusually so, that Alice was a brisk lively piece, the kind that gives the regular male patrons as good as she gets, and as his associate, Frank's acquaintance, had already put in a word for them, he did not hesitate to give them a month's trial as assistant waitresses to receive twenty-five shillings a week wages and a certain proportion of the pooled tips. The company made its own uniforms, and they were fitted at once. Two days after arriving in London, they were reporting to Miss Finberg, the manageress of the Halberd Street branch.

It did not take them three minutes to discover that the luck, which so far had been phenomenal, was no longer with them, and that Miss Finberg was not on their side. She was a tallish woman of thirty-five, the dark, smart, enamelled-looking type that is always managing something, and she seemed to them a figure of immense prestige, London itself with permanently waved hair and a black dress and keys. She was polite to them, rapidly explained their hours and duties, and handed them over to two senior waitresses. But they knew that she disapproved of them, and imagined that it was because they were little nobodies from Haliford. It was only later that they discovered that she objected to having waitresses appointed for her, without any consultation, by Mr. Smalley, and considered that as manageress she ought to be allowed to choose her own staff. (It was the old Oriental question, which has shattered armies and split empires before to-day, of "face.") So she saw them not as two eager youngsters from Haliford, anxious to learn the job and please everybody, but as the two girls that Mr. Smalley had had the nerve to push on to her, and so every time she noticed them she was reminded of grievances and injustice. Therefore, it was hard for them to satisfy her, impossible to please her.

Rose was shown what to do by a senior waitress, who had been carrying poached eggs on toast and pots of tea for the last ten years, called Wade, who had plump rouged cheeks, henna'd hair, and a wide, irregular-toothed smile. She was engaged to a steward on one of the ships that run to Australia, and was hoping to be married soon, which was one reason perhaps why she was so comfortable and friendly. She knew every labour-saving trick. She spoke of the customers always as if they were fairly amiable but occasionally dangerous lunatics. The people she knew outside the café obviously did not belong to the same species. To enter the Copper Kettle Café was practically to offer Miss Wade your certificate of mental incapacity. This was fortunate for Rose, who, in spite of her trembling anxiety at first, which made every trip to a table a terrific ordeal, could not help making a few mistakes, for it meant that Miss Wade was always lenient, her view being that the customer was always wrong, and more often than not wilfully wrong, a view directly opposed to that of Mr. Isaacson and his directors. Rose's chief difficulty was in understanding what people said. She was used to hearing people shout at the top of their broad Haliford voices. Here they either mumbled into their newspapers or rattled away in high birdlike London tones that made no sense at all. Some were disagreeable: they had been bossed about half the day themselves, and now it was their turn to be superior and unpleasant to somebody. Some of the women obviously hated the sight of her pretty eager face. Others brightened up at the sight of it, and asked Rose a question or two. The men either took no notice at all, hardly seemed to know where they were, or grinned, winked, showed off, chaffed, or in other ways kept on asserting their existence as grand males. Unlike Miss Wade, who took it easy and thought about the Red Sea, the impudent girls in Sydney, and bedroom suites in Stoke Newington, and had only the minimum of time and no real sympathy to spare for customers, Rose was not only willing but deeply sympathetic. She felt sorry for most of the people who came in; they looked so worried and tired; and she was only too anxious to rush away and bring them quarts of tea, and mounds of poached eggs. Some of them were exciting too; even the other girls, hardened Londoners though they were, agreed about that. Real actors and actresses, playing or rehearsing at the neighbouring theatres (and what a thrill it was to walk past those "Stage Doors" every morning and evening!) came in sometimes, and if there were more than two of them, they sat all together, talked loudly but mysteriously, and laughed a lot, not caring a bit if everybody else was staring at them. Twice Rose helped Miss Wade (who called them "theatricals," pretended they were nothing out of the ordinary, but was impressed) to serve them. And then on her third afternoon there, when the lunch-hour rush was over and the place was almost empty, she had quite a talk with one odd and exciting person. He came in, carrying a mass of typed sheets in a ragged blue cover, flopped into a chair, and instead of looking at the menu he stared gloomily at his typed sheets. He was an untidy fattish man; he had thick eyebrows, a turned-up nose, and a loose comical mouth; and he smelt strongly of tobacco and had ash all over his crumpled coat. When Rose, who was doing Miss Wade's work as well as her own, during this quiet time, asked him what he wanted, he did not even look up but groaned: "Anything."

"Well," said Rose, "but what's *anything?*" And silently she added: "Now tell me properly, please, Mr. Untidy Funnyface. It's bad enough looking after all this end of the place by myself, without you making it worse. Be sensible!"

"Oh, I dunno." He looked from his messy typed sheets, which Rose could see had names and speeches on them and must be something to do with a play, to the menu, and from the menu up at Rose. Then he smiled, quite cheerfully, and promptly gave an order for tongue and salad and a roll and coffee.

When she returned with her tray, he looked up at her again and said: "You're from Leeds, aren't you?"

"No, I'm not," she told him. "I'm from Haliford."

He shook his head over this. "Haliford. And—my God—what a place!" He said nothing more for a moment, while she was setting out his lunch. Then he asked: "And when did you leave Haliford?"

"Last week."

He laughed at that, though Rose saw nothing funny about it. But he was quite pleasant. "And what do you think of London, then, Miss Haliford?"

"Well," said Rose carefully, "I think I shall like it. Of course I haven't seen much of it yet."

"Of course," he said gravely, "you can't have. In fact, you haven't begun to see it yet, have you?"

No, she hadn't. She had really finished with him now, officially, until she gave him his bill, but as it was so quiet, and he seemed to want to talk and she was ready to listen, she contrived to linger on without looking as if she were merely gossiping.

"It isn't a town, a place like Haliford, this isn't, y'know," he continued slowly. "It's a wilderness. It's the Amazonian jungle. It's another Grand Canyon. Whole tribes live here, buried away, nobody knows much about 'em. One night you might wander into the middle of one of 'em, and never be heard of again. Just a rumour," he said, looking up solemnly at Rose, "of a great white queen—faraway—a throne built of human thigh-bones. That's London, lass—that's London." He sighed, and Rose, who could not make head or tail of this nonsense, looked vaguely sympathetic. Then he smiled, and so she smiled back at him, and the effect of this was to make his whole rather dingy and baggy face light up. "You're what this salad ought to have been—young and fresh and crisp and green. And where d'you live? Along what trail? Islington? And why Islington? Oh, you were recommended to go there? Well, be careful. There are old witches in Islington living on second floors behind lace curtains. They'll drink your blood, suck your marrow." He turned to his lunch, and Rose left him.

When she went to give him his bill, he stared gravely at her. "Promise me," he said mournfully, "you won't ever become an actress and have a temperament and a personality and a book of press cuttings and an agent and two big offers from Hollywood. Now promise!"

"You needn't worry," said Rose. "They wouldn't have me as an actress even if I wanted to be one."

"Probably they wouldn't. But one with your quality—this minute—would be worth a fortune to me. And we haven't one. Wish me luck."

Rose did, as he got up. He looked hard at her again. "Don't forget the unknown tribes. Or the old witches in Islington. And remember that Hell is supposed to have representatives in all the big cities. I've met several of them here. One or two probably come in this place. Watch out, watch out! And how," he concluded sharply, surprisingly, "is that young man from Haliford going to find you in this jungle?"

"There isn't one," said Rose quickly, though even then there was time to remember—quite unnecessarily—that boy, Edward Fielding.

"Of course there is. Be careful, I say. Turn down the wrong street, and you're lost for ever. Good-bye, my child."

As he said this, Rose, who was sometimes quite stupid but at other times saw everything in a flash, suddenly realised that though he was being clever and grand and patronising in a friendly middle-aged fashion, he was a desperately worried, unhappy man, as deeply lost as she could ever be in this ridiculous London he described. (And she was right, for he was an earnest and capable professional dramatist, working at a time when it was harder and harder to make any sense out of the theatre; and when he wrote a serious play, the critics treated it as flippantly as they did any two-hour song-and-dance entertainment, and when, in despair at such treatment, he wrote a comedy, the same critics asked why he was no longer serious. And his living seemed to depend upon the co-operation of a lot of mad babies. And he was beginning to feel slack and sagging and weary, and while the fun of things was not as funny as it used to be, all the vexations, disappointments, miseries, were just the same. And too much of the time he was sorry for himself, and then hated himself for being so sorry.) Good afternoon, sir, good afternoon.

Rose did not explain about this exciting man very well to Alice—Rose was not good at explaining, and thought a lot of things that she could find no words for—but even so, Alice might have been a bit more impressed. But Alice had noticed him, noticed that he was oldish and fattish and untidy, and had lost interest at once. Alice was deep in one of her boy moods again. London had made her much worse than she was in Haliford. Both girls had left home disappointed about a boy, Rose about Edward Fielding, who had never turned up, Alice about Gregory Porson, who had turned up once too often; but whereas Rose came to London wanting to forget about boys for the time being, Alice was more excited about them than ever. There were few in Haliford of her own age and kind she had not known or at least considered. But here in London, there were hundreds of thousands of brand-new ones. She saw dozens of them on her way to work; they came into the café; they passed by the score outside; and evening mobilised them by the thousand, paraded them right from Halberd Street to Islington, or wherever else she chose to go. She paid no attention to girls and women —except the occasional ones who were so smart that they were worth considering as examples of how to do it—and ignored all boys under twenty and men over thirty, as well as all those of the right age who looked dirty, wore no collar, were little and fat or very tall and thin, were grotesquely spectacled, very spotty, or were otherwise ineligible; but even with these broad reservations, there were so many young men about that the very sight of them, the mere knowledge that they were all so near, kept her excited, giggly, and—in Rose's view—downright silly. Whereas Rose wanted to spend her spare time looking at London itself, Alice wanted to spend hers looking at and for boys. At first, they were able to compromise, but very soon, after the first week-end had tested their friendship severely, there were differences, arguments, mutual accusations. Alice thought Rose was dull, and began to think that one or two of the other girls in the café, girls who were sports and knew their way about, would be more fun. Rose thought Alice silly, and though she did not want to go round by herself, there were times when she even began to consider that desperate step.

They had gone to Mrs. Burlow, 18, Pitt Square, Islington, because Mr. Smalley, who had a list of respectable women ready to let rooms to waitresses, had given her name and address to them and had explained how they found their way to Pitt Square, Islington. After the long squat streets of Haliford, the houses in this decayed eighteenth-century square seemed very tall, grand and fantastic. True, they were all rather dirty and were sadly in need of paint, but they were still fine houses. Rose had once seen a similar house in some English film, and she never went in or out of Mrs. Burlow's without feeling that she herself was half in a film. The steep staircase with its ornamental banisters did not quite belong to the real world. She and Alice shared a large double-bedded back room on the second floor. They had a gas-fire and a gas-ring, both worked from a shilling-in-the-slot meter. In the bathroom next door, which was a high, dark, smelly place, rather like an old empty tank, there was a gas meter. And all the rooms were lit with gas. So altogether it was a very gassy house, for ever hissing, wheezing, popping, and exploding. For years afterwards, the smell of gas always reminded Rose of those first days in London, at Mrs. Burlow's. Islington itself, away from the coloured glitter of the High Street and the Green, where all the big pubs and picture theatres and shops were, had a soft darkness and an autumn mixture of fog and smoke about it that were a bit gassy after the harsher nights of Haliford. It all seemed to Rose rather gentle and mournful, quite different from what she expected.

Mrs. Burlow herself was rather like that. She looked a widow, a perpetually distressed and inconsolable widow, but she was not, for there was a dim Mr. Burlow, whose mysterious business took him round to chemists' shops and hardly allowed him to return home at all. She had a round moist face, with swimmy eyes, and a large mouth that pouted and, as she looked at you, began to droop terribly on the left side, as if she was about to burst into tears. But she never did. Indeed, her voice was quite cheerful; it did not seem to belong to her; and when you heard it talking downstairs you felt that Mrs. Burlow had gone and that somebody else had suddenly taken charge of the house. She took a fancy to Rose at once, because Rose was "the image and living spit" of a great friend of hers who had spent her early life in Liverpool, which Mrs. Burlow persisted in regarding as being "a stone's throw" from Haliford. When Rose told her that she had never even seen Liverpool, she shook her head as if to say: "You have your own reasons for pretending not to know Liverpool, and I won't enquire what they are, but you can't deceive *me*." Indeed, at times, she spoke as if Rose and this friend of hers must be related and that some strange Liverpool-Haliford scandal must be at the back of it all. Rose rather liked her, but Alice thought she was "barmy." There were two other lodgers in the house, a Mr. Renton, who had the first-floor front but hardly ever seemed to be in it, a vague but important figure, and a Miss Hutchings, who was about forty, very short and square and deep-voiced, and the "chief sales" at a milliner's in the High Street. She had the second-floor front, shared the bathroom with the two girls, and said "Gur-hood murning" and "Gur-hood naight" to them regularly in a very stately fashion. She wore a purple wrap, and every second evening a strong smell of toasted cheese escaped from her room. The only other person in the house was a very small wild-eyed "help" called Vera, who always had a cold in the head, and, according to Mrs. Burlow, also had "moods." Rose was prepared to be deeply interested in all these people and to listen to all that Mrs.

Burlow had to say about them; but Alice, with her mind crowded and overheated with young men, refused to bother about them, and after the first day or two hinted that they had made a mistake in coming to Mrs. Burlow's at all. She had not left Haliford for this, she told Rose. This was not the real London at all.

They had made no plans for the Wednesday, when they would finish for the day early in the afternoon. Rose had said that she wanted to see more of London (they had been to St. Paul's and seen the outside of the Tower last Sunday, and Rose had written home to say so), but Alice had said nothing, had clearly avoided the subject; and when their work was done at the café, Alice came to her, a trifle shamefaced, and said: "I say, Rose, listen. D'you mind if I go out with Doris Lock to-day? She asked me to, and after all she's been very good to me, hasn't she? I mean, showing me how to do everything. You don't mind, do you?"

"No, of course not," said Rose, who did mind and thought it the limit. "You go, if you want to. I'll be all right."

"Oh, I know," cried Alice eagerly. "I wouldn't go if I didn't know you'd be all right, Rose." And off she went, with "boys" written all over her.

So Rose set out to be all right by herself. It was a fine afternoon, and this was the last week in September. There was a smokiness about the air, as there would be in Haliford this very afternoon, but here it had a soft golden quality, at once luxurious and melancholy. She turned into the Strand and walked slowly towards Trafalgar

Square, where the crimson buses went roaring round and round the immense column. There were just as many people as there always were: frowning, hurried people; chatterers in pairs; solitary slinkers; fat starers; and wizened little chaps with no teeth—and London seemed to have an endless supply of them—who stood at corners, waiting, just waiting. Rose was disappointed by the Strand, which did not seem to her much of an improvement upon Gladstone Lane, Haliford. But when she reached Trafalgar Square, with its flutter of pigeons, its stone lions, its loiterers, London began to look more important, more itself and far less like Haliford. The huge grey pillars of the buildings did the trick. After waiting for a break in the traffic, which ran unreasonably to buses, she slipped across and made for Whitehall. A lot of importance, in weathered grey stone, all down there. Prime ministers and all that. Rose did not care about them much. She might have known the names of two cabinet ministers, but beyond that could not have told you anything about the government, not even to which party it belonged. Politics were still to her something that men argued about with unnecessary noise and violence; one of their masculine fusses. She had no idea yet (but we must give her time) that anything that was said and done by political gentlemen behind those official-looking windows could possibly affect her own life. But she recognised the Cenotaph and looked with interest, though without emotion, at the fading flowers and curling wreaths massed round its base. Her Uncle Ben had been killed in the War, but she did not remember him. She was pleased, though, at the way in which some of the men who passed by raised their hats so nicely to the Cenotaph, and would have liked to have told one of them about her Uncle Ben.

She wandered on. There was the river, very broad, an oily look about it. Houses of Parliament. Big Ben. Westminster Abbey. Quite empty little streets and places round there. It was funny, she thought, how London, so jam-crammed with folks, would suddenly, as you turned a corner, empty a bit of itself for you, as if all the people had hurried away for ever. She sauntered through a tangle of little streets, where nothing much was happening except taxis starting up to go and biggish men in dark uniforms opening doors, and finally found herself in a park, quite a small park, with all its seats filled with authentic Londoners, mostly old and looking rather hopeless. But the grass and the trees and the water were nice. And the buildings of Whitehall, which she had just seen, suddenly appeared in the smoky-gold distance like white fairy palaces. She would have liked it all the better if she had felt that it belonged to her; but she felt it belonged to the rather hopeless-looking people sitting so dumbly on all the seats and not enjoying it much. Not all the people there were miserable. There were some children playing, lovely children too. And some soldiers with some girls, all laughing a lot. She came to some broad roads where cars were hurrying along as if the very sight of the grass annoyed them, negotiated the crossings carefully, and landed herself in another park. This was not so interesting. There was no water, and not so many nice old trees. People were lying about on the grass, many of them looking as if they had been dropped there, exhausted, almost lifeless, out of aeroplanes. They made her feel tired. Yes, she was tired. That was one thing about London: it made you feel tired in no time. At the top of this park was an important, crowded, gear-grinding street. Piccadilly—fancy! And there, almost at once, as if by magic, she found a familiar bus, Number 19, which would take her quite close to Pitt Square.

Once inside the bus, she did not notice very much. There descended upon her that vague but vast sadness which comes after we have observed thousands of strangers hurrying past on meaningless affairs of their own, a state of mind unknown to people who do not live in great towns. She felt very small and lost and weary. London seemed a mistake. She sat there, her eyes smarting a little, her head aching a little, with hands and feet that seemed to be swelling all the time, and saw without real attention the bright jumbling of shop windows, doorways, other bus windows, posters, and people, people, people. And now and again the opposite window, for she was sitting just inside the door and not facing the way the bus was going, showed her a watery reflection of herself, and the merest glimpse of this made her decide at once that the dress and hat she was wearing did not really suit her (her next-best too), that she looked foolishly young and swollen-faced and goggly-eyed and silly. Probably that was the real reason why Alice did not want to go out with her. And twice that morning, quite sharply, Miss Finberg (who did not seem to mind Alice very much) had found fault with her. And she realised that she was not a grand, pretty, dashing girl who had swept herself magnificently out of home and Haliford to have the most splendid adventures in London, but just a silly little thing, who did not know how to do her work properly, talked with a Haliford accent, was not smart, and would be better off back in Slater Street, where she belonged. And even there, that boy Edward Fielding had not bothered to turn up, after being so nice to her. At this point she told herself firmly to stop it. What she wanted was some tea, with other girls waiting upon her and having to be on their best behaviour; and when the bus stopped at "The Angel," as she knew it would, some tea she would have.

The teashop she patronised did not look at all like the Copper Kettle Café. It made no pretence at all to any Ye Olde Englande atmosphere. It did not bother about atmosphere of any kind. It was nearly as severely business-like as a power-house. It hastily and efficiently served mathematically regular portions of food and measures of drink on damp marble-topped tables. The waitresses made you feel that you must have a train to catch just outside. Rose tried to console herself by feeling superior to them, but did not succeed. She knew that, except in the splendour of her green and orange uniform, she was not superior to them, and would not have been given one of their jobs no matter how urgently she applied for it. The girl who served her, upon whom Rose turned a professional eye, was thin and sniffly and too liberally daubed with the wrong shade of face powder. But even though she set everything down on the marble-topped table with a little jarring bang, she was, Rose knew, her superior as a waitress. She could take ten orders while Rose was anxiously taking three. Rose would have liked to have talked to her, but the girl had too much to do. Odd, Rose reflected, that she was now herself a customer, and that this girl, if she was an old hand like Miss Wade, was probably lumping her with the rest of the idiots. Most of the other people in this place looked rather like the people on the seats in that park; they had the same air of uncomplaining hopelessness; if they read papers, they stared at them as if the news was the worst possible; and if they were not reading, they just stared into vacancy, as if nobody or nothing worth noticing could ever again come their way. In a Haliford teashop, people talked hard and loudly at one another, or looked about them to see who else was there. In London, it seemed, you gave all that up as a bad job. Either you shut everything out and brooded or put the *Evening Standard* or the *Star* between you and the rest of London. Rose herself had not yet acquired the newspaper habit. It was only rarely she bought a paper, and she could go cheerfully for days without looking at one. She was not entirely uninterested in what was going on, but she had found that other people always told her all the news worth bothering about. But that, of course, was when she was at home. Here in London it was so different that she might have to start reading newspapers. She bought an evening paper as she left the teashop.

She found a letter from home waiting for her at Mrs. Burlow's. As she took it upstairs, she met Miss Hutchings, all dressed up for the evening (her milliner's shop closed on Wednesdays), coming down. Miss Hutchings still looked too short and too square, but there was something very smart, very Londonish, about her. Rose imagined her going off to have the most mysterious metropolitan adventures. (She was actually going to meet the manageress of the boot shop in the High Street, then to have a ladylike glass of something together and to sit through the whole programme in the two-shilling balcony at the Finsbury Park Astoria.) Miss Hutchings was very friendly, and stopped for a moment.

"Jer-hust coming ho-o-ome, eh?" she asked in her deep voice. "The wayther is ster-hill ke-e-eeping up, is-ernt ait?"

"Yes, it is, isn't it?" said Rose, pleased by this attention.

"That's raight, that's raight. Wer-hell, jer-hust going out for the ev-ner-haing. Gur-hood naight, Miss Er——" And down she went, looking from the back view rather like a miniature Henry the Eighth.

As Rose turned in at her own door, she wished now that she too was going out for the evening. The joint bed-sitting-room, with far too many of Alice's things scattered about it, looked untidy and gloomy. Rose took off her shoes and had a wash, lit the gas and the gas-fire to try and make the place look cheerful, and then sat down in the one armchair, which had a high back pitted with sockets where velvet buttons had once been and a sloping and very slippery seat, to read her letter. It was a combined effort, in answer to her own first letter, from her mother and Nellie, and though there was nothing much in it and it ought to have made Haliford seem duller than ever, actually it made her feel home-sick. Slater Street seemed so far away, so dear and cosy. This large empty room, with its splutters of gas, its high dark corners, its suggestion of having seen dozens of girls like Rose and never caring much about them, seemed more unfriendly than ever. She stared down into the gloom of the back-yards below, across at the few windows opposite that had no curtains drawn and were lighted and open to the view; and found no comfort there. She returned to the letter, as if it had some magic words she might have missed, words with which she could pass the whole evening, words like her mother's face, Nellie's laugh, the cheerful noise of her father and brothers. But it was the same letter. She sat with it in her lap, her eyes heavy with tears, a miserable long time.

At the end of this time, and she did not know how long it had lasted, there came a knock. Mrs. Burlow peeped round the door, looked hard at Rose, let her face fall as if she were about to burst into heavy sobs, then entered, saying quite cheerfully: "All alone, Miss What's-it, eh? Well, well, well, well! Not pining, not grieving, are you? Where's your friend to-night?"

Rose, trying to look indifferent, explained about Alice.

"Not right," said Mrs. Burlow briskly, but looking moister and sadder than ever, "not right at all, though it's none of *my* business. Came to ask about the washing, but that'll keep. No, Miss Salfer," she went on, pleased that she had found some sort of name for her, "if you ask me, young girls like yourselves should stick together. And I'm sure you've got a sweet face, Miss Salfer, and I'll be bound you've a sweet nature, like my friend that came from your parts. And you're feeling lonely all by yourself in here, aren't you, having had your letter too? Yes, I know." She sat down opposite Rose, clasped her hands, and let the left side of her mouth droop lower than ever.

Rose had to admit that she was feeling rather lonely and not very cheerful. She also added, stoutly, that it was very silly to feel like that.

"Silly it may be, but it's natural, and I've felt like it myself many a time. Now do you know who's in this house besides us?" Mrs. Burlow asked, impressively.

Rather startled, wondering who on earth it could be, Rose said she didn't know.

"Nobody," replied Mrs. Burlow triumphantly, as if announcing the name of some celebrity. "Nobody at all. Your friend's out, isn't she? So is Miss Hutchings. Saw her go myself. Mr. Renton—well, he's away—on business —and I believe," she added, lowering her voice and looking very solemn, "in Stoke-on-Trent until Friday. My husband's out, but that's *no* news. And Vera—the girl—she's got her afternoon off, and in a proper mood too, wherever she's gone. So there's just us."

It did not sound very cheerful. Rose saw the two of them sitting there, the dark house all round them, and outside the soft melancholy of Pitt Square. She nodded and tried to smile.

"And I believe," said Mrs. Burlow slowly, "that if we've any sense, we'll go out too. Let the house look after itself. It's big enough. Yes, and old enough. We'll go out, just you and I. On the loose. That's right, Miss

Salfer, and you needn't look so alarmed. When I say 'on the loose,' I mean we'll enjoy ourselves in proper decent manner, of course. I'll take you, and you'll take me. Now where is it to be, that's the point, isn't it? Because I'm not one of them that likes just to go trapesing round. I like to be going somewhere." She stopped, then cried triumphantly: "I know. The music-hall up on the Green. Second house. Some varieties, that's what we want. I haven't been for months. What d'you say, Miss Salfer?"

Rose was delighted to be rescued like this from her long lonely evening. Mrs. Burlow stayed until Rose was ready, then she took Rose down into the kitchen, which was full of old biscuit tins and smelt of mice, to wait until she was ready, as if the house was so big that they might never find one another again if they each went and got ready at the same time. Mrs. Burlow returned, wearing a mauve hat that was so entirely unsuitable that for one dangerous moment Rose thought she had put it on for fun. Mrs. Burlow held herself very stiffly under this hat, as if she were balancing it on her head. When they got outside, she positively leaned back under it, which gave her a sinister look, that of a damp murderess. But there was nothing sinister in her conversation, and she entertained Rose all the way to the Green with descriptions of queer people who had lodged with her in the past. When they arrived at the music-hall, the doors for the second house were just opening, and they walked straight into the stalls, which were very cheap. The audience made a great deal of noise, especially in the balcony, where they trod heavily on peanut shells. Mrs. Burlow's hat led the way to the front, or as near to the front as it could get, and found two very good seats for them. Rose bought a programme for twopence, gave it to Mrs. Burlow, then looked about her brightly. It was a nice friendly little place, this music-hall, warmer and cosier and altogether more human than the picture theatres she usually attended. One thing she noticed. There were very few young people there. They were nearly all about Mrs. Burlow's age. So were the attendants. So were the members of the orchestra, who soon crept into their pit, wiping their mouths. Very few of the turns were young; they themselves, their creased and fading scenery, their worn properties, their jokes and many of their songs, were getting on in years. And the loudest applause always came when a performer said he would imitate "our dear old favourite" So-and-so, and name a music-hall star that Rose had never heard of, or when a singer would tell them that the new songs were all very well in their way but that the old songs were best and that "ne-ow with their ker-hind attention" he or she would "endeavour tew render" one of their old favourite ditties. The result of this was that though the whole place was so cosy and friendly, it was also rather sad. Youth had fled from it. The sap was drying up; the leaves withering. There was no bloom on anything here. Joints were stiff, voices wheezy, eyes anxious behind the mask of paint. One turn was an eccentric fellow with a grotesque make-up, a dead-white face and a very red nose, and his costume was that of a ragged tramp. He made little jokes, fell over himself, and then climbed on to the back of a chair, made more little jokes, and played the accordion. Rose thought him quite funny at first, but very soon she changed her mind about him. She was sitting near enough to see his real face, peering anxiously through that mask. It was old, weary, desolate. And from where she sat, she could see into the wings, and standing there, never taking her eyes off the performer, was an elderly woman, holding a dressing gown in one hand and a small medicine glass in the other. And then Rose wanted him to stop clowning for them, wanted the curtain to come down, so that he could put on that dressing gown, drink his medicine or whatever it is, and go away with the elderly woman, who looked like his wife, and rest and not worry any more. But she said nothing to Mrs. Burlow, who was enjoying herself, and laughing and clapping as hard as anyone there, perhaps because she too was no longer young and was being entertained by people of her own age.

In the middle of the second half, a conjurer appeared. He called himself Mr. Mantoni; was tall, rather stout, perhaps about sixty; had a slight squint, a large hooked nose, and a grimly humorous mouth; and his evening clothes were baggy and shabby. He was clever, and funny in a despairing kind of way. "When the deafening applause has subsided," he would say, in reply to the first feeble scattered clapping, "I will endeavour to perform another trick with the egg. The trick is real. The egg is not. Who is this fellow? Why doesn't he go off and let a proper turn come on? He can't be doing it for money." Everything about him was outworn and cynically shabby except his hands, his long dexterous conjurer's hands, now as rigid as if they were ossified, now fluttering like birds, as they squeezed packs of cards into nothing, removed eggs from behind his knees, pulled out strings of flags from empty hats. Rose was fascinated by those hands. Just to watch them fold a sheet of paper was a joy. And all the time his rusty voice went on and on, half jeering at himself, half mocking the audience, who were gradually beginning to like him. His last and most elaborate trick, he explained, was to make a table covered with crockery completely disappear; and as he began arranging the crockery on the table, and making disparaging remarks about it, a lady assistant appeared. She was a plump middle-aged woman, with some very queer curls on her forehead and what appeared to be a great quantity of pink lace curtaining wrapped round her. She was only there to hold and pass things to Mr. Mantoni, and was a figure of no importance, but at the sight of her Mrs. Burlow gave a gasping exclamation.

"What's the matter?" asked Rose.

"It's either Mrs. Gullane or I'm a Dutchman," Mrs. Burlow replied in a loud whisper.

"Do you know her?"

"Think I do! Known her for twenty years—longer. And that conjurer chap's her brother-in-law. Heard her talk of him. Well—Mrs. Gullane! Who'd have thought it? But her sister—that's his wife—gets arthritis bad, and that's why she's there."

By this time the table and all its crockery had been covered with a large Union Jack. "After I've counted three," said Mr. Mantoni, in his despairing voice, "the table, cups, saucers, plates, will have all gone. Where do they go to? God knows! And I do this twice nightly, six nights a week. Now you see why they have to pay me such enormous sums of money. Yes, ee-normous sums of money! One. Two. And a half. Ha ha, caught you that time! *Three—go!*" And he whisked away the Union Jack. The table and the crockery had gone, and in their place was a string of flags, which he and Mrs. Gullane pulled out, while the orchestra announced at the the top of its voice that it was a long way to Tipperary.

"Here," said Mrs. Burlow excitedly, "I must go round and see Mrs. Gullane. She'd never forgive me if I didn't. Never mind about these acrobacks. We can see acrobacks any time. Come on." And off she went, with Rose hurrying behind her. After consulting with the attendant at the front entrance, Mrs. Burlow led the way round to the back, where they found the Stage Door. The man there showed them how to find Mr. Mantoni and assistant, who by this time had removed themselves and their flags and eggs from the stage. They went down some stone steps, along a dim hot corridor, smelling of grease paint and gas and beer, and finally came to Mr. Mantoni's dressing-room. Mrs. Burlow knocked.

"You come in too," she said to Rose. "It'll be an experience for you. Professionals! I've known hundreds of 'em."

Mrs. Gullane and Mr. Mantoni, now in his shirt-sleeves, were sharing a bottle of stout. Mrs. Gullane recognised her old friend Mrs. Burlow at once and was delighted to see her. She was also pleased to meet Rose. Mr. Mantoni was also delighted and pleased, and conjured out another bottle of stout and two more glasses. Rose, who had once taken a sip of her mother's stout and loathed the taste of it, now found herself holding a full glass of the unpleasant stuff, under the admiring black-rimmed sharp eye of Mr. Mantoni.

"That's right, dear," Mrs. Gullane was saying. "Edith's down with her arthritis again, and so I said I'd help Fred out." She removed the queer curls, which appeared to be just as much the property of Mr. Mantoni as the flags and cards and disappearing eggs. "But business isn't too good, y'know, dear. Is it, Fred?"

"Five weeks in town this year, that's all I've had," said Mr. Mantoni gloomily. "And, mind you, the act's going as well as ever. Nothing wrong with the act. Any of 'em will tell you that. You saw how it went to-night, and, mind you, they're sticky to-night—all the boys were saying so. First house was better."

"That's right," said Mrs. Gullane. "You've no idea what it's like these days, dear. What with that and her arthritis, Edith doesn't know where to turn. Why, in the old days——"

But Mr. Mantoni took charge of the old days for her. "In the old days, when variety *was* variety, I've known myself booked up for two years. So many weeks out with the Moss Empires. So many weeks straight in town. Not a vacancy. 'Hello, Fred,' managers would say, 'here again. Glad to see you, my boy. Yes, we're still packing 'em in. You see you're middle o' the bill again?' And look at it now. When you do see a manager, his face is as long as a fiddle. Five weeks in town this year! I've had to make out this summer going to pier pavilions, in places I've never heard of in the old days, Punch-and-Judy-show places, I give you *my* word. This winter it'll have to be masonic jobs and children's parties, and there aren't as many of them as there used to be. And I hate children's parties. Ugh! They're death. Got the kids all round you, poking into your props, eyes like needles. 'What's that up your sleeve, Mister?' And there's always one kid in the front row who saw all the tricks last week at Mrs. Simpson's. And that's being a conjurer, these days." He turned to Rose, while the two women in low tense tones began to discuss the details of Edith's arthritis. "Enjoy the show?"

"Oh yes," cried Rose eagerly. "I thought you were very good."

"You were right. I am good. What's the matter with that stout?"

Rose was confused. "Nothing—only—you see, I don't——"

"Just a minute." He came forward, gravely, put a hand over the glass and then appeared to take out of it a mouse. Rose gave a little scream. He showed her the mouse; it was an imitation.

"You know," he said, regarding her appreciatively, "you'd make a good feed. Put you on in a nice costume —Oriental dancer style or something—and I might do the old girl-in-the-cabinet illusion. I still have the cabinet. Bought it from a German, just before the War. Remember the old cabinet illusion?" he asked Mrs.

Gullane. "Wouldn't this nice girl here look good in it?"

Mrs. Gullane looked Rose over carefully. "She would, Fred. You've got the right appearance, dear. What do you do, if I might ask?"

Rose explained shyly about the Copper Kettle Café. Then to cover her shyness and also because it was very hot in there and she was thirsty, she drank some stout. It was a bit better than last time.

"Well," said Mrs. Gullane, "if I was there, I'd stay there. You do know you can eat, whatever happens. It's all films now. They needn't eat. Better get into the films, dear."

"If she'll take my advice," said Mrs. Burlow briskly, "she'll leave films and theatricals and such-like well alone. She ought to stay where she is, till a nice young man comes along, and then say 'Yes.' And I wouldn't say it to the first neither, if I'd my time over again. Well, it's been a pleasure, I'm sure."

Mrs. Gullane said it had too. Mr. Mantoni said nothing because he had suddenly and surprisingly fallen asleep; a tired, elderly man, with a painted face, still holding the imitation mouse.

"Fred's dropped off," Mrs. Gullane whispered, as she came out of the dressing-room with them. "He gets tired now, especially when they're not very quick in front. It's hard work getting them going, though I'm sure he's only too glad to get the chance of doing it. Sometimes I don't know what'll become of him and our poor Edith. He can conjure anything nearly, but he can't bring three meals a day and nice lodgings and money for doctors' bills out of his hat. Good night, dear. Straight along and up the steps and round to the right."

The acrobats, three of them, with flat wide foreign faces, now dripping with sweat, were coming down as Rose and Mrs. Burlow went up. They were talking loudly and angrily in some strange language, but stopped suddenly as Rose passed. They looked at her with their queer foreign eyes. There was a strong animal smell about them. They were frightening, the kind of people who pop up again, infinitely menacing, in bad dreams. Rose hurried out. The Green outside, with the dispersing crowd laughing and chattering, a car or two starting up, the distant lights, the cool dark spread of night, seemed like a comfortable familiar room. She took in a deep sweet breath.

"Well, very enjoyable, I call it," said Mrs. Burlow, on their way home. "What do you say, Miss Salfer?"

Rose said it was very enjoyable too and thanked Mrs. Burlow for taking her. She did not say anything about its being curiously sad too, because obviously Mrs. Burlow had not seen it like that. This made Rose wish she had someone she could talk to properly. There was Alice, of course, but she did not feel like talking to Alice properly just now, and, anyhow, Alice would not understand what she meant. She was not clear about it herself, but she wanted to try and explain it all to somebody. Now that boy, Edward Fielding, had been quite good at understanding what you meant. He saw the point at once, and so it had been very easy talking properly to him. But he was still in Haliford. And even there he had not kept their appointment—silly fool! But what if it hadn't been his fault?"

"What's the matter?" asked Mrs. Burlow, turning round. "Did you drop something?"

"No, thanks. It's all right." Rose caught her up. This was the very first time it had occurred to her that it might not have been his fault. She had been so disappointed, so angry, that night when he did not keep their appointment, that ever since he had been lost in a cloud of disappointment and anger. Something to-night had blown away that cloud. She saw him clearly again. His eager voice sounded again in her ears. She began to think hard. Suppose——?

They were late, but Alice was still out, and when she came in, half an hour after Rose had got into bed, Rose had not stopped inventing perfectly sound excuses for Edward Fielding. But she stopped now. Alice looked tired and rather fed up. Serve her right.

"We went dancing with two boys," said Alice, throwing off her clothes as if she were heartily sick of them. "Hammersmith. It's miles and miles away. Thought I'd never get back. One of the boys was a lovely dancer. But I didn't see much of *him*, of course. I was there to keep the other chap going. Here, look at my shin. That's a bit of his work. Did you get on all right?"

"Oh yes," said Rose sweetly. "I had a lovely time. Mrs. Burlow took me to a music-hall show, and then afterwards we went behind the scenes——"

"You didn't?"

"We did. To see some friends of hers. I've always wanted to see what it's like behind the scenes, haven't you? I wouldn't have missed it for anything. You'd have loved it, Alice. I was sorry you weren't there," Rose concluded, softly and sweetly. "Good night, Alice. You'll turn the light out, won't you?"

Alice did. But she did not accept that "Good night." She had to have something to say for herself, even if she said it in the dark. "One chap kept staring at me," she said dreamily. "Then he came up and asked me to dance, but of course I couldn't. Tall and dark and very well-dressed, a bit like Gary Cooper. Just your style, Rose. He kept on staring at me all night. He smiled a lot too. The boy I was with got mad, but I didn't care. Kicker! Wouldn't it be funny if this chap—I mean the good-looking—came into the Copper Kettle one day? Oh—I say—Rose——"

The sound that Rose made was not very encouraging, but it was enough for Alice.

"I heard something to-night from Doris Lock about us," Alice went on, raising both herself and her voice. "Rose, listen, it's important. About us and the café. Doris Lock told me. She says there's been some sort of row about us being taken on. Miss Finberg says she'd been told she could find any new waitresses she wanted, and she wasn't asked about us. And Doris Lock says she heard Miss Finberg talking on the telephone this morning about us, and saying she wouldn't have it—and all that. And something about one of us having to go, because she'd promised some other girl—who'd worked for her before—a job in Halberd Street. So what's going to happen?"

"I don't know. We'll have to wait and see. Good

night, Alice." Rose refused to be alarmed and excited. Alice had chosen the wrong moment. Besides, Alice was given, particularly at such moments, to working up alarms of this kind.

And nothing happened the next day, Thursday, to suggest that Alice's story was more than a bit of idle café gossip. True, Miss Finberg was only there a short time. It was said that she had to attend a meeting of manageresses at the head office. But she was there on Friday morning, and so, at eleven o'clock, was Mr. Smalley. And he was asking for Rose, and asking for her in a blustering hasty manner that suggested he was not feeling very comfortable. There was a tiny room at the back of the café, just off the kitchen, that Miss Finberg called her office. Mr. Smalley, redder than ever at the back of his neck, walked in there; and Rose, feeling very small and cold and frightened, walked in after him, convinced that something was about to happen now.

VIII

THE Edward who arrived in London, a hesitating midget in the colossal glass case of King's Cross Station, realised that this was no time to be superior to his brother Herbert. He remembered with gratitude Herbert's careful instructions. He was anxious to be rid of his rather large suitcase as soon as possible, for this suitcase seemed to him an enormous and fantastically embarrassing responsibility, almost as if it were an elephant he had to convey through the streets of London. He did not take a taxi, because he did not know what crazy sum the driver might demand; he left the buses alone because they were confusing and he did not feel like experimenting with them while he had his suitcase with him; so he walked, in a slow, grim, lop-sided fashion, the suitcase weighing him down. It was the end of a rainy day; the roads and pavements were shining; the air was damp, thick, plummy. Edward soon found it quite warm, and began to sweat. Twice he had to ask the way. Crossing some dim square, as mysterious to him as a Siberian lake, the handle of his suitcase broke at one end. He arrived at the Lomond Hotel, Bloomsbury, very hot and sweaty and exhausted, and had an obscure feeling that they would take one look at him and his ridiculous suitcase and then ask him to go away.

The front door was open, so he walked straight into the

hall, which was long and narrow, had an office counter on one side, and a long narrow leather-covered settee on the other, and precious little room in between them. Further up was a potted palm, an umbrella stand, and the foot of a very steep staircase. Not a soul about. Not a sound. Edward hesitated, panting, a moment, then sat down on the settee, took off his hat and wiped his forehead. There were some theatre bills on the walls. He realised that now those bills were addressed to him. He could go to one of those theatres this very night, if he wanted to. But it was difficult to think about himself in London in this free-and-easy way while he still had the suitcase with him. Meanwhile, the Lomond Hotel gave no sign of life. Not a mouse stirred. He began to feel uneasy, looked about for a bell, and finally found one on the office counter. He gave it a timid little push. Nothing happened. Then he pushed it hard, and it responded sharply, alarmingly. It was as if the peace of long ages had been broken. It was a bell to fetch out fire engines, the Flying Squad, troops of cavalry. What it did bring, through some doorway that Edward could not see, was a small maid in a soiled blue uniform who came slopping up and stared hard at Edward.

"Oo," she said, "isn't there nobody? Where's Mrs. Parkinson?"

"I don't know," said Edward. "Isn't there anybody here?"

"Yes. You want Mrs. Parkinson. I'll find 'er."

She turned away, and seemed to do a vanishing act, disappearing into the potted palm. A few moments later, Mrs. Parkinson materialised, perhaps out of the umbrella stand. She was a large woman, nicely upholstered in black, and with a long, thickly powdered face that terrified Edward.

"What d'you—er—charge for a room?" he asked, hardly knowing what he was saying.

Mrs. Parkinson seemed surprised at this quite reasonable question; just as if this were not an hotel at all. "Well," she said slowly, closing her eyes, "how long would you be staying?"

"Oh—not long—just a day or two."

"Ah!" She opened her eyes, as if it was possible now to endure the sight of this visitor. "For bedroom, use of bath, breakfast—six and sixpence. For a longer stay and full board, we can quote weekly terms."

As six-and-six was what Edward had expected to pay, he was relieved, and said he would take a room. Everything became sensible now. Mrs. Parkinson rang a bell, produced the register for him to sign, and told a little old man, who must have been hiding behind one of the theatre bills, to take him to number forty-three. Edward was surprised to learn that the Lomond Hotel had at least forty-three bedrooms, and said so to the old man as they climbed the stairs together.

"Ar, yew got it all wrong, shir," said the old man. "Number forty-three—tha' meansh yew got the third bedroom on the fourth floor, shee? That'sh how they number 'em, shee? My word, shir, yew got shome shtuff in 'ere, 'aven't yew, shir?"

He put down the suitcase on the second landing, and puffed and blew. The rest of the journey upstairs, they carried the suitcase between them. It was a very tall, thin sort of house, not like a real hotel at all, and the stairs were the steepest Edward had ever known. Number forty-three was at the end of a corridor at the top, next to an angry old cistern.

"Well, shir," cried the old man, trying to be cheerful about it, " 'ere y'are, an' all on your ownshome, as yew might shay." He went and pulled down the blue blind with an important officious air, giving the guest the impression that there was a knack in pulling down these blinds. Then, apparently with a last despairing effort, he lifted the suitcase on to a folding stool. Then he lingered, rubbing his hands. "I'll tell yew what, shir," he whispered. "Yew couldn't have picked a better time for shtaying in thish perticler room, an' I'll tell yew for why, shir. In shummer—'ot as 'ell up 'ere. Winter—cold as the North Powl! But now, shir, jusht right, jusht right."

Even now he did not go, and Edward realised that something was expected of him. A tip? Ah!—that terrible tipping, which kept so many Haliford people safe at home, two hundred miles from London and its outstretched hands, its expectant calculating glances. He found a sixpence, which the old man received with dignity.

"Thank *yew*, shir," he said, moving to the door. "An' now I'll leave yew to it, shir." As if the moment he had gone Edward would be up to all manner of young monkey tricks in there.

The room did not suggest monkey tricks. It was high and narrow, and both the longer walls bulged inwards, to suggest that at any time now it might be narrower still.

It was furnished with a single brass bedstead, a wash-hand basin and jug, a squat brownish chest of drawers and a mirror, a brownish bedside cabinet with a cracked marble top, and two yellow cane-bottomed chairs. The uncompromising rules and regulations of the Lomond Hotel, which seemed to regard its guests as potential criminals, were tacked on the door. There were no pictures on the walls, only an endless pattern of pickled cabbages and decayed grapes. Young and hopeful and excited though he was, Edward was immediately cast down, instantly defeated, by this bedroom. Compared with this, the third-class railway carriage in which he had spent the last five hours had been a cosy home. There was a chill mustiness about the atmosphere of this bedroom, a cold contempt for its occupants, a vault-like air of being entirely removed from the real warm life of humanity, that took the heart out of him. He felt at once that he was only the latest of a long line of people, arriving here in high hopes, who had been desolated by this room. And he was right. The only flavour these inhuman boxes have is that of their occupants' accumulated misery. They smell of disappointment, loneliness, despair. They are not hotel bedrooms in the greatest city in the world; they are the narrow way, the dangerous gate, the ordeal, through which all newcomers must pass before they can reach the gold-paved streets. Mrs. Parkinson, that little maid, that gummy old man, with their sinister appearances and disappearances, are not real people waiting on travellers; they are infernal sentries, devilkins of the gate, goblin inspectors and examiners.

Edward's spirits rose a little when he had opened his

suitcase, for then it brought a glimpse of home into that bedroom. He felt better when he had had a refreshingly cold wash, had changed into his other shoes, had put on his raincoat, and hurried downstairs. Once outside, he felt better still. Free of that suitcase, he was no longer afraid of these London streets. It was not a fine night. There was a slight drizzle; but he knew all about drizzling, and this was warmer, softer, than the familiar Haliford variety. Above the dark ridge of roofs he could see a trembling brightness in the night air, a ruby glow, which could only be the reflection of the magical gay West End. This was his now. And it was Rose Salter's. It belonged to both of them. These were intoxicating thoughts.

After much debate with himself, he had decided that he would leave the Copper Kettle Café alone that night and try to find Rose at her lodgings in Islington. But first, he must eat. He found a teashop in Holborn, a fine big teashop yet snug too, and there he ordered a pot of tea, fried plaice and chips, toast, and some stewed fruit. The thought of Rose, so near now, a radiance just around the corner, put a golden bloom upon the whole place. The long room with its warmth and lights and appetising fragrances, went floating away, an indestructible bubble-like vessel, on a deep tide of happiness. Everything there, the diamond drops on the windows, the very crumbs on the tables, was precious and dear to him. All the people—the waitresses so trim in their black-and-white uniforms, the stout old chap gobbling boiled ham, the two middle-aged women carefully dividing fancy cakes, the man whose thick fingers rustled his evening paper, the pale mysterious girls over their cups of tea—were his friends, his companions in a glorious adventure. Outside, everything had been suddenly changed too, to match this new magnificence of life. Great peaks of achievement were shining there, with clearly defined tracks only waiting for his climbing feet. There were no limits now to what could be conquered, what could be enjoyed. Oh, ecstasy! What plaice and chips! What tea and toast! What stewed fruit! What a world of food and drink and adventure and friendship and love!

And many a time afterwards, up through the darkness, there returned to him a bitter bright image of himself sitting there in that Holborn teashop, so happy, so fantastically happy, eating plaice and chips in another world, a world that had come and gone in half an hour, a world lost in another time.

Meanwhile, he lingered, carefully finishing the last spoonful of fruit juice, the last half-inch of toast, the last dark drains of tea, manfully subduing the impulse to be off at once to Islington. He did not know how to get there. Neither did his waitress, who told him she lived at Fulham and would not know Islington if she saw it. But the other girl, the friendly understanding girl who might have known all that had happened to him, to whom he put his question as he paid for his meal at the cash desk, knew about Islington, and advised the Underground, from Holborn to King's Cross, then a change to a train for the "Angel." Oh, happy omen! A train to the "Angel!" So down into the earth he went, at Holborn Station, was shot through the very bowels of the Bloomsbury he had just left, perhaps hundreds of feet below that waiting bedroom and his suitcase, Mrs. Parkinson and the old man, until he came to the mysterious foundations of King's Cross, where after several adventures up and down short flights of stairs and along echoing tunnels of corridors, designed for midnight murder, he found a train for the "Angel." Rather dazed, he climbed up into a rainy, bustling, lighted world like a visitor from some subterranean kingdom. And where, in this drizzly show ot picture-house lights, red roaring buses, port and pale ale, was Pitt Square? Two men did not know; they were strangers themselves, they said, and the tone of their reply suggested there were millions of strangers, lost adventurers like himself, out and about that night. But a taximan, a strange jeering Cockney of a taximan, who would not look for Pitt Square or any other square unless he were paid to do it, told Edward where to go, rattling off his "first to the rights" and his "second to the lefts." So Edward came at last to 18, Pitt Square, Islington.

He was almost suffocating with excitement when he rang the bell, and yet before it was answered, something—perhaps the dark barren look of the house itself—whispered coldly that she would not be there. A goggle-eyed young girl, with a cold in her head, replied to his question.

"Miss Salder?" cried the girl. "Oo no. She's nod 'ere."

"D'you mean—she's out?"

"Oo no. She's god."

"Gone?"

"That's ride. She duzzud live 'ere eddy bor. Two days ago, she lefd."

"Where did she go? D'you know?"

"Oo no. I dode know."

"But hasn't she given you her new address?"

"No." Some impatience now.

"Look here," said Edward firmly, "is the landlady in—what's her name?—Mrs. Burlow?"

"Oo no, Mrs. Burlow's oud. An' I card dell you eddy bor. Miss Salder's god. She was odely 'ere aboud a weeg."

"All right," said Edward, turning away miserably. "Good night."

He was disappointed but not alarmed. He could see her at the café. After all, these girls might be always changing their lodgings, and that house, with its cold-in-the-head girl, looked rather dreary. A week had probably been quite enough there. Now, he did not like the look of Islington at all. He wanted to get out of it at once. He rode a mile or two on a bus that seemed to be going more or less in the right direction, and when he found himself once more in the neighbourhood of the great railway stations, he got off and wandered about. It was not very interesting. The evening now was flat. Simply to pass the time, he went into a picture theatre, which hardly differed in any respect from the picture theatres in Haliford. Once inside, he was sorry he had not been more ambitious and gone on to the West End, but having paid his money he sat through the programme, the only item of which he enjoyed was a short riotous comic, of a type that is becoming rare, which showed a lot of comfortable suburban people in California working themselves up to a glorious frenzy of anger and destructiveness, hurling bags of flour at one another, smashing the furniture, tearing down the banisters, and finally driving a car clean through the wrecked house. Nearly everybody in the scattered and rather indifferent audience enjoyed that comic film, which released some deep-seated feelings of frustration and anger in themselves, so that their roars of laughter towards the end, when the shadowy comic folk went berserk, had a loud lusty note in them. Laughing with the crowd, Edward felt for the first time—for he was hardly himself during that exalted half-hour in the teashop—that he was no longer a solitary young stranger, still staring at London out of Haliford, but one of the huge nameless Cockney swarm with their patient bearing and manners, with their sharp eyes and clipped cynical voices. He came out, a Londoner in embryo.

It was nearly eleven o'clock, and he missed the bite of supper he would have had at home before this, so he found a little shop that was also an eating place, with an urn at the far end of the counter, and a few little damp tables in the corner. Two taxi-drivers sat at one table, two railwaymen at another; a third was monopolised by an enormous woman in black, sitting like a wooden image with food and drink and paper parcels before her like propitiatory offerings; and at the fourth and last table there was a stringy little elderly man who had a long wet nose, a thin grey beard, and faded peering eyes. Edward took his sandwich and cup of tea to this fourth table. The elderly man, who had been looking at a paper folded into a small square, now glanced up, passed Edward the sugar, and then stared mournfully at Edward's sandwich, his cup of tea, and finally at his face. But he waited a minute or two before he began to talk. When he did begin he had all the merciless eagerness of the man who has been talking to himself for hours while moving among hordes of possible but escaping listeners.

"Wettish night," he observed perfunctorily.

Edward agreed that it was.

This was enough. The conventional opening move had been made: the real game could begin. "Now you look a sensible young feller," he said quickly, tapping the paper he had laid on the table, as if what was printed there gave him an excuse. "Has it ever occurred to you what we've become? And by 'us,' I mean the people of this city, perhaps of all our towns and cities. We've become——" and here he tapped harder than ever, to suggest it was all there, in print—"a race of bettors and gamblers. That's what we are. Bettors and gamblers. You can't deny it. Don't try to deny it, young feller. 'Orse-racing, going as strong as ever. These greyhound tracks! Football! Sweepstakes! Pontoons! Gamble, gamble, gamble! An' millions an' millions an' millions o' good money going down the gutter."

"All right, Dad," said one of the taxi-drivers. "What abaht it? They're not 'urting you."

"And 'ow do you know they're not 'urting me?" The old man was standing no nonsense from taxi-drivers.

"Well, 'ow are they? Their money, isn't it, Dad? If you don't want to 'ave a flutter, well an' good, nobody's asking you. But let them that does want to 'ave a flutter go an' ave one. It's their money."

" 'S'right," said the other taxi-driver.

"And I say it isn't right." And the old man, now trembling with passionate conviction, thumped the table. "Suppose everybody threw their money into the fire or the river? What then? It'ud be all right, accordin' to your argument, because it's their money——"

"You're talking silly now, Dad," said the first taxi-driver. "Who'd go and throw their money into the fire or the river?"

"A lot o' you men would," said the enormous woman in black, still like a wooden image, looking straight in front of her and hardly moving her lips. "You've no more sense."

The old man did not recognise this ally. "I tell you, money spent on betting and gambling—an' it runs into millions an' millions an' millions—is money wasted, thrown into the gutter. An' don't tell me they're not 'urting me. They are. 'Urting all of us as well as ruining themselves. When I was a young man, drink was the curse of this country. And now what is it? Bettin' an' gambling. I can live—I *do* live—on two shillings and ninepence a day, an' on that I live the life of a studying thinking man. I read. I look at the facts. I could give you figures." Now he turned to Edward again. "Young man, if I ask you a question, will you give me a truthful answer? Very well. 'Ow much a week do you spend on betting and gambling? Now be truthful."

"Nothing," replied Edward shyly. The two taxi-drivers and one of the railwaymen guffawed. The other railwaymen, who looked contemptuous, blew out cigarette smoke with a scornful hissing sound. The enormous woman did not even blink.

"If that's the truth you're tellin' me, young man, then I'll tell you—you're one in a thousand. Yes, one in a thousand. Keep it up. Don't start. We're betting and gambling our 'ealth, wealth and 'appiness away."

"Where to?" jeered the taxi-driver.

"Hell-fire." The old man, looking pleased and proud, now got up. "An' good night all." And out he went, to the accompaniment of much winking and nudging among the taxi-drivers and railwaymen. And the first taxi-driver added: "Poor old Dad!"

"Poor old nothing!" cried a scornful voice that must have come from the enormous woman, though she still stared straight ahead with a motionless face. "Speak for yourself!"

The Lomond Hotel was very quiet when Edward got back. He was admitted by a tallish, shambling chap who might have been the old day porter's eldest son, and might have been wearing the same black-sleeved waistcoat and green baize apron, both of which seemed too small for him. Like the others, he had appeared from nowhere, but he did not disappear when Edward went to the stairs but stood motionless, watching him. Just before the stairs vanished out of sight of the hall, Edward turned and looked down, and saw the porter still standing there, with the solitary overhead light giving his face a deceptive appearance of intellectuality, by throwing his forehead into sharp relief and sinking and darkening his foolish eyes.

Seen from there, he might have forgotten all about Edward and Mrs. Parkinson and the Lomond Hotel, and have been lost in some abstruse calculation concerning one of the more distant universes. Edward carried with him up the next three flights of stairs an image of Man the Thinker.

His bedroom received him coldly. Its one electric bulb, which had a curly white shade a size too small, had been carefully hung in the very centre of its space, to prevent any occupant from spending much time at the mirror, which reflected more of the bulb than it did of the occupant, and to stop any nonsense about reading in bed. Examined in this white glare, the room looked more inhospitable than ever. "Get to sleep," it snarled, "if you can." So Edward hastily undressed, banished the light and the room with it, and, shivering a little between the clammy sheets, rehearsed what he would say to Rose Salter in the morning.

And then it was morning, a strange, soft, dark, Londonish morning, with hot water in a brass jug with a lid on it. He did not try the bathroom at the other end of the corridor, chiefly because he did not possess a dressing-gown, and was too shy to venture out of his bedroom covered with his raincoat. (The Fielding family straddled that dressing-gown dividing-line between two great classes of English males, for Herbert, who was rising in the world, had achieved a dressing-gown, whereas Edward, who was still nobody, remained in the lower and larger and more naked section.) But he had what he told himself was a "sponge-down" (though he had no sponge) on the little mat in front of the wash-hand stand, rubbed himself hard to get warm, put on his underclothes, socks and trousers, and then, peering at the gloomy wavering reflection of himself, scraped away at his chin with a safety-razor that had been made so safe that it was hardly a razor at all. Feeling colder and cleaner than usual, not at all his customary self but a kind of half-crazy stranger carefully hidden behind a sedate appearance, a feeling shared by several thousand visitors to London that very same morning, he went down to breakfast. The dining-room, a room of no recognisable shape at all but so contrived that almost every guest could hide behind a dropsical pillar, had been conjured out of the back of the first floor, and had a very melancholy hidden-away air, as if it had no right to be there at all. But to Edward, who was not used to such places, it was not without a certain metropolitan impressiveness, which it shared with the dingy absent-minded waiter, and also with the breakfast menu that this waiter rather negligently and hopelessly put before him. On paper, here was a breakfast that made the reasonably substantial meals of Sutcliffe Place, Haliford, seem like pitiful improvised snacks. Edward ordered the lot: porridge, fish, bacon and egg, tea, toast, marmalade; and hoped that the waiter would not look surprised. The waiter did not look surprised, only sadder than ever. But there was something wrong with that breakfast. It ought to have been kept on paper and never translated into actual stuff on the table. Somehow, it all tasted the same, as if the various courses had been concocted out of a single synthetic substance, which was itself neither porridge nor fish nor bacon and egg. Just as there are now plastic materials, first achieved in a laboratory, that can be stamped or moulded indifferently into cups and saucers or plates or ashtrays or vases, so there must have been, in the kitchen of the Lomond Hotel, a tasteless greyish food substance that could be called anything on the menu. Edward rose from the table no longer feeling hungry, but the trick seemed to have been worked not by filling him with honest food but by giving him a disgust for the idea of eating. He decided to leave the Lomond Hotel as soon as possible, but first, he had to see Rose Salter.

It was about eleven o'clock when he found the Copper Kettle Café. He had not made up his mind whether to go in and pretend to be an ordinary customer or to enter boldly as a friend of one of the staff. What happened was that he drifted inside and found himself confronted at once by a formidable-looking woman in black, who was talking to the girl at the cash desk. This woman, who must have noticed something hesitant and enquiring about him, gave him a long level look, raised her fine dark eyebrows, and took a step towards him. This settled the matter.

"I just—er——" Edward began, stammering. "I mean —is Miss Rose Salter here, please?"

"Miss Salter?" The woman's eyebrows went half an inch higher. "No. Miss Salter *was* here, but she left last Saturday."

Edward stared at her miserably. "Could you—er—tell me where she is—please?"

"I'm afraid I couldn't." The woman sounded cold, unresponsive, quite unsympathetic to Rose Salter, Edward Fielding, the whole warm living race of mankind. And to show him that the matter was now disposed of, she turned again to the girl at the cash desk. There was nothing to do but to retreat, wretchedly, back into a Halberd Street that no longer had the slightest interest for him.

She had left her lodgings. She had left the café. Where, in all this wilderness, was she now? Had she gone back to Haliford? Edward decided fiercely that she had not gone back to Haliford. She was not the kind of girl, he was sure, who would make up her mind one week to leave home, and then go running back there less than a fortnight afterwards. She was somewhere in this desert of paving stones, this forest of chimney-pots, and he would find her. But how? That, he saw—and it was all he did see, for several times he bumped into people along Halberd Street and the turning into the Strand—would not be difficult, though it would ask patience. He had only to write to her sister Nellie, for Rose would be certain to write home and tell them of her change of work and address, and then Nellie could write to him. Obviously, this was something that must be done at once. So he bought a little packet of stationery at a Woolworth's in the Strand, wrote his letter in pencil over a cup of tea across the road, found the post office in Bedford Street, not far away, and thus sent his despairing query on the first stage of its long journey. And that was that. For a moment, standing there in Bedford Street, he felt the relief of a man who had just done a good day's work. Then he pointed out to himself that here he was in London, without a job, without the ghost of an idea where a job might be found, spending money all the time, and with nothing to return to but the Lomond Hotel. What was the next move?

Perhaps he ought not to have chosen to eat his dinner in the gigantic marble splendour of the Corner House, where a band sent great sugar-crested waves of Puccini over him and a thousand other diners, all people who looked as if they had homes and jobs to go to, who had everything comfortably settled for them, who had not to look for one golden needle in this colossal smoky haystack. He felt small, helpless, very young. It had been easy enough playing the snarling rebel, the bold adventurer, in the kitchen at Sutcliffe Place. But here, a homeless midget, eating stewed steak in the Corner House, it was very different. Perhaps the vast organisation of the place helped to diminish and frighten him, simply because it aptly symbolised the whole vast intricate organisation of our modern life, through which the individual, clutching a passport, insurance card, bank book, railway ticket, or some frail but essential bit of pasteboard or paper, moves so fearfully, knowing nothing except that he or she is not controlling the machinery and must suffer the effects of its operation without understanding its nature, plan and scope. Although all round him, from the smiling but intensely watchful floor manager in his morning coat and striped trousers to the policeman outside the street door in his helmet and uniform, there were people whose business it was to regiment him, to see that he behaved himself and to report him, take him away, lock him up if he didn't, there were no people whose duty it was to understand him, kind and wise persons, to whom he could cry: "Look here, I'm

Edward Fielding, of Haliford, and I'm twenty-three. And I've come to London because I've fallen in love with Rose Salter, and couldn't stay in Haliford, where, anyhow, I've nothing much to do and nobody particularly wants me, any longer when I knew she wasn't there. And I know, now that my life's really beginning, that I want to work hard at something—I don't quite know what, but I'm not really as silly as I may seem—and to be useful in the world. Here I am. What am I to do?" All this he himself felt obscurely: a dark, thin-faced youth, in a rather baggy and creased brown suit (not smart, but of good cloth, though; they attend to that in Haliford); a youth quite unlike the thick-set, aggressive-looking Yorkshireman of popular report, and yet with some indefinable suggestion of the West Riding about him, a north-country flavour that extended to more than his speech; a lonely, wondering youth, negligently performing the miracle of turning a stewed bit of a dead Argentine bullock's rump into so much bewilderment, fear, hope, and passion for a girl he had only seen twice; a young contemporary of ours—and therefore, with any luck, a unit in the future of our race—at whom most of us would give no more than half a glance and never a thought.

When his mother, a few days before, had told him to go and see his father's cousin, Alfred Fielding, who lived at Willesden, had given him the address of these relatives and had said she was writing to them about him, he had in his own mind contemptuously dismissed the very thought of the vague Willesden people; but now, with time on his hands, feeling so lost, he searched his pockets for their address, and, having found it, pretended to himself that he ought to go and see them if only for his mother's sake. The afternoon before him promised to be dull in every sense, for though it was not actually raining, there was over all the city a fuzzy and dirty grey blanket of cloud, blotting out the sun and the real sky. He had plenty of time to walk, bus, walk again, in the direction of Willesden, which he knew to be vaguely somewhere to the north-west, and manage it so that he arrived at his relatives' house in the late afternoon or early evening. At least, they would give him a cup of tea.

It was dusk when he arrived, a weary explorer, in Buckingham Grove, Willesden. He arrived with some notion of the real size of London. On the map, Willesden was simply one name among dozens, a name printed across a compact little area. Once there, he thought, he would make a turn or two and land in Buckingham Grove. But he soon discovered that Willesden itself was a jungle within a jungle, and no mere thicket. The afternoon darkened as he penetrated further and further into a mysterious region of residential streets that might have been planned in imitation of those Oriental nests of boxes. It was a bewildering maze of bricks and privet hedges and window curtains and lamp-posts. They were quiet, withdrawn streets that seemed to be closely guarding a million secrets. They gave you no sign of the kind of life that was being led in them. There might have been a dead man in every house. Buckingham Grove itself was no different from its neighbours. Its houses, which looked neither very new nor very old but had the same darkish middle-aged look of so many buildings in England, including nearly all railway stations, town halls, and public lavatories, were semi-detached, but miserably so, like houses that had once been in one long row but had since quarrelled and shrugged away from one another. Each had a tiny garden in front, and several of them had monkey-trees. Edward disliked these sinister-looking monkey-trees, and now felt prepared to dislike Buckingham Grove and everybody in it. But that did not prevent him from ringing the bell at the residence of Mr. Alfred Fielding.

He was invited into a comfortable dining-room, where there was a table laid for tea, by a girl about fourteen who was wearing the short blue dress and black stockings of a school uniform. This was Katherine. He did not like the look of her. She had dark eyes, a long sharp nose, a long sharp chin, and a quick jerky way of talking. Also, she stared so hard that she nearly squinted. She had just begun her homework, she explained, but she ignored Edward's suggestion that she could continue with it. "Mother'll be back in a minute," she said. "She'd a letter about you. From *your* mother. Your father died, didn't he?"

"Yes, he did," said Edward shortly, wishing that she wouldn't stare at him so hard. She was curled up in an arm-chair, like a cat, and stared at him across the curly black hearthrug as if he were a gigantic mouse.

"He came here once, your father did, but I don't remember him," she continued in her sharp jerky fashion. "What have you come to London for? I asked Mother that but she didn't know. But she's always so vague. We always laugh at her. She's a scream. Are you here on a visit or what?"

Edward nearly told her to mind her own business and get on with her homework. "Oh—well—I've sort of come to look round, y'know," he explained lamely.

"Look round what?"

"Oh—blow you!" said Edward to himself.

"What are you looking so annoyed about?" And she did not smile when she asked this, but simply looked sharp and impish—a hateful kid!

Edward decided that he would do the questioning. Why should this schoolgirl cross-examine *him?* "What time does your father generally come home?" he enquired in an aloof grown-up manner.

It did not impress her. "You haven't answered my question yet," she pointed out. "My turn first. I asked first."

"*What* question?"

"You said 'Look round' and I said 'Look round *what?*' I mean, you wouldn't come all this way to look round something if you didn't know what, would you? You sound just like Mother. Sort of thing she'd say. But she isn't related to you really, is she? So it can't be in the family. Do you know French?"

"Not much."

"Well, how much? Do you know the French for——"

"No, I don't," and Edward did not care if she did think him rude. "I learned French when I was at school, but it's a long time since I left school and I've forgotten most of it. And I've come to London—if you *must* know—to see if I can find a decent job here."

"You've got a hope," said Katherine cheerfully.

"How do you know I've got a hope?" Edward was beginning quite angrily, when there was a sound of somebody arriving. It was Mrs. Fielding. "Well I never did!" she cried. "I knew there was somebody here because I noticed the hat. So you're Edward, eh? Your mother—"

"I've told him," said Katherine.

Mrs. Fielding was not at all like her daughter. She was not dark and pointed and sharp, but one of those indeterminate-looking middle-aged women who might be figures in faded old water-colour drawings. The moment she left the room, as she did now to dispose of her little parcels, you could not remember what she looked like, and even when she returned she was still a blurred figure. But she seemed to be cheerful and kind. "Now you'll have a cup of tea with us, won't you? That's right. Your Uncle Alfred—I know he's not really your uncle, but that's near enough, isn't it, and I've got to call him something—he'll be home soon, and so will Arthur. That's my boy. He's just nineteen, younger than you, and going to be a chartered accountant. And Katherine—she's fourteen—and of course still at school——"

"He knows all that," said Katherine. And when she interrupted her mother in this fashion, she did not do it like a rude child but as an adult might do it to an infant who has been chattering too long. Her mother never showed any resentment.

"Sometimes Katherine and I have tea together before the men folk come home," Mrs. Fielding went on, in her vague but cheerful fashion, "just our cosy little selves. But to-day, as you're here, I think we ought to wait and all have it together, and I know they won't be long, though your Uncle Alfred is kept sometimes, but not so much now when business isn't as good as it used to be—and how is your poor mother keeping?"

Edward, who was always embarrassed by this class of question, as if there was something indecent about it, mumbled that his mother was all right.

"I'm very glad, very glad indeed. Such a long time since I saw her! And what a terrible thing—really, a terrible thing—it was about your father, wasn't it? I mean, so sudden and everything. It's that suddenness, I think, that's the worst, though of course you're often spared a great deal, I must say. Arthur—that's my boy——"

"He knows," said Katherine.

"Arthur had mastoid trouble three years ago—just three years ago next month, it was, you remember, Katherine?—and really I thought then at one time—but no, he pulled through splendidly, and since then we've been very fortunate—yes, you may look, Katherine, but if you knew as much as I know, you'd realise we *had* been very fortunate—though there's hardly a winter passes but what I don't get a little chest trouble—nothing serious, and goodness knows I ought to be thankful—but there it is, and I'm very glad we don't live lower down, because they can say what they like about Willesden, but it's high——" and she raised a hand, as if they were all now perched on some peak—"and because it's high, it's healthier than most parts."

There was a great deal more of this, and though Edward did not find it very interesting, he preferred listening idly to it to being cross-questioned by the unpleasant Katherine, who was now busy with her homework again. Arthur and his father arrived within a few minutes of each other. Arthur was like a longer Katherine in spectacles and trousers, with the same long nose and chin, and the same sharply enquiring manner. You felt at once that he had a great future before him as a chartered accountant. On first being introduced to Edward, he looked him over quickly as if he saw in front of him a column of dubious entries in a ledger. Mr. Alfred Fielding, who was now "Uncle Alfred," was not quite so sharp and Londonish as his children, and there was still about him a suggestion of the other Fieldings and Haliford, but he was a much more weighty and decided character than his cousin, Edward's father. He had been dark too, though now nearly grey; was bald in front; wore a neat moustache; and was very neatly dressed, in a manner that made him remind Edward of shopwalkers in very important expensive shops. He was a man who liked to repeat certain phrases, as if he liked the taste of them. One of these was "a moral certainty." Another was "a reasonable supposition." These gave his talk the same character as his appearance, that of a very responsible, serious-minded citizen. Edward thought him a bit dull and pompous, but preferred him to those dark ferrets, Arthur and Katherine.

As soon as the tea was poured out, Edward was popped into the witness-box. Uncle Alfred himself opened the cross-examination. "Well, Edward, your mother didn't say where you were staying, so I couldn't give you an invitation here myself. But I thought it was a moral certainty you'd come and see us. And we're very glad to see you, very glad indeed. We've been wondering what brought you to London. Your mother didn't say."

"He's come to look round—for a job," Katherine squeaked.

Mrs. Fielding nodded cheerfully, but Uncle Alfred looked graver than ever and Arthur stared and stared. Edward felt a fool.

"Is this true, Edward?" asked Uncle Alfred.

"Yes. You see—Uncle Alfred—I wasn't getting anywhere in Haliford—you know what things are like up there—and I wanted a change, and it just happened I had a little money given me—not much——"

"How much?" asked Arthur sharply.

"Oh!—less than a hundred pounds—but, you see, I thought it would give me a chance to look round here—and see if there was anything——" Edward's voice trailed off into a silence only one degree less foolish than his speech had sounded. God help him now! Mrs. Fielding was still nodding cheerfully, but the other three looked like fox-terriers that had been shown a plump lame rat.

"Well, well," said Uncle Alfred. "I must say, Edward, you're taking a risk, a big risk. And this money—well, if it's so little, I should disregard it. It's a reasonable supposition that a capital sum so small would not buy you an opening anywhere."

"I should think not," cried Arthur, as if he were ninety instead of nineteen. "Not a chance. What can you do?"

"I was going to ask him that." This, of course, from Katherine.

What could he do? His claims were never large at any time, and now they shrivelled to nothing. "Well," he mumbled, "I was with a noil and waste firm, y'know. Clerking and sampling and so forth."

"What's *so forth?*" Katherine got in, but this time she was unlucky.

"Can't expect to get much here on that," said Arthur. "Can he, Dad?"

"I'm afraid you can't, Edward. Almost impossible to find a good opening for an untrained man."

"Arthur's going to pass examinations to be a chartered accountant," his mother announced proudly. "Aren't you, dear?"

"Perhaps you had something in mind, had you?" asked Uncle Arthur.

No, Edward had nothing in mind.

"Where are you staying?" asked Mrs. Fielding. "Have you some nice friends here in London?"

"No, I'm staying at an hotel."

Arthur whistled. Uncle Alfred shook his head. They were all shocked. An hotel! Apparently he had now reached rock-bottom in their estimation. Edward hoped that they would conclude he was barmy, and let it go at that.

"If you're staying at an hotel, Edward," said Uncle Alfred, "it's a moral certainty you're spending a lot more money than you can afford to spend. You ought to get into rooms—cheap, decent rooms—as soon as you can. That is, if you really intend staying in London."

"I do," said Edward firmly.

"I'm only sorry you can't stay here until you've settled down a bit," cried Mrs. Fielding. "Only—you see—I haven't a spare room——"

Edward assured her promptly that he had never expected to be asked to stay. He did not add that the very thought of living in the same house with Arthur and Katherine made him shudder.

"I might be able to help you there. One or two of young fellows in our office," said Uncle Alfred, who was in a wholesale cloth merchant's in the City, where he had gone years ago from Haliford, "live in rooms—cheap, decent rooms—and I could find out from them if there might be a vacancy for you. In fact, Edward, I think you'd better come and see me at the office to-morrow, because there might be one or two matters I'd like to discuss with you. Here's the address." He handed over a business card.

Katherine, who had not taken her sharp little eyes off him for the last few minutes, now found an opening. "Are you engaged?"

"Katherine, what a question!" cried her mother, more amused than shocked.

"Well, look! He's blushing. Why are you blushing?"

It was touch-and-go whether or not he cried: "Mind your own damned business, you little monkey!" Fortunately, Uncle Alfred intervened. "That will do, Katherine. If you've finished your tea, you'd better get on with your homework." They had all finished tea now.

"Do you know about wireless?" asked Arthur. "Not much? How much is that? I'm just making a five-valve set. Think I'll get on with it." And off he went, clearly dismissing Edward as an uninteresting ignoramus.

While his wife cleared away the tea-things, Uncle Alfred carefully lit a very small thin cigar, sat himself in one arm-chair and Edward in the opposite one, and then as he smoked—and even his smoking was anxious and responsible, as if he had undertaken to make the little cigar last as long as possible—he asked Edward questions about his family and Haliford, gave his own views, freely sprinkled with moral certainties and reasonable suppositions, on the state of trade, the political situation, and other subjects for newspaper leading articles. Meanwhile, Mrs. Fielding popped in and out, sometimes returning still holding the thing she had just left the room to dispose of, nodded and smiled at them, as if to say: "What a fine cosy chat you men are having, aren't you?" Edward felt they were both being kind to him, and was grateful, as a homeless wanderer, but he also could not help feeling that it was all very dull. Just before nine, he got up to go.

"Yes, perhaps you ought," said Uncle Alfred, giving this—the umpteen thousandth problem of the day—his earnest consideration. "It's quite a way. But you ought to go back by Tube. Change at Baker Street or Oxford Circus. I'll take you along to our nearest Tube station."

To Edward's relief, Arthur and Katherine did not reappear, and he had only to say good-bye to Mrs. Fielding. On the way to the Tube station, as they cut briskly through various gloomy mysterious streets, Uncle Alfred carefully explained how Edward could find his way to the office in the City. He also hinted that he might possibly have some suggestion to make about a job. "Don't count on it,

Edward. But the idea has just occurred to me, and there may be something in it. Come along to-morrow about twelve, and I may be able to tell you something then. And—er—just remember that London isn't Haliford. Far more dangers of every kind here for a young man—drink—and—er—that sort of thing, you know, Edward. I think—er—your poor father—was—er——"

"Yes," said Edward. They were now standing outside the Tube station, which was very quiet. Odd to be standing here talking about his father!

"You never knew my father—your grandfather's younger brother—did you?" asked Uncle Alfred quietly.

"No, I never did. I've never heard much about him."

"No, you wouldn't. He was a drinker. Very wild. They found him one morning," said Uncle Alfred softly, "in Black Tarn—you know—on Langhead Moor—drowned. He'd been missing for three days. I was only twelve at the time. It made a great impression on me. I've been—well—careful, if you like, ever since. You be careful, too. Well, glad to have seen you, Edward. To-morrow, about twelve, at the office. That's right."

As Edward took his ticket, he turned and saw Uncle Alfred still standing there, a clearly defined, neat, precise figure in the light of the station entrance, apparently determined to see that Edward safely deposited himself in the lift. Somewhere behind him—but now what a world and age away!—were Black Tarn and Langhead Moor and the wild drinking wool men in straw hats and narrow-brimmed bowlers, high collars and cut-away coats, clattering up the moorland roads in brakes and traps, shouting and singing, drowning in the cold black water. Good night, Uncle Alfred!

When he awoke next morning, he remembered at once his letter to Nellie Salter. With any luck, she ought to be reading it that very moment. And if the girl had any heart at all, she would soon be writing to him to tell him where Rose was. That is, if she knew where Rose was. But of course, he told himself, she must know by this time. On that comforting thought, which warmed and fed him, he dressed and breakfasted. To-day the dining-room of the Lomond Hotel was not as quiet as it had been yesterday. An old lady, a thickly powdered skeleton of an old lady, a terrifying figure, complained about the toast, and did not complain once but went on and on, so that in the end Mrs. Parkinson herself, still securely upholstered in black, had to come in and try to quieten this noisy guest. But the old lady defeated Mrs. Parkinson, just as she had already defeated the waiter, by pretending to be deaf. "What? What? Can't hear you!" she shrieked. "I'm complaining about the toast. The toast! It's tough. You what? Well, that doesn't make it any the less tough, does it? Any fool can make good toast. Slice of bread, a fire and a fork. This is yesterday's, warmed up. I know. What? Speak up!" They were still at it when Edward left.

This was one of those mornings when the smoke and the Thames Valley mist decide to work a few miracles for their London, and especially for the oldest part of it, the City, where Edward went to find Uncle Alfred. The City, on these mornings, is an enchantment. There is a faintly luminous haze, now silver, now old gold, over everything.

The buildings have shape and solidity but no weight; they hang in the air, like palaces out of the *Arabian Nights;* you could topple the dome off St. Paul's with a forefinger, push back the Mansion House, send the Monument floating into space. On these mornings, the old churches cannot be counted; there are more of them than ever; ecclesiastical wizards are busy multiplying the fantastic steeples. There is no less traffic than usual; the scarlet stream of buses still flows through the ancient narrow streets; the pavements are still thronged with bank messengers, office boys, policemen, clerks, typists, caretakers, commissionaires, directors, secretaries, crooks, busy-bodies, idlers; but on these mornings all the buses, taxicabs, vans, lorries, drays, and all the pedestrians lose something of their ordinary solidity; they move behind gauze; they are shod and tyred in velvet; their voices are muted; their movement is in slow motion. Whatever is new and vulgar and foolish contrives to lose itself in the denser patches of mist. But all the glimpses of ancient loveliness are there, perfectly framed and lighted: round every corner somebody is whispering a line or two of Chaucer. And on these mornings, the river is simply not true; there is no geography, nothing but pure poetry, down there; the water has gone; and shapes out of an adventurous dream drift by on a tide of gilded and silvered air. Such is the City on one of these mornings, a place in a Gothic fairy tale, a mirage, a vision, Cockaigne made out of faint sunlight and vapour and smoke. It is hard to believe that somewhere behind this enchanting façade, directors are drawing their fees, debenture-holders are being taken care of, loans are being called in, compound interest is being calculated, mergers are being arranged between a *Partaga* and a *Corona Corona*, and suggestions are being put forward for little schemes that will eventually bring revolution into Central America and mass murder into the Near East.

Edward, who had an eye for the effects of such a morning though no tongue for them, wandered happily for an hour or so in this gorgeous unreality before he made for his Uncle Alfred's office, which was just off Cheapside. He found Uncle Alfred sitting importantly behind a desk in his own little room. Uncle Alfred was even more serious and responsible down here than he had been the night before at home. As soon as he had exchanged a few words with Edward, he consulted some notes on his desk. "Now, Edward, there's a chance, just a chance, that I may have found something for you to do. I don't pretend that it's very important or will get you anywhere. You can regard it as a temporary thing, if you like. But it's moral certainty that you'll find it better than doing nothing, and it will give you time to look about you."

Edward instantly agreed that it would, and added that he preferred doing almost anything to doing nothing.

"Quite so," said Uncle Alfred, with solemn approval. He looked at his notes again. "Well, there's a little concern we occasionally do business with here. As a matter of fact, they buy odd lengths and spoilt pieces from us. That's their line. Cheap odds and ends of anything, whatever they can pick up. There are two partners and they call themselves the Belvedere Trading Company. One of them was in here on Monday and I happened to remember him saying that they were short-handed, as one of their clerks had gone and they're pretty busy. So I rang them up this morning and they said if you went over this afternoon, there might be something for you. Now mind—don't expect too much. But I think it's a reasonable supposition you'll get something to do there, though what the money, hours, work, will be, I can't tell you. As a matter of fact, I must warn you, these two partners are—well, no doubt they're smart men of business in their own catchpenny line—but—well, you wouldn't call them gentlemen."

That did not bother Edward, who never gave a moment's thought to the question of calling or not calling anybody a gentleman. This was something Uncle Alfred had picked up since he left Haliford.

"Well, there's the address, and here's a note I've written about you to them. Now the next thing is this question of lodgings. Now one of our young men here—Lexden—tells me that there might be a room for you where he's staying, Chalk Farm way."

Chalk Farm way! "Is that a long way out?" asked Edward, who, now that he had come to London, wanted to stay in London.

"Chalk Farm? Good lord, no! There aren't any farms there now, y'know." And Uncle Alfred laughed. Edward could see him retailing this splendid joke to Arthur and Katherine. "Here's the address, and the best way to get to the house." It was all there in Uncle Alfred's neat handwriting. "You'd better go up there as soon as you've seen the Belvedere people. All right? Good! Well, that's the best I can do for you, just now, Edward."

He was grateful, and said so. Promising to let Uncle Alfred know what happened to him, at the first opportunity, he returned to Cheapside. He had a couple of hours to dispose of before calling on the Belvedere Trading Company, and he was able to dispose of them very pleasantly, wandering round the City, eating a one-and-threepenny lunch, then walking slowly along Newgate Street and Holborn Viaduct towards the Belvedere people, whose office was in one of the short streets between Holborn and the Clerkenwell Road. He had no difficulty in finding them: Uncle Alfred had seen to that.

The Belvedere Trading Company was on the first floor, above a shop that dealt in optical and other instruments. The staircase was dirty and dark, but, unlike those dark and dirty steps he had known so well in Pooley Road, Haliford, it had still about it a certain faded air of elegance, as if it was a staircase that had known much better days than these, which indeed it had. At the top was a chaotic litter that appeared to barricade the Belvedere Trading Company from the outside world. There were bundles of blankets, bales of shirts, dusty rolls of cloth, raincoats by the dozen, piles of boot boxes, mounds of socks and women's stockings, and burst cardboard cases spilling everything from field glasses to tobacco pipes, sets of collar studs to wax dolls. London might have been some equatorial forest and the Belvedere the first trading post, just established. You expected to find natives arriving with skins and pearls and rubber. Behind this barricade was a long room heaped with more boxes and bales and bundles, and, to one side, a small private office, partitioned off with match-boarding and glass. Out of this inner office bounced a large roaring fellow who smacked Edward on the shoulder.

"Morgans, eh?" he shouted. "You're just in time."

Edward stammered that he wasn't Morgans.

"Oh!" The large fellow, who had an inflamed and indented face, rather like an angry red full moon, was disappointed. "Then who the hell are you?" And he sucked his small ragged moustache, as if he had had enough of it and preferred to get rid of it that way. He smelt strongly of whisky.

Edward explained about Uncle Alfred and produced his letter.

"Yes, yes, I see. Old Fielding, eh? Careful old codger, isn't he? He didn't talk to me. Talked to my partner. Old man," he roared down the room, "just a minute, old man, just a minute."

"Old man" appeared, from behind a gigantic pile of hat boxes lower down the long room, and turned out to be a short dapper but foxy-looking man about forty, who peered at Edward—and indeed at everybody and everything, it seemed—through narrowed eyelids and a little mist of cigarette smoke.

"Old man," said the large fellow, "this is the kid old Fielding talked to you about—his cousin's wife's uncle's brother's nephew, from Oodersfield, by gum!"

The short one took the letter and peered at it in his own sceptical cunning fashion. Then he looked at Edward again as if he were a bale or bundle of something slightly damaged and going cheap. He nodded. "Righty-o. Seems okay. I'll leave it to you, Percy. I'm busy looking over that Dunstable stuff." He had a slightly nasal voice, rather reminiscent of those mysterious knowing men in American gangster films. Indeed, he appeared to have modelled himself on one of those men.

Percy took Edward in hand now. They went into the little private office, but no sooner had they got inside than the telephone demanded Percy. "Morgans?" he yelled hopefully. "Oh!—it's you, is it, George? Don't you know that I'm busy, blast you! Ha ha!—and the same to you, old boy. Well, listen. We'll all go. I'll get Madge and Beatie or one of the other girls, and you collect old What's-his-name and Dora. That's it. Cer-tain-lee, old boy. Ta ta!" Having finished with George, he now sat on the desk, which was a sad muddle of invoices and advice notes, and looked at Edward. "So you want to work here, eh? What for?"

"Well—you see—I've just come to London—and I want a job—and my uncle said——"

"Yes, I know all that part. What were you doing up north?"

Edward told him, and did not hesitate to throw in about half of Mr. Clark's work. He stressed the fact that he had left of his own accord.

"If you want to know how we do business in London," said Percy, "you've come to the right place. We can show you a thing or two here. Built this business up these last five years—right through the depression, clean through it—from nothing, absolutely damn-all. And look at it now.

Know what our business is? No? I'll tell you. The Belvedere Trading Company buys any line—bar battleships or cotton mills—that's going cheap, and—er—disposes of it in the proper market. And do we take chances? It makes horse-racing look like a whist drive. You've got to be so smart at this game, kid, that they haven't to catch you napping in the middle of the night. Fact! You've got to buy from Jews to sell to Scotsmen and make a profit. And half the time you're dealing with chaps who'd take the pennies out of a blind man's can and the milk out of your tea. You've got to work like hell. My partner—you just saw him out there—and I, we work like hell. We expect everybody else to do the same. Sink or swim!"

Edward did what was expected of him. He made a respectful agreeing sort of noise.

"Now I'll tell you what I'll do," said Percy, with a false heartiness that Edward recognised at once as part of his technique with customers. "You come to us. You don't know the business, don't even know the town. Straight out of the egg. You can add up a few figures, make out an invoice, answer the 'phone, but so can any little bit—and there are thousands of 'em—who wants a job at thirty bob a week. But I'll tell you what I'll do. I'll take you on here, practically teach you the business too, and you'll be on a month's trial—*but*—as we'd like to oblige old Fielding, who puts something in our way now and again—we'll pay you a couple of quid a week. Take it or leave it."

Edward took it. He knew it was miserable money, not enough to live on, but he would be doing something and this would give him time to look round and find something better.

"All right then," said his employer, suddenly becoming very dignified and grand. "The sooner you start, the better. I'll now show you our system of working here."

Even Edward, with his small experience of business methods, soon realised that the Belvedere Trading Company had no system worth calling one, that it simply muddled through with a kind of fierce energy, alternately kindled by optimism and despair. The two partners, Mr. Percy Cromford, the large one, and Mr. Kelso, the short gangster one, did all the buying and selling, but had a mysterious ally, on commission, called Cannock, who never came to the office and was nearly always out of London. The two partners, who were not lazy, whatever else they might be, also lent a hand with everything else. This was necessary, as Edward soon saw, for there were only three other people on the staff besides himself: a miserable elderly man called Rufus (this was his surname), half clerk and half warehouseman, who helped with everything in a slow but grimly conscientious fashion, as if he knew only too well that there was only this underpaid job between him and the workhouse; a warehouseman and porter, Bert Hewish, who did all the heavy lifting and carrying and sometimes drove an old Ford van; and a perky little shrimp of a Cockney girl, about eighteen, with dark, slightly squinting eyes and protruding teeth, called Queenie Broom, who did a bit of typing and telephoning and message-carrying and arranging and dusting. During the next two hours, Edward made the acquaintance of all these people, who seemed glad to see him, possibly because they had been short-handed. He also made the acquaintance of the sketchy book-keeping methods of the firm, and of its invoicing and other matters. Most of the goods it bought were not stored in this room but in railway warehouses and similar places, but it kept plenty of samples on hand, as well as complete odd stocks that had been unsold some time and were not worth warehousing. This explained the muddle of the place. It was Rufus's duty to keep a list of the samples and unsold stuff and to know where everything was, with the result that he himself looked like a dusty old sample of something that nobody wanted. Edward's job was the invoicing and transportation of stuff that had been sold; though in addition, of course, he had to do anything else that Mr. Cromford and Mr. Kelso told him to do. He had to be there at nine, could take an hour for lunch, and then worked on until the Belvedere Trading Company—as Mr. Cromford said—"called it a day." Sometimes, it appeared, they called it a day quite early, and the two partners rushed off to find double whiskies and new ideas; but at other times, with a fortune almost in sight, they all worked until eight or nine. They were fairly busy now, but this first afternoon, Edward was allowed to go about six.

As he found his way back to Holborn again, he felt a deep sense of satisfaction. He had a job. Even he knew very well that from every point of view it looked a poor sort of job; but that did not prevent him from feeling like a famishing man who has suddenly been given food and drink. London, though only in the dubious guise of the Belvedere Trading Company, had given him work to do. He was no longer a staring visitor, an idle hanger-on. In this vast ant-heap, he was now an ant that was busy carrying a half-inch of straw or fragment of leaf, like most of the other ants. He was satisfied.

The next thing to do was to get himself out of the Lomond Hotel as soon as possible. So he did not go back there but had something to eat and then set out for Chalk Farm, to the address Uncle Alfred had given him. Even with Uncle Alfred's elaborate directions to help him, he was some time before he found the house, for Chalk Farm seemed a dark wilderness of railway lines and canals. It was eight o'clock when he arrived there. The house was one of a short row of tall decayed melancholy mansions that had steep steps leading up to their front doors, noisy lighted basements, nasty little front gardens that were the haunts of complaining cats, a great deal of unpainted woodwork, and many upper windows that returned the light of the street lamps with a mad blank stare of their own. Any one of those houses looked the perfect setting for a famous unsolved murder mystery. Edward rang the bell at Number Four. The door was opened very cautiously, not more than a few inches, as if the house was in a state of siege. Could he see Mrs. Scrutton? This might have been a password he was giving, for immediately the door was thrown wide open, and the woman who stood there announced that she was Mrs. Scrutton and asked him to enter.

"Was it about a room?" asked Mrs. Scrutton, who seemed to think they had already had a long talk about something.

Edward said it was, and explained about Uncle Alfred

and the young man, Lexden, in Uncle Alfred's office.

"I have one," said Mrs. Scrutton, who had a large face with hardly any features on it, a pinkish prairie of a face. "It's at the top. Just a bed-sitting-room. You mightn't like it," she added, cheerfully.

He said he would like to see it.

"Well, if you would, you would," she replied, as if she was not responsible for such whimsies and rather deplored them. "We'll go up. It's quite a climb."

It was. By the time they arrived there, Mrs. Scrutton, who was short and rather stout, was puffing away like a little steam engine, and even Edward was breathless. The room seemed quite large to him, for it was bigger than his attic bedroom at home and much bigger than his room at the hotel. It was much shabbier than his room at the hotel, but somehow more cheerful, possibly because it gave the impression of having been really lived in. There were two chairs, a chest of drawers, a small brass bedstead, a miniature antique gas fire, a very worn carpet, and a very large pop-eyed portrait of Lord Kitchener.

"Books too," said Mrs. Scrutton, pointing, "if you're one who likes a read."

Yes, there were books, in a lop-sided little bookshelf in a corner. Three odd volumes of the *Library of International Literature*, two of *The Quiver*, an old *Illustrated Guide to Bristol, Bath, Etc.*, two paper-backed novels by Nat Gould, and *Everybody's Book of Electricity*. "Some nice reading there, I'll be bound," said Mrs. Scrutton, as they looked at the books together. "Though I'm not one for books myself. Now Mr. Finland—isn't that a funny name?—I thought it a scream, first time I heard it—he's got the room opposite—and he's got hundreds and hundreds o' books. But he's well edjucated, Mr. Finland is—a kind of professor in his own way—a really well edjucated gentleman. His only trouble is—well——" and she lifted her elbow significantly. "Can't leave it alone."

Edward enquired nervously about the rent.

"Well now, I'm one who likes to be fairly done by and I like to do fairly by others," announced Mrs. Scrutton. "And I'm particular who I have. Not like some I could mention, not a mile away from here. Take in anybody, and charge 'em fancy terms just because they wasn't—well—you know. None of that with me. It's my living and I don't pretend it isn't," she continued in a passionate strain just as if she and the now embarrassed Edward were in the middle of some heated argument, "but I'm particular, I keep a respectable house, I do fairly by others and expect to be fairly done by. You bring no girls up here. Mr. Lexden tried that, but I caught him at it, and I said, 'Mr. Lexden, I don't care who she is and where she comes from, but out she goes. And don't tell me she's your cousin from Manchester,' I said, 'because I've heard that before.' Now you look a very decent young fellow, I'm sure, but you might tell me a bit about yourself."

Mrs. Scrutton was fierce but not unfriendly, and Edward was ready to like her. So he told her a bit about himself, and she nodded as she listened, as if it was all what she expected and very right and proper.

"All right then. I think you'll suit me and I'll suit you, Mr. Fielding. It's fifteen shillings for the room, and if you want breakfast—just a nice plain breakfast, with an egg or bit of bacon—then it'll be a pound altogether. Both the gas for the fire and the electric light's on meters. All quite simple. Payable by the week and on a week's notice, unless otherwise arranged. You'll take it? Very well. You'd better come in to-morrow. No good your coming to-night, for you'll have that hotel bedroom to pay for now whether you sleep in it or not. Scandalous, I call it, that hotel business. Think people are made of money. I always tell young fellows like yourself, just starting in life here, as you might say, to be careful with your money——"

"I'll have to be careful with mine," said Edward, who had been trying to balance a budget for the last five minutes, and saw that he would have to spend some of his capital to live at all. They were now returning downstairs.

"Well, whatever you do," said Mrs. Scrutton, "never get behind with your rent. I'm not saying that because I'm your landlady. . . . I'd say it wherever you were staying. And why? Because you can always do without a suit of clothes or eat a bit less or not drink and smoke so much, but you've got to have a roof and a bed to sleep in. That's what I always say," she announced at the front door, as if Chalk Farm had asked her to make a public statement on this question, "and I don't care who knows it. Well, you come along to-morrow about this time or earlier and we'll have your room all ready for you. Good night."

And now that was done. All that was necessary, for life in London to begin properly, was the letter from Nellie Salter telling where Rose was. And by some enchanting accident, he might come across Rose any time now:

she was only round a corner somewhere. As the innumerable dim blobs in the dusk caught the lights of street lamps and shop windows and pubs and turned into faces, he examined them hopefully; and there began for him that procession of passing eyes which was to go on so long and come to an end at last in the strangest fashion.

IX

THE London Associated Drapers and Dress Stores Ltd.—known in the City and to the trade as "Ladds"—had been very fortunate. The combine had been capitalised at a monstrously high figure, but even so it could pay over ten per cent and a bonus. It could afford to laugh at the depression. Trade might decline, new wars might threaten, the very tenancy of civilised man on this globe might seem precarious, but women were more determined than ever to make the most of their attractions, and, being the modest sex that does not disdain any ally, were buying more and more dresses, stockings, hats, shoes, gloves, sets of underclothes, coats, scarves, bags, cosmetics, and hair and face treatments. "Ladds" had three large stores—one in Oxford Street, one in Kensington, and one in Brixton—and they were always crowded, so it built a fourth, in Marylebone Road, among the great new blocks of flats there. This new store was not brutally labelled *London Associated Drapers and Dress Stores Ltd.* Those five astute men on the board of directors knew better than that. Mr. Sanderson was one of the cleverest of them, a fine late specimen of the raiding Scot. The mind of the suburban shopping woman had been spread before him like a large-scale map for years, during which he had learned every tiny twist and turn of the business. The very day of the directors' meeting, he had bought a grand Raeburn at Christie's. There was the name for the new store. "Gentlemen," he had announced, "ye'll do no better. Raeburn's got a fine flavour. It's solid and at the same time it's got style. Say—Robert Raeburn. And ye can take it from me, they'll like it."

"They," of course, were the nameless hordes of women customers, fingering the pound notes and silver in their bags. All over London, clever men, conferring in a haze of smoke, were considering and talking about "they" and "them." Advertising men, newspaper men, film men, patent medicine men, company-promoting men, were all narrowing their hunters' and trappers' eyes, while in the streets below, swarming by the million, went "they" and their moving little mounds of silver and pence, soon to be diverted into this channel and that, then to be weighed and counted by those eyes. How lucky "they" are nowadays, when so many clever men consider their lightest prejudices and whims!

So the new store was called "Robert Raeburn's." And Mr. Sanderson had been right, as usual. They had liked Robert Raeburn. As they asked one another if they had been yet to Robert Raeburn's, or proudly announced that they "had got it at Robert Raeburn's, my dear," they had a vague but comforting vision of a tall, erect, slightly side-whiskered old Scot, a clever up-to-the-minute purveyor but also a whimsical character, who perhaps had a quaint sweet little grand-daughter who talked about fairies. The store itself was tremendously modern, all glass and stainless metal and geometry, and so it did not look like Robert Raeburn; but they felt that he had had it designed to suit their taste rather than his own, that he was always just round a corner somewhere in the building, seeing that everybody was attentive, careful and honest, rubbing his fine old hands, and throwing pawky Scots witticisms at the smiling heads of departments. If the worst came to the worst, they concluded, they could complain to Mr. Raeburn himself. They faced the assistants, many of them, with a "I'm capable of complaining to Mr. Raeburn" look in their eye, and it worked like magic. Indeed, the whole establishment and enterprise worked like magic, and everybody was satisfied.

It was a store on the American plan, designed for a world of rapid tempo and lightning changes, a world without any loyalty to material objects. Everything you saw at Robert Raeburn's was the smartest little piece of perfection for to-day, and in less than a year's time all those things would be out-moded, out-worn, only fit for the poorest dependant or the dustbin. Women were convinced that they could shop cheaply there because somehow the actual price on the ticket was always less than they expected; but in the end they spent much more than they ever intended to, because nothing they bought was in the fashion long or lasted for any time. Thousands of husbands and fathers were bewildered by Raeburn-haunted womenfolk who screamed with delight one day because they had bought so many nice cheap things there, and shortly afterwards were bitterly complaining that they had nothing to wear. Those five directors involved many a poor blundering man in a domestic argument that ended with door-slamming, curses, tears, and a final reconciliation that cost even more than the original demand. The five directors did not care. Robert Raeburn's was a gigantic success. Even the newspapers—or, at least, all those newspapers that had hopes of an occasional half-page advertisement—said it was. From nine in the morning until six at night, women streamed through those fine big doorways in the Marylebone Road, their heads humming with plans for matching this and that, their tongues forming millions of words, their feet hurrying inflexibly, any hundred of them throwing off enough energy to keep the dynamo at the Central Power Station busy for a week. They rushed into one department, lingered in another, charged like raiding cavalry into the bargain basement, ascended in silken and scented floods to the restaurant near the roof. The restaurant was very charming; it was in creamy yellow, with a few Euclidean designs picked out in vermilion; it offered you a dainty three-course lunch for two shillings and an equally dainty afternoon tea for one shilling; and mannequins, who at first sight looked like handsome young customers gone mad, slowly peacocked between the tables, exhibiting the very latest in everything; and even the waitresses, in russet-brown with frilly white collars and cuffs, were young and pretty. One of the youngest and prettiest of the waitresses, this first week of October, was Rose Salter.

When Mr. Smalley, redder than ever at the back of his neck, had walked into Miss Finberg's office at the Copper Kettle Café, and Rose, following him, had been convinced that something was about to happen, she had not been deceiving herself. Mr. Smalley had appointed two waitresses to Miss Finberg's staff without asking Miss Finberg's permission. Miss Finberg had complained to the head office. She had a candidate of her own for one of the new vacancies. Head office had agreed that Mr. Smalley had gone too far. One of the two girls he had appointed must go, and Miss Finberg had decided that it must be Rose, because she was the prettier and so was probably the little piece that Mr. Smalley had his eye on. Mr. Smalley was landed now with the task of telling his pretty piece that she must go. Miss Finberg was only too delighted to lend him her office for this unpleasant little scene.

"I'm sorry about this," said Mr. Smalley, not meeting Rose's eye. "It's nothing to do with you, kid. Not your fault at all. Just a little mistake, you see. Miss Finberg—well, never mind." There would be plenty of time, in the near future, to make a great deal of trouble for Miss Finberg. After this, it was war. He would show her.

Rose did not admire Mr. Smalley, but at this moment she felt sorrier for him, because there was loss of prestige written all over his very large red face, than she did for herself. So she murmured sympathetically that it was all right.

"It isn't all right," said Mr. Smalley hoarsely. "It's a dam' shame. But don't you worry. You'll have to leave us, of course, and I'm sorry because you seem to me a nice kid, just the type we want. But I've fixed something for you—something good." He waited for thanks, and got them. "A pal of mine, an old pal of mine, in the catering trade, has been looking after the restaurant at this new shop, Robert Raeburn's—see? Well, I had a little talk to him, and he's getting you in there. Only—don't let on you'd just started here—see? I told him you'd had plenty of experience."

"What will I have to do there?" asked Rose anxiously.

"Same thing as here, just waiting. Easy! If you ask me, it's a better job than this. Only thing is—you live in. Nearly all the waitresses there live in, then they're on the spot. Saves you a lot of trouble and expense. Wouldn't mind living in there myself," and he leered like an old Pasha.

Rose did not say anything. She did not know what to say—or to think. It was all too sudden and confusing. A waitress in the restaurant at Robert Raeburn's! Living in! What next?

"You'll have to get a move on," Mr. Smalley continued, "because they want you to start on Monday. You report to-morrow morning to Mrs. Furber—she's the manageress of the restaurant—before twelve. Employees' entrance, at the back, at Robert Raeburn's, Marylebone Road. Got that?"

Before Rose could decide whether she had got it or not, Mr. Smalley was holding her hand in one hot moist paw and patting her shoulder with the other, which seemed even hotter and moister. "And the best of luck, kid," he was saying. "You'll be all right at Raeburn's. You can go a long way there. Smart people, very smart people!"

That is how it happened. Once Rose had recovered from her first surprise, she began to feel pleased. She had never been into Raeburn's, but she had heard about this wonderful new shop. It was a cut, a distinct cut, above the

Copper Kettle Café. And this would show Alice, with whom Rose had begun to feel permanently displeased, that she, Rose, could get on very well without her, and was indeed getting on at a furious rate. While Alice was still slopping away at the Copper Kettle, Rose would be starting on another and superior adventure at Robert Raeburn's.

"Oh, I say, Rose," said Alice, later that morning, "I've just heard. You're going and I'm staying. I am sorry. What will you do?"

"It doesn't matter," said Rose, rather grandly, though not too grandly because she saw that Alice was genuinely disturbed, as indeed she ought to be, "I'm getting another job—at that new shop, Robert Raeburn's. In the restaurant. Living in."

"Well, I don't know!" cried Alice, returning, in her astonishment, to the true Haliford idiom.

It had been queer, very queer indeed, going down to the shop on Sunday morning to see this Mrs. Furber. To begin with, all London was so quiet. The bus rumbled down the streets of a dead city. The very places that were busiest on week-days were now the most silent and deserted. It was a dull, blanketed sort of morning, not wet, not fine, not warm, not quite cold, mysterious weather. The whole city might have been packed in dirty cottonwool. Rose felt unreal, and consequently was much less nervous than she might otherwise have been. It did not seem to matter, on a morning like this, so far removed from real mornings, that she should be going through the back door of this famous big new shop to see a possibly terrifying Mrs.

Furber and pretend to have had plenty of experience as a waitress. Raeburn's shop and Mrs. Furber could not be solidly terrifying. They too would be part of a grey chilly dream.

She found the *Employees' Entrance*. It was in a very quiet back street, where nobody was stirring. The door was shut and she could not see a bell. After hesitating a moment, she let herself in. Inside was a lift, and it was the kind you work yourself. Rose went in the cage, carefully examined the seven buttons and their labels, shut the doors in a hasty but gingerly fashion, pressed the button labelled *Hostel*, and then did a little vertical travelling. At the top, waiting to use the lift, were two girls, very smart Londony girls, who talked loudly, took no notice of her, and disappeared down the shaft before she could make up her mind to ask them about Mrs. Furber. It was very new up there, and still smelt of fresh paint. She went through a swing door on the left, and found a girl in a maid's uniform in the corridor. The girl took her to Mrs. Furber's room, which had two arm-chairs, a little desk, an electric fire, and quite an air of new grandeur.

Mrs. Furber was smoking a cigarette and reading the *Sunday Times*. She had grey waved hair, and a hard handsome look, like some of the older actresses you see in films. At any other time, Rose would have been frightened of her. But now she was not quite real, and it did not matter much what Mrs. Furber said or did.

"Yes, I remember," she said, after Rose had explained about herself. "Well, let me have a look at you." She had a good look. "Humph, yes. You could easily improve that hair of yours, though it's quite pretty. Pity you girls don't know how to make more of yourselves. A French girl or an American who was half as pretty as you are would turn herself into a beauty. You look good-tempered. Are you?"

"I'm supposed to be," said Rose, without getting very pink.

"Tact and good temper are essential here," said Mrs. Furber. "Much more important than at the—er—Copper Kettle places. If you annoy one of our patrons, you may be robbing the shop of one of its best customers, for all you know. You can see how important that is. And, please remember, here you're dealing with women most of the time, not with men, who'll put up with anything, especially from girls with your appearance. You've had experience, of course? Yes, I remember."

Not a lie to be told. And that, Rose said to herself, was simply because she didn't care. If she had arrived nervous and anxious, panting for the job, probably this woman would have asked her dozens of questions, and she would have had to lie like fury.

"You will live up here, very comfortably too, let me tell you," Mrs. Furber continued, in her brisk style. "You will be given breakfast, lunch and supper, and a certain allowance of free laundry. You will start at fifteen shillings a week, and will have a percentage of the pooled tips. We neither encourage nor discourage our patrons to tip you girls, but all the tips you receive must be put in the box. I am very strict about that. What you receive as your share will vary, of course, but it should amount to anything between fifteen and twenty-five shillings a week. You are also entitled to all the privileges enjoyed by the staff here—the use of the athletic ground, membership of the various societies we have, some free medical and dental attention, the use of the club room up here. Your name again? Rose Salter. Well, Rose, I think you will agree that you are a lucky girl to find yourself here, and I hope you will be a loyal member of our staff. We treat you in the best possible manner and we expect you to co-operate with us in the best possible manner. All our rules are sensible, and we do not allow any infringement of them. Now then——"

Mrs. Furber said all this very quickly, as if she had said it many times before, but nevertheless it was the most impressive speech anybody had ever made to Rose, and she did not fail to be impressed by it, even though it was Sunday morning in a cottonwool London and everything was unreal. She said she would do her best, and tried a smile on Mrs. Furber, who did not smile back, perhaps because she kept all her smiles for her private life. Now after not smiling, she was looking through some lists.

"Except for a few senior members of the staff, you girls up here share bed-sitting-rooms," Mrs. Furber said, looking up from her lists. "Perhaps I ought to explain that all the younger waitresses live in here, and a few of the girls from the other departments who have no home in London also live in. You will share a room with a girl from one of the dress departments. Her name is Beatrice Vintnor. Here is a list of our rules, which please read carefully. You will bring your insurance card to me in the morning and I will send it down to the office. Now I will show you your room."

They went down the corridor, turned a corner, walked past a number of doors, all bright with green paint, until they reached 39. Mrs. Furber knocked, was answered and admitted, and Rose found herself in a very nice new room, quite the nicest bedroom she had ever had. It even had running water in it, with nickel-plated taps. There was a fine new mirror above the wash-bowl. There were two white chests of drawers, two rugs, one in front of each bed, and two new little arm-chairs, upholstered in green, to match the paintwork. There was a small electric fire too. It was a wonderful room. Rose took it in at a glance, and was delighted by it. Beatrice Vintnor was there, making her bed.

"This is your room, Rose," said Mrs. Furber, without either friendliness or unfriendliness, like somebody in a hospital. "And this is your room-mate. You had better move in here some time to-day, and as I shall be out late to-night, you will please report to me—or to my assistant, Miss Drummond—at eight to-morrow morning outside the restaurant. I will arrange about your uniform then. Now I will leave you girls to get to know one another. Good morning."

"Good morning, Mrs. Furber," said Beatrice Vintnor dutifully.

Mrs. Furber nodded to them both, still without smiling, and left them. Rose stood rather awkwardly, looking at Beatrice Vintnor, and wondering if she would like her. Beatrice Vintnor stopped making her bed and sat on it, to stare at Rose. She was a thin girl, several years older than Rose, and she had fine dark eyes, a long and rather sharp nose, and a small discontented mouth. She was wearing a handsome thin woollen dress, of a dark red shade, which suited her admirably, and she seemed to Rose (who was foolish enough already to mistake her own sturdy shapeliness for an almost hopeless liability and so envied all these small-boned, lean creatures) a fashionable and intimidating figure, belonging to another and higher class. For a moment or two, while the two girls looked at one another, nothing was said.

"Where you do come from?" asked Beatrice, finally.

Rose told her, shyly.

"I'll bet you got that coat and dress there, didn't you?" said Beatrice.

Rose admitted, not without shame, that they had been bought in Haliford.

"And they look it," said Beatrice, with a short laugh.

This was not a friendly beginning. Yet there was nothing downright unfriendly about it, Rose guessed. Beatrice Vintnor seemed a nervous, jumpy sort of girl. She talked in quick jerks, and the short laugh, which Rose was soon to know only too well, appeared even then to be only a nervous trick. Rose did not reply to this remark about her clothes. She merely continued looking, perhaps a trifle reproachfully now, at the other girl.

There was a startling change of mood. Beatrice jumped up from the bed. "I'm sorry. I oughtn't to have said that. I don't suppose it's your fault. And anyhow, they're all right. You look sweet. Honestly, you do. It must be wonderful to have hair that shade—it's quite natural, isn't it?—with those eyes. I think you're lucky. Honestly, I do. Are you lucky? I expect you are. We need a bit of luck in this room. Did you notice the number? Thirty-nine. You see, three times thirteen. Ghastly! Can you tell fortunes? I'm always telling mine."

Rose stared at her in astonishment. This was a new kind of girl to her. She did not seem to be quite all there. Rose was so surprised at this outburst that she did not reply.

"Oh—all right," cried the other. "If you want to be sulky, you can be." She sounded quite offended.

"Here, wait a minute," cried Rose, whose voice sounded to herself now as broad and sensible as a farmer's. "I'm not sulky or anything. It's all right."

"Then why didn't you answer?" She still sounded cross.

"Well, you see—I mean—well, I didn't know quite what to say. But it's all right. Really, it is."

Beatrice said nothing but looked hard at her with those big dark eyes. They were curious eyes, too big and excitable for the rest of her, so that they seemed to be draining all the life out of her face, leaving it drawn, almost haggard. Altogether, a queer girl.

"It seems—very nice here," said Rose shyly. "You don't work in the restaurant, do you?"

"Good God, no!" said Beatrice, as if the very suggestion that she might do were an insult. "I'm down in the Dresses. I was in the Dresses at Burmages in Oxford Street. That's the same firm really, y'know. I'll bet you didn't know, did you? A lot of people don't." She gave the usual short laugh. "I've been working in London shops now for seven years. With luck, I may be a Head Sales soon. Then a Buyer. It's all luck, though. I've found that out. What experience have you had?"

"Oh—hardly any," said Rose cautiously.

"I thought not," said Beatrice, scornful again now. "I'm going to finish making this rotten bed."

"I'll help you if you like."

"Thanks." There was not much left to do, but somehow Rose did more of it than Beatrice did. When they had done, and had tidied up the room a bit, Beatrice was suddenly and embarrassingly grateful, coming quite close to Rose and telling her excitedly that she was perfectly sweet and just the kind of girl she had wanted to share the room. Rose left, to return to Mrs. Burlow's and pack her things. Mrs. Burlow for once showed a face that expressed her inner self. "It's always the same, Miss Salfer," she said tearfully. "Them you get attached to have to go. If it's happened once with me, it's happened a dozen times. Not that I blame you, Miss Salfer. You're doing well for yourself, even though living in's one thing and a home's another. But remember—in me you have a friend. And that's not a word," she concluded, wildly and dramatically, "lightly spoken."

It was queer leaving Alice, even though they were no longer the friends they had been. At the last moment Alice, who had been rather sulky and resentful when she had discovered that Rose would be better off at Raeburn's than she had been at the Copper Kettle, suddenly threw off her complicated unfriendliness as if it were an ugly cloak. She insisted upon going with Rose in the evening to the shop. All the way there, she was affectionate and melancholy, not at all her usual brisk self.

"It's because it's Sunday night," said Rose. "You never did like Sunday night, Alice."

"I know, but that's not it." Alice's voice was heavy with fatality. "Rosie, you know I never get queer feelings. You're the one for them. But I feel—we're separating for good. I feel that all sorts of things are going to happen to us, me especially, and we're not going to like them. And I feel you're going your way and I'm going mine." And with that, to the astonishment of the bus conductor, she suddenly burst into tears. This was an Alice that Rose had never seen before. What was the matter with her?

"But Alice, it's all right. We can see one another often, if you really want to. You talk as if I was going to Australia or something."

Alice refused to be comforted. "It's like that time my mother knew about my Uncle Harry. She *knew*. I didn't know I could get like that. But *I* know. You'll go your way, and I'll go mine. I don't believe we'll ever see one another again. It's never going to be the same after this. You see."

Rose replied sharply that that was all nonsense, but even as she was speaking, she suddenly felt that Alice was right. It was as if both of them had caught a glimpse of themselves, moving far away in the future, two small lonely figures in that dusk. Rose was not of a metaphysical turn of mind, but now she began thinking about the future, about the mystery of time. It was very queer. It was, indeed, quite frightening. Two days ago, Raeburn's had meant little or nothing to her. Now she was actually going to work and live there. Out of the darkness had popped that bed-sitting-room on the top floor, with Beatrice Vintnor sitting in it, staring at her. What else was being prepared for her in that darkness? Were they all there waiting, there in the future, until she arrived at them? The Copper Kettle Café and Mrs. Burlow's had once been waiting for her, and now already they were going, sinking into the haze of memory. It was all puzzling and rather frightening. Why didn't anybody really *know* about all these things?

She said good-bye to Alice at Raeburn's back door, and, feeling very small and subdued, went up to her room. Beatrice Vintnor was not in, much to her relief. Slowly and solemnly, she unpacked and put away her things. It really was a splendid room. There was even a big wardrobe cupboard with proper hangers for dresses. It was nearly full already, for Beatrice had an astonishing number of dresses, some of them real evening dresses, lovely wispy things. Adding her own modest contribution, Rose looked at Beatrice's things with admiration and awe. Beatrice ought not to have sneered at her clothes, but you could hardly blame her. Rose felt very humble and provincial. By ten o'clock she was in bed, and a very comfortable bed it was too, far better than the one at Mrs. Burlow's or the old one she had shared with Nellie at home. She thought about Nellie and home, and told herself it was time she had a letter from Nellie. But the letter, when it came, would have to be sent on from Mrs. Burlow's. To-morrow night she would write home herself, telling them what had happened.

She was just dozing off when Beatrice Vintnor dashed in, making a lot of noise. "Oh—so you're here," said Beatrice, flinging off her things.

"Yes," said Rose timidly.

Beatrice said nothing. She looked tired and rather cross.

"It seems awfully nice here," Rose ventured.

Beatrice did not reply. She did not seem to care whether Rose thought it nice or not. Perhaps she was angry about something that had happened to her outside that night. Rose did not say anything else.

Finally, Beatrice sat on the edge of her bed, and stared hungrily across at Rose, rather as she had done that morning. "Why is everything so devilish? Tell me that," she cried angrily. "What's the matter with everything? Why? Why? Why?" She was so fierce in her anger and despair that Rose was quite frightened.

"Has—something gone wrong?" Rose enquired, sympathetically.

"No, not something. Everything. And all the time. Yes, all the time, everything goes wrong. Why does it? What's the matter? When I was a kid, it wasn't bad. I can remember when it all seemed marvellous. Now it never is. Never, never! Oh, God!—is it going to be always like this? Until you're dead."

She looked as if she might burst into a passionate fit of weeping. Her face was all huge tragic eyes. What was the matter with her? She might be putting it on a bit—and Rose, a good Halifordian, suspected it—but there was something sincere about this outburst. Rose felt very uneasy. She had a sudden strong desire to get out of that bed, put her clothes on, and leave Raeburn's at once, going back to Mrs. Burlow's or to Haliford. That, of course, was silly. Why throw away a good job? Nevertheless, she had to control herself quite sharply to stay where she was.

The other girl, obviously a creature of the most quick and senseless changes of mood, now jumped up and said: "I suppose you think I'm a fool. Well, I'm not. I've had a stupid evening, that's all. Don't bother about me. Nobody does, anyhow. Naturally." She produced her usual disconcerting short laugh. "Catch them. The only thing to do in this world is to care about yourself. Probably you know that already. By the way, you have to be up at half-past seven in the morning. Good night."

It was a long time before Rose got to sleep. There was so much she could not forget. She could not forget the other girl, the newness and strangeness of her situation, in bed high above a big shop in the Marylebone Road, or the odd way in which things happened. And the next morning she had to begin all over again. It was frightening.

But it turned out to be not so bad, after all. Like most things, it shrank when you fairly tackled it; and Rose, though so often inclined to be dreamy, passive, gentle, could be a sturdy tackler. The work was no harder than that in the Copper Kettle Café, and now she had some experience behind her. Here there was no Miss Finberg resenting her. The restaurant itself was nicer. It was pleasant to see how impressed all the customers were. During the rush hours of lunch and tea, when there was never an empty place, you had to be very quick, and everybody was inclined to be short-tempered; but these periods did not last long, and the mornings and the middle of the afternoons were comparatively quiet and easy. Rose had to help an older waitress called Miss Jewson, who was much superior to Miss Wade at the Copper Kettle. She was tall, rather handsome, very ladylike, came from Gloucester, and had a great desire—for no reason that Rose could ever discover—to live in South Africa. Miss Jewson had never been to South Africa, had no relatives or friends there, but at some moment, when she was being less ladylike and aloof than usual, something she had heard or read about life in South Africa had caught and held her fancy, with the result that now she was planning and saving to go there. She did not say much about it. She did not say much about anything. But she was a very good waitress, very quick and neat, and with a fine professional air of being infinitely obliging. She taught Rose a good deal. Rose was easy to teach. At times she was forgetful or awkward, like every beginner, but she was so eager and fresh and pretty that her faults were soon forgiven both by the staff and the customers. The customers were not as varied and amusing as they had been at the café. There was nobody like that fattish untidy man, for example, the man who had been so funny that afternoon. There were too many women and not enough men. Rose soon found herself getting tired of her own sex. To begin with, she had to live entirely among girls. The hostel at the top, the bathrooms, corridors, dining and club rooms, were simply girls, girls, girls; too many stockings, breasts, powdered noses, heads of waved hair, feminine eyes, chattery high voices. Then women and girls by the thousand swarmed in and out of the restaurant, pushing and staring and chattering. They divided themselves into groups, just as they had done at the Copper Kettle. Some were very nice, and treated you in an easy, friendly manner. Some were half frightened, and pathetically grateful for being served at all: they came in as if they had no right to be there, sat on the very edges of chairs, looked about anxiously, and whispered an order. Sometimes you were sorry for them, but at other times they would irritate you. Then there were the usual bunches of misery who wanted to show how superior they were to mere waitresses, and so just made difficulties and extra work. A few of these always took an instant dislike to Rose, and Miss Jewson said it was because she was young and good-looking and the jealous cats couldn't stand it. But there were times when Rose was tired of even the best of them, simply because they were women and she was temporarily sick of her own sex. It was a relief to attend a sheepish male or two, as even Miss Jewson herself admitted. You never saw a man by himself in there, unless he was waiting for some woman to come up from the other departments. The tired ones who slumped into chairs like sullen little boys suddenly grown old, the cheeky ones who tried to catch your eye, like impudent little boys, were missing here. Rose found herself wishing there were a few of them about, as a change from this soft, scented, pink and powdery flood of females. As Grace, who worked at the next three tables, said to her at the end of one terribly crowded lunch hour: "Give you the pip! Silly old cows! Let me look at a few chaps for a change. Any chaps."

But that very morning, as it happened, a chap had been looking very hard at Rose. He sat at one of her tables with two elderly ladies, who had long horsy faces and commanding voices. She heard them call him "Fr-awn-cis." He was young, tall and thinnish, wore light tortoiseshell-rimmed spectacles and a very dark blue shirt, carried a wide-brimmed black hat, and looked vaguely artistic. He talked a lot in a rather high, hissing sort of voice that was quite new to Rose, who thought it sounded silly. He kept staring at her, and once or twice he smiled. This was nothing new, and Rose did not think much about him. But when they had finished and the two women moved away, he came over to her, to give her a tip. As he handed it to her, he said quite politely: "Would you mind telling me your name, please?"

Rose was so surprised that she blurted it out at once, without asking him what business it was of his.

He nodded and smiled, then said quickly: "Mine's Francis Woburn. Will you remember, please? Francis Woburn." And off he went, leaving Rose gaping after him.

What did it matter to her that he was called Francis Woburn? And why should he want to know her name? He was not her kind. What was the idea? She asked Miss Jewson, and that experienced young woman, who had no illusions about anything but South Africa, replied indifferently that he must have been "trying it on." But what, after all, had he tried on? Rose did not feel flattered, but neither could she work up any virtuous indignation about it. It was just senseless. Still, it was an event, something to think about.

But a letter that arrived that night, forwarded—and not in any hurry either—from Mrs. Burlow's, put an end to any idle speculations about eccentric young men in dark blue shirts. It was from Nellie, and it contained the most extraordinary and exciting news. That boy who never turned up, Edward Fielding, had actually called at the house to see her and explain why he was so late that night. He had been hanging about Slater Street for nights and nights, Nellie wrote. He was crazy about her, Nellie added. And such a nice kid too, Nellie said, and what did she mean by running away to London and leaving him? He had muttered something about going to London himself now, but Nellie was not sure whether he had actually left Haliford, was not even sure that he had definitely made up his mind to follow her to London. Never in all her life had Rose had a letter that excited her as this one did. Ever since that miserable night she had been trying to forget this Edward Fielding, who had been so disappointing. And it had not been his fault at all, poor boy. He was all that she thought he might be, when she left him after that happy Sunday. Crazy about her! Hanging round Slater Street, night after night! And when she was not even in Haliford! What a shame! She wanted to see Edward Fielding at once, to explain everything, to tell him how sorry she was, to discover exactly how crazy he was about her. Why, she was crazy about him too. Yes, she was. It came over her at once. An immense blank in her mind was now immediately filled with the thought of him. He had been there all the time, but she had pretended to herself that he wasn't. Now she must think and think about him again, go back over every minute of that Sunday they spent together. Everything was different. She must find out exactly where he was, for of course he was in love with her and she was in love with him, and it had been like that right from the beginning.

"And what's the matter with you, Rose?" asked Beatrice. They had arrived at Christian names and had shared the same room so far without a quarrel, but otherwise had made little progress since the first evening. "You look all excited."

Rose had to return a long way to reply. Beatrice, their bedroom, Raeburn's, London, all suddenly seemed unreal now. She replied cautiously: "I am—a bit. It's just something that's happened." But her heart sang behind the commonplace words.

Beatrice knew happiness when she saw it. "I wish it had happened to me," she muttered. She tore off a stocking and hurled it into a corner. She combined a passionate love of dress with a careless disregard for individual things, which made her a very untidy room-mate. "Oh, God!—I'm fed up. Everything's devilish."

"I'm sorry, Beatrice." But Rose was thinking about the letter she would write to Nellie, asking her to find out at once where Edward was.

"Do you mean it?" Beatrice's eyes were enormous and hungry. Her mouth was sceptical.

Rose looked at her, and felt genuinely sorry for her.

Poor Beatrice had no Edward Fielding, and on the other hand seemed to have all kinds of mysterious grievances. "Yes, I do mean it. I don't know what's the matter——"

"Everything's the matter," said Beatrice, for the fiftieth time that week.

"No, that can't be right," Rose continued. "But I know something must be wrong—whatever it is—and I really am sorry——"

"All right, we'll see," said Beatrice sharply, as if putting humanity to the test, perhaps for the last time. "I want you to do something for me. I want you to come with me to-morrow—and see my brother——"

"Your brother?" Rose was surprised.

"Yes. My brother—Lawrence. I went to see him yesterday and told him about you. He said he'd like to see you."

"But why should he? I mean——"

"I don't know," said Beatrice, quickly, impatiently. "What does that matter? If he thinks it would amuse him."

"But—but—where is he?"

"He's in a hospital," said Beatrice harshly. "He's been in a hospital for over a year. He can never get better. He's dying." And then suddenly her defiant manner left her, and she collapsed on the bed, shaking with great sobs.

Rose stared at her, horrified. She got up and moved uncertainly over to the bed, where Beatrice was still lying, her body jerking horribly in the spasms of her grief. Rose went nearer, wondering what to do. As suddenly as she had collapsed, Beatrice now sprang up and rushed over to the wash-basin. Nothing was said for a minute or two.

"Well?" said Beatrice, defiantly again. "Now you know. You needn't come if you don't want to. But you said you were sorry."

"Yes, I am," said Rose steadily.

"You won't like it, you know." Beatrice's eyes, like two dark birds of prey, were fixed on Rose's. "That hospital—it's hellish. If they were miserable, it wouldn't be so bad. But—but——" and her voice lifted and shook and took on a terrible intensity—"they're all so bloody bright."

No sooner had they entered the hospital, early the following evening, than Rose knew exactly what Beatrice had meant. It was not an ordinary hospital. You did not go in there to have a finger taken off or a broken bone mended. It was a hospital for those who were dying by inches. We are all dying by inches, we are all slowly rotting above our graves, but unlike the patients in that hospital, we are not constantly aware of the fact. But they knew all about their inches. They stared out of decaying bodies. Yet the whole institution, with its long corridors, its polished floors, its shining wards, its starched white uniforms, its little wagons of dressings and drugs, its trays and flowers and screens and framed notices, was determinedly bright. From floor to floor, ward to ward, with the doctors and attendant matrons, went thousands of little jokes, some of them the tiniest jokes known to man. The nurses wore a fixed smile, had loud cheerful voices, and told one another, over the beds they were straightening, what a ridiculously spoilt lot their patients were. And the patients themselves, while the mind kept watch at all in the crumbling tower of the body, chaffed the nurses, and exchanged among themselves, while the nurses could overhear them, merry little anecdotes about missing floor-brushes, belated sleeping draughts, cups of tea that had gone cold. Within these walls was a little world, and a world from which many things, such as sex, economics, politics, had been banished. Once inside there, it did not matter if democracy or autocracy should win, capitalism was as good as socialism, easy divorce as moral as divorce made difficult, and all systems of education were alike. Newspapers ceased to be important. A perpetual gentle birthday party seemed to be going on in there. When a guest was ready to leave it, screens were placed round his bed, and doctors and nurses, their set smiles fading for once, disappeared behind them, and very soon the male orderlies brought the stretcher from the mortuary. Next day, probably, there was a bewildered new face, a new guest, and the party went on, with a few new jokes in circulation. Even at parties in the best society some guests will be tactless, and it happened here now and then, often in the middle of the night, when the world might easily seem one vast torture chamber, with Pain lording it over the universe, for then somebody might suddenly scream and scream. But these little slips were never referred to, always carefully ignored. And on the third floor of this hospital, in a small ward with three other men, was Lawrence Vintnor, in the twenty-sixth and last year of his life.

"Lawrence," said Beatrice, and even she was brighter in here than she was outside, "this is Rose."

"Hello," said Lawrence, putting out a bloodless hand. It clung to Rose's as if it were feeding upon her vitality.

He was like Beatrice, with the same eyes, the same nose. He was so much like Beatrice that Rose never saw her again without being reminded of him, a fact of some importance, for her subsequent adventures would have been quite different if it had not been for this resemblance. But Lawrence was not merely thin, he was a shadow of a young man. All the life that was left to him was burning away in his great eyes. He was a staring, faintly smiling skeleton. Rose had had no experience at all of death, and very little of sickness, but she knew at once that Beatrice had been right: this brother of hers was dying. Even now he seemed to belong to Death rather than to Life. He was smiling at her out of the grave. At the first moment of their encounter, Rose had been startled and repelled, all the more so because there seemed to come from this wasted figure a faint but sickly sweet odour of decay and corruption. But no sooner had he smiled, had his hand clung to hers, had she looked into the great hollow eyes, than her feelings changed, and from some depths, unknown to her before, there came rushing a deep spring of emotion, almost sweeping her away. She felt ready to cradle him in her warm arms, to give him her own rich blood, to stay there and care for him day and night until he was cold for ever. This feeling was quite impersonal. To her he was not a person, but at once more and less than a person. She was so strongly moved that she could not speak, she could only look at him and try to smile at him. Beatrice turned away to speak to one of the other men. Lawrence still clung to her hand.

"It was decent of you to come here," said Lawrence. His voice was weak and rather hoarse, and seemed to be further away than he was, as if the thinking and speaking part of him was already half-gone. "Beatie told me about you. I thought I'd like to see you. Do you—want me to take my hand away?"

"No," said Rose, and then wondered if she had actually spoken.

"Thanks. It's—rather comforting. You've a beautiful face. Kind, too. I'll be able to dream about it. I dream a lot. I didn't like it at first, dreaming and then waking up here. Now I don't mind. I like it. I was going to be an architect. I dream about that. You'd be surprised what I've built. Whole cities. I think they must exist somewhere, don't you? Perhaps that's why there's so much space. You know, they say it's terribly empty, in the sky, space. And perhaps it really isn't. Perhaps I'm helping to fill it. Whole cities."

He did not speak for a minute or two. Probably he was exhausted. Rose said nothing, but tried to smile at him and tried to pour through the hand she still held, the hand so strangely large and light, all her strength and warmth and pity.

A slight movement of his head indicated that he wanted her to come nearer. She obeyed it. "About Beatie," he whispered. "I expect you find her—a bit difficult. She always was, and I suppose I've made it worse for her. Don't mind about her. Try to get on with her, will you?"

Here was something she could do. Rose promised earnestly that she would.

"We've been an unlucky lot," he continued, still whispering. "I won't bother you with it. You'll probably get plenty of it from Beatie. But try to help her."

"Yes, of course I will," said Rose softly. And meant it.

"Thanks." He smiled, very slowly. "Kind Rose. Sweet Rose. Beautiful Rose. Sorry—I'm being a fool. Didn't used to be like this, you know. But you get a bit queer in here after a time." He closed his eyes.

"Well, now," said a brisk bright voice that made Rose jump. There was a nurse at her elbow, a smiling but sharp-eyed young woman. "Aren't you lucky, Lawrence, having pretty girls coming in to see you?"

Lawrence opened his eyes, and made the required effort. "Yes, of course."

"I should think you are," cried the nurse in her brightest manner. She looked shrewdly at him, then caught Rose's eye and gave her a tiny shake of the head. Lawrence's hand had now withdrawn from hers. The nurse quickly and deftly settled him back on his pillows.

Beatrice returned. "Well, Lawrie," she said, in her unnaturally bright manner, "we'd better be going. Is there anything you want, next time?"

Lawrence looked at her, with the ghost of a smile. "Yes, everything."

"Now, Lawrence," said the nurse.

"Sorry. No, Beatie, nothing, thanks. Good-bye.

And good-bye, Rose. Thank you for coming to see me."

That was all. In two minutes they were back in the world outside. But to Rose it was not the same world they had left only a little time before. Perhaps it never would be the same world. As they went back to the shop by bus, sitting silently side by side, Rose stared out of the window at a different city, a city with disease and death hard at work in it. Before this she had never thought much about death, for it had never entered the house in Slater Street in her time. She herself and all the people round her had been going to live for ever. Now she realised that all those people down there on the pavements, those people staring at the shop windows, waiting for buses, going into public-houses, queueing up for the pictures, meeting and laughing and talking, were dying. By a miracle they were not dying as fast as Lawrence Vintnor, were still moving and chattering in the street instead of lying in bed in that hospital; but they too were on their way. She was given a glimpse of the vast tragic spectacle of life. She seemed to see on every face the marks of decay, the signs of the inevitable corruption. She was shaken with terror and pity. There were no more streets, no more people, there was only a blur of vague shapes. She could stare no longer through her tears.

And now Beatrice broke her long silence. "My God!" she cried. "Look at that hat. How some of these women can imagine they can get away with monstrosities like that——!"

Hats! What did hats matter? How could Beatrice even think about hats? She turned, blinking, to look at her in astonishment, but having looked at her could only think how like her brother she was. And then she saw that Beatrice was silently commanding her to say nothing about Lawrence. With an effort, she made some stupid reply about hats. She realised now that hats would do, anything would do. And they would go on for days talking about hats, about anything, with the shadow of Lawrence between them.

In their room that night, Beatrice began cursing the head sales down in the Dresses, and then as usual dropped from anger to despair, burying her head in her hands and beginning to cry hysterically. Now, remembering Lawrence, Rose went over to her, sat down beside her, and put an arm round her shaking shoulders. Beatrice at once clung to her, desperately. They sat there in silence, in their little room, high above the floors of dresses, underclothes, hats, stockings, shoes, the tables of dainty gifts, the glass and chromium plate and geometrical designs, the empty cash desks and locked doors, the buses and taxicabs, the crowds hurrying through the darkening streets to the grave.

Next morning, Rose had a letter, the first she had had in London that was not from home. It came from Doughty Street, and was signed Francis Woburn. She remembered at once; the young man in the dark blue shirt who had asked her to remember his name and had demanded hers. What on earth did he want? (Rose, like many people who do not have much correspondence, always let her mind wander all round a letter, sniffed at the postmark, the address, the signature, before actually reading it.) He wanted her to have dinner with him and then to go with him to the Russian Ballet at the Coliseum. He was, he explained respectfully, extremely interested in the ballet and was anxious to discover what her "reaction"—his own word—would be. If she was unable to come, would she please ring him up at the number above, but if she could come, she need not bother ringing him up, but could meet him at half-past seven that night at Merani's Restaurant, Old Compton Street, in Soho. Would you believe it? Didn't know her, hardly set eyes on her, and yet wanted to give her dinner at a restaurant and take her to see the ballet. And Rose, who had never had dinner at a foreign restaurant and had never seen a ballet, and who was an ordinary sensible healthy girl with an appetite for new and fashionable diversions, did not know what to say.

The trouble was that though she wanted the dinner and the ballet, she did not want Mr. Francis Woburn. All that she wanted in that line was Edward Fielding, and she was anxiously waiting for news of him. Francis Woburn might look artistic and have more money to spend than any of the young men she had ever known, but it was her experience that fellows who were ready to spend money on you were also determined to make love to you, usually in a very crude fashion, and she did not want Francis Woburn or anybody else—except Edward Fielding—making love to her. And she did not want to go to the restaurant and the ballet under false pretences. Unlike a lot of girls she knew, who took what they could get from the sex that had already taken all it could get, she liked to deal fairly with young men. It was possible, of course, that things were different in London, though she shrewdly suspected that in this matter they were not, that London and Haliford—and probably Paris and New York and Capetown and Shanghai—were all alike. She put the problem to Beatrice.

"Of course I'd go," said Beatrice. "I wish he'd asked me. What's worrying you?"

Rose explained, briefly and without mentioning Edward Fielding.

"What's this chap like?" asked Beatrice.

Rose did her best to remember exactly what he looked like.

"Oh—you needn't worry about him," said Beatrice. "I know these high-brow young men. They're easy. One little snub finishes them. They're too pleased with themselves to risk another. It's the tough older ones that are hard to handle. Let's have a look at his letter. Oh yes—he's all right. You go."

She did, and found him, still wearing his dark blue shirt, waiting for her in Merani's Restaurant. Rose had never been before to Soho, though she had heard about it. She found it very foreign and exciting. The strange things you saw in the little shop windows. The dark faces in the mysterious cafés. This was the romantic London of the films. Francis Woburn, whose voice seemed to be higher and more hissing than ever, explained very elaborately why he had asked her out for the evening. She was, it seemed, a new type to him, and as he had no chance of getting to know her in the ordinary way, he had taken the risk of writing to her. She had reminded him in Raeburn's restaurant of some girl in some picture by some famous old Italian whose name Rose did not catch. Rose did not much relish being a type—even though it was a new type—to anybody, but she was flattered at being compared with a girl in some famous old picture. (And she suddenly remembered poor old Major Beamish, that ridiculous night.) Francis Woburn asked her questions about herself all the time they were waiting for dinner, but, like many other people, seemed to be fonder of asking questions than listening to answers. He could talk fifteen to the dozen, and very soon Rose found it easy to pretend she was listening while she amused herself looking about her.

The restaurant was very small and warm and rather smelly. There was no doubt it was genuinely foreign. Whether it was reasonably clean was another matter, and Rose, now a sharp-eyed professional, had her suspicions. There were two yellow-faced waiters, and two fat yellow-faced waitresses, who had tried unsuccessfully to paint and powder the yellow out of their faces. The food was not bad, foreign but rather tasty, and probably concocted out of cheap scraps. They had wine out of straw-covered flasks, but it was rather sour and Rose did not much like it. The other people there were either like Francis Woburn, both male and female, or definitely foreign, with a marked resemblance to the waiters. The former lot all talked together in high hissing voices, while the foreigners growled at the back of their throats and furiously shovelled down their food. Francis Woburn knew some of the people there, and talked across tables to them. Rose felt a bit out of it, as there was nobody of her kind there. Two dirty-looking girls, wearing wide-brimmed black hats and thick knitted jumpers of the wrong colour, asked her companion to come over to their table, and when he shook his head, they stared hard and unpleasantly at Rose as if she was all wrong. But Rose knew she was all right, and refused to be put out of countenance by girls who had no more sense than to look untidy and dirty and wear the wrong colours.

"Of course," Francis Woburn was saying, "I'm practically a communist. Are you?"

Rose, who was thinking that it would be nice to be here with Edward Fielding, said that she wasn't.

"Aren't you class conscious at all? But, of course, you must be." He had a trick, new to Rose, of pulling out one word and making a great fuss of it, as if it was something very special. Thus he said "you me-er-ssst be." Rose listened for these words, which amused her. This gave her the appearance of being a most attentive and eager listener, so that her companion, who obviously enjoyed the sound of his own voice, was not dissatisfied. Meanwhile, they were eating and drinking away, and getting fuller and hotter.

"I'm most terribly keen," he was telling her now, "on a proletarian ballet. As a matter of fact, when I was in your place the other day—I'd been dragged there by a couple of aunts—and I was looking at you—by the way, did you notice I was looking at you?"

"Yes, I saw you," said Rose coolly. "We don't miss much, even though people are coming and going all the time."

"Quite. Well, I was thinking then, when I was looking at you, that it would be rather marvellous to have a scene in it with waitresses—I mean, in the ballet I'm trying to write." He waited for Rose to be impressed.

Rose was duly impressed. "Oh, are you writing one?" She did not know that people did write ballets, thought that you simply danced them, but was not going to say so.

"Yes, rather. I've written nearly half of one, and a friend of mine—absolutely brilliant chap who hasn't begun to be appreciated yet—is designing the costumes and sets. We're completely mad about it."

"When are you going to finish it?" asked Rose, anxious to show that she was interested.

Apparently this was not a very tactful question. A slight frown creased his fair forehead, immediately producing tiny valleys down which the miniature rivulets of sweat began to move. Rose watched them with interest, an interest he immediately mistook for an anxiety about his ballet. "The trouble is," he explained, "we began it, you see, in Catalonia, last year, at a simply heavenly little place on the *Costa Brava*. And now that we're back in town, we're finding it terribly difficult to recapture the mood. There, we were simply inspired. Here, we can't do a thing. He wants to get back to Catalonia, but just now I can't leave town—and—well, everything's rather difficult." He sighed heavily, like a man worn out with facing immense problems.

Rose decided now that he was rather nice, but, in spite of his ballets and *Costa Bravas* and foreign dinners and what not, very silly. As he still looked ready to sigh again, and had stopped talking for the first time since they met, she felt it was time she asked another question, if only to cheer him up and to show she was interested. "What do you do?"

"What do I do?" He seemed surprised. "Why——"

"I mean—you know—for a living. What do you work at?"

"Oh—I see. Well, I don't do anything for a living. I have a little money of my own, nothing much, of course. And then my aunts are pretty well off. But don't imagine I simply slack about. On the contrary, I'm always very busy, rushing about. There's the ballet, of course, and books and music and pictures—though there aren't many books and pictures nor much music that one can really enjoy. I've written a review or two for one of the better weeklies, and all that sort of thing. And then I've hosts—simply hosts—of friends who are doing things—artists of various kinds, you know. I'd like to introduce you to some of them."

Rose could not resist it. "Why?"

"Well, I don't know. But—perhaps I think you're a type that would interest them."

Type again! Type yourself!

"To begin with, you've got quite remarkable looks, really extraordinary. It's the amusing combination, I suppose, of fair hair and darkish eyes—very, very unusual and charming. And then there's a sort of—well, you might call it a noble simplicity——"

He was looking solemnly, almost owlishly, at her

through his large tortoiseshell-rimmed glasses, and Rose was annoyed to find herself getting hot—even hotter than she was already—in the face. Probably her nose was shining. That would be her bit of noble simplicity. She knew she was neither noble nor simple. But she liked what he said about her looks. It showed that Edward Fielding was perfectly right to be crazy about her, and justified his hanging about Slater Street night after night.

It was time to go. Francis Woburn put on his enormous hat, started talking about himself again, and they walked down to the Coliseum. He was much taller than she had supposed him to be—though perhaps it was the absurd hat—and she felt a little dumpy thing, though a nice sensible little dumpy thing, as she trotted along by his side, pretending to listen, but busy all the time telling herself that here she was, Rose Salter, with a foreign dinner inside her, and not too happy there either, now going to the Russian Ballet at the Coliseum, with a tall, hissing, superfine, very Londonish young man who could talk about her noble simplicity. It was all very strange indeed.

They climbed to one of the balconies of the gigantic theatre, which seemed to Rose the most splendid and exciting place she had ever seen. Dozens of players down below were tuning up. All round them, superfine persons, not unlike Francis Woburn, were studying their programmes or hissing away excitedly to one another. Then the lights died away, except those that illuminated the curtain so beautifully. The music began, and Francis Woburn stopped talking. Rose instantly forgot his very existence. The music was very strange, not like any she had heard before, and not at all comfortable and friendly and sweet. Rose did not know whether she liked it or not; she could not keep it at a distance to decide about it; she was simply carried away and half drowned by the colossal waves of sound; she was overwhelmed by its insistent beat and clang. The curtain was magically swept away, and the stage blazed at her. She was staring at a new country, a new world. It was as if the last great wave of music had taken her and flung her over the boundaries of this world. The little people in these new countries, people out of a fairy tale, exquisite princesses, wizards and witches, executioners, soldiers, leaping black slaves, lived their lives only in movement. Sometimes they were dull. Sometimes they were silly. But at other times they were so beautiful in their energy and grace, so obviously the creatures of another and better world than this, a world all of music and colour, that Rose choked and ached at the sight of them. People clapped. Francis Woburn clapped. But Rose did not clap. Just putting her hands together, making a silly noise, was not good enough for them. She gave them her heart. She surrendered. They would be dancing her away, somewhere at the back of her mind, for ever. She had been to their enchanted country and was now bewitched. Just outside—it was unbelievable—was St. Martin's Lane, and all the gloomy wilderness of London. And not far away, two pennies to a bus conductor, was that hospital and Lawrence Vintnor, and now she clutched that wasted hand again, gave her other hand into the warm comforting grasp of a distant Edward Fielding, and the music soared and throbbed and clashed, the magical figures twirled in ecstasy, the strange sunlight of their country grew brighter and brighter, and Rose Salter herself, blind and bewildered, not knowing whether she was aching with happiness or sorrow, seemed to be whirling in a dance, far above the miles of roofs, up to the stars, hand-in-hand with Life and Death.

Then it was over. They were all clapping like mad. Francis Woburn was saying that Somebody-or-other had been marvellous, simply marvellous. Then he was arguing with a youth in a black shirt and a bright yellow tie that somebody else was not too old—oldish perhaps, but still simply marvellous. And then they were out in the crowded street, quite a small shabby street, a street for dark gnomes and not exquisite princesses and tremendous wizards. And Francis Woburn was suggesting that they should have a drink and a sandwich at "the café," and that he would take her back to the shop afterwards in a taxi and see that she was in by twelve. She agreed to go, but hardly knew where they were going or what was happening. She was still far away. The music had not stopped, the magical sunlight and moonlight had not yet faded.

The café was very crowded, mostly with people rather like Francis Woburn. Room was made for them at a table where four other people, three men and a girl with a dead-white face, were already sitting, but they were friends of his, it seemed, and insisted upon their joining them. Two of the men had beards, and one of them, who had the larger and fiercer beard, actually had an ordinary deep male voice. It was he who almost pulled Rose down beside him. He told the others that he liked the look of her. Evidently he was the important one, for the others, even the white-faced girl, were very respectful to him. Rose was introduced to them but never caught their names. This large, smoky, crowded place seemed very dim and unreal to her. She was tired, for she had had a long day, and her adventure at the ballet had left her exhausted and absent-minded. This might have been a café in a dream. She could not even feel surprised to find herself there. She nibbled at a sandwich and drank some strong coffee. The others, who were drinking beer out of tall glasses, all talked and talked. The man sitting next to her, the one with the fierce beard and the deep voice, kept his leg firmly pressed against hers and occasionally ran a hairy finger along her forearm.

"That's all right for you people," he was booming at the others. "But I work. And when I say work, I mean work. And when I'm not working, I'm getting ready for more work. Pleasure doesn't mean anything to me. It hasn't meant anything these last ten years. I don't enjoy myself, don't even try. Through with it. I could live in a monastery or a gaol on bread and water, so long as they'd let me do my work."

All the time he was saying this, he was pressing a heavy hand upon Rose's knee under the table, and she decided that she had had enough of him. So now she freed herself and managed to stand up. She looked appealingly across at Francis Woburn.

"Don't go, sweetheart," said the bearded man, trying to grab her hand. "I haven't talked to you yet."

"She has to go," said Francis Woburn apologetically.

"Wouldn't you like to be my model?" asked the bearded one, with the air of a man conferring a favour.

"No, I wouldn't," said Rose shortly. "Good night."

As they went, they could hear the bearded one roaring with laughter.

"We were lucky catching Finklen," said Francis Woburn in the taxi. "He was in great form. Sometimes he doesn't talk all night. Sometimes he doesn't talk for days. Extraordinary personality, of course."

"I dare say," said Rose, "but I didn't like him."

"You didn't? Why, most girls simply adore him. He has the most amazing attraction for them, simply amazing."

"Well, he hasn't for me. If you want to know what I think, he's a big, hairy, conceited fool of a chap, who can't keep his hands to himself."

"Why should he keep—oh, I see. Sorry! I didn't realise. I suppose you'd like me to keep *my* hands to myself."

"I'd rather you did, if you don't mind," said Rose sleepily. She was thinking what a funny leathery sort of place the inside of a taxi was.

Francis Woburn was rather subdued now. "I hope you've enjoyed it."

"Yes, I have. Really I have," said Rose, feeling rather sorry for him now. "Specially the dancing. It was—oh!—well, I can't talk about it. Too tired, perhaps."

"Yes, I expect you have to work awfully hard in that place. And what a place! Those decorations—my God! I'm sorry you have to work all day there. But you needn't, you know."

"Yes, I need," but she was too sleepy to argue. She was

not too sleepy to guess that this was the moment when he would put an arm round her, and she was right. It was uncomfortable for them both, and there was no sense in it, but if he liked it, that was his affair. It did her no harm and seemed to please him, and after all he had been very kind to her. He was not a bad sort of chap, only nothing like so grand as he thought he was, rather silly and weak and conceited. When the taxi stopped, he let her go but made an ineffectual attempt to kiss her that ended in a feeble little dab on her cheek. (And quite enough too!)

"Thanks very much for an enjoyable evening," said Rose politely.

"Not at all. I say, I'll write to you again in a day or two. D'you mind? We could do something else together—hear some music or something, eh?"

Rose said that would be very nice, thank you, and left him. He did not write to her in a day or two, and, what was a great deal more important, neither did Nellie, to tell her where Edward Fielding was; but a day or two after that he wrote, and Rose found the letter waiting for her upstairs one night when she had been working later than usual, helping to clear away in the restaurant. But she did not read his letter then because she also found Beatrice there, and Beatrice was like a mad girl. Rose had never seen her in such a state before.

"What's the matter, Beatrice?"

The girl flung herself down on the floor in front of Rose, clutched Rose's skirt with both hands, and raised a wet tormented face. It was terrifying.

"What is it?" Rose stammered. "Is it—is it—Lawrence?"

"No, it's me. Oh, Rose, I don't know what to do, I don't know what to do. Oh God! You've got to help me, you've got to help me. Promise you will—promise. If you don't, I swear I'll kill myself. I will."

Rose was not looking at Beatrice. She was seeing again that face in the hospital, hearing Lawrence's voice, whispering to her about Beatrice. "Yes, of course, I'll help you."

"Promise. Promise before I tell you. I can't tell you unless you promise."

"All right. I promise."

Beatrice got up, sat down on the bed, wiped her streaming face, then looked steadily at Rose.

X

THERE was a pillar-box at the corner where he caught his bus every morning, and into it Edward dropped the letter he had been waiting—only a week or so, but it seemed a dreary age—to write and post. At last! Nellie Salter had been very slow in replying, but it was not altogether her fault. And anyhow, that was over now. No more Nellie, now that he knew where Rose herself was. Bolting his breakfast, he had just had time to write to Rose, at Robert Raeburn's, the big new shop in Marylebone Road, where she was working and living. Happy, blessed Robert Raeburn! There she was. Now he knew where to find her, and as soon as she had read his letter, she would know where to find him. He had told her where he lived and where he worked. That is all he had told her, except that he was very anxious to see her. It was not a love-letter at all. He had written dozens of love-letters to her in his head, but now he had decided, in his haste and joy, simply to let her know where he was and how anxious he was to see her again. And there, safe and snug in the pillar-box, was the letter, ready to work miracles. Waiting for the bus, he glowed with a sense of achievement.

The glow was needed. It was a raw morning, with a touch of fog thickening and chilling the air. Other people, not glowing, looked as if they had all got up too early or had been up all night. The men had reddened eyelids and noses. The women, powdering too freely as they peered into their dimly-lighted mirrors, were rather blue about the nose. Most members of both sexes looked disappointed and rather angry, as if they had just discovered that life had been cheating them for years, that all the gold in this forest was turning into dead leaves. The newspapers they were reading were angry too. Edward had no newspaper and was not sorry. There was no sense in being a happy man with an angry newspaper. He amused himself by looking at and thinking about the other people. They were nearly all office-workers, and they had stayed in bed an hour or two longer than the busmen, policemen, street-cleaners, hawkers, and porters, yet all these earlier risers looked far more contented and cheerful. Edward concluded, not for the first time, that there is something about office work that makes the people who do it peculiarly sorry for themselves. Miners and teachers, foundrymen and surgeons, all have hard days, but little is heard of them; the real weary worker, who may be seen in the advertisements demanding a certain sort of easy chair or mattress, who has to be nourished on a late cup of this or that, is always from an office. It is only offices that have the privilege of seeing that colossal figure, the Tired Business Man, at those times when presumably he is not tired. Edward felt sorry for his fellow-passengers, who looked as if they had too many nagging little responsibilities and not enough fun. He himself had not had much fun lately, but he could see a good time coming. The future dangled before him, a gigantic golden ripe plum, and his mouth watered.

The premises of the Belvedere Company, that trading post in the heart of darkness, were harder to get into than ever. Lately it had been buying more than it had been selling. When a good cheap line of stuff came along, Mr. Cromford and Mr. Kelso felt that they ought to snap it up. They had to take these risks. Last week, it had been hats, boxes and boxes of men's brown soft felt hats that had gone wrong in the final stages of manufacture. This week it was raincoats, a tremendous consignment from Manchester, which did not think them good enough for the regular trade. They did not look bad, these raincoats, and were probably all right so long as you did not take them out on a wet day. When he was feeling depressed—and it was not difficult to feel depressed at the Belvedere Trading Company's headquarters—Edward had begun to wonder whether the two partners and the staff—old Rufus, Bert Hewish, Queenie Broom, and himself—represented the human equivalent in rejects. Were they all darker on one side than the other, made in wrong sizes, had they loose joints, was their material faulty? This morning, not being depressed, he was sure that he himself was all right, but he still had his doubts about the others.

Bert Hewish, the warehouseman and porter, was trying on one of the new line of raincoats and already had one of last week's line in brown hats at the back of his large flat head. Old Rufus and Queenie were watching him.

"Wha's wrong wi' this ahtfit, eh?" Bert was demanding, in his heavy aggressive style. "A bloke could gow anywhere togged up in these."

"Thet's ri'," said Queenie.

"Well, he could and he couldn't," said old Rufus, who was slow and cautious in expressing an opinion as he was in doing anything else. He was the mystery man of the staff. Nobody knew what he had done before he came to the Belvedere Trading Company, or where he lived, or whether he was married or not, or anything. All that they did not know was that he did a great deal of work, in his own slow, grim, conscientious fashion, for very little money, and that he was old and without hope. He and Edward got on very well with one another, but the poor old chap had a bad time with the others.

"Ahr d'yer mean 'e could an' e' couldn't?" Bert snarled. Bert was a great snarler, especially to people like old Rufus. He was not one of your quick little smiling Cockneys, but the exceptional loutish type, who are either very aggressive or fearful and sycophantic.

"If those things come here," said Rufus, steadily and rather sadly, "then there's something wrong with 'em, isn't there? We all know that. All right. Now the people who know there's something wrong with them, you couldn't take them in, could you?" This looked like the beginning of one of those roundabout idiotic arguments that could go on between Bert Hewish and Rufus, who was mild but obstinate, for days. Edward had already heard bits of similar arguments, which never seemed to get anywhere or mean anything, in London pubs.

"Thet is so," said Queenie. "I'n't it, Mr. Fielding?" And she flashed her dark, slightly squinting eyes at Edward, whom she regarded with favour. But poor Queenie regarded nearly all young men with favour. She had protruding teeth, a slight squint, an undersized, under-nourished, almost deformed body, and was a very unattractive girl, who had had a lot of bad health already during her eighteen years of sparrow-like existence and would obviously have a lot more; but there burned in her, a steady bright flame, the feminine desire to come to terms with the other sex, and she would lead this forlorn hope until she dropped or until some astonished male capitulated out of gallant amazement.

"Nah listen," cried Bert contemptuously. "If the bloody clobber——"

"Language!" Queenie put in, tartly. As Bert Hewish, married already and no class at all, was not an eligible male, she could afford to treat him in her own natural sharp manner.

"I'm not talkin' to yew. Yew push orf," said Bert.

"Well, for Christ's sake!" cried an angry and despairing voice. It was Mr. Kelso, earlier than usual, and looking as if he had had what he and his partner called "a thick night." He was paler than ever, and there were great brown patches under his weary eyes. "Come on," he cried, glaring at them. "What the hell do you think this is? A Christmas party?"

"Sorry, Mr. Kelso," mumbled Bert, hastily removing the hat and coat.

"I'll make you all sorry in a minute. If you don't think you've any work to do, any of you, snap out of it and we can save your wages. And Rufus, the next time I catch you letting anybody mess about with the stock like that, you're out—see? Fielding, I want you."

And Mr. Kelso, still grumbling, led the way into the little private office, where he sat down, pushed his hat to the back of his head, rubbed his eyes violently as if he would just as soon spend the rest of his life without eyes, and groaned: "Just a minute. Can't think. What with one thing and another!"

Mr. Kelso was an unhappy man. He felt that he was an exceptionally smart man of business and that though he made the most of his chances, he had never yet had an opportunity to show the waiting world how really smart he was. All the time he met stupider men who made more money than he did, and as he was a man to whom money was all-important, for he was incapable of enjoying himself without spending money, he was constantly annoyed and irritated. Then again, he had a treacherous liver that resented the convivial life he liked to lead. If he tried to please his liver by living a quieter life, he was miserable. If he defied his liver, then it went—as he said—"back on him," and he was miserable again.

"I know," he said finally, struggling out of a yellow sea of nausea. "It's Barrons. We've got to try and get an offer out of them to-day for those damned hats. I don't want to ring them up again, it wouldn't look well. Now you ring them, Fielding, and you tell them that Mr. Cromford and I aren't here—see? And if they really want those hats, they've got to leave a firm offer here by twelve. If you like you can tell 'em we can easily sell the stuff later, but that if they buy it you get a commission and that's why you're ringing them."

"And do I get a commission?" asked Edward, who felt

that now he knew where Rose was, anything might happen.

"Don't be silly," said Mr. Kelso wearily. "We'll be lucky if we break even on the stuff. Commission! No, don't mention the commission. They wouldn't believe it, anyhow. Don't believe anything, those twisters. If you told 'em your mother was dead, they wouldn't believe you. No, you say you're responsible for the warehouse here, that you're expecting a big consignment of other stuff, and you want the space badly and so you're trying to rush this through on your own, see? That's the line."

There nearly always was a line of this kind. Possibly the Belvedere Trading Company and its customers did their business on those fundamental economic principles, buying in the cheapest market, selling in the dearest, and all the rest of it, that have made our modern world what it is to-day—though nobody seems to know what it is to-day—but nearly all their transactions involved a performance of some kind that had nothing to do with pure economics, a performance that had a rough-and-ready plot and then some clever improvising. Both Mr. Kelso and Mr. Cromford did more good acting in a day than most professional actors do in a week. And Edward had already been given several small parts, like this he had to play to Barrons.

He went to the telephone to play it, while Mr. Kelso, gloomily taking off his hat and overcoat, then lighting a cigarette he did not want, meditated over one or two other commercial comedies. Barrons, a firm that ran a small chain of shops under various names, all suggesting that the shops were there to dispose of lost property, salvage, army stores left over from mythical campaigns, were not enthusiastic about the hats, hinted that hats could hardly be given away these days, but said they would send their Mr. Furze over at eleven to give the stuff one last despairing glance. By this time, the other Belvedere partner, the large fat one, Mr. Percy Cromford, had arrived. He too had had a thick night, but either he had a better liver than Mr. Kelso or dispensed with that organ altogether, for as usual he was loud and hearty. He and Mr. Kelso made a good dramatic team. On one of his liverish days, Mr. Kelso could go and see some damaged stuff and buy it for next to nothing, for the manufacturers caught the infection of his deep pessimism. Just because his liver never went back on him, Mr. Cromford, if he was not dealing with astute old hands like Barrons, could loudly persuade customers that trade was improving, prices rising, and damaged stuff worth a generous offer. Between them, they ought to have made a lot of money. But somehow they didn't, as Edward had begun to suspect.

"You look a bit under the weather, old man," shouted Mr. Cromford. "What a night, eh? Pretty thick, old man, pretty thick!"

"Too thick," his partner grunted. "What are you going to do about Huntly?"

"See him this morning, old man. Take him out and give him a few drinks—and couldn't I do with one this minute?—and then sell him the stuff."

"Twenty-five bob a dozen?"

"Twenty-five bob it is. Or twenty-two-and-six if he's awkward. What did you think of Charlie last night? What a lad! What a lad! But where does he get the money from? That beats me, old man."

Mr. Kelso knew where Charlie got the money from. He always knew where people got their money from, and this probably only increased his irritation, when he remembered how little he had himself. "Commission," he replied now, half closing his eyes and looking very cunning.

"You think he touches, eh?"

"I know he touches."

Mr. Cromford, who was impressed, lowered his voice for once, and drew his partner out of the private office, whispering as he went. Edward remained behind, for he had some more telephoning to do. He could not be said to be learning much at the Belvedere Trading Company, but nevertheless the experience was not entirely without value. He had far more confidence now than when he had first come up those dusty stairs. He was not an outsider any longer. He knew something about commercial life in London, even if it was only that queer messy corner occupied by the Belvedere and its customers. He also told himself constantly that he was "keeping his eyes open," though he would have been hard put to it to describe exactly what he meant by that. This morning, however, London did not really exist for him as a place of business. He did what he had to do in the office in a dream. The solid reality was Rose in Raeburn's shop. There she was. He looked up the telephone number of the shop in the directory, and the very sight of it made him glow and feel excited. If he wanted to, he could ring her up. "I want to speak to Miss Rose Salter in the restaurant," he could say, firmly. And then her voice would cut through the drone of this smoky wilderness. Magic! He could go there at lunch-time, actually see her! This was a wildly exciting thought. Could it be done? He had only an hour, and would have to get to Marylebone Road and back, to say nothing of finding her in a big crowded shop. No, he didn't want a mere glance at her. And it would be awful if he didn't find her. But how glorious it was simply to consider these things! Life was beginning.

There was a public-house at the corner that offered you a cut off the joint and two vegetables, as well as beef and ham sandwiches, biscuits and cheese, and Edward often went there for lunch. To-day, old Rufus was there too, eating bread and cheese with a small glass of mild beer. Edward, happy and sociable, joined him. He found old Rufus rather fascinating. How old was he? What had his life been? There was something curiously empty and deadened about the old chap. The springs had been taken out, leaving only a few rusted wheels. His face told you nothing. It was covered with tiny wrinkles and a faint grey stubble; it was a mask, and a very dull mask. His eyes, which were a very light grey, never changed at all. His voice never rose or fell. The two partners bullied him unmercifully, Bert Hewish snarled at him, Queenie Broom was always making fun of him, and he endured them all with hardly a protest. He took stock of all the accumulated rubbish in his charge with a slow conscientiousness that could not have been improved upon if he had suddenly been called to look after all the gold in the vaults of the Bank of England. This time Edward was determined to get something out of him.

"Mr. Rufus," he began, with a respect that the old chap

never received, "tell me. What do you really think of those two—you know, Cromford and Kelso?"

There was a crumb of cheese left. Rufus carefully put it into his mouth. "Why d'you ask?"

"Oh, I don't know," said Edward, who didn't. "I just wondered—that's all."

Somewhere inside, the ancient rusty wheels began to turn. "Well, if you want to know," said Rufus, very softly, "not much."

"Neither do I."

"I dare say," said Rufus cautiously. His manner suggested that he did not live in the same world as Edward, a world where you could bounce about and shout your hasty opinions, a world of youth and hope.

"And I don't quite know why," Edward continued. "I mean to say, I can see there are a lot of things wrong with 'em but——" He paused.

"Not gentlemen," said old Rufus. "That's what wrong with them. Common as muck, the pair of 'em."

"Yes, I suppose so," said Edward, who remembered that Uncle Alfred had made the same point. It was not one he would have made himself. He had been born too late for it. Now he thought for a moment. "Do you think they make much out of this business?"

Rufus looked at the little pattern of froth in his glass. "More than you and me."

"They could easily do that."

"In my time," said Rufus, slowly and softly, "I've made more than them both put together, and then a bit more—a good bit more."

Here was something. "Have you? When was that?"

"A long time since." It sounded like centuries.

"I expect it was," said Edward, not very tactfully. "Where was that? Here in London?"

The old chap shook his head. "No, not here. Australia and the Federated States. Sydney and Penang, mostly. A long time since."

Edward stared at him. Who would have thought that the old boy had ever lived in such places and made money in them too? People were surprising. "What——" he began, but old Rufus cut him short, and it was the first time Edward remembered his cutting anybody short.

"Out there for years and years," he said deliberately. "Then I made a mistake. Came back. Shouldn't have done it. If you ever get away, don't come back. D'you know why?"

"You can make money out in those places?" Edward suggested.

"No, that's not it. Though I don't say you can't. But that's not it," he said, in a small faraway voice, staring just above Edward's head. "No sun here. When you're gettin' on, like me, you don't need a lot o'money. No women, no boozing, no monkey tricks. But you need the sun, boy. Look at it. And it'll be worse before it's better. Four or five months of it. Dark. Middle o' the night all day. No sun. Out there, in my time, I've thrown money to chaps on the beach, and there isn't one of 'em, not one, I wouldn't change places with now. They've got the sun, boy. I haven't. It's all you've got left when you're old. Warms your bones. Warms your blood. Pours the last bit o' life into you. If I could walk back there, where the sun is, I'd set off to-morrow. But I can't."

"Couldn't you go back somehow?"

"Wouldn't be here if I could. Put my money on the wrong card, boy. Look where you put yours." Old Rufus was more animated now than Edward had ever even guessed he could be. There was a spot of colour in his cheeks, a faint light in his eye, brought back perhaps by merely talking about the sun. "You think you've any God's amount of time in front of you, don't you, boy? And you haven't. My oath, you haven't. Suddenly you turn round, and the money's gone, you're old, and you're in the wrong place, and downstairs they're nailing your coffin. If you ever get into the sun, boy—and you're a fool not to go now, work or no work—see that you stay there. I must be getting back to the job. You please yourself." He went off without another word.

Several times that afternoon, Edward stared curiously at the old chap, moving slowly, dustily, obscurely, among his bales, and bundles and piles of dirty boxes, himself a cheap damaged remnant among a thousand other cheap damaged remnants. Was he dreaming about the sun at the other side of the world? Was this only the ghost of the Rufus they had known in Sydney and Penang? It was a darkish afternoon and very soon they had to light up, but except in the private office, where customers went to examine samples of stuff, the premises of the Belvedere Trading Company were badly lit, with three old electric bulbs. And by the time the afternoon was wearing away, Edward always found himself wearying of the shabby little company and its shabby little trade, for somehow by that time nothing it bought seemed worth buying and nothing it sold worth selling; the place was little better than a huge dustbin; the goods in it ought to have been burned long ago; it was a trade in mistakes and lies and bits of cheating; and the mind and the heart both turned away from it all. Perhaps that was why Mr. Cromford and Mr. Kelso now found it necessary to have so many double-whiskies. To-day, after doing a deal with Barrons and preparing the market for the new crop of raincoats, the partners went off early, as soon as double-whiskies were available; and Edward and the others did not remain behind very long.

There was no letter from Rose, in reply to his, waiting for him at his lodgings. But of course there couldn't be. She would probably be hard at work in the shop all day and might not have seen his letter yet. Patience, patience! Plenty of time! Before he went upstairs to his room, he ran into Mrs. Scrutton's only son, Jack, a youth about his own age. Jack was looking very important and pleased with himself.

"Got a nice date for next week," he announced at once. "Big football dance out Barnet way."

"That ought to be good," said Edward politely, though he knew nothing about football dances out Barnet way.

"I'll say it ought," cried Jack. "And that makes seven dates now, and the season's not got going. Oh boy!—we're on the up and up."

Edward left him to go on the up and up himself, to his room at the top of the house. He never knew whether Jack Scrutton did anything for a living during the day: but at night Jack was the pianist of a jazz band that called itself "The London Rhythmic Collegians," although none of its members had ever seen the inside of a college. There were six of them and sometimes they practised downstairs. They were all exactly like Jack, that is, they were London youths who had transformed themselves into young Americans. They sang American songs in an American style. They talked American slang with an American accent. Sometimes they must have been surprised to find themselves still in London, with not a campus, levee, coffee-shop, gipsy tea-room, a Broadway, a Forty-Second Street, a ranch, a round-up, a hay-ride or a barbecue, within two thousand miles. When they were not out playing or practising, they went to picture theatres, music-halls, and other places where well-known dance bands might be performing, and listened critically. They also heard dance music on the radio and the gramophone. They read all the American and English theatrical periodicals, and would exchange with one another and discuss such important news items as "Joe Delvini's Ten-Piece Combine Slated for the Air in Chi," or "Webster's Hot Musicoes and Hoofers Make the Grade on Coast." They would assemble in a back room in Chalk Farm and shake their heads because a dance band had recently been transferred from the Cocoanut Grove in Los Angeles to the Paramount Theatre, Portland, Oregon. Edward had met all these Rhythmic Collegians, after a rehearsal downstairs and could not make head or tail of them, they were so solemn and professional and American. (They always called a tune "a strain," and some strains were "sweet," some "hot," and a few "hot and scat.") Though they were only too delighted to help other people to be gay, and would sing and play for hours about their imaginary American love affairs and their hot nights in the old town, and though they were tremendously admired—in their blue pullovers, white flannel trousers, blue socks, white shoes—by all the more impressionable girls in the suburbs where they played, they were anything but gay themselves. Except when they were professionally crooning at them, they ignored the girls. They did not drink and rarely smoked. They brought to their service of the great scarlet goddess of jazz the pure white devotion of the neophyte. And Edward never knew whether to envy them or to laugh at them, and usually succeeded in doing a little of both. As he did now, having just left the single-minded, happy Jack Scrutton.

There were four other lodgers at Mrs. Scrutton's. First, there was Edward's neighbour on the top floor, Mr. Finland, mentioned by Mrs. Scrutton during their first interview as the educated gentleman who unfortunately "could not leave it alone." Then, on the floor below, was Lexden, the young man who worked at Uncle Alfred's place. The other two men Edward did not know at all. One was a commercial traveller he had never even seen. The other, a very short-sighted middle-aged chap, did something in the L.N.E.R. offices. It was very queer living in such close proximity to strangers, to be constantly climbing stairs that did not belong to you, to know nothing whatever about the people who lived in neighbouring houses. It made you feel very small and solitary, an insect crawling about in an immense jungle.

Edward made himself some tea in his room. It was cheaper than eating out all the time. It was also a bit messy and depressing, but that could not be helped. He had only just finished when Lexden bounced in. He was a red-faced, pug-nosed young man, two or three years older than Edward, who came from the Midlands, where his father, a manufacturer, had once made and then lost a great deal of money. Lexden had suddenly found himself pitchforked into a clerk's job in London and a bed-sitting-room overlooking a dingy back street in Chalk Farm. But he did not—as he was fond of saying—"give a damn." He was one of those people who are thoroughly at home in the insecure, scatter-brained, violent world of to-day. He was energetic, cheerful, and quite insensitive. He was an authority on all the livelier pleasures of London, and when he was tired of them, he mounted a stinking old motor-cycle and went roaring out on one of the arterial roads to pick up a girl or drink beer in some distant market town. He always seemed to have plenty of money, though only Mr. Kelso would know where he found it, for his job was not worth much. Edward had been once or twice with Lexden—he was the kind of young man who never forms real friendships, only wants a pal for the evening and almost anybody would do—but Edward did not much care for him. It was like going about with a half-crazy retriever that could talk.

"Well, Fielding, you young stinker," shouted Lexden, after bouncing in and banging the door behind him and kicking a chair, "I've just made four quid. Newmarket.

What are you doing to-night?"

"Sorry," said Edward, "but I've got to go somewhere."

"Where?"

Well, he didn't propose to tell Lexden that he was going to hang round the back door of a big shop, in the hope of seeing a girl. "Oh—just—somewhere——"

"A piece, eh? Careful, careful, Young Fielding! Some of these London bits, y'know! Whoa, boy, whoa!" Lexden, sprawling in Edward's one comfortable chair, with his legs dangling over the arm, lit a cigarette. "Four quid I made. Not bad, eh? Got in at eight to one. Chap I used to know at home put me on to it. Somebody always knows what'll win. All you've got to do is to find the right fellow. Do you have a flutter?"

"No."

"Why not?"

"Because I haven't much money and I don't know anything about horses," Edward replied, very sensibly.

"Spoken like a man and a twirp," roared Lexden, and then shouted with laughter.

There was a knock. Mr. Finland peered in.

"Come in, Dominie," cried Lexden, who was fond of giving people nicknames. "Let's have a look at you."

They had their look at him. Mr. Finland was a tall man in his fifties, shabby but vaguely imposing. He had a fine head of grey hair and a large grey moustache. He held himself erect, with an air of conscious dignity. And when he was sober, as he was now, he was very much the schoolmaster. He had been the head of an elementary school somewhere in the provinces, but had been summarily dismissed. Nobody knew why, though Lexden often amused himself by putting forward the most wildly obscene explanations of this dismissal. Now he made a meagre living out of correcting papers for a correspondence school and doing other odd jobs. When he had any money, he spent it on drink, chiefly whisky, and often quietly, steadily, sadly got drunk in his room. Lexden regarded him as a great joke, but Edward, to whom men like Mr. Finland had been the most awe-inspiring figures only a few years before, was secretly bewildered and rather saddened by the mere sight of him.

"Well, Dominie," said Lexden, blowing smoke at him. "How goes it?"

"I regret to say, Mr. Lexden, that it does not go very well. And what are you two going to do with yourselves this evening?"

"My young friend Fielding," said Lexden, with an impudent parody of Mr. Finland's manner, "is going out with a girl—otherwise, a bit, piece, totty, skirt, fluff, or even tart."

"I didn't say so," said Edward, rather sharply.

"You needn't," said Lexden. "We know, don't we, Dominie?"

"We can infer certain things," said Mr. Finland. "We can draw our conclusions."

"I wanted to show him the—er—ways of this great city," said Lexden, continuing his parody.

"Excellent," said Mr. Finland, with grave approval. "And what a city it is! I was only reading, a few minutes ago, that the number of printers—just printers—in

Greater London exceeds the whole population of Oxford and Cambridge. Printers alone, mark you."

"We mark," said Lexden, winking at Edward and at once making him feel uncomfortable. Surely poor Mr. Finland could see that Lexden was pulling his leg?

"The Metropolitan Water Board," said Mr. Finland impressively, "now supplies per day more than two hundred million gallons of water—pure water—to the area under its control. Astonishing figures—really astonishing."

"But we don't care about water, Dominie, you know damned well we don't. You haven't a drink in that room of yours, have you?"

"Unfortunately, no."

"Then you'd better come out with me, Dominie, and we'll tank up."

"Well, that's very kind of you, Mr. Lexden. But I must explain——"

"That's all right," said Lexden brutally. "I've just won four quid. We're all right."

"Excellent," said Mr. Finland hastily. "Some day, when we all have leisure, you must allow me to show you both some of the lesser-known historical sights of the city, relics of its—er—hoary past. Roman London, for example. Very few people realise," he continued, getting into his stride, "that Roman London—Londinium—has not entirely vanished. Only a few yards from the Strand—you may be surprised to learn—are the remains of a Roman bath. It's some time since I first saw it——"

"And I've never seen it and don't intend to," cried

Lexden heartily. "If it's much older than the bath Ma Scrutton keeps for us, I'll be surprised. Fetches the skin off your backside. Come on, Dominie. Have a wash and brush-up and put the old gown and mortar-board on and then we'll go and shift a few."

"I'll be ready in a few minutes. Mr. Fielding, I hope you will not regret your evening in pursuit of the—er—fair sex. Good night." He smiled gravely, nodded, then went out, a fine dignified figure.

"And I'll bet that by the time I get him back," said Lexden, "the old boy's stewed to the ears. Have a look at us, Fielding, if we're in. Sometimes he's in great form when he's tight. I'll get him going on education committees. He knocks hell out of 'em. Gets his own back."

The evening was slightly warmer than the morning had been, and now there was a bit of fog about, just enough to dim the lights and enlarge the gloomy immensity of the city. Raeburn's shop was closed now, of course, but its great windows were still lit up, and lots of women were lingering in front of them, looking at the dresses and hats and shoes and stockings and cosmetics all cunningly arranged against backgrounds of dark velvet. It seemed very rich and grand and impressive to Edward, who hastily abandoned the idea of boldly going to the employees' entrance and asking for Rose. She herself took on a certain richness, grandeur, impressiveness, so that he began to wonder, dismally, whether she would want to have anything to do with him now. After all, they were no longer in Haliford, and even in Haliford, which had its manufacturers' sons with sports cars and bank clerks who wore white flannels for tennis, Edward was no great catch. And here in London, which suddenly seemed crowded with rich handsome young men, she might not think anything of him at all. Why should she? He asked himself this, not very hopefully, while he walked slowly past the lighted windows in search of the employees' entrance. Edward alternated between having a magnificent opinion of himself and having no opinion of himself at all. He could not take a sensible middle view. Either he was so extraordinarily gifted and intelligent in a rather mysterious but very effective fashion that it was astonishing everybody did not at once recognise the fact, or he was nothing at all, a silly-looking, sulky, brainless, ignorant fool not worth anybody's notice. For some time, he had assumed that in Rose's eyes he was the grand fellow he ought to be, but now, diminished by the tall splendour of Raeburn's, which had accepted Rose at once, he dropped immediately into the most despairing humility. Why should she bother her head about him? Who was he? Here there were thousands and thousands just like him, and thousands and thousands better off, more likely to appeal to a girl. Hadn't he better go home?

Nevertheless, he found the door, the magic door through which Rose must pass. *Robert Raeburn's Ltd. Employees' Entrance.* He choked with excitement, there in the side street, at the very sight of it. There were not many people about. After the light and bustle of the main road, it seemed strangely, almost menacingly quiet. The door itself had an unfriendly look. It was closed tight, and looked as if it proposed to remain so for a long time.

Perhaps this was not the only door? Perhaps even now Rose was walking out of some other door. Hastily he searched, but could find no other back entrance, and returned in even greater haste to his original square yard of greasy pavement, under a street lamp, and a few yards lower down, nearer Marylebone Road, than the door itself. A policeman came, and looked at the door and then looked at Edward, and moved on majestically. From somewhere high up there was the sound of a gramophone or a wireless set, a tiny tinny sound of music, a quivering point of gaiety, far away, out of his world altogether. A dark bundle moved slowly towards him, and turned itself into a little elderly woman carrying a large shopping bag. She looked like a weary old witch. Perhaps she was. Then the door opened and out came two girls, talking in quick high voices. Rose? No. Both dark girls, rather pretty, smart. They took no notice of him, but went tripping away to Marylebone Road, perhaps to have the most magnificent social adventures, completely denied to him though no doubt quite open to Rose. Something very depressing about those two girls. He hated them. But not so much as he hated the young man who suddenly arrived, two minutes afterwards, to wait at the door, only a few yards away. This young man obviously had an appointment and was no miserable hanger-about like Edward. He looked at his watch, then whistled softly but impatiently. He was taller than Edward, wore a very smart overcoat, very broad in the shoulder then sharply waisted, and might have been the kind of young man you see in advertisements. And he might be waiting there for Rose?

He was not waiting for Rose. The next girl who came out, a tall girl, was his; and to prove there was no mistake he at once tucked her under his arm. "Where are we going, my duck?" Edward heard the girl ask, as they moved off. And the young man replied, loudly and confidently: "Just wait. I've got a surprise for you."

They left Edward feeling very small and inferior, some grubby little thing on the pavement. Young men like that, chaps with wonderful overcoats, loud and confident voices, and surprises all over the place, probably waited at this door all the time, and a girl like Rose had only to show her face outside for one of them, promising surprises by the dozen, to take her away. Edward had plenty of time for these gloomy reflections because for the next ten minutes nothing happened in that street. Then two more girls came out, and were not Rose, and behaved exactly like the first two. It was getting colder. He took a turn or two up and down the street, which cost him threepence, for that was the sum demanded by a wheezy old chap at the bottom of the street. He needed it, he said, for a night's lodging. Edward felt no glow of virtue after parting with this threepence. The old chap was probably a fraud. Two more girls came out, not a bit like Rose. One was thin and dark, and the other small and no particular colour that Edward could determine. He heard the smaller one say: "Well, if you're going to Clapham, Beatrice, we can get the bus together as far as Victoria." So the other one, the thin dark one, was called Beatrice and was going to Clapham. And who cared about that? A miserable stupid job, this, hanging about a door! He decided he had had enough, and walked away, only to turn and hurry back when he heard some more girls come out. Several of them this time, all giggling away. One had lingered behind the others, to fasten her coat. He would ask her about Rose. He took a step forward. "Er—excuse——" But she gave him one severe glance and hurried after the others. Thought he was trying to pick her up! She would! Edward told her retreating back that he wouldn't have anything to do with her if she was the last girl left, that anyhow he had always disliked girls with bulging eyes and parrot noses, that the girl he was waiting for was worth fifty of her, and a great many other bitter things. But it was not very amusing.

He lingered in the neighbourhood of that door for another hour, sometimes standing under the lamp, sometimes moving uneasily up and down the street. Nothing happened. It was as if all life had ebbed away from that corner of the city. He could still hear it roaring elsewhere. He was alternately moved by the self-contempt and the self-pity of those who wait and wait in vain. At one moment he was the solitary neglected fool among nine million wise beings. The next moment he was the one creature among them who was decent and kind and not the slave of the most selfish and degrading pleasures, and he recognised a certain fine austerity in this waiting. Then once again he was disgusted with himself, and saw in his inability to drop the silly business nothing but weakness. Nothing may have happened in the street, but a great deal happened inside his head, where one Edward after another took the stage, only to be cheered or hooted by an audience of Edwards. But there came an end, with numbing cold, even to this internal drama. There was no sense in waiting any longer. If Rose wanted to see him, she would answer his letter. If she didn't—well? Well what? He went off to find a bite of food and something hot to drink.

But all along Marylebone Road he was still searching for that one face. It was a procession of eyes. All London now was a procession of eyes. He was rapidly becoming an authority on eyes. Men's were quite different from women's, which were somehow further forward in the face, so that they could see more without obviously turning them. Young women's eyes—and of course it was these that he noticed most—were of many different kinds, from the large dull glassy to the fierce little starers. Rose, he remembered, had beautiful mild soft eyes. You saw very few of that kind about, just as you saw extraordinarily few happy faces, smiling faces, even contented faces. The Metropolitan Water Board, as old Finland said, might supply two hundred million gallons of water a day to this city, but very little of that water seemed to wash happy faces, smiling faces, contented faces. That water was used for worry, for anxiety, for discontent, for despair. These were not the very words he used to himself, sitting in the little teashop near Euston, but they express shortly his feelings, which were dark and confused. He felt himself growing up very quickly here in London, and the Edward who had left Haliford seemed now a mere baby. The very pressure of life in these streets was hardening him. In some ways he was shyer than he had been at home, but that was merely because he was new here, hardly knew his way about, was always conscious of his youth and ignorance, but underneath this superficial shyness he was maturing.

When he arrived on his top landing, the door of Mr. Finland's room was open, and obviously Lexden and Mr. Finland were in there. Lexden heard him, popped his head out, and insisted upon his going in. "The old boy's tight as an owl and in great form," Lexden whispered. He himself was not drunk, but clearly he had been drinking hard.

Edward went in, more in the hope of preventing any mischief than of enjoying it. Mr. Finland was now very different from the precise and pompous old chap who had walked into Edward's room several hours before. He was sprawling in a lop-sided arm-chair, among a sad litter of papers and dingy textbooks. His hair was ruffled, his face red and creased, and his eyes had a glazed look. The little room was thick with smoke and the reek of whisky.

"Come in, my boy," said Mr. Finland in a wobbly-pobbly sort of voice. "Come in. Glad to see you. Sit down."

Edward did not sit down but remained standing just inside the door, but Mr. Finland, who had closed his eyes, took no further notice of him.

"Now, Dominie," said Lexden, mischievously, "are you sure you know what you're talking about?"

"I know what I'm talking about," cried Mr. Finland, in a surprisingly loud voice. He opened his eyes to glare at them. "No man better. Please un'erstand that. No man better." With some difficulty he struck a match and held it to his pipe, which did not respond, obviously because there was no tobacco in it. This did not seem to worry him.

"Go on, Dominie," said Lexden. "Tell us the truth. Spill the ruddy beans."

"The beans—that's t'say—the truth—the truth is," replied Mr. Finland very solemnly, "there are in this country—our country—England—various and numerous collections of blockheads, ignoramuses, dolts, charlatans, hypocrites——"

"And twirps."

"And twirps, not to speak of prudes, blackguards, old washerwomen, and scoundrels, who call 'emselves education committees. Education committees!" Mr. Finland laughed with great bitterness, then glared at his listeners again. "What do they know about education? I'll tell you. Nothing, sir. They know ab-so-lutely nothing. And why? No minds. No knowledge. No ability to impart knowledge. Nothing. Yet those same people—those very same people, mark you—have the power of life and death. I repeat it, the power of life and death. Where did they send me? They sent me here. The worst day's work they ever did. And why? Because I have in my mind—nearly all planned out—a book on our educational system, our so-called educational system—which I don't hesitate to say, gentlemen, is rotten, rotten to the core—a book that will set this country on fire. Yes, on fire!" Having shouted the last few words, he suddenly collapsed, and mumbled something about Parliament and Committees of Enquiry.

"Now, Dominie," said Lexden mercilessly, "tell us what really happened. Come on, spill it."

Mr. Finland, who had closed his eyes again, slowly opened them, and looked vaguely at the two young men as if he was not quite sure who they were or what they were doing there. "My father was a poor man," he began, quietly now, almost as if talking to himself. "Market gardener. Worked hard. No money. But he sent me to school. Sent me to college. Hard for him. Hard for me. Hard for us all. But before he died, he'd seen me go through college—first in my family, all poor, to do that—get a post, get a better post, and then in the end get a school of my own, good school. 'Richard,' he said to me—he was an old man then, old market gardener, worn out, end of his time—'Richard, you've done well. Knew you would. Done well, you have. All proud of you, lad.' That's what he said. Last thing I ever heard him say. School of my own. Good school. Headmaster—Richard Finland."

Something strange was happening. Mr. Finland's lips were quivering underneath that great grey moustache; and he was making unpleasant noises; his face was wet. Mr. Finland was crying.

"Now then, Dominie, what happened?" said Lexden.

"Come on, Lexden," whispered Edward sharply, putting out a hand.

"Wait a minute. He's only tight. My expense too."

Edward could have hit him. "Blast you, no," he cried fiercely. "I'm going and so are you. For God's sake, leave him alone."

Lexden stared pugnaciously. "What's the matter with you?"

Edward held the door open. "Never mind what's the matter with me," he replied, steadily, answering the other's stare. "The point is, you've got to leave him alone." This brought Lexden outside, and Edward was able to shut the door.

"I've half a mind," said Lexden, "to give you a punch on the nose for your damned impudence."

Edward knew very well that Lexden was quite capable of giving him a very unpleasant punch on the nose, for he was a strong fellow and the kind that becomes very aggressive at the end of an evening's drinking. But he was still so worked up that he hardly felt afraid.

"Please yourself, but you're not going to worry that poor old chap any more to-night."

They stood on the little landing, glaring at one another. Fortunately, at that moment, there was the sound of voices, Mrs. Scrutton's among them, from below; and Lexden, after making a rude noise at Edward, was content to turn and stand, looking down the stairs. A moment later he went down himself, not very steadily, and Edward was free to go into his own room. There was no letter for him. It was still too soon, though. Patience, patience! To-morrow was the time. Half an hour afterwards, when he was in bed and nearly asleep, he heard sounds from the neighbouring room that suggested that Mr. Finland was falling over things and sending piles of his dirty little text-books crashing down. Edward wondered whether he ought to go in and help the old chap into bed, but decided that Mr. Finland was best left alone, even if it meant that he was now lying on the floor, still dressed, in a drunken stupor, his tousled grey head among the textbooks. Soon, Mr. Finland would be dreaming or unconscious. Let him be.

Next morning, there was still no letter for Edward. Now he was disappointed, even though there had not been much time for a reply. The world immediately shrank and lost colour. It was a dismal morning, dark and wet. Edward was one of those people who feel strongly that periods of time have characters and moods of their own, who think in terms of hostile Mondays or friendly Thursdays, who remember hateful Aprils and tender Junes. He knew at once that this was a day with a character of its own, and a bad character, one of those days that do not dislike this person and that but the whole race of men. Everybody at the Belvedere Trading Company was out of temper. The unsold stuff seemed to take up more room than ever, seemed more soiled and dustier, and the prospect of selling it infinitely remote. Mr. Kelso, very yellow in the face, very liverish, found fault with everybody. Mr. Cromford dashed out about the middle of the morning, to pull off a deal with the raincoats—and nobody could say that raincoats were not wanted, a day like this—but he came back before lunch, very wet and annoyed, with not a coat sold. Old Rufus, who must have felt exiled from the sun for ever, was slower than usual, maddening in his ghostly deliberation. Queenie Broom was starting a cold in the head, and everybody who went near felt she was bombarding him with germs. Bert Hewish, who had nothing to do outside, hung about lumpishly, did as little as possible, and was obviously in one of his sullen moods. A horrible morning.

It was the same at lunch-time. Edward went to the tea-shop in Holborn where he had been several times before; in fact, it was the very teashop he had gone to his first evening in London, the very place where he had felt so wonderfully happy. To-day the place lay under a curse. Everything was wrong. The customers did not know what to order, and when they received what they finally did order, they obviously wished they had chosen something else. They got in one another's way, and glared, without apology. They resented each other's wet steaming clothes. They shook and rustled newspapers fiercely into one another's faces. Timid ones were almost pushed off tables. The waitresses were impatient, clumsy, forgetful, and filled with resentment. They snapped at the customers. They grumbled and screamed at the service window. Plates were put down with a bang. Tea and coffee were spilled. Tables were left wet and crumby. The room reeked of steaming coats and hats, boiled cabbage, stew, cigarette ends, and too many disagreeable people. Nobody wanted to stay there long. But nobody wanted to go out into dark and dripping Holborn. Edward knew very well that there was nothing really wrong with the place, that it was still the same establishment in which he had fed before in peace and comfort, where indeed he had once been gloriously happy. What was wrong was the day itself, the malevolent day, whose grey wet face had perhaps been cursed by the stars ages before it had made its first appearance in any calendar. Edward did not know anything about astrology, but he felt that the existence of such days, almost universal in their evil, was an argument in its favour. The more people tried to do, on a day like this, the more they would encounter misfortune: signals would be missed; wing struts would give way; wheels would skid; brakes refuse to come on; children would run into the traffic; old men would have strokes; burning cigarettes and curtains would creep towards each other; safety belts would snap; its opportunities were endless and immense. The only way to defeat such a day, he reflected, was for everybody to stay in bed.

The day was not long in showing what it really could do. At a few minutes to four, that afternoon, a well-set-up youngish man, wearing a dark overcoat and a bowler, confidently entered the premises of the Belvedere Trading Company and demanded to see one Edward Fielding. Fortunately, Edward himself had asked him his business, and was now able to take him to a small private space, between a wall of piled raincoats and a curved parapet of shoes and hat-boxes, bundles of socks and stockings, and cases of damaged toys, without disturbing the two partners who were doing some gloomy telephoning in the private office.

The visitor looked about him in a rather amused fashion. "Rum sort of business, this," he said finally. "What do you sell—everything?"

"Nearly," said Edward, wondering what the man wanted. "We buy cheap lines—stuff that's been damaged or isn't quite right—and then sell it off to retailers."

"And then they palm off on to me," said the visitor, grinning. "Which explains why I'm always getting taken in. Now I'd like a few words with you. And I ought to explain that I'm Detective-Sergeant MacMurray, of the Criminal Investigation Department."

Edward stared at him as if he had just said he had come from the moon. "Is that Scotland Yard?" he asked.

"It is."

He was a pleasant-looking chap about thirty-five or so, with a small dark moustache, a blunt nose, and a dimple in his chin. He did not look a bit like somebody from Scotland Yard, though Edward did not doubt for a moment that he was speaking the truth. But there was something hugely idiotic about a chap with a dimple in his chin suddenly arriving from Scotland Yard and wanting to talk to him, Edward Fielding. No sense in it at all. Edward stood there, foolishly, with his mouth open.

"Now," said the detective in a very quiet friendly tone, "you've just written a letter to a young woman by the name of Rose Salter, lately employed at Robert Raeburn's in Marylebone Road, haven't you?"

Edward did not feel a bit alarmed. He simply felt that there was no sense in this at all.

"I might as well tell you that that letter was handed over to us this morning."

"What, my letter!" Edward was indignant now. There might be no sense in this, but they had no right to mess his letters about.

"Yes, your letter," said the detective, grinning. "Bit thick, eh?"

"Yes, it is."

"Well, never mind about that," he continued, in a firm

but not unfriendly tone. "What I want you to do is to tell me what you know about this Rose Salter."

This Rose Salter! That was a bit thick too. Edward stared at the detective's blunt nose and moustache and dimple as if something might be interpreted from them. What was the idea? "Look here, I don't understand."

"You're not, by any chance, one of these clever young fellows, are you?" asked the detective, quite gently. "We see a lot of them. They just try and make it as awkward as they can for us. Mistake, too, in the long run."

"I'm not trying to be clever or anything," said Edward earnestly. "I'll tell you what you want to know—if I can—if you'll tell me what it's all about."

"Fair enough," said the detective, who had been looking hard at Edward. "Well, you see, there's a charge against this friend of yours, Rose Salter—a serious charge."

The very foundations of the city opened now and down Edward went, to grope in the darkness. A serious charge! This was sheer lunacy.

"Some days ago," the detective continued, after noticing Edward's dazed look, "certain property belonging to the shop was missing, and some of that property was discovered in her room, and at the same time she herself disappeared, without giving notice or asking for her money or anything. Now you write to her, telling her you're anxious to see her."

"I am," said Edward sharply.

"And so are we." The detective grinned. "So we come to you."

"But—you see—it's silly," said Edward, as if continuing

an argument that had been going on for some time. "I mean—about Rose—Rose Salter. It's silly."

"You may not know it," said the detective, as if he too were continuing an argument of his own, "but certain young women who give us a lot of trouble—smart girls, pretty girls, many of 'em——" he smiled appreciatively, as if he was as fond of smart pretty girls as the next man—"manage to get jobs in these big shops just for the purpose of stealing. It's a system. They're put up to it. They take what they can, and then clear out——"

"But it isn't true," cried Edward desperately. "Rose—she wouldn't steal anything. I *know* she wouldn't."

"You'd be surprised what some of 'em'll do," said the detective, who evidently felt that Edward knew nothing about the sex. "I've been surprised in my time. They look at you with big eyes. What, me? How dare you? And the same ones would take the milk out of your tea. Mind you, I don't say this girl's like that. All I know is that the stuff was found in her room and that she disappeared. Now you tell me about her."

"She comes from Haliford, where I come from——"

This obviously confirmed something the detective had already heard, for he nodded. "What's her address there? You might as well tell me, y'know. We'll find out anyhow. They may have it now. Besides, if she is a wrong 'un, you don't want to have anything to do with her. And if she isn't——"

"I'm sure she isn't. I know she isn't."

"You may be right. But what's the address, laddie?"

Edward told him. He also told him all that he knew

about Rose, some of which was carefully taken down in a notebook. But only one small part of Edward was occupied with this business of answering questions and giving information. The rest of him, at fever heat, was asking himself questions. He could not believe she had stolen anything. Never, never! But why had she disappeared? In his painful bewilderment, he did not hesitate to ask the detective about this disappearance of hers.

"All we know," was the reply, "is that she went. She didn't tell anybody she was going—not even the girl who shared her room——"

"But couldn't she have had an accident or something?"

"She packed up and took her things," said the detective. "You don't take your suitcase to an accident. No, she obviously meant to go. I'm afraid there's no doubt about that, laddie."

He did not say any more because at that moment, Mr. Kelso and Mr. Cromford appeared round the screen of hat and shoe-boxes and bundles of socks and stockings, and looked enquiringly at them. If this chap, their glance said, really wants to buy something, we're the men to sell it to him.

"Good afternoon," said the detective politely. "Sorry to take up this young man's time."

"Depends what your business is, eh?" shouted Mr. Cromford, in his best hearty manner.

"I'm Detective-Sergeant MacMurray of the Criminal Investigation Department."

The two partners looked startled. No doubt they were

honest men themselves, and no doubt all the goods they bought were the property of the men who sold them, but the fact remains that they looked startled.

"It's all right," said the detective. "He hasn't done anything wrong. I'm asking him a few questions about somebody else, that's all. And, in fact, I've finished. Nothing else?" he added, looking at Edward.

"No, except I know it's all a mistake," Edward told him, very earnestly.

"Might be. I've known 'em happen. Well—good afternoon. Good afternoon, gentlemen."

As he went off, the partners looked at one another, and then, when he had gone, they looked at Edward, who realised that the air was heavy with doubt and suspicion.

"What's this?" asked Mr. Kelso, not very pleasantly.

"Look here, Fielding, you've not been getting mixed up in any funny games, have you?" said Mr. Cromford.

"Because if you have," said Mr. Kelso, half closing his eyes, "you're out—now."

"No, I haven't," said Edward sharply. "I wrote a letter to a girl who comes from the same place I do, and—and—she's missing—that's all. And the police are trying to find her."

"Humph!" And Mr. Kelso disappeared.

"And where is she?" asked Mr. Cromford, with the air of a man who could do with a little cheerful scandal. "Gone on the razzle?"

"No, I don't know. Mr. Cromford, can I go now, please? I want to send a telegram to her sister. And I want to go to the shop where she worked, to see if I can find out anything. It's—it's—urgent, or I wouldn't ask."

"All right. Pop off."

Edward, his heart thumping away, descended into the glitter and darkness of the rain-streaked lighted city, which had now changed its character for him. In these stone mazes went the hunters and the hunted. Your name found its way on to a printed form or two, was copied into note-books, and there were men searching every thicket and path for you. Even he could feel a certain shrinking of the spirit, as if he had just caught a glimpse of the iron skeleton of the social body. And what was Rose feeling now? Where was she? Haunted by that lost golden face, he hurried through the rain.

XI

"WELL, my dear," Mrs. Wilber was saying, "it's what I expected, so I'm not surprised. Beatie Vintnor's not been my cousin all these years for nothing. And I say—you've been very, very silly. I must speak my mind, mustn't I?"

"Yes," said Rose, cheerlessly. "But—you see—there was Lawrence. And I'd promised."

"As for poor Lawrence, nobody's sorrier for him than I am," said Mrs. Wilber, popping a fair-sized piece of rich chocolate cake into her mouth, then licking her lips. "It's wicked what's happened to that boy. Worth ten of Beatie too. But he's one thing, and she's another thing. She's always been the same. Gets herself into trouble—can't keep out of it—never could—and then expects somebody else to take the blame. Now she's landed you."

"Yes, I suppose so," said Rose, who certainly felt landed. "Only—well, as she said—after all I didn't take the things. And nobody can say I did. If they'd any sense, they'd know I *couldn't* have taken them. I was in the restaurant all the time, and never went near the Dress Department."

"Do you want that one with the walnut on?" asked Mrs. Wilber earnestly. "Because if you don't, I do. I love walnuts. Well, I've no doubt it's all been worked out very nicely—for Beatie."

"If they did catch me," said Rose, repeating another of Beatrice's arguments, "I could always say I left because I couldn't stick it there any longer. I could tell them I didn't know anything about the things."

"You could tell 'em a lot of things, I've no doubt," said Mrs. Wilber calmly, "but whether they'd believe you is another matter. Have another cup of tea?"

Rose passed her cup, and said nothing until it had been filled. Never in her life before had she felt so remote and unreal as she did now. She was still in London, but this London across the river, with its Clapham Common, which you could just see from Mrs. Wilber's sitting-room, was quite unlike the other London she knew, and might have been a city hundreds of miles away. Mrs. Wilber, who was Beatrice's cousin and the wife of a commercial traveller, had the upper half of a dark brick house near this Clapham Common. Rose had not a clear idea where she was, for Beatrice had rushed her there after dark, after a frantic talk on the telephone with her cousin. A good-natured plump little woman, with a husband who was away for weeks at a time, no children, a good daily char to do most of the modest housework, few friends, nothing much to do, Mrs. Wilber had been quite glad to have her there for a day or two. She and Rose got on very well. Indeed, she seemed to like Rose much better than she liked Beatrice, whom she regarded with the exasperated disapproval common among relatives. Beatrice had promised to explain everything as soon as she could get across from the shop again—there had been no time for explanations that night—and Mrs. Wilber, after leaving Rose alone for nearly twenty-four hours, was now discovering the whole foolish story for herself from Rose, who felt that she had no right to hide anything from this kind stranger who had sheltered her.

"I suppose," said Rose, doubtfully, "the best thing I can do now is to go back home—to Haliford."

Mrs. Wilber's eyes and plump little mouth opened wide; in horror, it seemed. "My dear, you can't do that."

"Why can't I?"

"You disappeared, didn't you? And they think it's because you took those things and were frightened of being found out. Well then! They'll tell the police, and the police will find out all about you—where you live at home and everything——"

"But they don't know."

"Of course they do. Or they will. They get to know everything. They ferret it out. I was only reading the other day a piece in a paper about how they do it—you'd never believe how clever they are—give 'em a button or anything, and they have you. And the first thing they'll do is to watch for you going home. I should think so indeed! And I'll bet Beatie didn't mention that, did she?"

"No, she didn't." Rose was terribly dismayed.

"She wouldn't!"

Rose stared across the little table at Mrs. Wilber, but did not see her very plainly. She had known before that she had done something silly, thrown away a good job, to say the least of it, but now for the first time, with all this talk of the police, and the police actually waiting for her at home, she felt as if she really had done something wrong, as if it was she and not Beatrice who had taken those dresses. It was awful.

"What can I do then?"

Mrs. Wilber was genuinely sorry for Rose, clearly an innocent, sweet-natured child who had gone and let herself in for this because of that pilfering, half-crazy monkey of a Beatrice. She was ready to do anything she could to comfort the poor girl. But at the same time, she could not help enjoying the situation, which had brought vivid life and drama into the dreary solitude of her maisonette. This beat the pictures.

"Well," said Mrs. Wilber, unable to keep that enjoyment out of her voice, "you've got to face the fact that they'll be after you."

Rose, feeling hunted already, nodded dismally.

"They know your name, and they know—or they soon will—where you live at home. Now, do they know what you look like? Have they a photograph? Could they get one from your home?"

"There are only a few little snaps there," said Rose, who could see big bullying policemen in Slater Street, shouting at her poor mother, grabbing the snapshots. Her knowledge of police procedure was derived entirely from films, and as these were mostly American, it was American policemen and detectives—loud-voiced bullies with hats at the backs of their heads and cigars stuck in their mouths—she saw.

"If they're like most snaps," said Mrs. Wilber, "they won't tell 'em much. I shouldn't worry much about that." She thought hard for a moment, while absently putting a few crumbs of icing into her mouth. "Your best plan," she said finally, "is not to leave London. I've always read that's the best thing to do. It's when you try to leave London—they get you. London's so big, they can't find you here. But the first thing you'll have to do is to change your name." She looked at Rose with great satisfaction.

Rose for once was not dismayed. She had no great objection to changing her name. Like most girls, she had often trifled with the notion of changing it just for fun. She felt there was a very deep and interesting side of her nature that somehow was not expressed by the name Rose Salter.

"Now," and Mrs. Wilber held up a sticky warning finger, "don't go in for anything too fancy."

"What do you think, then?" asked Rose, glad of this not unpleasant interlude.

Mrs. Wilber looked critically at her, as if she were privately measuring her for a name. "How about Alice?"

"Oh no, I've a friend called Alice."

Evidently Mrs. Wilber understood at once that you cannot go about with a friend's name tacked on to you, for she nodded and thought again. "Phyllis?"

"No, I don't like that. Do you?"

"Not much. What about Hilda?"

Rose shook her head quickly. "I used to know a girl called Hilda and I couldn't stand her."

They tried a dozen names but there was something wrong with every one. Either Rose or Mrs. Wilber had known a bad example of the name or one of them simply didn't fancy it. They had quite a cosy half-hour, sitting over the tea-things, with this name business, and Rose felt quite cheered up.

"Well, dear, my opinion is this," said Mrs. Wilber finally. "The simpler the better. What about Mary?"

Rose tasted it.

"My mother was called Mary," said Mrs. Wilber.

Rose felt it would be rude to offer any objection, after that statement. She did not want to insult her hostess's mother. Mary it was, then.

"Now, for your other name," said Mrs. Wilber, getting up and then looking vaguely round, "you want something simple too."

"Like Smith?"

"Well—yes. But Smith's a bit—well, anyone would call themselves Smith, wouldn't they?" As if looking for an idea, Mrs. Wilber gazed at a large photogravure on the wall. It was called "Lovers' Tiff" and showed you an old-fashioned young couple, apparently about eight feet tall, standing with their backs to one another in a rose garden. These lovers leaving her still blank, Mrs. Wilber had a look at a neighbouring picture, which was called "Best of Friends," these being a little girl, two puppies, and two kittens. Nothing came of this lot. So Mrs. Wilber picked up a book, and glanced at a page or two. "All these names are silly, though," she said, throwing the book down.

"What about—Pearson?" asked Rose.

"Pearson? Mary Pearson?" She tried it several times. "Yes, that'll do. Now then, dear, from now on—at least till all this has blown over—you're Mary Pearson."

Well, that was that. The fun was over. The question

now was—what was Mary Pearson going to do?

Mrs. Wilber sat down comfortably for another cosy little chat. "That's the point, isn't it? You'll have to work at something."

"Of course I will. I haven't any money. Only about three pounds altogether."

"And you do see—don't you, dear?—that if you try to get another place in a shop or a café, they'll want to know where you've been and all about you? In fact, if I were you, I wouldn't even try it. Too risky altogether."

Yes, Rose saw all that.

"The more public—so to speak—the work is, the more they'll want to know, the more people will notice you, and the more likely it is you'll be found out. And you can't go home. And you've no money. You'll have to do something."

Rose saw all this too. It was painfully clear to her. What she could not see was a possible solution.

But Mrs. Wilber was thinking hard, with her eyes closed and her plump little face all screwed up. Rose watched her anxiously. She herself seemed incapable of thought. She was bewildered, lost. She might have just fallen off a cliff.

Mrs. Wilber opened her eyes wide. They were alight with triumph. "Now I'll tell you what to do. You've got to hide yourself away—as Mary Pearson—somewhere in London. And you've got your living to earn. Well, you're a nice-looking girl and you've done some waitressing—so it oughtn't to be hard for you to get a place, if it's worked properly—you ought, just for the time being, while they're still on the look-out for you, to go into service."

"Service?"

"Yes, you know. Domestic service."

"Oh, I couldn't," cried Rose, thoroughly dismayed and shocked. Domestic service was the very last resort of girls in Haliford, who would accept the lowest possible wages and the worst hours and conditions in mills and shops before they would go and work in other people's houses, put on the uniforms of servitude, answer bells. All the Haliford traditions were against being a domestic servant. Rose felt as if she were listening to some indecent proposal.

"Now I call that silly," said Mrs. Wilber, almost sharply. "It's the one thing that'll keep you out of the way and where too many questions won't be asked. And all kinds of girls do it now. I was reading a piece the other day by a daughter of a baronet who'd been in service—enjoyed it too, I mean she had—some of it."

Rose did not reply. She was trying to readjust rapidly the Salter opinion of domestic service and servants. And it was hard work. Mrs. Wilber began to assemble the tea-things, before taking them away, and Rose sprang up to help her. In the little scullery, as they washed up together, they began talking again.

"You'll have to have references," said Mrs. Wilber. "Now for any other kind of work, they wouldn't be easy. But for domestic service, it's all right. Half of 'em are faked anyhow. I can give you one—and if they want to ring me up, they *can* do. And I've a friend, Mrs. Brunch, who keeps a very nice private hotel at Eastbourne, and she'd stand for another—if I asked her. Once you've been in a nice place, the rest is easy after that. You can get an ordinary job then, and say you've been in service. Anyhow, I expect you'll be getting married, sooner or later. You're the marrying kind. Like me."

By this time, after much thought and inward struggle, Rose had become reconciled to the idea of becoming a servant. She realised that there was a definite advantage now in doing her work hidden away in a private house and not in some public place where dozens of policemen might notice her. She was all for secrecy and safety now, as Mary Pearson.

"But I don't know how I'd set about it," she confessed. "Have you to answer advertisements in the paper?"

"Better not. Go to one of these registries, that's the thing. A West End one too, and the bigger the better. You ought to try for a big house too."

"Oh no," cried Rose. "I'd much rather be in a little one. I wouldn't know what to do in a big house. Too posh altogether!"

"Yes, dear, but don't you see there's little chance of them finding out anything about you in a big house, where they keep plenty of servants and there's always some coming and going? Too nosy in a small place. Want to know all about you. As for the work, you try for a parlourmaid's place—we'll say you've been one, see?—because it's only what you've just been doing, except it's in a private house instead of a restaurant. Now I'm not going to say any more. Just you think it over, dear."

They went back into the sitting-room and listened to the wireless, with which Mrs. Wilber passed a good deal of her solitude. "And they can say what they like about it," she remarked, during a lull, "but it makes things a lot more human. You hear a voice or two, and a bit of entertainment and news and suchlike, and it cheers you up when you're on your own so much, like me. I tell you, it's been a godsend to a lot of us, and I could name half a dozen in this street—grass widows half their time. Of course some of it's silly—with their music that hasn't a tune, and fat cattle prices, and prime ministers of Roumania, and how to win a bicycle race, and education, and what not. But it's better than just sitting waiting for the postman or bedtime, and you can't always be going out, can you? Oh—listen to her! I hate them airy-fairy sopranos, all pretending to know German and Italian—don't you?"

So they sat listening, with frequent comments from Mrs. Wilber, who could not keep quiet long. Rose felt very safe and snug, and liked Mrs. Wilber's sitting-room, which had dark red walls and two very fat browny-leathery easy chairs and a swollen settee, a great many photographs, chiefly of people at the seaside, a big standard lamp with a pink shade, and a nice well-grate, in which Mrs. Wilber, who liked to be warm, kept a good fire. But though, after the madness of that escape from Raeburn's and their subsequent sinister talk, Rose felt safe and snug here, she did not feel her normal self at all. She was lost. The old sensible world had completely vanished. She was sitting, temporarily and comparatively at ease, in a dream. Mary Pearson listening to the wireless. And what about Edward Fielding now? A tiny lost Rose

Salter, hiding somewhere behind Mary Pearson, called frantically to him.

They were interrupted, about nine o'clock, by a sharp ring downstairs. Mrs. Wilber had one of those bells that ring just behind the door and have a most alarming sound. Rose jumped. Policemen for her!

It was Beatrice, looking very pale and thinner than ever. "I got away as soon as I could," she began, after greeting Rose.

But Mrs. Wilber, who had kept silent until the two of them were safely in her room, would not let her say any more. "If you want to know what I think, Beatie," she cried sharply, "I'll tell you. I know what you've been up to, and you ought to be ashamed of yourself. It was bad enough taking the things——"

"I didn't steal them, honestly I didn't. It was silly, I know. But I took one to wear, and I took the other two to show to a girl I know——"

"I don't care," said her cousin stoutly. "I know you've plenty of excuses. You always have. But whatever you did, you'd no right to persuade Rose here to land herself into such a mess——"

"But what could I do? Don't you see——"

"Owned up to it."

Beatrice burst into tears. "I daren't. I'd have lost my job—at the very least—and never got another in a London shop. I'll swear I'll never do it again. I'm safe now——"

"Yes, I'll bet you are," said Mrs. Wilber grimly. "Trust you. Well, it's the last time I help you, Lawrence or no Lawrence. If that boy only knew——"

"Oh, don't, don't," Beatrice wailed. "You didn't mind, did you, Rose? You see, Lou, it's different for her. She'd only just come, and didn't much care, and she's young and——"

Rose stopped her now. She did not want a repetition of that last scene in their room at Raeburn's. She had had enough. "Oh, do stop, please. It's done now."

Beatrice stopped, and dried her eyes, and sniffed a good deal.

"Well, what's happened about it?" asked Mrs. Wilber, regarding her with very little sympathy. "And the truth, mind. It's important Rose should know."

Beatrice looked appealingly from Mrs. Wilber to Rose, and then back to Mrs. Wilber. "They're sure it was Rose," she replied in a loud voice. "And they've had the police in. I don't know exactly what's happened, but I heard our Head Sales say the police thought Rose—you know, I don't really mean Rose, but the girl they think did it—must be a sort of professional crook, a girl who works in a shop just to be able to steal things."

"Nice look-out for poor Rose, isn't it?" said Mrs. Wilber, grim again.

Beatrice looked across at Rose with those enormous hungry eyes that had already done so much damage. "I'm sorry, Rose, and ever so grateful. And I'll do anything I can——"

"And a fat lot that is," said Mrs. Wilber. "Well, I'd better tell you what we've been deciding." Which she did, at some length.

"It's the very best thing," cried Beatrice, cheerful again.

"And honestly, Rose, it won't be bad—just for a time until things settle down. All sorts of girls do it now, as Lou says. And you're just the kind who'll get on well with everybody. I think it ought to be fun."

Mrs. Wilber, now basking in the sunshine of her admirable plan, thought it ought to be fun too. Both of them were so enthusiastic about domestic service that Rose could not help wondering why they had never tried it themselves, but she was too polite to say anything. Mrs. Wilber began to concoct a reference, which announced that Mary Pearson had been her parlourmaid for the last twelve months and was only leaving now because she did not like Clapham. When, after several attempts, it was finally written, it looked a splendid reference. A warning note about Mary Pearson was sent to Mrs. Wilber's friend at Eastbourne, who would have to answer for her if necessary. Rose had no uniform, of course, and now there was a good deal of talk about that, talk that both Beatrice and Mrs. Wilber, who did most of it, thoroughly enjoyed. None of them knew a servants' registry office in the West End—for it had been agreed that the West End was the best field of operations—but after some talk of looking in the next morning's *Times* Mrs. Wilber remembered the telephone trade directory, and out of that, after much profitless discussion, they selected, as first choice, a very aristocratic-sounding one, the *Curzon-Lansdowne Domestic Employment Agency*, in the very heart of Mayfair.

The journey there, next morning, was not pleasant, even though Mrs. Wilber was with her most of the way.

It was the first time she had been out since her flight from Raeburn's. And now—the police were looking for her; she could not go home; she had to have a false name; she was a hunted creature. This would be all right and might turn out to be grand fun, once she had got used to it. But at first it was not pleasant. You could no longer look at policemen and think what nice big comfortable friendly men they looked. It was hard now to meet their eye. And that eye was not what it was; no longer blue, innocent, beaming; it was now smaller, shrewder, a murky grey, nasty eye. Rose could feel it boring into her back, once or twice that morning. At any moment, a gigantic hand would come—clop!—on her shoulder. "Here, you!" the voice behind would say. Then police courts and trials and black vans and prisons and Edward Fielding looking sorrowfully at her through the bars on visiting day—a scene she knew well from the films. Thus, in secret terror, came Salter *alias* Pearson, carrying a faked reference, to the *Curzon-Lansdowne Domestic Employment Agency*.

Once inside the *Curzon-Lansdowne*, she suddenly lost all her fear and not only did not care but was actually amused. In fact, it was not long before she wanted to giggle. She had to spend some time in a waiting-room. (There was another waiting-room across the corridor for mistresses.) There were several girls, as well as a man or two, in this waiting-room, and then others came and went. She noticed almost at once that there were two main types, the ones who were so grand, so haughty, so completely super-de-luxe that they would not talk to anybody, looked as if they had almost forgotten how to talk, and the others who from the moment they entered were anxious to tell everybody everything about themselves and to hear, if time permitted, everything about everybody else. It was the first lot who really seemed to suit the *Curzon-Lansdowne*, which was itself very grand, haughty, and completely super-de-luxe. All the women who worked there walked about with their noses in the air and talked in very mincing, "refaned" tones. They seemed quite idiotic to Rose, who more and more wanted to giggle. And it was worse when she was finally shown into the large room.

There, the women clerks sat at desks, some dealing with butlers or cooks, others with housekeepers, parlourmaids or housemaids. The parlourmaid expert, before whom Rose appeared, was called Miss Clonbrook. She had light green hair—or so it looked in that light—and eyeglasses on a gold chain and an orange-coloured mouth and the largest silver brooch Rose had ever seen. When she spoke, she pulled her mouth in and her nostrils quivered, as if there was a bad smell about. Probably she was so important and refined that to her a parlourmaid was a sort of bad smell.

"The neem?" said Miss Clonbrook.

"What did you say?" asked Rose.

Miss Clonbrook closed her eyes, as if in great pain, then opened them to stare disdainfully at Rose, who might have been suffering from one of the more obvious skin diseases. "Your neem?"

"Oh! Sorry! Ro—— I mean, Mary Pearson."

"Mar—ay Peahs'n." Miss Clonbrook, with an air of vast condescension, wrote it down on a form in front of her. "And what ex-pay-ri-aunce?"

Rose had to do a bit of quick lying. "Three years," she answered hastily, hoping she wasn't red in the face.

"As par-lah-med?"

"Er—yes."

"You're very yang," said Miss Clonbrook severely, staring hard at Rose's collar.

"Well—yes—I am."

"North-cantry, Ai imagine?"

"Yes." Rose hesitated. "This is my last reference."

Miss Clonbrook took hold of one corner of Mrs. Wilber's letter very gingerly, as if she thought there might be smallpox germs on it, and then held it well away from herself as she read it, to avoid contamination. However, after reading it, she risked another look at Rose's face.

"Yang, but nace appeahraunce," she said. "What wages?"

"Oh—I don't know—the usual, I suppose."

This hurt Miss Clonbrook, who had to close her eyes again. "Fortay-fave pernds? Fiftay pernds?" Her voice seemed to come from faraway, out of a distant agony. "Ai have a clayent—Laday Holt-Ibstock—who maight care to see you. Very nace familay. We have sent several peepal theah. Four in familay. Cumberland Squayah, Hayde Park. Jast a small staff of six," she added, with a touch of disdain, as if she did not approve of the Holt-Ibstocks, nice family though it might be, roughing it in this fashion.

Lady Holt-Ibstock, it appeared, was actually there, and now Rose was solemnly conducted to her, introduced as if she were some little bit of rubbish found on the premises that morning, and left to be interviewed by the client in a little wooden cubby-hole, which was very bare and cold. Lady Holt-Ibstock herself also seemed rather bare and cold. She was a tall middle-aged woman, wearing a depressed-looking hat that did not suit her and could hardly have suited anybody. She had a rather large bluish nose, faded eyes, and a loud confident sort of voice that was in startling contrast to her manner, which was not loud and confident at all.

"Well," she shouted, making Rose jump. "You're rather young—as that woman said—but if you've had the right sort of experience, I don't know that that matters." She did not look at Rose as she spoke, and Rose came at once to the conclusion that this Lady Holt-Ibstock, for all her title and grandeur and loud voice, was just as shy as she was.

Fortunately, Rose had not much lying to do, even though she had to answer a lot of questions, for she was asked if she knew how to wait at table and clean things and so forth, and that was all right. After working in a café and a restaurant, Rose felt quite professional about this kind of work, though she suspected that once she was inside this mysterious big house, there would be a lot to learn. She admitted, however, that she had never worked in so large a house before. Lady Holt-Ibstock was obviously anxious to get out of this arctic cubby-hole. The wages were three pounds fifteen shillings a month, to start with. One afternoon and evening off every week, and alternate Sundays. She would have to share a bedroom with the second housemaid. Could she start at once? Rose agreed to go that very evening to 7, Cumberland Square, Hyde Park.

She returned to Miss Clonbrook and had to wait until that superior person had finished interviewing an employer, a miserable woman who had a staff of four, only four, to look after herself and her husband, which fact kept Miss Clonbrook's eyes closed for minutes on end. When Miss Clonbrook had condescendingly promised to see what she could do for this timid suppliant, who by this time looked thoroughly ashamed of herself and her sordid little existence, she faintly acknowledged the presence of one of the lower orders, Pearson the parlourmaid, and took down the particulars that Rose gave her. The *Curzon-Lansdowne* would now extract a fee from Lady Holt-Ibstock and a commission from Rose, and was in fact doing very well for itself.

Rose decided now she must have some sort of uniform of her own, and after much hesitation—for she felt that shops were particularly dangerous ground—went into one of the smaller places in Oxford Street and spent half of what she had left in the world on a demure, dark green outfit that made her look very pretty indeed. Mary Pearson looked as attractive a parlourmaid as you could wish to see, but Rose Salter, staring at her, felt herself blushing. All her Haliford blood rushed to her cheeks in revolt against this descent into servitude. She might be going into the house of the grand Holt-Ibstocks in Cumberland Square, Hyde Park. Nevertheless, she was going as a servant. A skivvy! What would her father and mother and Nellie think? Suppose Edward Fielding found out! All this came of being sorry for people and letting yourself in for them. Never again! As she thanked Mrs. Wilber for being so kind to her and then said good-bye, Mrs. Wilber assured her once more that she would find it all great fun, but it was a very subdued Rose who replied that she hoped so. And it was quite a frightened Rose who rang the bell, that night, at the side door of the basement of the house in Cumberland Square. It was a tall, frowning sort of house, with big iron railings in front, and iron bars guarding the basement windows. This might, as Mrs. Wilber and Beatrice had said, be better than working somewhere outside, where the police might find her, but at this moment the house itself looked horribly like a prison. And as she waited for somebody to answer the door, she told herself that she was saying good-bye to Rose Salter of Haliford. Enter Pearson the parlourmaid.

What she chiefly remembered afterwards of those first few days in Cumberland Square was that she felt cold all the time. During her first interview with Lady Holt-Ibstock, in that wooden cubby-hole, she had felt cold, and Lady Holt-Ibstock had looked cold. Once inside the Holt-Ibstock house, she felt colder still. Rose and her family had always lived in small rooms, and those rooms, if they were downstairs, had good big fires in them from September to the end of May. The Salters believed in being snug. They did not mind being over-warm, and sometimes they and their guests fairly sweated in the glare of the roaring coals; but they always took every possible precaution against the cold, from filling the coal cellar to buying plenty of thick woollen blankets. Now, for the first time, Rose had stepped out of this hearty snug tradition. She was so far removed from any familiar cosiness that she might almost be living at the bottom of the sea. Although it was hardly winter yet, these were bitterly raw days. But the square outside was no colder than the house, and possibly a bit warmer in the early afternoon. The house had been recently redecorated and partly refurnished; its predominating shades were cream and pale blue; and there was a good deal of unpainted wood about; and very few carpets. Nearly everything she saw there gave Rose the shivers. There was a little white statue of a naked girl on the first landing that made Rose ache. It was better, of course, down in the basement, where the servants had a little sitting-room—sometimes referred to as "the servants' hall"—opposite the kitchen. The kitchen itself, with its big stove, was warm enough, but Rose did not often find her way in there, because her work was upstairs in the dining-room or the butler's pantry, and also because the cook, Mrs. Penner, did not like people to go uninvited into her kitchen. As for Rose's bedroom on the top floor, a room she shared with the second housemaid, Eva, it was a little ice-house, and the bedclothes failed miserably to keep out the cold. Eva said that she and the last parlourmaid (who had left to get married and warm again) used to cram themselves into one bed, just for warmth; but Rose, who did not much like the look of Eva, a messy sort of girl, was having none, and preferred to shiver alone. Downstairs, there were plenty of fires, but somehow they never seemed big and fierce enough even to take the chill off the large rooms. And all the stairs and landings, which had some secret but direct connection with the arctic regions, were permanently glacial.

Such was the home of the Holt-Ibstock family, and, in Rose's view, it suited them perfectly. All four looked as if they had been kept in cold storage a long time and had then never been properly thawed out. Sir Edwin Holt-Ibstock, who was a Member of Parliament and a very important personage who sat on committees and received deputations and who was very much on the Blue side and dead against the Red side, was very tall and thin and had scanty grey hair and a close-cropped grey moustache and a high complaining voice. He did not look quite as blue as his wife, perhaps because he could wear more clothes in the evening, but nevertheless he was thoroughly frosted. Mr. Raymond, the son, was also tall and thin, a rather colourless young man, but was not so bad as the other three because he went out and played games. Miss Diana, only twenty-three, was perhaps the worst of the lot. She was thin but not so tall as the others, and she had chilly blue eyes, pale hair, and a little button of a nose that was nearly always reddish, no matter how much powder she put on it. When Rose saw her in evening clothes, with bones and gooseflesh showing all over the place, rather like a plucked turkey on a frosty Christmas Eve, Rose could have cried out in pity, and wanted to wrap her in hot blankets. Miss Diana's voice was the highest and most complaining of them all. All their voices, high-pitched, clear and loud, were cold too. They were like people out of a refrigerator. Rose felt very sorry for them at first, because they seemed to get so little cosiness and comfort and fun for their money. And they were always grumbling. Sir Edwin grumbled about the state of the country; Mr. Raymond grumbled about the City, where he worked, and golf and such things; Lady Holt-Ibstock complained about "the servant class"—even when it was handing her potatoes and listening to her—and the vulgar pushing people there were about nowadays; and Miss Diana, who was always rushing in and out and telephoning and writing notes and cancelling one engagement and accepting another and quarrelling with her friends and making it up again and saying she had nothing to wear and then complaining because she had to go for a fitting, was the most dissatisfied of them all and was always screaming that everything was "foul." Except in the matter of Miss Diana's clothes, Rose did not envy them at all. They had nothing like the fun and jokes her family had at home. They hardly ever seemed to do anything because they liked doing it. Even their amusements, which must have been very costly, appeared to be forced on them, like a sort of homework. When they had people to dinner, they all ate and drank an astonishing number of different things, and pretended to laugh and be jolly; but Rose, busy helping Mr. Penner, the butler, could see that Lady Holt-Ibstock was anxious all the time, Sir Edwin indifferent, and Miss Diana and Mr. Raymond, if they were at home, just bored. It seemed to Rose a silly sort of life and a terrible waste of money.

There was much more excitement, more drama, more life, downstairs among the staff. There were six of them, including Rose—or Pearson, as the family called her. First, Mr. and Mrs. Penner. Rose had to see a lot of Mr. Penner because she had to help him. He was not her idea of a butler at all, because instead of being a large, fat, oldish man with side-whiskers and a comical manner—like the butlers in films—he was rather small and thin, very dark, with queer pale eyes, lighter than his skin. And there was nothing comical about him. He was rather frightening, not because he was difficult to work with, for Rose got on with him quite well and he was very patient in teaching her the various things she did not know, but because he had been a sergeant in the War—and had been blown up or something awful—and he was fond of referring, in an odd frightening way, to what had happened in that War and would happen—bombs and poison gas and all kinds of horrors—in the next war, over which he brooded darkly. At all sorts of odd times, as Rose could see by the look in his eyes, he would be thinking about these nightmares. When he was serving the family and their guests with wine—and he fancied himself as a server of wine—he would be wondering, as he confided to Rose, what would happen to some of these people soon. He could see them all poisoned with gas fumes or blown to bits. Apart from these queer brooding spells, he was a quiet and decent man, easy to work with. Mrs. Penner was the snag. She was a very good cook, who could work wonders when she set herself to it, but she had a violent, almost insane temper, and was a terribly jealous woman. She was bigger than her husband, and had a flat, unhealthy-looking face and blazing eyes. There was some sort of madness working in her, just as there was in Mr. Penner, but she was much more dangerous than he was. You never knew when she might flare up. Sometimes nobody dare go near the kitchen. It was like having a tigress in there. You could hear her banging about and talking to herself. If the door flew open, you would see her standing there, a large kitchen knife in her hand, her eyes blazing away. She frightened Rose, of whom she was rather jealous, because Rose and her husband had to work together upstairs.

Mrs. Penner's chief jealousy, however, was reserved for Dorothy Crowle, the older housemaid, who was really more of a personal maid to Lady Holt-Ibstock and Miss Diana. Mrs. Penner believed that Dorothy, who saw more of her mistress than Mrs. Penner did, was always busy "turning the family against her." She also said that Dorothy had been spoilt and did not know her place, which really was far below a cook's. Dorothy was not so loud in her dislike of and opposition to Mrs. Penner, but she did not hesitate to say that Mrs. Penner was a very disagreeable and dangerous woman, not quite right in the head, and that the house would be better without her. Dorothy herself was a sandy sort of woman in her thirties, plain and stringy, reserved and very respectable, and said to be religious, a keen Wesleyan. The struggle for authority that went on endlessly between Dorothy and Mrs. Penner, the plots and counterplots, the alliances and leagues they formed, the wild charges that flew about, were all something quite new and startling to Rose. The mere business of learning to do a new job upstairs paled and shrank into insignificance when compared with this roaring drama downstairs. Rose's own sympathies were on the whole with Dorothy, who seemed to her not particularly likeable but at least fairly harmless. But Eva Newton, the younger housemaid, who had to work with Dorothy, did not like her and said she was sly. So Eva always sided with Mrs. Penner. On the other hand, little Connie Ball, the kitchenmaid, swore to anybody who would listen to her that Mrs. Penner was a devil, more than half-mad, and would, before she had finished, "do in" somebody—probably Connie herself—with that largest kitchen knife. So Dorothy could always depend on Connie's support, though it did not amount to much, because Connie was very young and unimportant, and nobody believed half she said. Little Connie had had a romantic history, for she had been found, when a young baby, on the doorstep of an orphanage, which had been then compelled to adopt her. She still looked rather lost and bewildered, and not at all like the heroine of a romantic story, who might afterwards turn out to be the illegitimate daughter of a duke. Rose saw very little of her. She saw most of Eva, because they shared a bedroom. Eva was a ginger-haired girl, with greenish eyes, a spreading sort of nose, and a very wide loose mouth, and she came from Watford, where her father, when he worked, was a paper-hanger. She was an easy-going, kind-hearted girl, but Rose did not like her in the same bedroom—and was determined not to have her in the same bed, even if the temperature went down to zero—because she was untidy and rather dirty and talked all the time about boys and the first nights of honeymoons and the be-diamonded and doped adventuresses in Paris she read about in Sunday papers. She had four different admirers, only alike in the fact that they all "tried it on" (and she loved to give exact details of the trying-on, spluttering and giggling), and she dodged from one to the other in what seemed to Rose a silly dreary fashion. She and Rose could have had the same nights out, but Rose saw to it that they didn't. It was nice having the bedroom to oneself for an hour or two on the nights when Eva was out. Rose did not like it much in the sitting-room downstairs, where Mr. Penner ran a gloomy and cynical eye over the paper; Mrs. Penner, jabbing away at a penny bottle of ink, wrote angry letters to her relatives, and Eva and Connie sat giggling over old copies of illustrated papers that came down from the drawing-room. (Dorothy hardly went in there, except for meals. It was the headquarters of the Penner lot.) It was not that anybody was unpleasant to her—though sometimes Mrs. Penner stared dreadfully—but sitting there made her feel lost and sad. It was like an awful parody of home. And it was difficult for Rose not to feel lost and sad during these first days. She was not even Rose Salter, but Mary Pearson. She was buried away, among strangers, in this tall cold house. Everything was unfamiliar, hardly real.

She spent her first off day, and after that her first Sunday evening out, over at Mrs. Wilber's at Clapham, and that had been all right, because Mrs. Wilber knew all about her and was comfortable and kind. Rose told her all about the Holt-Ibstocks and the quarrels of the staff; Mrs. Wilber gave her all the bits of news *she* could think of; they had long cosy chats over the teapot about everything and nothing; Mrs. Wilber told her fortune with cards (a dark young man coming back into her life, and an accident or something, then a strange bed), and they listened to the wireless. It was nice. But it made going back to cold Cumberland Square all the worse. She moved among the frozen Holt-Ibstocks and through the complaints and charges and ultimatums downstairs like a girl in a slow sad dream. Where was Edward Fielding? Where were her mother and father and Nellie, and Haliford? Where was life, with the sun, moon, stars, kisses and singing and fun? It was as if her whole world had been put under some icy spell.

She did her work—turning out the drawing-room and dining-room, helping Mr. Penner in his pantry and at the table—as best she could, and fortunately, though she was new to much of it, she did not find it hard after the fierce rush of the restaurant. Mr. Penner said that Lady Holt-Ibstock was pleased with her, but somehow that did not matter, if only because Lady Holt-Ibstock did not seem a real person. It was more important that Mr. Penner himself, in his own queer we're-not-long-for-this-world fashion, was pleased with her, but even that was not really important. They were pleased with Pearson the parlour-maid, and she was not really Pearson the parlourmaid, was only playing a long chilly game of pretence. Because of this constant feeling of unreality, she had no desire to make friends with anybody in the house. And Cumberland Square could never be even the shadow of a home. It was only her hiding-place. And London itself had retreated, turned quiet and ghostly in the distance. The noisy crowded days at the Copper Kettle and in the restaurant at Raeburn's seemed far away, behind some remote veil that had suddenly shut off nearly all the warmth and light of life.

Yet actually she had not been there quite a fortnight when something happened that changed everything, in a flash, flooding her world with warmth and light. It was quite unexpected. Not the least sign of its coming had been given her. There was not the slightest quiver in that very ordinary day to suggest that it would blow up gloriously. It was one of her harder days because the Penners were out, though even that afterwards turned out to be a wonderful stroke of luck. When the Penners were out, she had to lay the table for dinner and do the waiting, and also see that Connie downstairs had properly warmed up the food Mrs. Penner had left prepared and had also done the simple cooking—chiefly of vegetables—expected of her. Fortunately, on these nights, the family did not expect anything grand. This particular evening, both Sir Edwin and Mr. Raymond were out to dinner, and though an aunt of Lady Holt-Ibstock's was coming to dine with her and Miss Diana, she was, it appeared, of no importance.

"Who is it?" Mr. Penner had asked Rose. "Oh—that aunt. I'll tell the wife. Anything 'll do for her. The other one's different. They're expecting the other one to leave 'em something. This one's got nothing to leave. Not that it won't be all the same," he added darkly. "They'll all get a lot more than what they expect, and not from aunts neither. By the way, this one doesn't take any wine, or if she does, they don't let her have it. Never seen her with any. You'll have it easy, Mary."

It was too. There was soup to serve. Then veal in a casserole, with mashed potatoes and Brussels sprouts. No sweet, only a savoury, and then some mingy-looking fruit. The old aunt looked as if she lived in the country, and had a raw, red, rather kind face. She and Lady Holt-Ibstock argued about a man called Jim, probably another relative. Miss Diana looked very bored. (Dorothy said that a young man she was after had just had to go to Africa, so that might be it.) They all drank barley water. The dining-room was cold, of course, but the aunt did not seem to mind, perhaps because she came from the country and was so red and healthy, and of course Lady Holt-Ibstock and Miss Diana did not notice because they were now perpetually cold and had forgotten what it was to be warm. Nothing cosy about this dinner. The table, a lot of naked wood with a few mats and plates on it, looked cheerless. But Lady Holt-Ibstock and the aunt talked away in their loud high voices, and finally got Jim settled. Miss Diana kept closing her eyes, to show that it was all painfully boring. She was wearing one of her oldest dresses, and looked very scraggy in it. "I wish I had it," said Rose to herself, as she went round with the sprouts. "I'd show you something, Miss Diana Holt-Ibstock." Oddly enough, the next moment, after she had put the dish back on the serving table, she and Miss Diana looked one another straight in the eye, the chill light blue fairly meeting the warm goldeny brown. Something ought to have passed between these eyes. There they were, two girls looking at one another. But nothing did pass. Miss Diana slowly closed her eyes, and by the time they opened again they were looking somewhere else. There seemed to Rose something deeply insulting about this. She was glad the young man had gone to Africa, and hoped he would stay there. At least it would be warm in Africa. "Miss North Pole, that's you," Rose said to Miss Diana's goose-fleshy back, as she went out to the pantry.

She served coffee in the drawing-room, which was a very long room, so that Rose always felt nervous carrying the tray from the door to the distant region near the fireplace.

"Oh—Pearson—put out the card table," said Lady Holt-Ibstock.

This was easy. Rose had done it before. You unfolded the top, which was covered with apricot velvet and very pretty, and then you pulled out a third leg. She did this, and then brought up three straight-backed chairs, for these people liked to sit bolt upright when they played cards, not like Dad and the boys at home, who played Nap and Solo leaning back and sprawling and throwing the cards at the table. So far, so good. But then Miss Diana told her to get out the Something (there was an "eek" in it) cards and markers, and Rose was promptly dished. She went to the top drawer of the curved walnut chest of drawers, where they kept all the cards and counters and little pencils and what not, wondering what on earth the Something-eek cards and markers were. Lady Holt-Ibstock and the aunt were shouting to each other about Hilary now.

"I don't agree," Lady Holt-Ibstock was shouting. "Hilary was never the same after Malta."

"My dear, it was long before that," cried the aunt, bellowing like a farmer. "It was before Gib. *She* began it."

"You're probably right. Of course, she wasn't quite——"

"I should think not. About three drawers down from the top."

For a moment Rose, standing helplessly, wondered whether this last observation was meant for her, though it did not seem likely that the old aunt would know where the Something-eek cards and markers were.

"Have you got them, Pearson?" asked Miss Diana.

Rose in her despair grabbed the nearest lot of cards and came away with them. She looked appealingly at Miss Diana. No good. That young lady gave the cards and her one glance of supreme disgust, got up, saying, "Good God! No," took the cards away from her, and went to the drawer herself. Rose, half ashamed, half indignant, was a burning scarlet.

"You can clear the coffee things, Pearson," said Lady Holt-Ibstock, as if from the top of some distant mountain.

Rose caught the old aunt's glance, shrewd, amused, and not unsympathetic, resting on her. Still burning, Rose took the tray down the room.

"Really, these maids——" Miss Diana was beginning.

"Now, please, Diana," said her mother.

And as Rose opened the door, she heard the old aunt saying: "New one, isn't she? Pretty little thing. Very pretty little thing."

And Miss Diana replying, in haughty surprise: "Oh, do you think so? I must say——"

Now she was safe outside. She had only to clear the dining-room table and take the things into the butler's pantry, where she could wash up some of them herself and send the others down the little lift into the kitchen. Among the pictures in the dining-room was one of an oldish man, who wore a wig and a lace collar. He had a round red face, a long smiling mouth, and sharp little eyes. You knew at once he had enjoyed himself in his time, had not cared tuppence what anybody thought of him, and was nobody's fool. There was more richness of character in the mere picture of him than there was in all four living Holt-Ibstocks. He was all right. Rose could have got on with him, though she knew intuitively that he would have wanted watching. Now the two of them had a good look at each other. His eyes seemed to twinkle and wink. "Take it easy, Rose," they said. "Don't worry. You're worth ten frozen scraggy stuck-up Dianas. You'll have a good life yet. I had one. I know." And Rose, standing there, holding her tray, did something she had not done for a long time, she winked herself, winked back at him. Then she felt a lot better.

But it was when she was finally tidying up the sink in the butler's pantry that the first coloured rocket went up and the wintry spell was broken. She had just sunk back again into her usual cheerless passivity, was looking forward to nothing but the faint possibility of being warm in bed within the next two hours, when Connie came scuttling up the stairs and burst into the pantry, her eyes enormous, her mouth wide open. "Ooh, I say," she cried, in a loud whisper, "there's a chap downstairs and he's asking for you."

"For me?" She was instantly alarmed. She could only think of the police.

Connie nodded very quickly a great many times, her eyes bigger than ever. This was drama and she meant to enjoy it.

"What—what's he like?" Rose swallowed hard.

"Ooh—well—I couldn't see 'im properly—not down there at the back door—but he's a young chap—and he seemed very nice—bit nervous, y'know—and—and—let's see—he talks a bit like you."

This did not sound like the police. She hurried down to the basement, thinking like mad all the way. And there he was, standing just inside the dimly-lit passage to the back door. A yard away from him she stopped, and for a moment they said nothing but just stared at one another.

After all, she had only seen him twice, counting that first glimpse of him on the Park seat as a time. His actual presence was still strange to her. As a name in her thoughts, as a vague figure in her day-dreams and idle speculations, he was familiar enough, nobody more so; in this shadowy form he was already part of herself; but not as a solid person, standing in front of her, wearing a damp raincoat, nervously twisting the hat in his hand.

"Yes, it's me," he announced, in a low voice, not looking at her now but looking down. "I hope it's all right—I mean—coming here like this. I had to see you." He was terribly nervous.

It was this that suddenly gave her self-confidence. She took charge of the situation at once. "Wait a minute," she commanded, with a quick nod and smile. She found Connie, still palpitating with drama. There were only the two of them down there, for Eva was out that night, and Dorothy was upstairs, probably sewing in her own room. "Connie, will you listen for the bell and run down and tell me? I'll be in the sitting-room." Connie, all eyes and rapid nods again, hurried away, and Rose took Edward Fielding into the sitting-room.

As soon as they got in there, under the sharp light, she felt ashamed. Many and many a time she had dreamed of this meeting, but never like this, in a servants' sitting-room in the basement of a strange unfriendly house, herself a servant, plainly to be seen—in uniform. She could hardly meet his eyes, which were now fixed hungrily upon her. No sign of disgust in them.

"But, I say," she said, as if they had already had some talk, "how did you know I was here?" He was thinner and untidier than she had remembered, but she had been right in thinking he had lovely dark eyes.

"I wrote a letter to you at that shop," he explained, not smiling, very serious. "Nellie told me where you were. A detective came to see me where I work. He said they were looking for you——"

"Oh!" she gasped, ashamed again.

"I knew you hadn't really done anything, of course," he said sturdily, now looking fairly and squarely at her. "I told him so. Anyhow, I sent a telegram to Nellie, and she told me the police had been there. I know—but don't you worry. Then I went to the shop, and kept asking in that café place. And in the end a girl put me on to that girl you shared a room with——"

"Oh, Beatrice! Did you like her?" she asked, inconsequently.

"No, I didn't. She tried hard to put me off, but I wasn't having any, and before I'd finished I made her tell me where you were. Mary Pearson," he added, with a faint grin.

"I didn't want to do this," she told him, looking hard at his tie, which was a black one with thin red stripes, worn at one edge. She would like to buy him a nicer tie. "But I couldn't help it. There didn't seem to be anything else to do."

"No, I know." He did not appear to be at all concerned about her being there, a servant under a false name, and she was immensely relieved. A new eagerness suddenly lit up his face, and in a way she remembered, with a rush of feeling, so that the sight of it caught at her heart.

"Y'know, I couldn't help being late that night," he began.

"No, that's all right," she said quickly. As if she didn't know all that. And hanging about Slater Street night after night, and seeing Nellie, who said he was crazy about her! She knew, she knew!

"I came to London because you did," he went on eagerly. "I've been thinking about you and looking for you ever since that Sunday—you remember?"

Yes, she remembered. And although she knew all this, had turned it over and over in her mind so many times, now when she heard him say it, she was so deeply moved that the tears rushed to her eyes. Now that he was actually here, telling her all this, she wanted to rush away, straight up to her bedroom, and cry and glow and wonder in peace.

"I suppose I'd better not stay here long, had I?" he said, uneasily.

"No, not long."

"Oh!—Rose—Rose——"

That unbearable cry from the heart swept her towards him, and the next moment they were kissing, clumsily, saltily, with a great deal of damp raincoat mixed up in everything.

"I'd better go," he said at last.

"Yes."

"When do they—I mean—when can I see you?"

"Thursday."

"What time?"

"I get off after lunch—about half-past—but you——"

"Never mind about me, Rose. I'll be there whatever time you say."

"Three o'clock, then. Let's see. Not just outside. There's a pillar-box the other side of the square. You can't miss it."

"All right. There, three o'clock on Thursday."

They were now nearly at the back door. A bell was ringing. Connie was rushing downstairs. "Good night, Edward."

"Good night, Rose."

XII

NOTHING much happened on that Thursday. Two youngsters went out on a little jaunt and enjoyed themselves, because they were so young and in love. But they will remember it all their lives, just as we all remember certain days all our lives, and as this is their book, the day must not go unrecorded. Those who do not wish to read about happiness may be quickly assured that there is even now enough misery in print to last them until their eye-sight goes. Happiness cannot be adequately described, and that is why we read so little about it, while the dark wastes that lie around it are strewn with millions of words. But the day shall have its chapter, even though the bloom is not there, nor the deep tender mystery of it. This happiness is the rare blossom upon the tree of our life, as rare as the suns of warmth and light in the black cold inter-stellar spaces. It is also a mystery, for though it seems to spring from the core of life, it does not quite belong to this world, which is bewildering enough if, as we are told, we are the children of this planet and the centre of our being is here. So now for happiness, for the flower that comes at last out of the dark ground; the fragrance of primrose and violet after the rotted leaf reek of winter; the flash of the fabled blue-wing; blackbirds fluting it in misty orchards; the ship long overdue entering the harbour mouth; all the sheaves bound and the vast moon rising;

garlanded landfalls in the South Pacific; the fog lifting and the landing-ground clear; the sudden smile of a friend in some God-forsaken hole; moonlight among the Meister-singers; a brick wall in the enchanted country of Vermeer; the last experiment finished and not a loophole anywhere; an eight-pound son turning his face to suck; the epic written and outside a glitter of stars; the bulge and weight of stockings in the dark of Christmas morning; the *Cease Fire* and not a lad missing; the last task completed and every promise kept and your grandchild putting your chair out in the sun. You will not understand the happiness of these two unless you remember your own, and set it glowing behind the pages, turning the poor dim picture into a glorious transparency.

The day itself was good; not very bright or warm, of course, for now it was November; but when you have made every allowance for the latitude and the season, it was a good day. There was no rain. If there was fog, it was a friendly little fog, with a bit of sunlight somewhere in it, that made all interiors snug and cosy and yet at the same time gave the streets themselves a kind of cosiness too, not enlarging and darkening the city but keeping it small and elfish, just the very setting for one of the happier passages in a fairy tale. All the morning, both Rose and Edward, who were keeping an eye on it, liked the look of the day. They knew very soon that it was on their side. (This cannot be helped. Even the most splendidly dis-illusioned contemporary must admit that something must be on somebody's side some time.) Edward was busy all morning deciding where they ought to go and what he would say to her. Rose was busy trying to make up her mind what to wear—she had not a lot of clothes, but they could be variously combined in the most bewildering fashion—and thinking what she would say to Edward. Each of them was now quite unable to remember what the other looked like. This was most tantalising. They could remember with disgusting clearness all sorts of ridiculous faces of people who did not matter at all, people they had bought apples from or sat opposite to in railway carriages. But the most important face in the world refused to appear. Each talked earnestly to a smiling blur. Apart from this inability, they had not a care, in spite of the fact that one of them was still degrading herself, under a false name too, in domestic service and was still wanted by the police, and the fact that the other had just been sacked by the Belvedere Trading Company, had no further job in view, and not much left out of his windfall. These matters were now seen in their true perspective; they were mere details; fairly entertaining subjects for discussion later. A few learned and conscientious persons, here and there, were even now planning how to turn such careless young people into good citizens, just as a great many other persons were even now planning how to take their money away from them, even if it meant cheating, when they should become good citizens; but they themselves were not bothering at all, and might have been a mediæval hind and his lass preparing to walk together in one of the giant forests of that old leafy England.

The pillar-box was there, waiting for Edward. (You never know—some fool might have ordered its removal.)

He arrived only twenty minutes too soon. Rose arrived early too; that is, she arrived at the appointed time, which is early for the female, with her queer time lag. The final combination of garments, thrown on in despair, after hours of indecision and at least half an hour of trying on and taking off, was tremendously effective, making Edward at first feel very humble and shabby, and doing him a lot of good. Rose herself, breathless and bright-eyed, was radiant, and people noticed her, and she noticed people noticing her, and thought how nice this was for Edward. They walked towards Marble Arch, through the hazy, faintly golden streets, talking fifteen to the dozen. There were so many questions to ask and answer, so many adventures to recount, so many mysterious gaps to be filled. So when they came to the buses, they had not even begun to decide where they were going. It did not matter. Wherever it was, they were both going there. They ran up the steps of the nearest bus; and when the conductor came for the fares, he reminded them both of a funny-looking chap who gave out programmes for the military band concerts in Ackroyd Park, Haliford; and when he had gone, they both said so and laughed a lot and thought how wonderful everything was, and one lady sitting near smiled at them, and another looked sadly their way, and a grumpy old fellow, who was trying to decide if it was worth while doing a deal in Burmese Tin, hated the sight of them. When at last Edward looked out of the window instead of looking at Rose, he saw they were in New Oxford Street, and there was a sign pointing to the British Museum. He asked Rose if she had ever been there, and she hadn't, and he hadn't, so off they jumped. At a foreign shop at the corner, Edward bought a shilling's worth of chocolates—grand big ones, put up in an aristocratic cardboard container, but not so many of them for your shilling—and they both tried one. Then, with that rich tropical adventure going on inside their mouths, they walked up to the British Museum.

It looked so enormous and important and official that at first they were rather afraid of going in; but a number of other people, no better than they were, calmly crossed the courtyard, so they went too. There was a policeman standing quite near, and Rose's heart thumped a bit as they passed him, but it was all right. It was fine. Nothing to pay either. There is a special little thrill of pleasure nowadays, when you seem to pay out money every time you want a little amusement, in walking into a big important building without being charged anything. All you had to do was to leave your umbrella, and as Rose had not brought hers and Edward had never had one in his life, that was all right too. It was very solemn inside, and so quiet after the din of the streets that they could hear people's footsteps quite distinctly, and began to walk about, rather tiringly, on their tiptoes, for fear of making a clatter. They kept very close together, feeling a cosy little pair under that high roof and in front of that tremendous staircase. As they stood for a moment, wondering where to go first, Edward's hand clasped Rose's arm, and the thrill of that was terrific, so terrific that perhaps it radiated through the whole Museum, and the mummies upstairs, remembering what life had been, faintly stirred.

"You'd like to go round a bit, wouldn't you?" asked Edward, speaking very quietly.

"Yes, I would," whispered Rose, who would not have missed it for anything now.

There were not too many other people there, but just enough to make them feel they were not lost among these solemnities.

"Fancy being here all by yourself," whispered Rose. "Wouldn't it be awful?"

And Edward, though bluff and brave about it, admitted it would be pretty bad; not in the afternoon, but late at night, with the great stone beasts watching you climb the staircase.

Some foreigners, of course. They had both noticed before that you were likely to see foreigners in places like this, all reading guide-books and looking very serious and conscientious and exchanging remarks in their fantastic languages, and all, no doubt, wishing it were done with and dinner-time. They had a good look at these foreigners, who were, after all, part of the exhibits. There were three tall youths with pale eyes, stiff chaps, like men made of wood; and Edward was sure they were Germans. Then two little Japanese, like yellow squeaky gnomes, and more mysterious than any of the Museum things. And a whole dark, jabbering, gesticulating family, women and all with moustaches, with a fat father who led the way and looked so quickly and eagerly first in front and then behind at his family that he was more like a whiskery top than a man.

"I don't think I'd have liked this much with anybody else," said Rose, "but it's fun—with you."

He stopped then—they had a whole place to themselves—and told her it was ever so much more fun for him and that he had thought hundreds of times about being with her in places like this and that London had been nothing at all just because he had been looking for her all the time. And then she admitted that Nellie had said he was crazy about her, and looked quickly at him to see if this was all right. And he said it was all right, because he *was* crazy about her, and didn't care who knew it. All this happened in front of a long row of Roman Emperors, who stared out blindly and stonily, and had, most of them, fierce cruel features.

"If you ask me, they're a nasty-looking lot," said Rose thoughtfully. "You can imagine them—look at that one—ordering your head to be cut off or a lion tearing you to pieces or whatever they did. They're all better dead and finished with. There's nothing like that anywhere now, is there?"

"I'm not so sure," said Edward dubiously. "You read all sorts of things, don't you?"

She looked at him so solemnly then that he kissed her very quickly, right in front of an emperor, but they discovered that this one, who was called Caracalla, had turned his face away; and Edward explained how this emperor had turned away on purpose, and made Rose laugh, though she did not like to laugh out loud in there.

After that there were a lot of Greek and Roman statues, far too many of them. Some of them were lovely to look at, of course; the women in their long slim perfection; the men with their broad shoulders and curves of muscle;

they made you realise how fine people could look when they were well-made and had their silly clothes off; but there were far too many of them, and you got tired of their whiteness and blind eyes. And they hurried through the rooms filled with "rare fragments," bits of tombs and what not.

"Though, mind you," said Edward, "I believe when you know all about it, some of these bits of stone are the most important of all the things they've got. Chaps spend years looking for them."

"Well, I must say," said Rose, "it seems dotty to me. I can't see why anybody should bother with these broken old pieces of stone when real life's going on all round. Do you see what I mean, Edward? If I had a tombstone—and I hope I shan't have—but if I had, I wouldn't want people in thousands of years' time to spend years messing about with bits of it. I'd rather they got on with their own lives, and never mind about me."

They began lingering again when they came to the Egyptians, who were much better than the Greeks and Romans, more frightening perhaps but more exciting. The Greeks and Romans reminded Rose of the Holt-Ibstocks.

"They're all so stiff and frozen up," she explained. "And so pleased with themselves. Now these old Egyptians—of course they're terribly foreign and far away—like the people in the Bible——"

"They are in the Bible, some of 'em," said Edward. "I got a prize for Scripture when I was at school, though I never liked it much. I hated the Israelites. Nasty crowd!"

"Well, these Egyptians may be as old and far away," said Rose, looking earnestly at several of them, "but somehow there's more life about them, isn't there? You know what sort of people they were. You could live amongst them."

"Look at all those busy little chaps going like billy-ho," said Edward, pointing. "Kind of Mickey Mouse effect, isn't it?"

They looked about them, wonderingly. Those half-animal, half-human gods and goddesses, ready to frighten your life out, but understandable in a queer way! These kings! What chaps! The huge heads, like those of stone giants buried up to the neck, staring out, waiting to be released, to stump straight out into Great Russell Street, with half the gallery hanging round their shoulders!

"You know, Edward," said Rose, shyly and earnestly, "I think you can tell about these emperors and kings or whatever they were, just by looking at these heads of them. You know that some were nice and kind, and some were terrible and cruel. There's something about them that tells you. Look at that one."

"He's a fierce one."

"I'll bet he was a human devil. And still is, if you give him half a chance. I wouldn't come here at night by myself and stand looking at him—not for anything. He'd come alive again, and start ordering the others to do all kinds of devilish things. Honestly, he would, Edward."

She took his arm and squeezed it. He looked to see if anybody was coming, and then drew her behind the gigantic head and arm of *Thothmes III*. When he tried to kiss her, she made a little face at him and escaped by turning away, but when she saw his look of disappointment, she turned back, rested in his arms, and sweetly raised her lips to his. And for several moments they stayed there, pygmies in the shadow of that head and arm, but so rapt and oblivious in the trembling primrose ecstasy of first love that it is a wonder that all those gigantic heads did not turn towards them and open despairing eyes, that the granite and black marble fists did not clash together, that all the vast litter and ruin of dead-and-gone life there did not quiver in ghostly reawakening and cry: "We too, we too! We remember. At Thebes and Memphis, Babylon and Nineveh, Xanthus and Halicarnassus, in temples that are dust, and gardens that are desert, long ago, long ago. But we too, we remember."

Hand in hand, these children of our day, which has a streaked red sky that might mean sunrise or sunset, stared at Sennacherib and Ashur-nasir-pal and Shalmaneser and Ashur-bani-pal, and made little or nothing of them and their victories and their conquests and their tributary kings and their palaces and horsemen and footmen. The long bearded faces spoke never a word. The kings of kings were silent for ever. Yet the happiness Rose and Edward knew might never have flowered, the two of them might never have met, never even have existed, if one of these kings had not boasted in his cups, if one of these horsemen had not fallen wounded far from Assyria, and who shall trace that path and write that chronicle? And though we know who Sennacherib was and what came of him, who knows who we are and where we are going? Those winged lions from Ashur-nasir-pal's doorway have survived nearly three thousand years. Where will they be in another thousand years, and who will be looking at them then?

It was while Edward and Rose were examining a pair of tweezers and a head-scratcher from Ur of the Chaldees that they were joined by a middle-aged man who suddenly looked hard at Rose.

"Met you somewhere, haven't I?" he said, smiling.

Rose glanced at him—a tall, rather stout man, with a large hooked nose and a wide humorous mouth—and then remembered. It was Mr. Mantoni, the conjurer, whom she had met the night she had gone to the music-hall with Mrs. Burlow.

"That's right," said Mr. Mantoni. "Knew we'd met somewhere."

He was introduced to Edward, who did not look any too pleased to meet him, though he said he was. But Mr. Mantoni, who had probably had enough of his own company that afternoon, was not to be so easily put off. "Often pop in here," he explained. "It's warm and you can't spend any money. Get ideas here too, now and again, though mostly for big illusion acts that I couldn't afford to put on, even if anybody wanted me to, and anyhow they don't—but still, I get ideas. Egyptian's the best. Very fruity. Where are you going now, you two?"

"Well, we don't know," said Rose. "Do we, Edward? We've finished looking round. We haven't seen everything, of course, but we've had about enough."

"Same here," said Mr. Mantoni. "For one thing, I could do with a cup of tea and a smoke. Matter of fact, I'm on my way to see an old friend of mine. Near here. Killing two birds with one stone, I am, and he's bird number two. He's a magician. Or *was*. Used to be on the halls. Called himself Prince Chang Lung. Remember him? Oriental illusion act. Then he had a breakdown—after nearly getting killed in a revolver trick he was working—and now he keeps a little shop near here. Sells cheap tricks. Take you there if you like. Glad to see you. Bit lonely, old Alf is. Never married. Makes a good cup of tea too in his back room. What do you say?"

Edward looked at Rose, and Rose looked at Edward. Neither of them signalled either Yes or No. They hesitated. This was good enough for Mr. Mantoni.

"Come on then," he said, taking charge of them at once. "Not ten minutes' walk from here. He'll amuse you, old Alf will. He's amusing. Not like me."

He said this so gloomily that Edward laughed, and then Rose had to laugh too. She remembered now that this was how Mr. Mantoni talked on the stage.

"How is——?" Rose began, as they were walking out. She hesitated because Mrs. Mantoni, which was probably only a stage name, sounded so queer.

"The wife? Not so good, though I've known her worse. Still got my sister-in-law helping with the act. I've a banquet to-night—that's what they call 'em, banquets, and I suppose they ought to know—out at Tottenham. Another one on Saturday—at Ilford. Then I put in a week at a picture palace at Lewisham. Hate picture palaces. Too big. Half of 'em can't see you, and the other half don't want to. But here we are," he announced as they came out, as if all the world outside the Museum belonged to him. "A few minutes' walk and we're there. And now I can light my pipe."

Edward lit a cigarette. Rose did not find it necessary to light anything. It had been nice inside the Museum, and now it was nicer still to be back in the world again, walking along with Edward to have a cup of tea with two conjurers. Even the noise of the streets, the chill in the air, the deepening dusk, were welcome and precious. There was an infinite exciting promise in the lights of the shops—though on closer examination these shops near the Museum were not the kind she liked—and in the growing feeling that the whole great city, now filling the air above it with a quivering red glow, was theirs to wander about in and explore. But any other place would have done. Haliford, really, would have been better still. To walk down Slater Street arm-in-arm with Edward, to have burst in and cried to them all, "Here we are!" But this was good. She was alive again, and so warmly and deliciously alive.

Edward was thinking that Mr. Mantoni was probably a mistake, but otherwise was deeply content. A restlessness that seemed to have been gnawing at him for years was no longer there now. He was not lost and lonely. London was all different. It had no objection to him, was positively friendly, and hinted at magical possibilities. Rose had done it. She had taken with her that glorious day of theirs on the moors, had kept it alive, and now had brought it into these streets. But it was all more wonderful to-day than it had been then, because all the time when he could not find her, though he had clung to the belief that she was the perfect girl for him, he had never been quite sure, whereas now that she had reappeared, so vividly out of the dark of that disappearance, he was quite sure, rapturously sure. And this disappearance, these London adventures of hers, which belonged to her as his belonged so intimately to him, gave her in his eyes an air of enchanting mystery that she had not had in Haliford, although she had not been without mystery there. Now, you might say, she was doubly mysterious. He looked at her, walking beside him, and instantly, knowing at once that he was looking at her, she turned and smiled, a quick, sweet, intimate little smile that said more than any words they had so far exchanged. Out of this mystery came this smile.

Meanwhile Mr. Mantoni, who was enjoying none of these fine feelings, talked away. Probably neither of these dreamy kids was listening to him, but that was no great matter. He had spent years talking to people who were not listening. If you went on long enough, they listened.

Alf's shop was in a turning off New Oxford Street and not far from the top end of Drury Lane. It was a small shop, with one window, over which was his sign, *Tricks, Jokes and Novelties*. The window was filled with a fascinating assortment of the tricks, jokes and novelties. There were perpetually overturned ink bottles, dinner buns that squeaked, cigars that exploded, pencils that would do anything but write, imitation beetles and spiders and bluebottles, match-boxes that went hopping away if you touched them, false noses and popping eyes and sets of moustaches on cards. But the best thing of all was a little hand-printed notice at the side of the window, saying, simply and superbly: *Magic Taught.*

"And what more do you want?" said Mr. Mantoni, pointing to this notice. "Magic Taught. After the third lesson, you're allowed to use Aladdin's ring, and after the sixth you're given Aladdin's lamp. By the time you've had ten lessons, you've had a go with the ring, the lamp, magic carpet, various invisible cloaks, and know all the chief *geni* by name. There's Alf, demonstrating a trick. Won't disturb him for a minute."

They were all in the doorway now, looking through the glass upper half of the door into the shop. The interior was even more fascinating than the window. It too was small and very crowded with strange things. There was a full-size imitation skeleton. There were dozens of masks, clowns and Chinese, wolves and bears. There were strings of silk flags, gigantic dice, playing cards a foot high, and mysterious cabinets. On one side of the counter was a youth with his mouth wide open and staring hard. On the other side was Alf, a little thin man, with a big head and a flat wizened face. He looked like a gnome. But there was also still something rather Chinese about him, some remaining traces of Prince Chang Lung. He was holding in front of the youth, who looked as if he were about to taste it, a shining little metal box with collapsible sides. Very quickly and neatly Alf flipped the sides down, then peered through the framework of the box at the youth, to show that there could not possibly be anything inside the box. With three deft movements, Alf closed the sides of the box again, tapped the top with an air of negligent wizardry, then opened the top and took out of the box a bright green square of silk. Then he winked at the youth, and Edward and Rose nudged one another happily. This was all right, this was going to be fun. Alf then repeated the process, opening and closing the box, but this time taking out of it a square of scarlet silk.

"I don't see how he does that, do you?" said Rose.

"Yes," said Mr. Mantoni. with a groan. "Terrible little trick. Not that poor old Alf doesn't do it very nicely, considering that that young fellow there is smelling and almost licking the box. But—bless me!—I've known the time when Alf would have made that young chap himself disappear in five seconds. However, he's sold it—the deal's done—and we can go in."

They waited until the young man, who was now clutching the box but had not closed his mouth yet, opened the door, and then they crowded in and seemed to fill the shop. The two magicians, so very different in appearance and yet with something in common, a something that belonged to their profession, perhaps an odd combination of shrewd glances, quick hands, and a rather detached, whimsical air, greeted one another gravely, cordially, two wizards meeting in the depths of the forest.

"Fred, old boy," said Alf, shaking hands.

"Alf, old boy," said Mr. Mantoni. "Thought I'd look you up."

"Very glad to see you, Fred."

"And I've brought a pretty girl to see you—Miss—er——"

"Salter," said Rose.

"You have, Fred, a very pretty girl," said Alf, smiling at Rose, and making her blush as they shook hands. "And this is her young man. Don't deny it. I can tell. Glad to see you too. Come into the back and we'll have a cup of tea." He led the way, opening a door with frosted glass panels, into a back room that was a delightful higgledy-piggledy. Very snug too, with a bright fire and an old cooking range and a kettle singing away on the hob. A tall shambling lad rose from the hearth, where he had been making toast.

"Roger," Alf said to him, "you look after the shop now. If they just want jokes and stuff, you can look after 'em, but if they want a trick, you'd better tell me. Funny thing about that lad," he added, as Roger disappeared, "can't do the simplest trick—and you know what these tricks are, Fred, they get out for amateurs—not to save his life. Wants to be a conjurer. Give his ears for it. But ruins every trick he tries to show 'em. Born clumsy. Now make yourselves at home."

Rose and Edward looked about them delightedly. This was much better than the shop, for not only had it some of the same queer things in it, but it also had a bench with fine litter of tools and pots of glue on it, scores of mysterious professional photographs and blueprints, Oriental furnishings that were shabby but still vaguely magnificent, all mixed up with a cosy elfish domesticity. Rose was given the only arm-chair; Edward and Mr.

Mantoni perched themselves on Prince Chang Lung's painted stools, while Alf hopped about, producing out of nothing various cups and saucers and plates and a butter dish and a pot of jam.

"We all met in the British Museum, Alf," said Mr. Mantoni. "I still like to go there."

"I used to," said Alf, without pausing in his tea-for-four illusion. "Wonderful props in there. And y'know, lot of those old chaps were just illusionists, like us. Called themselves priests then, but that's what they were."

"I believe you're right too, Alf. We'd have done well out of it then. Running our own temple and plenty of burnt offerings and what not."

Alf, turning round, the teapot in his hand, looked solemnly at Rose and Edward. "As I've said to Fred here more than once, there's a lot of conjuring goes on in this world that isn't called that. Haven't I, Fred? Now *we're* honest with it. Quickness of the hand deceives the eye. You know we're cheating you. Don't make any bones about it. These other chaps say nothing."

"Do you mean card-sharpers?" asked Edward.

"Oh—that's nothing. Card-sharpers! Make me laugh. Fred, you remember that time we both got on the train to Liverpool just before the Grand National——?"

"I do, Alf. You were on at the Empire and I was going to the Argyle."

"That's it. And those three fellows—sharpers written all over 'em—asked us—*us*—to have a game with 'em. Oh, dear, dear, dear! We had a game with 'em all right, all right." And Alf chuckled.

Mr. Mantoni chuckled too. "They thought they'd take us on at Nap. Alf had a trick pack in his pocket, and ended—just when they'd begun to wonder where they were—by showing 'em a Nap hand with five aces of spades in it."

"But I'm not talking about sharpers," Alf continued, looking solemn now. "I'm thinking about a lot of other people. Illusionists, and they never let on. Doctors and lawyers and politicians and financiers. What are they doing half their time? Tricks—pulling the rabbit out of the hat—sawing the lady in two—asking you to watch their right hands while their left hands are making your money disappear—and not telling you anything about it. We're honest. We tell you."

"Alf's right," said Mr. Mantoni. "Funny thing is too—we make our living by deceiving people, but I never knew a good magician yet who wasn't as straight as a die. Isn't that so, Alf?"

"It is so, Fred. Only dishonest for fun, we are."

"Well, then, give this nice girl a good cup of tea," said Mr. Mantoni, in a droll way.

"Just what I was going to do. Now," he said to Rose, passing the cup, "I think you'll like that."

"Oh!" cried Rose, after thanking him and taking the cup.

"What's the matter?" The two magicians leaned forward, gravely. Edward looked too. The liquid in Rose's cup, which certainly appeared to have been poured out of the teapot a minute ago, was bright blue.

"Something wrong there," said Mr. Mantoni solemnly.

"Doesn't look right, does it?" said Alf anxiously.

Rose began laughing, not so much at the trick and at her own surprise as at the whole scene, this queer little room and its owner, like an elf, and Mr. Mantoni, the large magician, funny and yet a trifle sinister, and Edward looking across and not knowing whether to be annoyed or amused, and the firelight playing on the Chinese things and the masks and old photographs and flags and bunches of artificial flowers. Many a time afterwards she returned in memory to this room again, remote as a room buried in some city on another planet, and she could hardly believe she had been there in reality, that it was not a cosy episode in some old dream. Even now, it had a dreamlike quality. One shiver, and it might be gone, and she would be back in the pantry at Cumberland Square or at Raeburn's shop or—and this was more likely, for all these London places had been touched, misted over, with unreality—solidly back in the kitchen in Slater Street. So although she laughed, there was a tenderness, a little catch of the heart and the throat, in her laughter.

They all laughed, and Rose was given an ordinary and quite nice cup of tea, and they all had tea and toast and jam. It was very cosy and friendly. Edward and Rose were content to munch and listen, frequently exchanging glances that were better than words, while Mr. Mantoni and his friend asked one another what had become of old So-and-so, and were reminiscent over the good old days when music-halls were crowded to the roof and all the boys and girls in the profession who were any good were out on the road, with hardly a vacant date. Mr. Mantoni, the gloomier of the two, had nothing good to say about the days since the War, the only days that Rose and Edward had really known.

"It's no use, Alf," he said finally. "You can't get away from it. Those were good days. These aren't. I don't mean just for us, but for everybody. That war did something. It's never been the same since. There isn't the fun and the easiness and the character. Too many machines. Too much of this American stuff. Too much of a rush for nowhere, and to hell with it when you get there. Too many forms to fill up. Too much dope of all kinds, and not enough honest booze. Too much sex and sex appeal, and not enough larks and sprees. Not enough variety, our sort and every other sort." He lit his pipe, blew out a cloud of smoke, and stared gloomily into it. "It was all right then. Nothing waiting for you round the corner. At least we thought there wasn't. Now there's something round the corner all the time. Everybody knows it. You can see it in their faces. What's next? What's coming this time? So they all go running round in circles, kidding themselves they're having a good time, all doing the same things, taking the word of command from the papers and the wireless and Hollywood. And they know that just round the corner, there's something waiting for 'em. So there's no easiness, no fun, and nobody has time to get ripe. No, it's no use, Alf."

Alf had lit his pipe too—it was a large curved pipe, with a Turk's head carved on the bowl—and now he took it out of his mouth, blew three magnificent rings, and pointed the stem at his old friend. "I know what you mean, Fred. And I expect that's more than these two do. Eh?"

Edward admitted that he didn't quite understand. Rose said nothing, and felt very young and feminine.

"Quite so," said Alf. "But I know what he means. Yes, Fred, but it won't do, it won't do. It's just old man's talk."

"Speak for yourself, Alf," Mr. Mantoni protested. "I'm no old man."

"Well, you're no chicken, and neither am I," said Alf, regarding him quizzically. "But anyhow, you're talking like an old man. Don't blame you. Hard for us to talk any other way. You see, Fred, the world's moving on and we aren't. We don't belong any more. This shop doesn't. Nobody'd really miss it, if it burned down to-night. Same for us. Our bit of magic's all right, but now they've got their own kind. Remember the time, Fred, when the old Bioscope was a turn, and the least important turn on the bill——?"

"Yes, they all used to go out to the bar."

"Well, look at it now. The films!"

"You look at it. I don't want to."

"No, but everybody else does. They've moved on, and you haven't. I don't know where they're all going to, but my old Dad—he worked in a vinegar brewery in Bermondsey—told me he didn't know what would become of me when I went into the profession——"

"That's different."

"Not it. Open your eyes, Fred. You look at the boys and girls walking round to-day. Look at these two—if you don't mind me being personal. What's wrong with 'em? What's wrong with all of 'em? Nothing, except they're twenty and we're sixty, that's all. I can remember—and so can you, Fred—when the old folks—they were all chapel-goers, then, and strict—thought music-halls were samples of hell. Now you're talking like them, except that where they said chapels, you say music-halls, and where they said music-halls, you say picture theatres. There isn't much of your kind of fun any longer, but there's plenty of another kind. They're just as free and easy in their own way as we were in ours. And as for not waiting for things round corners, I think we'd have done better if, instead of singing 'The Soldiers of the Queen,' we'd have done a bit of wondering what there was round the corner. Some of those old Union Jack patriotic please-give-me-your-kind-applause turns we knew would make these boys and girls sick. And you know, Fred, just forget the good times—everybody'll have good times whenever they live—and remember some of the others. Lot of dirt about, all kinds, too much booze, too much bullying, all sorts of nastiness. These two wouldn't stand for it. Would you, dear? Just stand up there a minute."

Rose, very pink, stood where he placed her, wondering what was going happen. Edward wondered too, but was busy admiring her. And so, indeed, were the other two men.

"Not going to hurt you, dear," said Alf in a professional tone. "If I had the act going now, I'd make this little lady a good offer."

"Make a fine feed," said Mr. Mantoni. "Said it the first time I saw her. In my dressing room, wasn't it, up at Islington? I remember."

"Now take this hat," said Alf, producing one from nowhere. It was an old silk hat, much the worse for wear, or rather for its long professional life, during which it had probably never been properly worn. "Nothing in it, is there? Make sure, dear, make sure. Never take the magician's word for it. Nothing in it, eh? Let your young man have a peep inside it. Absolutely nothing, eh? All right then. Give the word, Fred."

"With pleasure, *maestro,*" said Mr. Mantoni gravely, standing to one side. "One! Two! *Three!*"

Alf plunged both hands into the hat, which Rose was still holding, and out of it, in lightning succession, brought strings of little flags and coloured silks, artificial blossoms by the dozen, several flowering plants, and, at the end, a large Oriental umbrella that looked far too big to have been hidden up his sleeve or hidden anywhere.

"Very neat, Alf," said Mr. Mantoni, with solemn professional approval. "I always said you never had an equal with that stuff. Lasting well, too."

"And that, ladies and gentlemen, concludes our afternoon's entertainment," said Alf.

"Thanking you for your kind attention and appreciation," said Mr. Mantoni, in the same tone. "Well, it's about time I went home to put the rabbit in my tail coat pocket for the Tottenham Freemasons."

"And any time you're round here," said Alf to Edward and Rose, shaking hands, "just pop in."

They thanked him and went out with Mr. Mantoni, who left them, to catch his bus, in New Oxford Street. It had been nice in there, but it was nicer still to be alone again, walking arm-in-arm, looking at the shops and talking about themselves. It was about half-past five now, and they had a whole evening in front of them. Edward would have liked to have left these lighted streets far behind, to have plunged into the friendly darkness of some country lane, but this was London, not Haliford. They knew that round them for miles and miles the streets went on and on, the houses and lamp-posts and buses and tram-lines and shops were still there, and there was no reasonable end to the city. They were lost in its dense heart for this evening, at least. There were parks, of course, but both of them dismissed the idea of visiting them, very quickly and without giving a reason, which was the same in each of their minds, namely, a suspicion that there was something rather sinister about London parks after dusk. They agreed that it would be nice, very soon, to have a proper meal, because the magician's tea and toast would not last them through the evening, and neither of them had eaten much earlier in the day. And then they would have to decide where to spend the evening. To help them, Edward bought an evening paper, but did not look at it then. They walked slowly along New Oxford Street, got bumped a bit now and then, for it was the time when people leave their work and go charging along in their newly found freedom, not caring whom they bump. But Rose and Edward did not mind.

They turned down Charing Cross Road and had a look at the shops where all the latest "song hits" fill the windows, and Rose wished they could buy some and then go home—a vague but delicious little home of their own with a piano in the corner—and pick out the notes together. And Edward told her about Jack Scrutton and his "London Rhythmic Collegians," and Rose said she would like to meet them, and Edward, feeling a trifle jealous, described them in such a way as to make them look very silly, and Rose laughed, and so it was all right. This brought them to Cambridge Circus, and they crossed there and walked round the Palace Theatre and so came into the lower half of Shaftesbury Avenue, where there are so many theatres, and shops that sell foreign papers, and all manner of strange exciting places and things. All the theatres had their signs lit up, and one or two of them had people waiting already at the Pit doors. They stopped once or twice to look at the photographs of the actors and actresses and scenes from the plays, and Rose told him about the actors and actresses who used to come into the Copper Kettle Café, and Edward, secretly impressed by this mysterious rich experience of hers and perhaps a bit jealous too because he was not part of it, felt all kinds of queer confused emotions, but only said it must have been very interesting, and gripped her hand tightly in the crook of his bent arm. There are times when Piccadilly Circus really looks like some kind of gigantic circus, with the buses roaring round and round like well-trained monsters, and the coloured lights flashing above them; and this was one of the times. They stood at the corner, watching everything. It did seem, at that moment, the very centre of the world—and a very delightful, gay, spangled world too. It was a clear evening, but no stars were to be seen above the glittering signs, the fiery goblets pouring out wines of golden light. Piccadilly Circus itself was now a sort of star.

They had their evening meal in that very Corner House where Edward had eaten before going to see Uncle Alfred. The same marble splendour; the same band sending out its sugar-crested waves of Puccini; the same thousand-headed crowd of diners; but now what a difference! Here he was, sitting with Rose. Remembering that other time so vividly, looking back at that smaller, pathetic Edward, he began telling her about those first few days in London. And then about that night when he had waited so long outside the back door of Robert Raeburn's shop, and how he had imagined her out with some other fellow.

"And I wasn't even there at all," cried Rose, looking at him with great tender eyes. "I'd left then. Run away—like the silly chump I was. And you were waiting."

"Hours and hours."

"Isn't it funny nothing told you I wasn't there?"

"Oh—I don't know. Why should it be?"

"Well—somehow—we ought to know—when we're thinking so much about somebody," she said slowly, struggling with the thought that there was something ill-managed, curiously lop-sided about a world in which you could flash messages from England to Australia in a second or two but in which two lovers, in the same city, busy thinking about one another, could not exchange the most urgent signals across a few streets.

"I remember when I was ever so little," she continued. "I hadn't gone to school because of something, and it was winter, and I was in the kitchen with mother and she was baking—I used to like it when she was baking, and I used to make a little loaf for myself—and I was looking out of the window and it was beginning to snow. There were big flakes, I remember. It was all blue and white and cold outside, and nice and warm and red—with the big fire—inside, you know. And I was staring and a bit dreamy and thinking about the Hans Andersen fairy stories I used to read then—there was a lot of snow in them—and then all of a sudden I didn't see the snow at all, I saw my Aunt Edith's back room—I used to go there a lot because I was very fond of my Aunt Edith—she's dead now—and saw her too, and she was all twisted up and moaning, and I said: 'Oh—mother—my Aunt Edith's hurt herself. I've just seen her.' And mother said: 'Go on with you. Don't tell me them tales.' And I started crying, and said I really had seen her. And then mother didn't know what to do, but when she'd got all the loaves into the oven, she told me to stay there, and she went to my Aunt Edith's and she had hurt herself, just as I said, and she never properly got over it. Wasn't that strange?"

And the eyes that looked across at him were the eyes of the little girl who stared out of the window at the falling snow, and, though he was busy eating a steak-and-kidney pudding and had his mouth full of that delectable richness, though the two of them were on a tiny island in a loud sea of dining and chattering and Italian opera, he wanted there and then to gather into his arms the Rose sitting there, the Rose who had looked out of that window long ago, all the Roses there had ever been. He realised that the vision she had had of her aunt—something unknown in his experience—was nothing compared with the sheer magic of her life to him, that there was nothing in Hans Andersen that had more of the true fairy-tale feeling than the simple picture he had of her sitting there on that distant baking day watching the snow. He did not use any of these words to himself, but what they convey—indeed, a great deal more than they can convey—was what he richly felt at that instant.

"Where shall we go afterwards?" asked Rose, with that deeply feminine combination of passivity and sharp expectation—that look of what-wonderful-thing-is-to-happen-to-me-next?—which always enchants the attendant male, and helps to explain why so many confident and aggressively know-their-own-mind women are so often left to entertain themselves.

Edward picked up the paper he had bought. There was enough explosive material on its front page—a conference had broken down here, there was a crisis somewhere else, grave warnings had been issued in yet another place—to blow Rose and Edward and any possible children and grandchildren they might have, clean off the face of this planet—but Edward never gave a glance at it but plunged straight into the middle, where he knew the entertainments were advertised. He gave these advertisements a shrewd Haliford look, but even so he did not notice that their size and fervour were in exact disproportion to the importance and merit of the wares they advertised, that a foolish film, travestying history and human nature, here to-day and forgotten in six months, needed a whole quarter page of superlatives, was "the triumph and wonder of the year"; that a bad play, made out of bits of former successes, falsely written and acted, announced itself as "the season's best offering . . . a masterpiece"; while a good play, composed and produced with honesty and real care, was merely "well worth seeing" in small print; and Beethoven's Ninth Symphony had a bald line or two to say that it would be performed at 8.15.

"Are they"—Rose hesitated—"still doing those dances at the Coliseum? I'd like to see them again."

"Oh, did you go there?"

"I was taken."

Edward looked hard at her.

She had to explain now about Francis Woburn, and it took her some time. She had hardly started before she realised with a shock, partly of fear, partly of delight, that Edward was jealous. This was absurd, of course, because she hadn't thought anything at all of Francis Woburn, had not the least desire ever to see him again; and yet while she told herself how ridiculous this jealousy was, and was rather frightened to see a certain sharpening and hardening of the dark young face opposite, she could not help feeling a delicious little thrill. He was jealous.

"Did he write to you again?" Edward asked, rather sharply.

"I don't know, you see—because I ran away just after that," she explained hastily. "As a matter of fact, there was a letter—but with Beatrice carrying on so, I forgot about it. I mean, it might have come from him. I don't know."

"If you had stayed on, and he had written," Edward

pursued, "would you have gone out with him again?"

"Oh—I don't know. It doesn't matter, does it?"

"No," said Edward, looking intensely miserable, "it doesn't."

"But it doesn't."

"No, I suppose not."

"Edward, you *are* silly. It really doesn't. All the time I was out with him, I was wishing it was you. I didn't care at all about him. Not the least bit. And I don't think," though she did, but this was clearly not the time to say so, "he cared anything about me. It was just a fancy. Because he'd noticed me that morning. I expect he'd plenty of money, and had to have somebody to go with, every night."

"I'm glad I didn't see you," said Edward darkly.

"I'm not," cried Rose, sparkling away, trying to lighten that darkness. "I'd have come running to you, never mind Mr. Fancy Woburn, honestly I would!" And that did it. The face lit up again. The whole Corner House went on to a higher voltage.

"Now where shall we go?"

"You have a look," he said, handing over the paper. "There doesn't seem much."

Not much indeed! In one place, there was this Ninth Symphony, life taken through the shadows of death and then transfigured and resurrected, in immortal sound. In another place, four string players, the greatest of their kind in the world, men who had slaved together perfecting into a miracle their technique, four men who had become like one passionate voice, were performing their quartets.

In yet another hall, a stout middle-aged German woman, who had turned herself into a kind of great humanised bird, was offering an hour of the magical winters and springs, the cold dead maidens, the wandering festive students, the eternal romantic youth of Schubert. In one theatre, there was a production of *Twelfth Night*; and for a few shillings you could wander again in the bright Illyrian gardens, divide your heart between Viola and Olivia, laugh and wonder again at Sir Toby and Malvolio, Aguecheek and the bitter-sweet singing clown—"What is love? 'tis not hereafter." In another theatre, there were half a dozen Bernard Shaws, in a rich variety of costume and make-up, debating among themselves with clashing steely wit and at a white heat of intellectual passion. In another theatre, hard to get at and nearly bankrupt, you could hear the snapping harp string and the thuds of the axes destroying the cherry orchard, and be moved to the deepest tenderness you had ever known in a playhouse. Nor was that all. It was only the beginning. That night, a precise little man, peering through his glasses at his notes on the table and shyly avoiding any direct glance at the faces in front of him, would undertake to prove, by complicated mathematical reasoning, that we are undying creatures in an endless adventure among new dimensions; and elsewhere, a young scientist, scarlet-faced and mumbling, would tell his audience that he had found evidence of bacterial life in the very heart of the meteorites that have come to us from outer space and that therefore life is not confined to this planet but exists, at some stage, everywhere in the universe; and a retired engineer, speaking in a suburban town hall, would outline his new economic theory and show that as things are we are busy cheating and starving ourselves; and a poet and scholar would take his handful of listeners into the clear wonderland of the Chinese art of the great periods, so that they would forget themselves and London and all this age, would know a new delight, simply because a Mongolian artist was enraptured by the sight of a branch of peach blossom, one morning a thousand years ago. And that was not all, still only the beginning. There are fruit trees in this forest of a city.

But Rose and Edward, being children of their age, decided in favour of a large picture theatre, not far away. The prices were monstrous, but Edward, defying a whole ancestry of West Riding Fieldings, cheerfully bought two seats in the balcony. In that huge, soft, cushioned dimness, sitting very close, they felt cosily alone. There they were, almost sharing one arm-chair, and before them was the gigantic magic window of the screen. In a theatre or at a concert, they would have become part of an audience, would have been compelled to surrender themselves, but there is not this compulsion—only a fraction of it—with the films, which, if they find you solitary, still leave you solitary, but if, as so often happens, they find you one of an entranced pair, do not disturb that entrancement. It is probably for this reason that an evening at the films is seldom a waste and an irritation, just as it is seldom, perhaps never, a glorious event. Rose and Edward, occasionally clasping hands, always pressed close together, were far more acutely conscious of one another than they were of the entertainment offered them. But they enjoyed that too. There was a coloured Silly Symphony, which was, like so much of life, at once rather beautiful and grotesquely silly; it was life seen quickly and simply, and set to music. The chief film of the evening, which was a Hollywood musical comedy affair, was not at all like life, and had been more carefully removed from it than the wildest of Mr. Disney's fancies. It was all about a lively young man (who was more eloquent with his feet than with any other part of him) who pretended to be a millionaire, and a rich young girl (who also preferred dancing to conversation as a possible means of exchanging ideas) who pretended to be a poor manicurist; and they fell in love in an impossible hotel in a seaside resort that was probably on Venus; and they and the staff of this hotel and some of its guests (nearly all good-looking girls) danced a lot, ran in and out of bedrooms, and sang the very newest of those American dance-tune songs that Rose liked so much, songs that did not really belong to her own life and character at all but that did, in their own banal fashion, express something deeply American and very real, a sort of dark inner despair lit with stabs and glitterings of sexual excitement. She and Edward, in a state of mind far removed from this of the songs, listened to them with great pleasure, and enjoyed the rapid but smooth nonsense of the film, which was indeed a triumph of skill and organisation, of clever men working together for one end, men with everything at their finger-tips but real art, the desire to reveal the vision of life, the honest unfolding of the mind, the cry from the heart, all of which they had never known or had said good-bye to, long ago, on *The Chief* between Chicago and Los Angeles. Rose and Edward, however, being children of this age, may have found more in the film than would superficially appear from this description of it; there may have been an almost profound appeal in the rapidity of its tempo alone; its cheerful irresponsibility, dimmed only by the easiest sentiment, may have meant more to them than we can guess; and even its world may have been an amusing parody of the world that they preferred to see, a world of quick change, of easy light relations with people and things, without rigid standards and heavy responsibilities, cleansed of despair and madness and death. We cannot tell—and neither could they—what exactly it meant to them. But they told one another they had enjoyed it. And certainly, in the truest sense, they had enjoyed themselves.

It was nearly half-past ten when they left, and time for Rose to be hurrying back to Cumberland Square. They came out into that extra-dimensional, oddly solid world that lies in wait for us all after the films, and which is at once curiously exciting and intimidating and promising, as perhaps those extra-dimensional worlds of the little lecturer will be for us all one distant day. It was that hour when there is a lull—like those mysterious pauses in a roomful of talk—in London's evening, long after the theatres have opened but before they have closed, well past dinner and not yet supper-time; and the West End, though by no means deserted, yet had a rather vacant air, as if the streets were illuminated for some still distant event; and the bus they found let them half its top to themselves.

They told one another that the afternoon and evening had gone all too quickly—"flown" was the word—yet actually each of them could look back, and did, without mentioning it, upon a rich crowded tract of time they had had together, seemingly as long as all the weeks when they had not found one another again. The meeting at the pillar-box, the bus ride, the British Museum, Mr. Mantoni, his friend Alf, the walk through the streets, the meal at the Corner House, the pictures—it was stupendous. They had spent a little lifetime together, and now they had to say good-bye to it, to die a little death.

Cumberland Square was deserted, misty, cold. They stood close to the railings round the bit of garden and lawn in the centre, now a mere dead-leaf smell in the dark. The warm sweet weight of Rose was in Edward's tightened arms. Her face was a mysterious pale oval. There was something faintly salty about her cheek and lips when he kissed her, as if they were already haunted by tears. There they clung together in the last dumb ecstasy of the day. Now was the time for Edward to utter great and memorable things, for Rose to treasure and repeat to herself during the long days, the cold nights, of her exile into the wilderness of Holt-Ibstocks'. But he could not say them.

"I must be going," she told him. "Say something, Edward."

He did his best. She had to be content with it.

Then: "What about Sunday?" he asked.

"I can't, this Sunday. It isn't my day," she said, not without hesitation and shame.

"Oh—that's rotten. You oughtn't to stay there,

Rose, really you oughtn't."

"I won't long. But don't let's talk about that now. I'll have to be going in."

"But when am I going to see you?" cried Edward, the despairing male, who did not want merely to treasure things said and repeat them to himself, but wanted the living creature beside him.

"Listen," said Rose, and very unnecessarily, for if there was one person in London that night who was being listened to, it was she at that moment, "I believe I could get off Tuesday. Not in the afternoon. But at night, I believe I could work it. I'll be outside that Corner House about seven—if you really want me to."

"Don't be silly. I'll be there."

"I must go."

"Oh!" A sharp cry of misery from Edward.

It was she now who kissed him, and there were both passion and pity in this last kiss. It was so long for him to wait, and he was so impatient. She could wait now, warming herself in that cold house with the thought of him. And having kissed him, she broke away and ran across to the gate into the basement, turned as she opened it, waved to the dim figure, and ran down the steps. He heard the door down there close sharply after her. Immediately that tall house was touched by a glamour that all the city round it had lost. He waited a moment, perhaps for some last miracle. Nothing happened. He turned away, and now already was adrift on a confused dark tide of feeling that would keep running until he saw her again. So ended their day.

XIII

THERE was nothing friendly about that Tuesday. It was not blanketed in November fog, but it was a darkish, wettish, thick, sodden sort of day. There was no sky above the old stone forest. Night had never left its narrower tracks and deeper hollows. Little patches of darkness there waited for the great darkness to return. It had not retreated far. The sun never showed its face. This was no day for woodcutters' children to be out wandering. Goblins were peering and pointing and gibbering. The witches were mumbling over their brews. In the depths of the maze there was a reek of boiled rat and toad, a whiff of the curdling fat of hanged men. In the shadows here, through the steam there, faintly lit with hellfire, we may catch a glimpse or two of a goblin face, a witch's eye. But we may not know what we are looking at. And there will be nothing in the newspapers to tell us.

Oddly enough, on that Tuesday afternoon, only a few hours before they were due to meet again, Edward was not thinking about Rose, nor Rose about Edward. For once, both of them had other things to think about. And if we begin with Edward, perhaps we can find our way somehow through the dark tangle to Rose.

Edward was trying to see Mr. Baddeley of the Mawson Office Equipment Company, in Westminster. He had an introduction to Mr. Baddeley from a pupil of Mr. Finland's.

It was, as might be expected of a pupil of Mr. Finland's, a very slender, shaky little introduction. Even Edward knew that, but he was determined to make use of it. He might be a tremendous fellow now as a lover, but he was still a unit in the economic system, one who demanded goods and services and must therefore also supply them. And London at present did not seem to have much use for the services of Edward Fielding, who was beginning to feel that he would be better off back home, where at least a few people knew him. London might be more prosperous than Haliford, but it did not seem anxious to share its prosperity with Edward. Nor, for that matter, with a great many other people, whose depressing acquaintance he was now making. This last week he had discovered that he was one of a great legion of the workless, all going to and from the labour exchanges, all looking up and answering advertisements, all waiting and waiting outside doors and *Enquiries* windows, all men who were finding it harder and harder to look "experienced, keen, efficient, and public school preferred," and easier and easier to look forlorn, unwanted. The state of most of them, Edward knew, was far worse than his, for he had nobody to keep but himself, and he still had some money left; but nevertheless he began to share their growing apathy and deepening despair. He had not felt much respect for himself as an employee of the Belvedere Trading Company; but now, as nobody's employee, an answerer of advertisements, a hanger-about, he felt even less respect for himself. He began to understand why old Rufus had allowed himself to be bullied so monstrously.

So far, all that London wanted him to do, it seemed, was either to invest a hundred pounds or so in some dubious project or to try and sell on commission, from door to door ("And don't forget," one chap had said, "you have to keep your foot against it or they'll shut the damned door in your face"), articles that were cheaper in the shops or that nobody in their senses would want to buy. Mr. Finland's pupil had told Mr. Finland that there was "an off chance" that Mr. Baddeley of the Mawson Office Equipment might want somebody, and Edward was in no mood to despise off chances. So here he was, in Westminster, with his shaky little letter of introduction.

Mr. Baddeley was a thin dark man, with brown stains under his eyes, not unlike Mr. Kelso of the Belvedere. When at last he came out, he glanced at Edward's letter of introduction with contempt, glanced at Edward with hardly less contempt, and then said, shortly, that he was sorry but there was nothing doing. His "sorry" was quite mechanical, obviously. He did not see Edward as an eager and anxious young man, deeply in love, desperate to make his way in the world. He did not really see him at all. As a real person, a fellow soul in the astounding adventure of life, Edward was simply not present in Mr. Baddeley's field of consciousness. Edward was merely a ghostly shape holding a ridiculous letter, and one of the minor nuisances of a beastly afternoon. Mr. Baddeley was in trouble, and worried. (He had recently bought a house out Harrow way, and was wondering now if he could really afford those monthly payments. He had also a son at a minor public school, and that took a bit of keeping up too.) One of his best customers, the Westminster Imperial Development Company, had given him a magnificent order for new office equipment, and was now complaining that its instructions had not been obeyed. Both filing cabinets were the wrong size; the two chairs were not of the requisite pattern; the handles of the desk drawers were not chromium-plated, as ordered. The Westminster Imperial had given precise instructions; and refused to take delivery of any odd filing cabinets, chairs, desks, that the Mawson Office Equipment Company saw fit to leave on its premises. "My God!" it exclaimed privately, "what a bad show!" And Mr. Baddeley had to admit that it was. So he was worried. This made him dismiss Edward at once and contemptuously, so that Edward left the place feeling hurt and angry, and was still feeling hurt and angry that night when he had to meet Rose.

The Westminster Imperial Development Company was also worried, but not, of course, about some trumpery order for office equipment. The Westminster Imperial worked on a big scale. It did not call itself *Imperial* for nothing. Men of all shades, from lemon-yellow to a purple-black, in all manner of distant places, planned and toiled to feed it. The word went out from those fine dignified office buildings, and deserts were torn open, little steamers disappeared up rivers into the dim rotting jungle, whole towns were built in the wilderness, hosts of people—managers, clerks, labourers, pimps, prostitutes—suddenly arrived or as suddenly vanished, machine-guns slashed the façades of tropical palaces. From any reasonable and civilised point of view, a good deal of its activity was sheer brigandage, but most of it was brigandage in a nice, neat, clean-handed style. You could even be a director of the Westminster Imperial and have the clearest conscience. This was because, following the refinements of our civilisation, you and it worked on the limited liability principle. All you did was to demand a certain result—a higher tariff, an increased turn-over, some little monopoly or other, a firm agreement, a definite concession—and then the people under you sent out their instructions demanding this same result, and so it went on, until perhaps somebody, somewhere—but of course a long way from the decencies of Westminster, probably in some God-forsaken place where, after all, nobody knows any better—might be compelled, in order to bring about this result, to do some rather dirty work. But whose fault was that? You did not ask for bribery, corruption, robbery, murder, massacre, revolution, war: had none of these things in your mind; you simply, in the way of business, asked for a certain result, merely a higher tariff or increased turn-over and so on, that you were surely entitled to demand by the very nature of your enterprise. This is the limited liability system, without which we should never get anywhere at all, and the Westminster Imperial people knew all about it. Sir Alfred Skidmore, the directing spirit of the vast concern, was naturally an old master of this limited liability. If he was worried, as he undoubtedly was, this Tuesday afternoon, it was not because his conscience was troubling him.

At a first glance, Sir Alfred looked the very pink and shining embodiment of a clear conscience. He was a rosy man about sixty, with a fine head of grey hair, eyes of the blue of distant ice, beautifully shaven cheeks, and an eighteen-guinea suit of dark West of England cloth. The most sceptical shareholder would have taken heart at once at the very sight of him. He produced the immediate vivid impression that a good character actor aims at. He was, in fact, one of the best and most highly paid character actors in London. The play had been going on for years, and nobody, not even Sir Alfred himself, knew what the fifth act would be like. Sitting at his desk, which was a genuine Chippendale (though its top was covered with devices that Chippendale never dreamed of), he frowned at the little gold pencil that had just stopped writing down figures, then pressed a button, spoke into a small black box, and asked for his confidential secretary and assistant, Gerald Ruthvere. Within a minute, a tall, exquisite figure of a young man had entered the room. He had a small head, crisp fair hair, restless smoky-grey eyes, a short upper lip, and a charming smile. Sir Alfred, who was old-fashioned enough to have enormous greenhouses at his place in Surrey, where he grew orchids, might have entertained the fancy, if he had been a fanciful man, that there was now standing by his side the largest and most successful of his hot-house growths, a talking and smiling orchid, beautiful and faintly rotten. Many generations of aristocratic and really distinguished personages, as far removed from the common bargaining and grabbing of life as Brahmans, had given this young man a superb outward stamp, so that at the first glance, or regarded hazily, he seemed the very peak and flower of young manhood; but on closer inspection, there appeared to be something wrong with the material that had taken that stamp, a slackness, a profound debility, a hint of corruption. He seemed a charming but fatal parody of those aristocratic ancestors, whose features he had taken and faintly blurred, just as his life here in this office—and his life outside, which often was by no means unconnected with the life inside it—was a shameful parody of their lives, passed at the side of kings. Having sold himself for money, this young man, like many of his kind, gave the impression that he had fewer reservations about what he was prepared to do for money than the commissionaire downstairs or the man selling newspapers outside the front door.

"Antill lands to-day, Gerald," said Sir Alfred. "He has that Columbian concession in his pocket. We had confirmation of that yesterday from our fellow at Bogotá. The French are after him, of course, but he's coming here first."

"I'm afraid he won't stay long, sir," said Ruthvere, with a faint smile. "I met him the last time he was over, and he told me then he didn't like London. Paris is his little holiday resort. It would be, of course."

"Of course," said Sir Alfred, somewhat absently. These two used the phrase a great deal in their conversations, possibly out of politeness—for each had a special world of his own and it was polite to assume that the other knew all about that world—but now and again with various shades of irony. "Well, we must keep him here a few days. It's imperative. We've come to no agreement yet with the

Dutch group, and until we do, we can't make a definite move."

"Quite," said Ruthvere, smiling again.

"If he gets over to Paris—well, we don't know what might happen. So he mustn't go, not before the end of the week. And that's up to you, Gerald. You know him, know the sort of fellow he is, and you must take him in hand—keep him amused here somehow."

"All right, sir. I can try. But——" And he paused, to let himself be interrupted.

"It's got to be done, Gerald. Absolutely imperative. And you know how to do that sort of thing. Can't do it myself, so it's no use my trying."

"Antill," said Ruthvere slowly, his smile reminiscent now, "has peculiar tastes, sir——"

"Yes, yes, I dare say." Sir Alfred waved a hand impatiently. This was limited liability operating. He did not want to know anything about Antill's peculiar tastes, would have nothing to do with them. All he asked was that the fellow should be kept amused for a day or two. "But that's your affair."

"I might be able to arrange one or two things that would amuse him," Ruthvere continued, softly. "The only thing is, sir, these things are apt to be rather expensive here——"

Sir Afred held up a hand, and looked up steadily at the young man. He read a faint mockery—perhaps of the limited liability principle—in that face, and called to his aid all his dignity and authority. "So long as you keep him here, Gerald, the Board will be prepared to be generous in the matter of an entertaining allowance. This is a very big thing indeed. I'll be getting into touch with him myself to-night, and you'd better come along, and in the meantime go ahead and make your—er—arrangements——"

The young man smiled once more, delightfully this time, and then returned to his own room, where the smile still remained while he turned the pages of a small notebook. Finally, he took up the telephone, and asked for a private line.

"Mrs. Hubarth, please. Mr. Gerald Ruthvere. Oh—hello, Violet! No, it's ages, isn't it? But we men of business, y'know—eh? By the way, how *is* business, Violet? I see. Well, now, am I wrong in imagining that you've run across a fellow called Antill? That's what he calls himself, though I doubt if it's his real name. Probably had dozens. Yes, that's the fellow. Yes, oil. South America, chiefly. Ah—you sound brighter already. Yes, he lands here to-day, and I have to keep him amused for a night or two, very much amused, and I thought you might have an idea or two. Good! Well then, Violet, let's meet for a cocktail or two and talk about it. What time? Excellent!"

In her small sitting-room in St. John's Wood, Mrs. Hubarth, having put down the receiver and scribbled a line on the pad, looked thoughtful. She was a handsome woman of indeterminate age. Her rather long, smooth face curved back slightly from the cheek-bones. A full red mouth was painted on it. The thin arched eyebrows, expressing a perpetual surprise at the world that their owner did not feel, were also painted on it. The whole face was as unwrinkled as a peach. If it had been a porcelain mask, the years could not have left fewer records on its surface. And when the heavy white-and-blue eyelids were nearly closed, as they were at this moment, this was a face bewildering in its combined suggestion of ripe feminine maturity and complete lack of experience; it was that of a life-sized and faintly ageing doll. But when she opened her eyes, as she did now, the arched brows, the painted meaningless mouth, the whole blank page of her face, might have been nothing but a decorated little window through which she stared at the world. All the subtle little signs and marks of experience that should have been visible on her face had somehow taken refuge in those full, hazel-green eyes, had alternately frozen their surface and set fire to their depths, until they looked out with chrysolite hardness. But being eyes and not stones, they remembered what they had seen, and what they had seen had not been good to see.

She rang, and then went nearer the fire, making herself comfortable in a low chair. It was a house of some size; this small sitting-room of hers was on the second floor; and so it was some time before the bell was answered. The woman who finally appeared was middle-aged, dressed in black, and had the rather square, tough, leathery face, with prominent cheek-bones, that seems to belong to so many Frenchwomen of a certain class. This one had cunning little eyes, a great gash of a mouth, and an evil chronicle of wrinkles. She looked like a housekeeper who was at once more and less than a housekeeper. She had a conspiratorial air. The room grew stuffy with dirty secrets the moment she had entered it. Mrs. Hubarth immediately repeated to her the substance of her conversation over the telephone with Gerald Ruthvere. The woman listened carefully, with her eyes fixed on those of her mistress or employer, who looked straight at her. No limited liability nonsense here.

"I am seeing Gerald Ruthvere later to-day," Mrs. Hubarth continued, "and I'll know more then. But in the meantime we've got to be thinking. This has come at an awkward time, Toinette."

The woman, whose very name, Toinette, must have been dragged down leagues of grimy corridors from some bright lost world of youth and gaiety, nodded grimly. Then she added, reflectively: "But, Madame, it shood be olright. We can get—oh!—Pheelees, Mabell——"

"No, they're no good," said Mrs. Hubarth sharply. "Not for this man. Don't you remember him? Let me see." She closed her eyes, as if to find him in that darkness. "He's biggish. Clean-shaven. No particular features . . ."

The man who was staring out of the boat train, as it slid into Waterloo, at that very moment, might be said to have no particular features. His large face might have been hastily modelled in putty. Only the eyes were alive. They were very full and an odd light brown. He was one of those men without nationality, without background, without roots, who are for ever travelling by aeroplane or express liner from Ritz to Ritz, who make money without having any offices or warehouses or factories or even employees of any kind, who speak four or five languages fluently but always with a slight puzzling accent, who are not known to any public or newspapers anywhere but are known to certain financial magnates and politicians, are dimly recognised by head-waiters and passport officials and pursers, and who seem to have no relatives and no friends. They are one of the peculiar minor products of our age. They seem to belong to it as the nervous currencies, the armies of workless, the talking films, cocktails, international dance bands, dictators with fancy salutes, and the ceaseless battle for oil-fields, all belong to it. Ferdinand Antill knew something about currencies, the unemployed, films, cocktails, dance bands and dictators, and he knew a great deal more about the struggle for oil, for it was mainly on this that he thrived, if such personages can be said to thrive. He left the train for the platform with the indifferent air of a man who is neither coming home nor arriving abroad. There was nobody to meet him. He did not expect anybody. Nevertheless, once or twice he looked about him sharply.

There were two men on the platform whom Ferdinand Antill did not notice. They saw him, however, and at once contrived to efface themselves. But when he finally got into a taxi, they were not far away. The larger of the two nodded to the other, who muttered: "Okay. I got him," and then took a taxi himself. The one who remained and who had spoken stood for a moment in the gloom of that Waterloo exit, and lit a cigarette. In the sudden flare of the match, his face looked horrible. It was almost a concave face. The cheek-bones and the ridge of the square chin stood out, while the cheeks themselves were hollow, the nose very flat, and the mouth merely a thin line. It was a face without colour but with an almost phosphorescent pallor. It was more than unhealthy. It looked as if it existed, and had always existed, in a world far removed from all questions of health or illness, an underground of skeletons, giant fungi, blind worms. The commonplace description—"a figure of the underworld"—was here a phrase of genius. The man was still young, but there was no known quality of youth to be observed in him. His childhood could not have been more than twenty years away, yet it seemed impossible that it had ever been there at all. His cigarette alight, he stayed where he was for a moment or two longer, looking in front of him with narrowed eyes. He might have been fixing in his memory, beyond the possibility of error, the appearance of Ferdinand Antill, who had just been carefully pointed out to him. And any policeman of experience—certainly, any policeman of experience in the United States, where so many of these drugged rats still flourish—seeing him there, would have recognised him at once as "a killer."

The London police, however, were not interested yet either in this fellow or in Ferdinand Antill, who was not yet even a name to them. That afternoon, Scotland Yard was thinking about its neighbour, Trafalgar Square, where there might soon be trouble. The Communists had arranged to hold a demonstration against Fascism in Trafalgar Square, this Tuesday evening, and the Fascists were hastily organising a counter-demonstration.

Major Manisty was in charge of the counter-demonstration, and at that moment, already wearing his black shirt, was giving orders. He was as proud and happy as it was possible for him to be. He was a wiry, tough man in his early forties, and had a rather narrow, twisted face, with prominent eyebrows, a clipped dark moustache, and a thrusting pointed chin. He had a military appearance, but it was not quite genuine; it had a quality at once theatrical and passionate. Genuine soldiers rarely look as militant as Major Manisty did; they are usually simple, rather mild, comfortable, thoroughly extroverted men; whereas Major Manisty was tangled, introverted, neurotic, in his militarism. He was the son of a fairly well-to-do stock-broker who had suddenly gone bankrupt; he had been to a public school and had been compelled to leave early and spend three unhappy years in an estate agent's office; he had joined the army at the beginning of the War, been rapidly promoted, commissioned, then promoted again; had seen a good deal of fighting, and had lived through those years, which seemed to him more like real life than any of the years he had known before, in a curious mixed mood of growing self-importance, terror and ecstasy; had stayed as long as he could after the Armistice and had then come home to find himself rapidly dwindling; had secured through a brother officer a job on a tea plantation, which had been fun while it lasted; had returned to England to dwindle again, with no salaaming servants, no smiling little brown beauties, no high jinks at the club; had listened to a violent Fascist tirade against Jews, Communists, Socialists, Pacifists, all kinds of swine he had always disliked, had joined up at once and been quickly promoted again. His promotion had been earned, for he was a useful man in the Fascist ranks, and would be still more useful if Fascism grew. He had the combative energy and bitter courage of the man to whom ordinary quiet reality is bewildering and depressing; it was only in a world of violence and gigantic simple hatreds that he discovered himself. He was ready to be knocked on the head or to be shot himself so long as there was a good chance of knocking other people on the head or lining them up against a wall. He really hated all these people he denounced—the Jews, Communists, and the rest—because they had come to represent all the difficulties, snubs, disappointments, injuries, that had ever come his way. And perhaps, deep down, he realised that a world without violence, a world of measured appeals, calm thought, patient work, meant the end of him.

"Now you understand," he was saying, in a sharp high-pitched voice to the four black-shirted young men who stood before him, who were his subordinate officers, "you've got your orders. Tell your fellows not to hesitate. If the bastards ask for it, they're going to get it, to-night. We'll show 'em how to demonstrate. All right. Get going."

Over at the Communist headquarters, that afternoon, they were busy organising too. Fred Blair was in charge. He was a year or two younger than Major Manisty. He had not long black hair, a permanent scowl, a sinister blue chin; did not look at all Russian. He was a stocky, broad-faced North-countryman, who fancied himself, on convivial occasions, as a bit of a baritone singer. He had a plump little wife, who called him "Fred lad," and a plump little boy, of whom he was very proud. Fred Blair's father, a heavy drinker, had been killed by the sudden snapping of an old belt in the engineering shed where he worked; and Fred had been brought up by his mother, whose intelligence and character were superior to those of her husband and of most of her neighbours. Fred, a fitter in those days, had stayed at home during the War. Afterwards, he had gone to evening classes run by the Workers' Educational Association, and had turned socialist. He was a shop steward. The failure of a big engineering strike, in which he had been prominent, led him to the Communist Party. He had been to Russia, tried vodka and caviare and disliked them; had hobnobbed, mostly in smiling dumb show, with Kommissars. He had gone grimly through all the works of Karl Marx that have been translated into English, and they were for him what the Bible had been for his Puritan grandfathers: all his history, philosophy, record of the past, prophetic revelation of the future. It never occurred to him to question the metaphysical assumptions of Marx, simply because these were the only metaphysics he was acquainted with, and so they seemed to him wonderfully deep and penetrating. In his view, anybody who did not accept the Marxian account of this life either had not the brains to understand it (and into this class he contemptuously shovelled many of the workers) or was debarred by villainous self-interest, bourgeois hypocrisy. He was quite savagely realistic about actual members of his own class, which had to be mystically elevated into "the proletariat" before it received his devotion. He had no illusions about elected persons and officials, even those with whom he often had to work, but he believed that under Communism all this fetid mass of jobbery, vanity, jealousy, intrigue, self-seeking, would vanish in a twinkling. He also believed that all persons possessing more than a few hundred pounds of capital were dark conspirators of immense cunning and entirely without scruples. The smallest action of theirs was always directed against the workers. So he could talk cheerfully of their "liquidation," just as his Russian comrades did, simply because he did not see them as real people and had never sharply imagined, translated into vivid mental pictures, this process of their "liquidation," had had no vision of them penned like starving cattle into vast concentration camps, lined up and bloodily pulped with machine guns, hurled into pits of quicklime. From all this he would have shrunk, revolted. There was no cruelty, no sadistic twist, in him. And in his simple enthusiasm, he had never noticed in the glances of his Russian comrades a certain glimmer of Oriental irony when he talked to them so cheerfully of the inevitable revolution in Britain. Nor did they tell him, even if they knew, that, good Marxian though he was, the famous fog of London, that dark elfin haze, was still drifting through his mind. Such was Fred Blair, who was now telling various cell leaders, the few who were free at this hour, what they might expect to encounter that night. They did not shrink, but looked at him steadily. One was a widow of forty-five, a little peaked woman who obviously overrated the nourishing properties of cups of tea at odd hours; and of the remaining five, two were young girls, slender, big-eyed creatures who had recently and contemptuously marched out of Girton and Newnham to hoist the Red Flag, which they actually proposed to carry that night.

"Mind you," said Fred Blair, in his broad accent, "it'll be rough. Mak' no mistake about that, onny of you. Bobbies'ull be there, you can bet on that, but you can bet an' all they'll tak' their time while they see them black-shirted bullies knocking such as you about. They have their orders, like a lot more——"

The telephone rang. It was a call for one of the two girls from Cambridge, and when she answered it and learned who was calling her, immediately her face, so young, frail, transparent that her heart seemed to beat just behind it, lit up wonderfully. But then the light quickly faded. She was having a love affair—a delirious mixture of revolution, now-I-am-free-at-last-to-live-my-own-life, and quite old-fashioned, bourgeois, romantic passion—with a handsome young doctor, attached to one of the London hospitals. He was not a member of the Party, for he was far too busy, but he too, when he had time to think of it, had communistic tendencies, and he had told her that he would try to be there at the demonstration that night. Now he was explaining, hastily and apologetically, that it could not be managed. There was too much to do at the hospital. And one of his patients, pretty grim case—chap called Vintnor, he'd mentioned him, did she remember?—could not be left at all now. Then he simply said: "Darling!" in a gobbly, shamefaced sort of voice that she liked, and she said: "Darling!" in a thrilling intense way, and she returned to Fred Blair's table, while he hurried back to the ward in which Lawrence Vintnor lay dying.

The chain, one of many hundreds of thousands linking people that afternoon throughout the city, is now almost complete. The witch web in the gathering gloom of the stone forest has been woven, with sticky fibres radiating from Mr. Baddeley, Sir Alfred Skidmore, Gerald Ruthvere, Mrs. Hubarth, Ferdinand Antill, the men who followed, Major Manisty and his Fascists, Fred Blair and his comrades, and some fainter threads from the handsome young doctor and the dying Lawrence Vintnor. It was of him, Lawrence, that Rose was thinking, not because he had recently ousted Edward from her memory and imagination, but because, that very Tuesday morning, she had received a letter—an urgent, declamatory letter, very characteristic of its writer—from Beatrice Vintnor, begging her to see her brother Lawrence, who had been asking for her. At first, she had decided it was impossible. Her only spare time for several days to come was this evening, and this evening belonged naturally to her and Edward. She felt annoyed with Beatrice for asking her at all. She hardly knew these Vintnors, did not really care very much for Beatrice, for whose sake she had already done one gigantic silly thing; and yet somehow these Vintnors—as she said to herself, in her resentful bewilderment—"made these claims" upon her. And she found, as so many other people have found in similar circumstances, that in some mysterious fashion she could not help feeling responsible, simply could not dismiss them. If she had something to give that they asked for, then somehow she had to give it. And then gradually, she forgot Beatrice and began to remember Lawrence, returned in memory again to his bedside. She could see his wasted face quite clearly, although she could not remember exactly what Edward looked like. It was annoying, but there it was. Lawrence kept staring at her throughout the day. She would have to go and see him that night before she met Edward, to whom she had never mentioned Lawrence at all, though she could not have explained what had prevented her. But though it was all going to be difficult—for she could not get a message through now to Edward to tell him she would be late, and she could not finish work, go to the hospital, see Lawrence, and be at the Corner House about seven, as she had arranged—she saw that she simply could not race off to a happy evening with Edward and ignore Lawrence's appeal. She felt obscurely but profoundly that her happiness was impossible on those easy terms, that to be happy with Edward that night she would have to see Lawrence, though why it should be so, she did not know, did not even ask herself. She was a creature of intuitions and instincts, and during these last few weeks, she had suddenly grown up, and those intuitions were more subtle and those instincts more profound. But she had no more words for what went on in her mind than she had before, and a careless observer would have noticed little change in her and would probably not have given her credit for one-half of what passed somewhere behind that smooth fresh face and those velvety eyes.

No sooner had she decided to go to the hospital, which meant that she must leave the house earlier than ever, than the smouldering Dorothy-Penner feud suddenly blazed furiously. In one hour, behind their domestic scenes, there was more energy consumed, more vital drama created, than the Holt-Ibstock family itself had consumed and created in a month. It was all about a teapot, which Dorothy claimed for her own private use in her room, and which Mrs. Penner, working through her ally, Eva, removed from that room and restored to the kitchen. Dorothy went down and took it away, saying that she had Lady Holt-Ibstock's permission to use it for herself. Eva declared she had nothing of the kind. Little Connie, the kitchenmaid, always ready to get a little of her own back on Mrs. Penner, piped up that she knew for certain what Dorothy said was true. Mrs. Penner, more like a madwoman than ever, with a grey face and snapping red eyes, gesticulated with the largest kitchen knife, stormed without ceasing, and drove everybody out of the kitchen. Mr. Penner, wearing his old Front Line face, wandered uneasily between his pantry and the madhouse below, and occasionally took Rose on one side to tell her in a whisper that Mrs. Penner took things hard but that she had more to contend with than people realised. With the exception of Rose, who was still a newcomer and so not deeply involved, all of them were too busy with this gigantic affair, too angry, too much upset, too dramatic altogether, to do any real work. They were far more violent than any of the quarrelsome people Rose had known in Haliford. As servants they had to pretend to be quieter than they really were, less human, merely wheels in a smooth domestic machine, but once the lid was off—and the lid had to come off at frequent intervals—they let themselves go further than ordinary working people did, became all too human, plunged at once into terrific melodrama, cursing and weeping in one breath. Rose had no patience with them and their tantrums. She thought they were silly. And, of course, they must start all this now, when she was desperately trying to get done. She was so impatient, so sick of this house that was either a glacier or a spouting volcano, that if this had been merely a job, if she had not still felt she was in hiding, she would have walked out there and then. As it was, feeling something dark and hampering, even menacing, about this day, to which she had looked forward so eagerly for the last four days, she struggled along, her mind racing ahead of her hands, which seemed maddeningly clumsy.

It was just after six when she put on her little green hat and green woollen coat and hurried out into the muffled foggy dampness of Cumberland Square, and it was a good deal after six by the time she reached the hospital. It looked very formidable, with its rows of lighted windows glimmering through the haze, and the bulk of it towering into the night and losing itself there. Before, she had been with Beatrice, who was always going. Now she had to do it all herself. The very fact that she knew what was going on behind those walls, how different it was in there from outside, made it seem difficult to penetrate, like going from one life to another. The oldish man in uniform looked busy and worried, and she felt he had far more important things to attend to than any question of hers. There were several other visitors hanging about, and they had an uneasy look. Nurses and orderlies in white coats walked quickly past, as if they knew exactly what they had to do, and that what they had to do was the only thing worth doing, and they made her feel a foolish breathless intruder. Meanwhile, the precious minutes were ticking away on the face of that large clock, above the head, now bent to the telephone, of the oldish porter. At last he was free, and gave her a dubious enquiring glance. She gave him Lawrence's name. He asked her what block, what ward, Lawrence was in, and if she ever knew, she could not remember now. He grunted, then drew a long breath, as if asking heaven for a little more patience for such ignorant, time-wasting callers, then turned away, sat down by his telephone again, and looked in a book. Rose hoped fervently he was looking for Lawrence in that book, but he had not said he was going to, had simply grunted and turned away, and for all she knew, he might have done with her and be going on with something else. It was humiliating and exasperating. And time was running away. She told herself she would not look at that clock again. But finally, he got up slowly, and explained, in a dragging, reproachful manner, where she must go. She went so quickly across the big courtyard that she nearly bumped into two men carrying a stretcher, and was horrified, shaken, by the nearness of the possible catastrophe.

She realised now that a large hospital, filled with dangerous cases, is the last place in the world to be impatient in, for she was only there on sufferance, had no possible concerns of her own that could be regarded as being of the slightest importance there, had no justification for stopping or addressing a word to any of the people, all so preoccupied and active and uninterested in her. At last, she found the right waiting-room. There were only two people in there, a shabby, middle-aged couple, who sat very close together, never saying a word, simply staring sadly in front of them, the man ceaselessly twisting his cap between his short thick hands, the woman nervously fingering the catch on her bag. They looked as if they had been sitting there in that little room, just like that, staring in front of them at nothing, for days and days. It was very queer in that waiting-room. First, there was the world outside; then the hospital, withdrawn from that world, remote as a distant city; and then, inside the hospital, in the very dead centre of it, this room, still more remote, removed from everything. Even Time was lost there. Rose could not have said how long she was in there before the nurse came in, beckoned to the couple, and then glanced enquiringly at her. Rose told her she wanted to see Lawrence Vintnor. The nurse merely nodded, and led out the little man and his wife, who seemed smaller, shabbier, more forlorn than ever as they passed through the doorway. Left alone in this remotest of rooms, Rose seemed to fill it, make it throb, with the beating of her heart. The place seemed stifling now. Quite apart from seeing Lawrence, from hurrying to Edward, she longed to get out of it.

A young man in a long white coat came in. He closed the door carefully behind him without even giving Rose a glance. Then he looked at her. He was a handsome young man, with a broad face and eyes unusually wide apart, but at this moment he looked tired, not merely as a man would look who had just been working hard, but also spiritually exhausted. He gave a slight frown.

"But—are you his sister?" he asked, frowning harder, not out of annoyance but as if he found everything, including Rose in that room, much too perplexing.

Rose felt very small and apologetic. "Do you mean Lawrence Vintnor's sister? Well—no, I'm not. You see," she continued hastily and breathlessly, "I know her and I know him—and she wrote to me—and said he wanted to see me——"

"We sent for her some time ago." He rubbed his head. "Several hours ago. Must have been. She doesn't seem to have turned up. When they said—a girl was waiting, I thought it must be his sister at last, and I said I'd do it—and so—er——"

He broke off here, and rubbed his head again, as if that helped him in some mysterious way. Rose, more herself now, looked at him gravely and said, as a serious child might have said it: "I'm very sorry. But I don't know what you mean. Can't I see him?"

"Well, he's dead, you know. Died about three quarters of an hour ago."

Rose sat silent, looking at him. Then her eyes, which seemed to act independently at this news, to take it in before her mind did, suddenly filled with tears.

"It's a rotten business, of course," said the young doctor, gently but hastily. "But best thing that could have happened, though of course we did all we could to prevent it. He hadn't a chance, not a dog's chance, right from the first. Operation after operation too. Tried everything.

Not his fault at all. Just bad luck. Something as thick as that——" and he held out two fingers—"in most people's insides—well, by some curious freak, was as thin as paper in his, so everything went. No stopping it. Just bad luck, poor chap! Why he should have been like that, and go through what he did, God only knows! And even if He does know, it's still a damned shame."

"Yes. I—oh, I don't know," said Rose, hardly aware of what she was trying to say. "I'd better go, hadn't I?"

"Might as well, you know," said the doctor, brisker now. "But if you know where his sister is——?"

"I don't," replied Rose, hastily, getting up. The doctor held the door open for her, and smiled nicely at her as she passed him. There was a new hospital kind of smell in the corridor outside that had not been there before. Also, some lovely chrysanthemums, great golden-brown blooms, outside one of the doors. Two women, visitors, going down in the lift talked eagerly about "what a good long rest would do for him." At the bottom, a lot of nurses were standing in a row, like soldiers on parade, waiting to be inspected. Did nurses have to do that? The open courtyard was awfully cold now. But she walked slowly. The oldish porter was still telephoning. The clock above him insisted upon telling her that it was now half-past seven. Almost without thinking, like a galvanised automaton, she hurried away and found a bus that would take her to the Strand.

In the bus, which now seemed to crawl, now to race horribly, she could not make up her mind whether she wanted to see Edward at once, just to be with him, to be sure he was still there, or whether she wanted to run away and be by herself, not see Edward at all that night. She knew she could not begin to talk about Lawrence now to Edward, because she felt incapable of making him understand—could not understand herself in any form that could be given words—what she had thought about Lawrence, who had somehow been at once less and more than a person to her. She did not want even to try and find the words necessary for the most simplified explanation of what she had just been doing. Yet not only was she going to be terribly late, but she was also in a queer state of mind, with a great numbed spot in it surrounded by crackling excitement. How could she begin to answer questions? She sat there, bewildered, turned towards the steamy window, but seeing nothing of the passing panorama of Life and Death.

XIV

THERE are those who will not wait for anybody or anything. There are those who, with an Oriental indifference to the passing of time, can wait in peace. Both classes show a strength of mind not possessed by all the others in between, who can neither refuse to wait nor wait in peace, who ache to be off yet dare not go, who hear time wasting itself in great roaring cataracts, who feel themselves insulted, scorned, diminished, by every empty minute, who condemn themselves to the torture of a thousand cuts but still remain, spiritually bleeding, at the rendezvous. Edward was one of these unfortunate souls. He was outside the Corner House before seven, and there he waited a long hour. Of its sixty minutes, only the first five had been even tolerable. The others were misery. The pitiful failure of that interview with Mr. Baddeley had left him worried and feeling small. He had arrived at the Corner House rather low in self-esteem. He spent the second half-hour of his waiting in violent alternations of scorn and pity for himself, so that by the time Rose did come he was in a most wretched condition of mind. And not only of mind. He had chosen a bad place to wait in. People were always bumping up against him. It was cold. And he was hungry.

All his resentment ought to have vanished at the sight of her. But it did not. The sinister day saw to that. It increased, or became sharply focused, at the sight of her. There she was, and it was her fault. If she could have carried off the situation coolly or gaily—if she had been one of those women who are incapable of appreciating the difference between seven o'clock and eight o'clock—then she would probably have swung him out of his resentment. But she was in no state of mind to do this. She was timid, placating, and this only made him worse.

"Oh—Edward," she cried, putting a hand on his arm, "I'm sorry. I—I couldn't help it."

"Well, I must say, I think it's a bit thick," he muttered, not looking at her properly, keeping himself far away from her. "It was you who said 'seven,' wasn't it?"

"I said 'about seven,' Edward," she reminded him, but not boldly, gaily, but still timidly.

"Well, do you call this 'about seven'?" he asked savagely. "Because if you do, I don't."

There they stood, with traffic, people, lights, swirling about them, miserable stony lumps of humanity. Rose, the more miserable and the less stony, could have cried.

"Do you want something to eat?" he enquired, in a surly perfunctory way.

Now Rose could have done with something to eat, would have liked nothing better than to have marched straight into the Corner House, which looked very gay and inviting, and have ordered a cosy pot of tea for them both, but Edward's tone suggested that if she did want food and drink, this would only be a further delay and grievance, and she imagined that he did not want anything himself; so she replied that she didn't. Dismayed, she saw at once that this had done no good at all. He looked sulkier than ever.

"If you like," she ventured, after a tiny wretched silence, "we can have something."

"No, it doesn't matter. I don't want anything." Annoyed with her, he was ready now to annoy himself, to shout a gigantic snarling *No* to everybody and everything. "Let's get away from here. I'm fed up with standing about here. And so would you be."

They moved on, slowly, and miserably separate. Rose found herself wishing that she had obeyed her first impulse, after leaving the hospital, and had given up this evening with Edward. She could have made it right with him afterwards. This was awful, much worse than not meeting at all. But because she was hiding something from him, she felt she must make every effort to put things right between them, even if he was being so silly.

Forcing herself to be bright and eager, she said: "Where shall we go?" She said it in the very tone that had enchanted him last week.

It did not enchant him now. "I dunno," he mumbled, staring straight ahead. That sour mumble suggested that there was nowhere to go. At one stroke, it flattened out the whole glittering edifice of pleasure.

They had come to the end of the Strand and joined the people who were waiting at the edge of the stream of traffic for an opportunity to cross the road. There were a good many of these people. Above the steady roar of the buses, they could hear sounds of shouting and singing. When the break in the traffic came, they crossed with the others. Trafalgar Square, with its columns and great lions, even in that dark haze, catching the light from all the illuminated signs, was a mysterious confusion of crowds and stormy sounds. Something was happening there.

"Let's see what it is," said Edward.

"No, don't," said Rose, suddenly and unaccountably afraid. She could not have said what it was that frightened her, but she knew at once that she did not want to go a step nearer.

"Aw, come on," cried Edward disgustedly, as if he had lost all patience with her. He moved forward, nearer the Square proper, and she followed him, sick at heart. A lot of other people, drawn by the noises, were moving that way, towards the great lions.

She managed to catch him by the sleeve. He turned so impatiently that her hand fell away from him. There was light enough for her to see that he was looking angrily at her, as if she was an interfering stranger. "Edward, let's go away from here. It's nothing to do with us. And I don't like it. Let's go."

"Why should we?" he asked her, sharply, accusingly. "We're not going anywhere. I don't know what's the matter with you to-night, Rose."

"I don't know what's the matter with you," she replied, sadly.

"There's nothing the matter with me. Only I want to see what's happening, that's all."

All this with people all round them, which made it all the more hateful. Once more, Rose wished she had never come to meet him. She ought to have gone straight back to

Cumberland Square—or, for that matter, anywhere where she could be quiet, by herself—after she had left the hospital.

Then Edward, goaded by something he caught in her look, said roughly: "If you want to go—well, go then."

This was more than she could bear. Saying no more, she turned and pushed blindly past a couple arm-in-arm at her elbow, past some more people, all thick lumpy shadows, hurrying she did not know where. And it seemed as if this decisive movement of hers brought to life something violent and evil in the whole throng there. There were terrifying shouts. A scream or two. Then a huge dark upheaval on her left, where the big crowd was. People were backing furiously from some disturbance there, and at the same time newcomers were pressing forward, and in a second or two there were no empty spaces and she was struggling in a mad mass. Through this mass, coming nearer every moment, there came a wedge of whirling arms, furious faces, yells and screams. They were fighting. Edward! Where was Edward? She looked round desperately, hemmed in as she was, and saw a hundred strange faces, but not Edward's. Once she thought she heard him calling her, but there was so much noise, she could not be sure. She could not be sure of anything now, felt completely helpless, at the mercy of people who had stopped being people and had turned themselves into a huge, yelling, squirming monster, bigger than all the lions and columns. Indeed, she was now part of this monster. She felt herself being carried over to the right, so solidly jammed that her feet hardly touched the ground. She was carried into the road itself, higher up than the end of the Strand. Cars and buses were there, hooting to pass, but they could not, there were too many people being forced across in front of them. There was a sharp elbow wedged into her ribs. It belonged to a little man, with a dirty pointed face, a cheerful squint, and an old cap much too big for him at the back of his head. "Sorry, kid," he panted, "but can't flaming well help it, see? Too many flaming people." But he tried hard to free himself and her. The next moment, however, she and the little man and a hundred others were all tangled up, suddenly swept further out by another movement, the biggest yet, from the crowd in the Square, which was making lunatic noises. This time, Rose's right foot not only touched the ground but tried to stay where it touched, owing to some obstruction down there, and as the tons of crazy humanity surged on, she felt a stab of pain in that ankle, and would have fallen if there had been room to fall. As it was, her weight fell on the little man. The few people on their right scattered this way and that, and then both Rose and the little man had collapsed against the running board of a car. Rose cried out with pain and fright, then felt faint.

"Here, take her inside, for Christ's sake," she thought she heard the little man cry. "Hurt herself, she has. Come on, or I'll push your flaming window in, lady, see?"

And that was the last she saw of the little man. Now she was inside the car, half on the floor, half on the seat, which was covered with crimson leather. It was not a large car but it was a very fine one, the best she had ever been in. There was only room at the back for her, sprawling there, and the lady who was looking curiously at her, and who was wonderfully scented with violets. She saw the chauffeur turn round, and thought he was a black man who was rolling his eyes. The car was moving now. There were policemen on horseback. Then it all went.

Not that she was quite unconscious, though the pain in her ankle, the fright she had had, the whole dark horrible confusion of it, together kept her in a half-fainting condition, so that for some time everything seemed to be happening at some distance from her real self, went on without her acquiescence and responsibility, and had the unreality of some other person's dream. Afterwards, she remembered vaguely riding some distance in that car, trying to answer the lady's questions, and finally being almost carried into a house, remote, mysterious, by the lady and the chauffeur between them.

Nothing was clear until after she had swallowed that burning, choking stuff, which must have been brandy. She did not like it, and she felt rather sick, but very soon afterwards the mists thinned, things came nearer and became solid and real again. She was lying on a sofa, under a pink shaded light, in a small sitting-room. Her hat and coat were off, and so was her right shoe. Everything was very still, after the noise and struggle of Trafalgar Square, which might have been thousands of miles and months away. The room was all pinkish, and quite pretty, nicer than any at the Holt-Ibstocks'. It was very warm, rather drowsy. A clock ticked pleasantly.

The lady of the car was sitting opposite. She was smoking a cigarette, and smiling through the blue wisps of smoke at her. It was not easy to see this lady's face, but she looked very smart and handsome. A lot of make-up, though. And with full, staring kind of eyes. Brownish? Greenish?

"Like a cigarette?" And the lady smiled. She might be very smart and handsome and rich and have a lot of make-up and staring eyes, but she was quite friendly.

Rose shook her head. She did not feel up to talking yet.

"More brandy?"

Again Rose shook her head. She felt she ought to say something now, but could not manage it. So she smiled instead, and the lady smiled.

"Attractive child, aren't you?" said the lady, calmly and cheerfully.

Rose felt anything but an attractive child at that moment, but she was glad that the lady thought she looked like one. And then she thought about Edward.

It was as if the lady could read her thoughts. "By the way, who is Edward?"

Rose found her voice, but it was very rusty. "He's—he's—a friend," she began, stammering.

"Your young man, eh?" Another smile.

She nodded. "We had a quarrel—not much of one—and then got separated in the crowd," she explained. "How did you know about him?"

"You kept saying something about your Edward in the car. It's the only thing I know about you yet, that you have an Edward. I don't even know your name."

"It's Rose Salter—I mean," she added hastily, suddenly remembering, "—Mary Pearson."

"Rose Salter *and* Mary Pearson?"

"Well—you see—I changed it——" Rose looked across, confused and apologetic.

The lady smiled again, as if she quite understood that it might be necessary to have two quite different names. "I'd better call you Rosemary—and then we have them both—hadn't I? Well, Rosemary, as you've probably guessed, you're in my house. I brought you here because you seemed to have hurt yourself—we're going to attend to that ankle in a minute—I've sent my housekeeper for some things—and there didn't seem anything else to do."

"No," said Rose, politely. "Thank you very much. My ankle must have got twisted when they all pushed so hard."

"Yes, so I imagined. You don't sound like a London girl. Are you?"

Rose explained shyly that she came from Haliford. And this seemed to please the lady, though Rose could not think why it should. But perhaps she was only trying to be nice and friendly.

"And what are you doing in London then?"

"Well, you see——" and now Rose felt ashamed of herself all over again—"I'm a parlourmaid at Lady Holt-Ibstock's in Cumberland Square. I'm not really a parlourmaid—I mean I haven't been there long—and before that I was working in one of the big shops——"

"Which?"

"Well—I'd rather not say."

The other laughed. "You're a mysterious girl, aren't you? Two names. A parlourmaid and yet not a parlourmaid. Worked in one of the big shops but you'd rather not say which. Really!" There was nothing unfriendly in this. Indeed, she seemed more pleased than ever.

"It does sound a bit funny," Rose admitted ruefully. "But it isn't really. I haven't done anything wrong. Oh!—I say—is it getting late? I'll have to go soon."

"What! With that ankle! You can't possibly, my dear child. We had to carry you in here. No, you'll have to stay."

"But they'll wonder what's become of me."

"That's all right. If you're worried about it, I can easily ring up—who is it?—Lady Holt-Ibstock—and explain. Do you like it there?"

"Not much."

"I should think not. Tell me about it."

Rose told her a little about it—wages, hours, what she did, who the others were—and the lady listened with a sort of scornful incredulity that made Rose feel even more ashamed of herself.

"Miserable existence!" she cried, when Rose had done. "Why, it's absurd. A pretty child like you! If I'd only the same kind of work to offer you here, I'd pay you twice as much. And you can do much better than that. Now don't talk." She got up and rang a bell. "We're going to attend to that ankle now. And before we do, you'd better have some more brandy. Certainly, you must."

She poured some out and stood over Rose, who was still lying on the couch, and made her drink it. A woman in black, with a creased, sombre face, came in with some things while she was drinking the brandy. It did not make her choke so much or feel sick this time. It gave her a sort of glow, and then she felt swimmy, and rather light-hearted and careless.

"Now," cried the lady gaily. "If you don't want that pretty little dress spoiled, we'd better take it off. Don't be absurd. Nobody but us here. Now then!"

So between them, they got her dress off. Feeling rather dizzy, she stretched herself out on the couch again. The lady sat opposite to her again, and stared and smiled. The woman in black, who appeared to be a foreigner, unloosed and peeled off Rose's right stocking, and began bathing the ankle in cold water, which she had brought with her in a little flat enamel dish. Rose felt silly, stetched out there, with her dress off and one bare leg, in front of these two strange women. They were both tremendous starers. Once or twice, she thought she saw them exchanging glances; very queer glances, with something secret and significant about them, and somehow—ridiculous as it might seem—the bare leg came into it. And then Rose told herself not to be foolish. She realised that her own state of mind was queer enough. The evening had been too much for her: first, the hospital and the news of Lawrence Vintnor's death; then the quarrel with Edward; the crowd and the fighting in Trafalgar Square; the pain in her ankle; then fainting and brandy and these women and this house; enough to make anybody feel queer, ready to imagine anything. She didn't even know where she was. But this lady was being very kind, taking so much trouble.

As if to prove it conclusively, the lady asked now if she had had anything to eat during the evening. Rose admitted she hadn't, but said she wasn't very hungry.

The woman in black, who was not very pleasant to look at but was deft with her fingers, and who was now wrapping the ankle in a very tight cold-water bandage, spoke quickly to the lady in a foreign language, probably French. Her mistress replied briefly in the same tongue, whereupon the woman in black collected her things, nodded and smiled at Rose, put a startlingly cold hand upon her bare leg for one second, then waddled out.

"She's going to make you a cup of good hot soup," said the lady. "You can drink it in bed and it will help to make you sleep."

Rose did not know what to say. She felt helpless and bewildered. It seemed so queer to be brought like this into a strange house and to be expected to stay. It was not as if she was really badly hurt. She could have hobbled down into a taxi, and easily got back to Cumberland Square.

"What's the matter, child?"

"Well—it's only that—my ankle isn't very bad, you know. I mean, I can easily get back. I'm putting you to a lot of trouble."

"And you can't imagine why I'm taking all that trouble, eh? Now admit it, isn't that what you're thinking?" The lady laughed. "Well, I'll tell you. In the first place, you really ought to rest that ankle, and you've had so much excitement to-night, you're not fit to move. But that isn't all, of course. I'm not running a free nursing home for girls I've never set eyes on before. The fact is, I'm going to try and steal you." She laughed again.

Rose did not laugh, but she smiled. She did not know yet what the lady meant, but already she felt better about it all, because obviously the lady was going to explain why she was taking all this trouble. And for the last few minutes, dazed though she might be, Rose had felt some explanation was necessary.

"At the moment, I've got no staff here but the housekeeper, who's been with me a long time, and a daily woman who does the rough work, and of course Sam, my chauffeur——"

"Is he a black man?" Rose enquired earnestly.

The other laughed. "What a solemn face! Yes, he is. Why do you ask?"

"I thought he was. Then I thought he couldn't be, and I must have been dreaming. You know, I was so muddled. And it seemed so funny, a black man driving the car."

"I found Sam in Paris. There are a lot of black men in Paris. Some of them came over with rich Americans. Sam did. He worked for a friend of mine. I had two maids, but I had to get rid of them quite recently—you know what some of these dreadful London girls are like—and as I like to do a good deal of entertaining, it's been very awkward these last two or three weeks."

"Yes, I'm sure," said Rose sympathetically. She was flattered by these confidences. Lady Holt-Ibstock would never talk to her like this, probably did not even talk to Dorothy—her favourite—like this. It was nice.

"I like my maids to be attractive, can't bear these horrible little sluts one sees about, and when I saw what an attractive child you were, I thought what a pity it was you weren't working here, and then when you told me you were a parlourmaid at Lady Holt-Ibstock's, I made up my mind

I must steal you. It's absurd the wages the woman is paying you. I'll give you twice as much, and probably for half the work, because I'm away a good deal. And I'm rather unconventional, as you see, and I think we'd get along very well together. There! Now you understand it all."

And Rose felt she did, and was vaguely reassured, though she could not have said what had made her feel uneasy before. It would be much better here than in Cumberland Square. Warmer, to begin with. And then, not all that quarrelling. She remembered, for the first time since she had left the house, the tremendous bust-up of that very afternoon, the insane antics of Mrs. Penner, and felt she did not want to go back there. Besides, she could probably see Edward here.

"It sounds nice," she said. "The only thing is—I don't really want to be a parlourmaid. You see——" But she hesitated.

The other looked searchingly at her. "Something happened at that shop, I imagine. And you went into service to get out of the way." She laughed. "All right. It doesn't matter to me. But you'd be out of the way here, and it wouldn't be like ordinary service at all."

"Where is—this?"

The lady laughed again. "Oh—you don't even know where you are, do you? Well, you're still in London. This is St. John's Wood."

"I see. Thank you. And—I don't know what to call you, do I?"

"I am Mrs. Hubarth. Now you ought to be getting to bed."

"I'd like," said Rose hesitantly, "to write to Edward—my boy friend—to tell him where I am. You see, he might be worried. When we—separated, the crowd came in between us, and he won't know where I've got to."

"No, he won't," cried Mrs. Hubarth, with friendly mockery. "And that's terrible. But it'll do him good to wonder for a day, so you can write to him to-morrow. Now I'll ring for Toinette, and we'll get you to bed."

The bedroom was on the next floor, the third and top floor, and Rose, assisted by the woman in black, managed to hop up the short flight of stairs without putting any weight on her injured ankle, which was now numbed by the tight bandaging. The housekeeper never said a word, so Rose did not try to talk to her. The bedroom must have been used by one of the maids who had recently left. It was much nicer than the room she shared with Eva Newton at Lady Holt-Ibstock's. She had it to herself, and anyhow, it was a larger room, and better furnished. The things in it obviously had not been bought specially for a maid's room, but were old things that had been brought out of one of the chief bedrooms. There was a faded pinkish carpet covering all the floor. The bed was a large wooden one, and the ends were carved, though some of the carving had broken off. The chest of drawers had fancy painting all down the front, but the patterns were blurred. The mirror was fancy too, and framed in faded gilt. The curtains, though old and a trifle shabby, were a rich dark red. There were two little gilded chairs, rather stained and scratched. The two electric lights had pink silk shades, like those in the little sitting-room, but of course older. It looked very cosy and nice, all the more so because a small gas fire was burning. It was, taking it all round, the nicest room Rose had ever slept in. The only thing wrong with it was that it smelled stuffy and not very clean. In that subdued pinky light, it was impossible to see if there was much dirt about; but it did not smell fresh and clean. There was about it somehow a vague reminder of somebody else's unmade bed. And the last girl who had slept there—and Rose had a feeling that quite a number of girls had occupied this room—must have used a very strongly-perfumed face powder, and not opened the window since she last threw it about. Over and above all this, there was something not quite right about the room, something to which Rose could not put a name. Yet the fact remained that it was a nice, comfortable, cosy bedroom.

Moreover, it had a little bathroom of its own too, a luxury that Rose had never known before. The housekeeper showed her this bathroom, turning the light on in there, and muttered a few words to the effect that this bathroom could be entered through the other bedroom but that the door—and she rattled the handle to show exactly what she meant—was locked on the far side. So Rose had this bathroom for her very own. It was a very small bathroom—with everything in it a bit rusted and cracked—and it was not very clean, but there it was, her own bathroom. Grand!

There was a suit of pyjamas—fancy but faded, like so many of the things here—waiting for her on the bed. And on a little table at the bedside were some biscuits and a little bowl of soup that was steaming away and had a most savoury and enticing smell. Really, they were being wonderfully good to her. Oh—and there were some slippers by the bed. And a wrap on the chair. And a hair-brush and comb by the mirror. So thoughtful too! And yet this foreigner housekeeper, with her creased, yellowish, drawn-in sort of face, did not look as if she would want to bother two minutes about a strange girl who arrived in the house. Perhaps it was Mrs. Hubarth herself who thought of everything.

Rose took up the pyjamas. She was now sitting on the edge of the bed. The housekeeper moved forward, as if to help her to undress, but Rose, who did not fancy being undressed by this woman, shook her head. Then for a moment or two, they just looked at one another. Rose decided that she did not like this housekeeper, not because she was a foreigner and ugly and not inclined to talk, but because she had cunning little eyes, too many crafty wrinkles, and a horrid mouth. When you looked at her steadily like this, and she took shape as a real person and not just a figure in black, there was something unpleasant, even rather frightening, about her. But of course that might be because she was foreign. Anyhow, Rose felt she had had quite enough of this woman's queer staring and pawing round. She would undress herself, decently and out of sight, thank you!

She worked it by suddenly scrambling up, taking the pyjamas with her, and hobbling quickly across to the bathroom. Once in there, it was all right. She took her time. Indeed, it was not easy to undress in that little bathroom, with only one leg to stand on. She bumped herself a bit. Twice she heard the door open and close in the bedroom, and once she heard Mrs. Hubarth and the housekeeper talking. It was after that that the door closed again, and then there was silence. They must have both gone and left her to it. The pyjamas were rather too big for her, but they had been good ones in their time. She looked very funny in them in the glass. Bed now. She hopped back into the bedroom.

To her surprise, Mrs. Hubarth was standing there, holding something. "My dear child," she cried, "you look a sight. I knew those things wouldn't do at all. Look! I've brought you some really nice ones." She held out another suit of pyjamas, made of the palest pink silky mesh, very pretty, and quite the flimsiest Rose had ever seen.

"Oh no, thank you. It's quite all right," stammered Rose, who was embarrassed, not knowing what to make of all this palaver. Pyjamas like that for her!

"It's not a bit all right," cried Mrs. Hubarth forcefully. "I simply won't have it. Take those ridiculous things off now, and put these on. I insist. I brought them up specially."

Well, that was that. She had brought them up specially—these lovely things, which must have cost no end of money. Rose did not know whether she had wandered into a fairy tale or a lunatic asylum.

"Come along now, I won't go until you do." She said it cheerfully, humorously, but obviously she meant what she said. "Off with them." And this was quite a command. Rose had either to obey or make herself look ridiculous.

In another moment or two, she was sitting on the edge of the bed, embarrassed, blushing, and stark naked, for Mrs. Hubarth, instead of handing her the new suit of pyjamas and then taking herself off, had calmly kept them and walked round to have a good stare. There was no possible doubt about this stare. It was taking in every detail of the shrinking golden-white body. Rose met it, and felt terribly hot and uncomfortable.

"I say——" she began, protestingly.

"Don't be absurd, child," said Mrs. Hubarth, in a cool amused tone. "I'm only having a look at you. Yes, you've got quite a pretty figure. I don't know how long it'll last. With those breasts and thighs, you'll probably be fat by the time you're thirty, but now—you're nearly perfect. Here, put these on. Well, have a good night. That stuff ought to make you sleep. And to-morrow morning, I'll ring up Lady Holt-Ibstock, and then you and I will have a talk. I'll turn this light out, and you can turn out the other when you're in bed. Good night, Rosemary."

It was all very strange—and the staring wasn't even decent, though that was probably the way some of these smart people went on—but in a way it was fun, an adventure, something to wonder at now and talk about afterwards. She had an exciting glimpse of herself as the heroine of an amusing little story. Things like this didn't happen to every girl. Here she was, in pyjamas you could see through but that felt very nice, in a comfortable big bed in a mysterious house, and with a bandaged ankle, and not knowing what was going to happen. The soup was good, except down at the bottom of the bowl, where it was rather thick and had a bitterish flavour. Two biscuits. She didn't feel empty any longer, but beautifully warm and sleepy. And she had a very pretty figure (and she felt she had one, in those pyjamas) and was an attractive child; and this fanciful—what did she call herself?—unconventional, that was it—unconventional Mrs. Hubarth wanted her to stay there. Twice the wages. Nothing like so much work.

She turned out the remaining light, and was no longer a large creature in a pinky room but something tiny in an immense, rather stuffy darkness. Memories of the day returned, like a vague and very jumpy news reel. Mrs. Penner shouting. Mr. Penner whispering uneasily. That waiting-room in the hospital. The good-looking young doctor who rubbed his head. "Well, he's dead, you know . . ." Edward. Grumpy, stupid, sulky, silly Edward. Dear Edward. . . .

XV

AS soon as Edward had spoken so roughly to Rose, he realised that he had gone too far. He was sorry. But he was also in that state of mind which makes it impossible for a person to act quickly. He watched her turn away so sharply and push past those people, and never made a move himself. He might have been made of wood. And when he did move, it was too late. A moment or two before, there had been openings in the crowd, like the narrow lane down which Rose had disappeared, but now there was a solid mass of people. As he struggled to get through, he caught a tantalising glimpse or two of Rose's little green hat. Then the people in front began backing away, the people behind tried to push forward, and then nobody could move. He could not even catch a glimpse of Rose now.

There was a harder push than ever from behind and it happened that at that moment there was a mysterious thinning in the crowd to his left in front, with the result that he was swept forward, further into the Square, nearer the centre of the disturbance. He wanted to cut through to his right, in the direction that Rose had gone, but there was no chance of that. He was pushing against a solid wall of people. His only hope was that Rose was now out of it, on the edge of the crowd, and would wait for him there. And he had plenty of time to remember that it was he who had insisted upon coming here. But what exactly was happening? He asked the man next to him.

"Bloody Reds an' Blackshirts 'aving a barney," was the reply. "Silly muckers! But I wish I could see 'em."

He had his wish. He and Edward and all those standing near them were swept forward again, and this time they reached the area of battle. The Communists were making more noise, but the Blackshirts, better disciplined and more combative, seemed to be doing more damage. A lot of them, standing on steps or perhaps on improvised platforms, were raised above the general mob, and were easily seen. Among these was a tall slender girl, not much older than Rose, who was holding a red flag. Two young men in black shirts were trying to snatch it away from her. Edward saw one of them hit her between the breasts, saw her crumple, while the other young man wrenched away the flag and shouted in triumph. A little middle-aged woman, screaming hysterically, tried to take the flag away from him, but he put his free hand flat against her face and pushed her away, and she fell and disappeared from sight. And then the fight seemed to be going on all round him. He saw two spectacled youths and a woman clawing at a Fascist, tearing the black shirt off his back. Several Fascists came charging to his rescue, down went the two spectacled youths, and down went the woman, who had been kicked off her feet. Somewhere near was the noise of somebody vomiting. There were shouts of "Police! Police." Heads were being cracked further along. Those who were mere spectators, in a panic now, were backing away as hard as they could.

Edward found himself entangled with a little squad of blackshirts, who seemed to be under the orders of a dark thin fellow with a short moustache, a fellow older than most of them. They appeared to be knocking about anybody who happened to be in their way, and twice Edward, who could not get out of their way, got pushed and sworn at. He had taken a great dislike to these bullying young men. All his growing anger, fed by his enforced separation from Rose, the idiotic sheep-like behaviour of the crowd, the sight of their brutality to the women of the other side, was now focused upon them. It had been a hell of a day, what with one thing and another, and this was its grim peak. So huge was his resentment that he began to feel reckless. The second push he got sent him backing into the leader of the squad, who was still bawling his orders.

"Get out, you young——!" cried this fellow with the moustache, and contemptuously flung him away.

Maddened beyond endurance, hardly knowing or caring what he was doing, seeing in that one contemptuous figure all the obstacles, all the derision, of the world, Edward jumped and put all his strength, all his protest, into one vast punch at that dark face. And down went Major Manisty.

Down went Edward too, with his head singing. Nor could he get up for some minutes. People were stumbling, falling over him. He felt sick, terrified. More shouts of "Police!" He pushed against the stone, sat up slowly and painfully, and held his aching head in his arms while he slowly looked about him. There were dozens of policemen about, and the big crowd had retreated from the Square.

Of the people who were left, some were being helped or carried away, others were being held and questioned by the police.

There was a large heavy hand on his arm. A policeman, looking enormous, was lifting him to his feet. He was also asking what his particular little game had been.

"Nothing to do with me," said Edward, not without bitterness. "I just happened to get mixed up in it, that's all." He rubbed his head, and then realised that it had had a hat on it. "Lost my hat now."

"Don't see one here," said the policeman. "You'd better go home before you get mixed up in anything else. What do they do it for? Tell me that."

"I don't know," replied Edward irritably, still looking about for his hat. "I didn't even know what was going on here when I first got shoved into it."

"Well, you'll know better next time." And the policeman moved off ponderously, leaving Edward still looking for his hat. It must have fallen off when he was knocked down, and then kicked away during the subsequent rush. It was no use going further into the Square. If the hat was kicked anywhere, it must have been kicked the other way, so he began searching further and further in that direction. The police were quietly dispersing the crowd round the edge of the late battlefield. There was no more shouting. It seemed very quiet. The deep irony that seems to follow all scenes of useless violence was present. Even the illuminated signs, asking everybody left there to try certain beef extracts, table waters and steamship lines, appeared to be touched with this irony. And so was Edward. He remembered that this was the evening he had been anticipating with almost painful eagerness ever since last Thursday, and now his head ached horribly, he was shaken and bruised, he had lost his hat—and where was Rose? He had now arrived in his search not far from the place where she had originally disappeared from his view. It was near a statue, which he found, impelled by what seemed a senseless curiosity, to be that of Sir Henry Havelock, hero of the Indian Mutiny.

It was more important to find Rose than to recover his hat, and anyhow, she might help him to recover his hat. So he dodged through the traffic, which was still not returning in a full stream, and reached the pavement on the other side, hoping to find her waiting there. He went down to the end of the Strand. He went up, past the end of Duncannon Street, as far as St. Martin's. No Rose. She must have been so angry that she had gone straight back to Cumberland Square, and now, thinking it over, he could not blame her. If their evening had been wrecked, it was his fault. And it was after nine. If she had gone home, she would not come out again. He might as well try to find his hat. So back he went.

There was another fellow looking for something, a little man with a cap too big for him. They nearly bumped into one another.

"Looking for something, mate?" asked the little man.

"Yes. My hat."

"Crumbs! Y'ought to be able to find your flaming hat. I'm looking for a flaming badge. Might have dropped it 'ere, might be on the road. 'Ow can I flaming well tell? Got a fag?"

Edward gave him one, and had one himself. The little man pulled away at his in silence for a moment, shutting his eyes as he filled his lungs with smoke. He had a dirty, battered but still cheerful face. When he opened his eyes again, he squinted in a friendly fashion at Edward through the smoke. Then he made a tut-tutting noise, to show his disapproval of things. "Go and lose my flaming badge! Just like me! I needn't have poked my flaming nose in this, need I?"

"I needn't, either, but I did. Got in the middle of it."

"Well, I didn't, see? But what I did was to flaming well go and do somebody a good turn—sheer kindness of 'eart—and then what 'appens? Does God love me? I go and lose my flaming badge. And," he added darkly, "it's not the first time them things has 'appened to yours truly. Doing somebody a good turn!"

Seeing that they were smoking together, Edward thought they might as well go on talking a little longer, so he asked what had happened.

"Well, I'll tell yer. I'm standing here—see?—and next to me's a little piece in green—and I'm jammed right up against her—see?—an' I must say if I'd have picked the one to be jammed up against, that's the one. Well, we're all flaming well pushed up this way—can't 'elp it, we 'ave to go—see?—and then there's another bull's rush, an' we're 'alfway across the road—see?—me an' this fair piece in green an' lots more. Well, she's 'urt her flaming ankle in the rush, an' she's white as a sheet an' nearly faintin' an' by this time we're up against a car that's over there, an' this kid's dropping on the flaming running board—see? Well, this is a posh car—not big but posh—with a shover in front and a posh woman in the back—an' I see her plain 'cos she's got the light on—see? So I says: 'Here, take her inside, for Christ's sake'—to this posh woman—see?—'Hurt herself, she has,' I says—and then when she didn't make a move—I opened the door an' says: 'Come on, or I'll push your flaming window in, lady, see?' An' then I got the kid in. An' then, of course, I go an' flaming well lose my badge. T-t-t-t!"

"The girl?" cried Edward excitedly. "She hadn't a green hat and coat on, had she? And was she a fair girl but with brownish eyes? Very pretty. About so big? And about twenty?"

"Right every time. That's the very piece or her spit image. Just shows yer, doesn't it?"

"But that's my girl. I've just been looking for her. We got separated."

"More fool you, mate! If she'd been my bit, we wouldn't 'ave got separated. Not flaming well likely!"

"And this car? You're sure she went off in it?"

"Saw it go. An' if you happened to 'ave a couple o' bob on you, mate—'cos I'm short, an' I've lost my flaming badge into the bargain—I'd tell yer about that car. And it wasn't no ordinary car neither."

"Well, I suppose they took her home, so it doesn't matter. Still—I'd like to know." And Edward found two shillings.

"Thanks, mate. Y'ought to know about that car, just

in case. I'd know it again, all right, I believe it was one of these fancy foreign jobs. It was all silvery outside, believe me or believe me not! And it was all red inside—y'know, this fancy red leather. And the shover was a nigger—big buck nig, black as your boots——"

"Here," Edward protested, "you're not making this up, are you?"

"Mate, it's the flaming truth. Silver outside, red inside, nigger driver. An' belonged to a posh woman, all dolled up—with a face on her like an expensive tart who's just retiring—an' I don't care 'ow posh an' dolled up she was—she 'ad an old tart's face—I've seen 'em an' I know—see? An' I wouldn't like any bit of mine to 'ave much to do with a painted piece like that—I give you my word——"

"But it was you who put her into the car," cried Edward angrily.

"An' what of it, what of it? Did yer want to see the kid lying out on the flaming road? I'd got to do something, hadn't I? Now there's a bit o' gratitude for yer! Tell me next I ought to mind my own business! And lose my flaming badge into the flaming bargain!"

"I'm going to see if she's back home. Good night."

The wild-looking, hatless young man who arrived at the basement door of 7, Cumberland Square, to ask for Mary Pearson, was not given an enthusiastic welcome by Mr. Penner, who looked at him very suspiciously round the door, which he held open about six inches.

"She's out."

"Hasn't she come back yet?"

"That's her young man." This was from Connie,

who had managed to peep through the narrow opening.

"Yes," said Edward desperately. "You see—I was with her to-night——"

"Better come in." And Mr. Penner held the door open.

They went into the little sitting-room. Mr. Penner turned off the wireless. Mrs. Penner and Eva Newton were there, and of course Connie. Edward recognised them all from Rose's account of them. It was like suddenly meeting characters you had read about in a book. He was introduced as Mary Pearson's friend, Mr. Fielding.

"Something's happened, hasn't it? I know it has," said Mrs. Penner, in a dark prophetical tone. "I said an hour ago—didn't I, Eva?—some trouble was on its way for somebody here. Now wait a minute. Will you have a cup of tea and a bit of cake?"

Edward was very glad to have some tea and cake. While he was refreshing himself, he told them what had happened, only omitting the quarrel. He could not have asked for a better audience. A dead calm had followed the storm of the afternoon down here, and all four of them had been feeling bored. And now here was drama, and of a welcome non-partisan kind too; here was mystery; and all complete with a hero and a heroine and a strong love interest. Their eyes shone.

"Well, I can tell you this," cried Eva Newton, looking at once noble and defiant, "Mary's a good girl, a real good girl, she is."

"That's right, Eva," said Mrs. Penner approvingly.

"What's that got to do with it?" Mr. Penner showed some irritation at this new example of feminine inconsequence. He had had a day of it and did not want any more. "Nobody's asking whether she's good or not——"

"She *is* a good girl," Eva repeated, reproachfully.

"Nobody's saying she isn't. That's not the point. The point is—where is she?" And Mr. Penner looked across at Edward, as from one tower of reason to another.

"That's it," said Edward earnestly. "You see—if that woman brought her home, then she'd have been here now."

"Long since," said Mr. Penner, with a kind of gloomy gusto. "Couldn't have taken 'em more than quarter of an hour—say, twenty minutes at the outside. And look at the time now."

"Yes, and time you were off to bed, Connie," said Mrs. Penner severely.

"Oh, what for?"

"Because it is," said Mr. Penner severely. And Connie, protesting, had to go.

"I suppose she couldn't have come in without one of you knowing about it?" Edward asked the remaining three, who gave him the impression that this matter could be thoroughly discussed now that Connie had gone.

"No," replied Mr. Penner. "The family's out to-night. She'd have had to come in this way. Bad ankle too. Couldn't have done it."

"I'll go and see," said Eva, and hurried out.

"Wasting her time, that's all," was Mr. Penner's comment.

Mrs. Penner, looking like an immense prophetess of woe, glanced burningly from her husband to Edward.

"If you ask me, that poor girl's been kidnapped."

"Not she!" cried Mr. Penner.

"Well, what then? Where is she? Tell me that, Penner," said his wife, with a pitying side-glance at Edward.

"The only thing I can think of," said Edward, while Mr. Penner was darkly cogitating, "is that her ankle must have been so bad, that woman took her to one of the hospitals, and that's where she is."

"That sounds a bit of sense to me," cried Mr. Penner.

Eva returned, dramatic and gasping. "Not there!"

"Of course not," said Mr. Penner. "She's been taken to one of the hospitals. And the question is—which?"

Edward felt helpless. He knew nothing about London hospitals. He had seen one or two of them—immense buildings with posters in front of them, urgently demanding funds—and the thought of Rose lying helpless behind one of those great blank walls was not pleasant. He searched for another explanation of her disappearance. "There's another thing," he announced, while the Penners were remembering all the hospitals. "This woman in the car might have been going home herself—probably was—and she might have taken Rose——"

"Who's Rose?" asked Mrs. Penner sharply.

"I mean Mary. I call her Rose. She might have taken her home with her, just to let her rest a bit."

This not unreasonable and hopeful explanation did not commend itself to the other three, perhaps because it was not dramatic enough.

"If she were mine," said Mrs. Penner, in a deep thrilling tone, "I'd go to the police. Then there'd be *no* mistake."

Edward saw that this would not do at all, and was instantly alarmed. He came down heavily on Mr. Penner's side, and asked about hospitals. Mr. Penner had his list ready by this time. "What you do," he said, with a gloomy relish, "is to ring up the accident wards. I'll go up to my pantry and do it now. You'd better come with me."

They were half an hour in that pantry, which was bitterly cold and depressing, ringing up hospitals. It was a miserable business. At the end of it, Edward did not know whether to be relieved or sorry that not one of them had any news of Rose. He clung to the opinion that the woman in the car had taken Rose to her own home, and might probably be keeping her there until she had rested her ankle and was fit to return to Cumberland Square. He said so to Mr. Penner, who was now rather blue about the hands and face but seemed to have enjoyed his chats with the accident wards.

"It's after eleven now," said Mr. Penner. "Getting late for a maid to be out. If she wasn't fit to come back, they'd ring us up and tell us."

"She may he here any minute," said Edward desperately.

They went downstairs again, and reported their failure to Mrs. Penner and Eva, who instantly said they were not surprised. Both of them were in favour of going to the police, and Edward had to work hard to argue them out of it without appearing to be arguing them out of it. At half-past eleven he got up to go. Mr. Penner agreed to wait up until Edward had telephoned from his lodgings to enquire if Mary Pearson had then returned.

It was after twelve when Edward, at the telephone

downstairs at Mrs. Scrutton's, learned from Mr. Penner that Mary Pearson was still missing. They arranged that one of them should ring up the other, early the next morning. Oddly enough, Edward did not feel as worried now as he had done earlier. The very strangeness of his visit to the house in Cumberland Square had perhaps unbalanced his judgment then, whereas now that he was back in his own familiar surroundings at Chalk Farm, he felt that there was some ordinary sensible reason for Rose's continued absence and that everything would be all right in the morning. He still ached from the clout on the head and the odd kicks he had been given during the rumpus in Trafalgar Square, but he was desperately tired and was soon asleep. His dreams, which were singularly clear and happy, took him back to Haliford and Sutcliffe Place; showed him his father again, still hopeful; a younger and less pompous Herbert; restored some blazing July when school was breaking up for the long holidays and there was cricket in Ackroyd Park; and there was no Rose, no London, no Mrs. Scrutton's and Cumberland Squares, and the blackshirts and the reds had not begun to think of fighting in Trafalgar Square. The days to which he went back in these dreams had had no special quality at the time he had first lived them, but now when they returned, or when he travelled indifferently back to them, they were ecstatic, magical.

The morning was all the greyer and colder. Half-dressed and shivering, he ran down to the telephone in the hall, paid his twopence to it, only to be told by Mr. Penner that Mary Pearson had neither returned nor sent any message and that Lady Holt-Ibstock was extremely annoyed. Mr. Penner added that he was now of Mrs. Penner's opinion, that it was a job for the police. Edward earnestly assured him that he would attend to all that. He returned slowly to his room, thinking hard. Rose knew his address now and had had time to write to him, but there was no letter for him. True, they had quarrelled, but he could not believe that her side of the quarrel could have lasted much longer than his did, and his had collapsed less than a minute after she had gone. Her resentment, justified by his sulkiness and rudeness, may have lasted longer than that, but he could not believe that she could keep steadily on being angry with him through all her adventures last night. And she must know he would be feeling anxious. She might be paying him out for his silliness last night, but that did not seem like her. Besides, she would have let them know something at Cumberland Square.

He ate an absent-minded, messy little breakfast, then stared into his little gas-fire, wondering what to do. Before he had arrived at any decision, Mr. Finland looked in to borrow a few matches. (Mr. Finland may be said to have *smoked* matches, for he was one of those men who are for ever lighting and relighting their pipes.) Mr. Finland was quite ready to have a chat. They were the only two on that top floor, and Edward, unlike Lexden below, treated the battered old chap with something like respect, was sorry for him but did not show it, so that they got along very well together. Indeed, Edward had come to like Mr. Finland. Looked at from one point of view,

Mr. Finland was a hopeless sort of person, who had made a mess of his life and now had to get drunk two or three times a week, simply to keep going at all. From another point of view, however, he was a better kind of man to have about than most successful ones, because although, when sober, he was too grandly dignified and rather pompous—perhaps to make up for being drunk and undignified so often—he was really simple and helpful and humbly anxious to understand all about you, and by no means unintelligent. Unlike the people who have done all they want to and have got on, he always realised that there was a lot of trouble about in this world and that folks are bound to be weak and silly sometimes. So Edward was quite glad to see him.

"You look worried, Fielding," said Mr. Finland gravely. "I have been meaning to ask you if the letter of introduction to the office equipment concern brought any result."

Edward laughed, not very cheerfully. "Do you know, I'd forgotten about that. I took it round yesterday afternoon, and the chap turned me down flat."

"Don't be discouraged, my dear boy. These things must happen. The only thing to do is to—er—approach every possible channel. Let no opportunity pass. I had the same difficulty when I—er—first decided to try independent tutoring work here. Every conceivable obstacle—including some I'd never thought of, such as the deplorable state of one's collars and boots during these periods—every obstacle was placed in my way, but I persevered. My motto was *Nil desperandum*, and it should be yours too.

Have you ever considered the possibilities of employment in some capacity in one of the moving picture studios? One of my pupils, an electrician, who has a brother, also an electrician, in one of the studios, is very optimistic indeed, and speaks highly of the business."

"No, it isn't work that's worrying me, Mr. Finland. It's—my girl."

"Ah, yes, the one you mentioned. A tiff, perhaps? A lovers' quarrel."

"Well, we did have a bit of a row," Edward admitted, "but that's not it. The fact is—she seems to have disappeared."

"Tell me the facts," said Mr. Finland, rather as if he were Sherlock Holmes or somebody of that kind. And in order to improve the likeness, he sat down and lit his pipe, and very soon filled the room with the smoke and reek of his strong cheap tobacco.

Edward, not sorry to be confiding in somebody, told the whole story, so that at the end Mr. Finland knew as much about it as he did.

"Extraordinary! Though this is, of course, an extraordinary city. Anything might happen here. But the butler is right, you know, Fielding. You must communicate with the police. I have no particular enthusiasm for the police—and indeed once or twice I've found them absurdly officious—but in this instance it is the only sensible course."

"I don't want to do it, Mr. Finland. You see, Rose, when she worked at the shop, took the blame for something she didn't do, to help another girl—I don't know why—it was a barmy thing to do—and she ran away, and the police were looking for her. That's why she changed her name and went to that house as a parlourmaid. So I can't bring the police into it—not yet, anyhow."

"Quite so. I see your difficulty." It was typical of Mr. Finland that he did not condemn Rose for doing something silly, or hint that there was something fishy about it all, or anything of that kind, but went on trying to be helpful. That was why he was a good person to confide in, far better than most people, who would begin to pass judgment at once. "Well, then, we must bring some reasonable method to this question. The girl is injured—not, I imagine, very seriously—and is helped into a car. It is," he added, enjoying himself, "a car of unusual appearance, with a silvered body, red leather upholstering, and driven by a negro chauffeur. The car takes her away. The problem is then, simply, where did the car take her to?"

"Yes, that's it, of course," said Edward, rather impatiently. "She may have been taken to a hospital because her ankle was very bad or there was something else wrong. But we tried the most likely hospitals, last night."

"Then she may be in some other you did not telephone," said Mr. Finland. "Or, alternatively, in a private nursing home. There are a great many private nursing homes."

"But it isn't likely, is it? I mean, a stranger wouldn't take a girl with a bad ankle to a nursing home, would she?"

"It's a possibility rather than a probability. Have you a

sheet of paper, my dear boy? We ought to jot down these alternatives—under their proper headings—Possible—Probable—and so forth—and then, working along these methodical lines, you can investigate without any further waste of time."

The jotting down on paper seemed to Edward rather a waste of time in itself, but he did not say so. He got up to find a sheet of paper, while Mr. Finland, with great gusto, sharpened a pencil.

"You know, Mr. Finland, it's queer," he said slowly, as he looked about for the paper, "but Rose has been a funny disappearing kind of person to me. We had that grand day on the moors I told you about, and then she disappeared—came to London—and I came to London—and it was weeks before I found her again. Well, when I did, we had all that afternoon and evening together, last week, and then it looked as if it was going to last for ever. Perhaps I took advantage of that, being so silly and sulky last night when we met, just because she'd kept me waiting, and now she's disappeared again. I don't suppose you know what I'm talking about—I'm not explaining it very well—I'm a bit mixed up about it myself. But it's as if, just when I think Rose is an ordinary girl, she disappears, and then I have to go looking for her. In one way, I hardly know her—we've been together so little—and yet I've spent so much time thinking about her and looking for her, I seem to know her better than anybody in the world. And I think why I don't like London any more is not because of work, but because all it seems to do is to swallow up Rose. She's somewhere behind the fogs and the houses and the crowds nearly all the time."

"I think," said Mr. Finland mildly, taking the sheet of paper, "it would be better if we kept more strictly to this actual matter of her disappearance last night. These last observations of yours, which I couldn't follow closely, seemed to have certain mystical—or possibly pseudo-mystical—trend——"

"Yes, of course. Well then, she might have been taken to a hospital or nursing home, but it isn't likely."

"Alternatively," said Mr. Finland, who was now happily writing, "to the house of some relative or close friend."

"Not likely."

"Possible but not probable," murmured Mr. Finland, making a note of it.

"This woman may have taken her to her own home, to rest or something. That's quite likely."

"Highly probable. You notice, Fielding," said Mr. Finland, quite the master detective now, "one link throughout here. The car. Wherever she went, this car took her there. In short, we must concentrate upon the car. And of course upon its owner."

"Yes, of course. If I could find this woman, I'd jolly well soon find out where she took Rose."

"Exactly, Fielding." Mr. Finland was quite triumphant, as if they had just made some remarkable discovery, much to the surprise of Edward, who could not see that they had got any further. "Find the car and the owner of the car."

"Yes, I know. But how?"

"I will reply by asking you a question, my dear boy. How many cars, even in this city, are driven by a negro chauffeur, have silvered bodies, and red leather upholstery? Undoubtedly, there are several have one feature, several another, but all three—no. Only one car, in my opinion, will fully answer to this description. And fortunately, we live in a time when people notice motorcars when they notice nothing else. The car, Fielding, my dear boy, can be found. Moreover, as I believe you still have a little money left—and would be willing to spend some of it——"

"Yes, of course, but I don't see——"

"Then," said Mr. Finland firmly interrupting, "I think I know the very people who could help you, and who would ask only a modest honorarium for their services. The Foreign Legion."

"What?" The old chap must be trying to be funny.

"It's a name—facetious but a trifle bitter too, I fancy—given to themselves by a small group of middle-aged men you may have met at the local Labour Exchange. Do you know Torroni's Café—known locally as a 'caff'—a few doors further down than the Labour Exchange? It's a very modest establishment, patronised by taxi-drivers and bus conductors, where one can get a cup of tea or coffee and a sandwich or piece of cake for a few pence. That is the headquarters of the group."

Edward was bewildered. "What are they? What do they do?"

Mr. Finland replied carefully and with dignity: "They

are middle-aged men who have been unfortunate, like many of us. They cannot find regular employment. If they do, they drop out of the Legion. For the most part, they stay in. They are decent, intelligent, thoughtful men who have been unlucky. I do not mean to say they have no faults, no weaknesses, but if they have, they have been unlucky in possessing those faults, those weaknesses. We can't all have a clocklike perfection. We are men, not guaranteed pieces of mechanism. I spent a good deal of my time with the Legion when I was not so busy as I am now, and when it looks as if work is not coming my way, it is my one consolation that I shall be able to go to Torroni's again, spend my threepence or fourpence, and exchange opinions and experiences with the others there. One or two of them are men of unusual ability, who have held good positions. Between them, they ought to be able to trace that car."

"It sounds a terrific job," said Edward, not very hopefully, "even if half a dozen of them tackle it. When are they there at the café?"

"Usually, any time between half-past eleven and two," replied Mr. Finland. "I shall not be free myself this morning until twelve, but if you would like to go along with me then, we will see what can be done." He stood up and solemnly handed Edward the sheet of notes. "I am extremely happy to be of any small service to you in this matter, Fielding, my dear boy. We meet at twelve, then."

Edward went downstairs, and spent some time vainly trying to speak to Mr. Penner again on the telephone.

The number was engaged so long that he began to wonder if Mr. Penner had been told to ring up half London in search of Rose, forgetting that Sir Edwin Holt-Ibstock and his family might want to use the telephone at times for their own affairs. When finally he got through, Mr. Penner had no news at all, except that Lady Holt-Ibstock was still annoyed. To this Edward, irritated, retorted that he hoped it would keep fine for her. Not knowing what move to make next, until he saw the Foreign Legion at lunch-time, he cut through the dark maze of little streets behind his lodgings to Camden Town, where he bought a cheap brown hat to replace the one, his only one, that he had lost the night before. This new one reminded him of those they had had at the Belvedere Trading Company, and he felt suspicious about it, did not take to it, gave it no entry into his real life, just wore it. By the time he got back to Mrs. Scrutton's, he had a good excuse to ring up Cumberland Square again. He was not long getting the number, but Mr. Penner did not answer this time. He heard a rather loud, important female voice, probably Lady Holt-Ibstock's.

"Would you mind telling me, please," he said cautiously, "if Mary Pearson, the parlourmaid, has come back?"

"Pearson? No, Pearson hasn't returned," the voice shouted, nearly deafening him. "She hasn't given notice. She's left all her things here. I can't understand it at all. More tiresome. I say—most tiresome. This is Lady Holt-Ibstock speaking. Who is that? I say—who is that?"

"Nobody," said Edward in a tiny ironical voice, and at once rang off.

The head of his landlady, Mrs. Scrutton, now appeared over the banisters. "You're having a good go at that telephone this morning, aren't you? Enjoying yourself?"

"No, I'm not."

"Well, if you don't now, you never will." Mrs. Scrutton was fond of such maxims, all tending to prove that life is a wretched business and that the young had better try and enjoy it before they discover what it is really like.

"All right, then, I never will," said Edward sulkily. He was in no mood for this rubbish. "What time's the next post?"

"When it comes," retorted Mrs. Scrutton sharply, withdrawing her head very quickly, like a Punch-and-Judy character. Edward waited for Mr. Finland, who appeared very soon, looking very dignified and important.

They went to the region Edward had visited once already that morning, a region of cheap shops and rubbishy Belvedere Trading Company garments, of dusty meat and flyblown biscuits and rotting oranges, of pawnbrokers' shops and funeral parlours and dingy little pubs, of Racing Specials and cough mixtures and barrowloads of bananas, of morning queues for films about an imaginary Wild West, of colds and adenoids and pregnancy and prolapsus. The café was a typical establishment of its kind; neither pleasantly foreign nor decently English; the result of dreary cross-purposes, the exiled Italian peasants who kept it being under the impression that it was very English, and its Cockney customers firmly believing that this was the Italian way of doing things. It began as a shop, selling the usual packets of cigarettes and slabs of chocolate; then it sprouted an urn or two and displayed some soggy buns; and then it changed altogether into a place of refreshment. In the far corner was a table longer than the others, and at this table half a dozen middle-aged men were sitting, with cups and crumbs in front of them. This was the Foreign Legion, and they were a shabby lot. With the cruel physical snobbery of youth, Edward took an instant dislike to their appearance, and was rather sorry he had come to see them. Too many unshaven chins, red and bulbous noses, goggly eyes, coat collars thick with dandruff and tobacco ash. Yet in here these men had temporarily lost their usual wandering and unwanted look. Being regular customers, here at least they had some status, and so they expanded again into personalities. They greeted Mr. Finland warmly but politely. There were quite punctilious introductions all round. Perhaps because they had so little else to stand on, these battered old chaps stood on ceremony. There was Mr. Sewell, a thinnish, sharp-chinned fellow who looked shrewdly through iron-rimmed spectacles, who had been a journalist of some kind and the victim of one of those tremendous Fleet Street amalgamations. There was Mr. Findhorn, who was short of breath, short of hair, short of almost everything, and had once been an assistant cashier. There was Mr. Moffat, who had once managed a milk business and still had a vaguely rural air. There was Mr. Scawton, a little bushy man, who had been a solicitor's clerk, and who was still deliberate and precise. There was Mr. Ravenglass, who had been a traveller for a firm of manufacturing chemists, and who was now very shabby indeed, a blurred and tattered sketch of a middle-aged citizen, but who yet retained a manner in which were combined the austerity of the scientist and the bonhomie of the commercial traveller. And, lastly, there was Mr. Colsterworth, who seemed to be the oldest there, and had a twisted blue-lipped face, and never spoke above a whisper, so that it appeared as if he had already almost taken leave of this world. Edward never learned if they had wives and families. Mr. Finland did not seem to know. But here they were, six middle-aged men, clean outside the profit-making and wage-earning scheme, rusting away like old and disused engines at some railway siding, reported Dead or Missing in the economic casualty lists, yet still very much alive, able to think, remember, and feel—a section of the Foreign Legion camped far out on the social desert.

It was to Mr. Sewell, the fellow-professional man, that Mr. Finland explained what had brought Edward there, though the other five listened carefully. Mr. Finland did not tell the whole story, but concentrated upon the car they had to find.

"We can find it," said Mr. Sewell without any hesitation. "That is, if it's a car that has been here some time, and not one from outside. Of course——" He stopped, and looked at Edward.

"I haven't a lot of money, you know," said Edward. "But—well, what do you think?"

"What do *you* think, Mr. Finland?"

Mr. Finland and Mr. Sewell looked earnestly at each other, while the other members of the Legion looked earnestly at the pair of them.

"How many of you can—er—take part in this?" asked Mr. Finland.

They all could and would, except Mr. Colsterworth. "Better leave me out," he whispered faintly. "Sorry. Not strong enough now—padding round—asking for cars. Sorry."

"Then I suggest, gentlemen," said Mr. Finland gravely, "five shillings each for expenses, and two pounds for the one who discovers the car—or, to be more accurate, the owner of the car."

"Fair enough," said Mr. Moffat heartily.

"Though, of course, gentlemen," said Mr. Scawton, the legal member, "we might consider it advisable to pool the reward. But that can be settled later."

They all looked at Edward, who felt hot and red-faced. He could not make up his mind—it was one of those occasions known to everybody—whether he was making an inspired decision or merely a fool of himself. The whole scene, his very presence there, had a dreamlike unreality. Mr. Finland and his Foreign Legion! It was all worlds away from Rose and himself. Yet the fact remained that she had vanished, and presumably in this car. But even the car had a dubious, fairy-tale quality about it, and more than once he had doubted its existence. That little man in Trafalgar Square might have been making it all up. The whole thing, with the solid exception of Rose's absence, might be a tangle of unrealities. Nevertheless, he agreed.

"I shall try too, of course, though I must say it seems a pretty hopeless job." And Edward looked round, almost apologetically.

Mr. Findhorn and Mr. Ravenglass were beginning to express their doubts, but they were cut short by Mr. Sewell. "Don't agree at all. Not if the car's been here some time. Now some of us here like to think we can use our heads——"

"Always talking about it," chuckled Mr. Scawton, rubbing the end of his nose vigorously.

"Exactly, Mr. Scawton," Mr. Sewell continued. "Well, here's a chance. Now, let's see. And to start with, I vote we pool the reward. Otherwise, we can't work together properly."

"Co-operation every time," said Mr. Moffat. "Nothing like it."

"Except in the milk business, eh, Mr. Moffat?" said Mr. Scawton, chuckling again. "But we agree, eh, gentlemen?"

"All right. Now look at it," said Mr. Sewell, beginning to enjoy himself. "Here's a car. Silvery body, red leather inside, driven by a negro chauffeur."

"Ought to be able to find that all right," said Mr. Scawton. "Even if the woman has her own garage, it has to call somewhere for petrol and oil and what not."

"Exactly," cried Mr. Sewell. "Ten to one, they go to the nearest garage. The chaps there will know all about a car like that."

Even Mr. Ravenglass agreed with this.

"I thought of all that," said Edward, who had, "but look how many garages there are in London—even if this woman lives in London—and we don't even know that."

"Just what I was thinking," said Mr. Findhorn.

"Wait a minute," cried Mr. Sewell, brightening all the time now. "This is where we start using our heads. Now what sort of woman would have a car like that—and a black chauffeur?"

"One of these fancy, smart, fashionable women, I say," said Mr. Scawton.

"You're right, Mr. Scawton. And it's ten to one she lives in London. It's ten to one she lives—now, wait a minute."

"What we want," said Mr. Moffat, "is a map. And we haven't got one."

"Oh yes, we have," cried Mr. Sewell. "Carried one for years." He pulled out of his inside pocket a thick wad of miscellaneous papers, and found among them a folded, crumpled map of London, which he spread out carefully on the table. "It's going to be useful now. You look here." He put the other papers back in his pocket and found a stub of pencil. "We can wash out everything south of the river."

"Wimbledon and Blackheath?" asked Mr. Scawton, looking dubious.

"They're just a possibility, but only just."

"Begin with Probables before Possibles," said Mr. Finland gravely. "That's always been my own system of working."

"You're quite right, Mr. Finland," said Mr. Sewell, on fire now, his eyes flashing through his spectacles. "Look. We can also wash out everything east of here. Then, to start with, wash out everything west of a line here—running down from Ladbroke Grove to Earl's Court Road."

"Eliminate Paddington, Kilburn, and everything north of Hampstead Heath," cried Mr. Scawton, vainly trying to obtain the pencil.

"Right. That narrows it down a bit, doesn't it?" And Mr. Sewell began drawing thick lines on the map. "Now then. First there's the West End proper, chiefly the big hotels and service flats. Right? Then there's Belgravia, South Kensington and Chelsea. Then there's Mayfair. Then there's Lancaster Gate, north of Marble Arch, and St. John's Wood. Then there's Maida Vale and Hampstead. Then there's Regent's Park and Bloomsbury. I make that six districts. We might improve on 'em."

They all bent over the map, which now had a great many thick pencil marks on it. The unwanted men came to life. The Legion was on the march. They all had a good knowledge of the city that had used them so badly, even if they were not so ready with tongue and pencil as Mr. Sewell. The map itself also came to life for them. They began pointing and talking all at once. Even Mr. Finland, who would not be able to join in the search, eagerly joined in the discussion. Edward himself, though he knew less than the others did, though he still felt himself lost in the great forest, plunged in too. And two taxi-drivers, who knew the Foreign Legion and usually threw it an ironical word or two, catching a glimpse of the map and overhearing the topographical references, now came over and insisted upon giving advice. The proprietor's daughter, who had glorious black eyes and a shrill meaningless laugh, was drawn by the noise and excitement in that corner, and left her counter to look on, with the half-wondering, half-ironical stare of the young female at the mad old males. The proprietor himself, all hair, yellow fat and wide grin, waddled out of the back room, where he had been doing his endless accounts, and shouted encouragingly into the corner. The three remaining customers were staring hard and grinning. Two astonished children and a little dirty wisp of a newspaper man were looking in through the open doorway. And behind them, majestic but faintly curious, was a policeman, opening his eyes at the sight of the "caff" suddenly boiling with life. So the search began.

XVI

ROSE awakened very slowly, as if she had come to from an immense distance of sleep. She opened her eyes, saw nothing in the gloom of any interest, and so closed her eyes again and retreated a little way into that distance. A tiny and obscure feeling that she had been asleep a long time now crept into her consciousness. She opened her eyes wide, forced them to stare, to collect information. Where was she? Long before she had completely recognised the room, which was still darkened by the heavy curtains, she remembered. She was having an adventure, with a twisted ankle and a kind lady playing their parts in it. She had thought of it as an adventure late last night, so it must still be an adventure this morning. But somehow, it did not seem as light-hearted now, perhaps because this was not the time of day for adventures. What time was it? She had no watch. Very carefully, still feeling her ankle, she got out of bed, put on the wrap, then groped her way to the curtains and managed to draw them. It was daylight, and she knew at once that it was not early morning, although it was rather dark outside. There was nothing much to be seen. She looked down, through a thick greyness of atmosphere, at a leafless tree, at the top of a brick wall, at the back of tall houses beyond the wall. The room, though still stuffy and rather smelly, was cold, and she lit the gas-fire. Her head ached a little, and she had a nasty taste in her mouth; rather as if she was just recovering from a long illness. But she was also very hungry, and she knew that she must have slept a long time. She went into the bathroom, and thought of taking a nice lazy hot bath—for she decided that she might as well make the most of these luxuries—when she remembered her clothes. Last night, she had left them in the bathroom. Now they were not there. Somebody must have put them in the wardrobe or the drawers. She had a quick wash, just to make herself feel more wide-awake, and then went to explore the wardrobe and the drawers.

Her clothes were not there. But the wardrobe was not empty. There were two fancy old wraps in it, a fur, three odd shoes, and quite a nice little black hat that had been tossed into a corner. The interior smelt as she remembered the room itself smelling when she first came into it, last night, of over-scented and not over-clean girls, perhaps lots of them. There were things in the drawers too: odd torn stockings, a few soiled bits of underclothing, two or three powder-puffs, handkerchiefs stained with lipstick, and a mess of curling squeezed-out tubes, empty powder boxes and rouge pots and jars of face cream, hairpins and safety pins, torn letters and bills. And in the last drawer she looked in, the top right-hand one, there were some drawings that seemed to have been cut out of foreign papers. These drawings were of a kind she had never seen before. She did not know such things existed. They were not only obscene, putting into hard lines what before had only existed dimly in her imagination, but they were so ugly and lunatic in their obscenity that they were frightening. She looked at them all quickly, and then hurriedly shut them away, tried to banish them for ever. She stood leaning against the chest of drawers, trembling. It was as if she had just been looking at and listening to a madman. He was in that drawer, commanding her to open it again and let him out. And now it seemed as if everything she had felt about this room, from the moment when she first entered its stuffy, smelly pinkiness, was focused to a sharp point by what she had just seen. Perhaps all the time she had known somehow that that mad filth was somewhere about, just waiting for her. For the last five years, Rose had been earning her living among crowds of women and girls, and many of them did not care what they said, so that there was not much about men and women that she did not know, and what she did know did not disgust her in the least. She was neither very curious nor prudish. But those drawings were something quite different, belonging to some strange world. They did not turn men and women into animals but into grinning devils; they had nothing to do with fun and making love; they came from some region of disease and torture and insanity. The man who had done those drawings—and instinctively she knew that it must be a man—had hated himself and everybody else. They were his revenge on life.

Rose decided that if she did stay with Mrs. Hubarth, she would not sleep in this room. The maids who had had it before—probably foreigners—were obviously nasty girls, and the room would take a long time to recover from them. Meanwhile, she wanted her clothes, and felt very silly standing there, in a strange house, dressed in a thin wrap and the flimsiest pyjamas, with no clothes in sight. That housekeeper must have taken them away, though why she should have done so was a mystery. The ankle still did not feel quite right, and as she wondered what to do now, Rose limped back to the bed and sat on the edge of it.

The door opened, quietly, cautiously. A head came round, and it was a strange head, a middle-aged woman's, with a swollen red face.

"Well, then," it wheezed at her, "if yer not wakened up at last, an' sittin' there pretty as a picter. Back to bed, dearie, or yer'll be catchin' yer death o' cold." The woman, who was short and fat, and was wearing an immense cleaning apron, came a step or two into the room. This must be the charwoman.

"What time is it, please?"

"Time? It'll be nearer one than twelve, dearie. An' if ever a girl 'ad a good sleep, then it's you, isn't it? I was just the same at your age, dearie. I could lie in, an' sleep it all off. An' now I can't, never mind what time I gets to bed. An' hungry too, I'll be bound."

Rose admitted she was hungry.

"That's right, dearie. Well, get back into yer nice bed, an' I'll bring something upon a tray, just like yer might be a little queen."

"I've been looking for my clothes," said Rose, who felt she would rather get up than be treated like a little queen.

"Never mind yer clothes, dearie," replied the

charwoman vaguely. "Make the best of things as yer find 'em, I always say, an' if they want to make a nice fuss of yer, let 'em while yer've got the chance. Wait till yer see what I brings yer, dearie."

Evidently Mrs. Hubarth thought she ought not to get up yet, which was very nice of her. Rose remembered that she must write to Edward, who would be wondering what had become of her. But there were no writing materials in this room. She mentioned this to the charwoman.

"Quite all right, dearie. If yer wants to write a nice little letter, we can see to that. Now just get back into bed, an' I shan't be long." And she waited until Rose, still wearing the wrap, got into bed before she went away.

Rose waited uneasily. She was annoyed with herself because she felt uneasy. Here, for once in her life, she was being waited on grandly, being made a fuss of, and yet she could not enjoy it properly. She told herself that she was a little fool. But the uneasiness remained. Perhaps it was because she had come to dislike this particular room. And it would be difficult to tell Mrs. Hubarth, who had been so kind, that she hated this room of hers.

The fat little char returned in triumph carrying a large tray, on which were two cutlets, potatoes, French beans, toast, some fruit, and a glass of red wine. "An' yer couldn't wish for nothin' nicer," she remarked, as she put the tray in front of Rose. "I'll say that for that Frenchy 'ousekeeper. A queer one she *may* be, but she can pop into that kitchen an' dish yer up something nice in quick-sticks. An' look what I brought, dearie. Paper an' envelope an' a nice pencil, all to write to yer boy friend with. An' if he's not a lucky young feller, I've never seen one. What does he do to yer, dearie?" The woman put a fat hand to Rose's cheek, and wagged her head leeringly. Rose drew back sharply, and realised now that she had hated this woman right from the first.

They stared at one another for a moment, during which the woman's fat wheezy geniality suddenly vanished and her little pig eyes were hard and resentful. She was about to say something, but apparently thought better of it, and suddenly went off without another word or look. When the door closed, there was a little click outside. Nearly upsetting her tray, Rose scrambled out of bed to test her sudden suspicion. Yes, the door had been locked outside. This discovery gave Rose quite a queer feeling, but she decided that the hateful charwoman must have locked the door just to annoy her, and that it was silly to worry.

There was certainly nothing wrong with the lunch or dinner or whatever it was on that tray. Feeling luxurious and spoilt, Rose ate it all up, and drank the wine, which made her feel very warm and comfortable inside. After that, it was fun to push the things to one side, use the tray as a writing desk, and decide what she would say to Edward. This was her very first letter to him. He had been very stupid and cross, they had even quarrelled, but now she was not going to bother about that. Some girls would have paid him out for behaving so badly, but she had forgiven him and would not pretend she hadn't. And the very sight of the notepaper made her feel less uneasy about everything, because it was nice notepaper and it had the address of the house and the telephone number on it, in neat red print. Somehow this made a great difference. All her silly little uneasinesses looked sillier than ever now, just childishness.

It took her quite a time to write a letter that did not seem foolish, and it was a good thing she had been given several sheets of notepaper. The final version, which was not quite right but would have to do, ran as follows:

Darling Edward,—

I am very sorry about last night though it was mostly your fault and I expect now you are sorry too! When I walked away there was a lot of pushing and fighting and then I hurt my ankle and a very kind lady took me into her car and made me stay at her house which is where I am at present. She is trying to get me to work for her! I think I will too though I am not quite sure. She is very taken with me and calls me a very attractive child! Do you think I am? Anyhow this is where I am and my ankle is nearly alright now and you need not worry about me. I have been thinking a lot about you and I hope you have about me too because I love you very much and I hope we will not quarrel any more!

Your loving,

Rose.

When this was safely inside the addressed envelope, Rose did not feel shut away and lonely any more, even though the door was still locked, for now she knew exactly where she was and Edward seemed to be just round the corner. It must be getting on for the middle of the afternoon now, for she had eaten slowly and had taken a long time over the letter, and somebody would be coming in for the tray and could take the letter to be posted. It was a dark afternoon, and she could not have written much longer without turning on the light. It was nice and cosy with the room dimming round her and the gas-fire turning into little bars of bright red-gold. She snuggled down, gloriously lazy and opulent, wondering idly when somebody would take the letter and when Mrs. Hubarth would come in to see her.

She had not long to wait. And Mrs. Hubarth's first words were very reassuring. "Why that stupid woman should have locked this door, I can't imagine. Well, well, my dear child, and how is your ankle now? I can't see you. Toinette, close the curtains. There!" She had turned on the light, while the housekeeper attended to the curtains.

Mrs. Hubarth was still wearing a very handsome Russian sable coat, as if she had only just come in. Rose, blinking a little, saw that she was the woman of her remembrance of last night, very smart, good-looking in a hard sort of way, and with curious eyes. She was smiling now, but her eyes did not smile. They stared at Rose, speculatively. The housekeeper, who looked sulky, like a woman who had just been found fault with, took the tray, but Rose did not give her the letter.

"You look rather pale, my dear child," said Mrs. Hubarth, as soon as the housekeeper had gone out with the tray. "Is the ankle still painful?"

Rose said that it wasn't, not very.

"Well, we'll see," said Mrs. Hubarth, still looking critically at Rose. "What you need at this moment is a little make-up. Not much, of course. But it's absurd to look like that. Now wait a minute." She hurried out, to Rose's astonishment, and returned a few moments later with a hand mirror, some rouge, powder and a new lipstick. "If you know how to use these things, use them," she said, rather sharply.

"But it doesn't matter—thanks," Rose stammered.

"Certainly it does. Because you're pretty and still very young, that's no reason why you should do nothing about your face. And you're looking washed out, not as attractive as you did last night. Now then, try this lipstick."

She held the mirror for Rose, and then insisted upon her using the lipstick, rouge and powder, telling her exactly what to do. Rose did not like to protest again, and could not help being flattered by this deep interest in her appearance, though there was something oddly and disquieteningly impersonal about it, as if Mrs. Hubarth were far more interested in Rose's face than she was in Rose herself. But perhaps, Rose concluded, these very smart, fashionable ladies were far more interested in faces than in people. Perhaps Mrs. Hubarth's maids had to look just so.

"And you needn't worry about Lady Holt-Ibstock. I telephoned her this morning and explained about you, and she's quite willing to let you go, if you want to stay here. I said you did, of course."

Rose was relieved to learn that the people in Cumberland Square knew where she was. This, like the address on the notepaper, made everything seem at once less mysterious and vaguely threatening. It was all right. Her trouble was, she told herself, that she knew so little about people like Mrs. Hubarth that she simply imagined things were mysterious and threatening when actually they were quite ordinary in this different world.

"About your ankle," said Mrs. Hubarth briskly. "I'm not going to risk your getting up too early, simply because I don't want a lame maid on my hands for weeks and weeks —naturally."

This was reasonable enough, and Rose nodded, and tried a little smile. She caught a glimpse of this smile in the mirror that Mrs. Hubarth was still holding before her, and there it looked a tremendous flashing thing, bright red lips parting to reveal the whitest teeth. What an exciting girl that was in the mirror! Herself and yet not herself. A new, saucy, rather wicked-looking Rose.

"That's much better, isn't it? Of course it is. Well now, it happens that a friend of mine—who also happens to be a doctor—is calling here this afternoon, and I'm going to ask him to have a look at your ankle. Then we can be sure of not making any stupid mistakes. You see, Rosemary? And as he happens to be a charming young man—though he *is* a doctor—I'm sure you won't mind."

Overwhelmed by these attentions, feeling more the little queen than ever, Rose hastened to say that of course she wouldn't mind, was very grateful.

"Splendid! And you can amuse yourself, until he comes, by brushing your hair. Here's a brush, and I'll leave the mirror. Your kind of hair, my dear child, needs the most tremendous brushing. See what you can do to it, and then he'll see what an attractive maid I've been able to find.

And don't be too shy with him. Doctors—especially these brilliant young ones—are always annoyed when their patients are absurdly shy. Now, remember."

Rose had meant to give her the letter to Edward, but she was gone before Rose had a chance to mention it. Rose found herself almost a trifle relieved. Edward seemed a rather smaller and less important figure in her imagination than he had been before Mrs. Hubarth came in, and made such a fuss of her. He was still Edward, of course, but he had dwindled a little during these last ten minutes, and there persisted in clinging to her thought of him now something that made him dwindle, a faint suggestion of shabbiness and absurdity. As she brushed her hair, which crisped and took on new colour and light, she dismissed him from her thoughts with a certain impatience, an impatience that was partly directed at him for diminishing himself, and partly at herself for suddenly seeing him differently. She might not look her usual self in this mirror, but she had never looked so pretty before. Now, with her hair like springing gold, her eyes so bright, her lips so moistly red, Mrs. Hubarth could not say she did not look an attractive child. And she found herself wondering what the doctor would think of her, which was something quite new, for the doctors she had known in Haliford were grumpy, barking middle-aged men who behaved as if they thought everybody silly and childish. If you told them you were ill, they said at once there was nothing wrong with you, but if you said you were all right, they told you sharply that you were in a wretched condition. In short, they were always determined to disagree with you and to show you they knew a lot more than you did.

She had finished brushing her hair but was still sitting up in bed thinking about doctors, when she heard voices outside the door. One was Mrs. Hubarth's, and the other a man's. They seemed to be laughing together about something, and Rose hoped that it was not about her. Then the laughter stopped suddenly, and there was a knock.

The young man who followed Mrs. Hubarth and said "Good afternoon" so pleasantly was startlingly unlike any doctor Rose had ever seen or imagined. The young doctor who had told her that Lawrence Vintnor was dead had been quite good-looking, but he had been good-looking in a doctorish sort of way. But this young man might have been a film star. He was tall, and had a small head, with hair as crisp and fair as her own, smoky-grey eyes, a short upper lip, and a charming smile. After he had first smiled, he tried to look solemn, but Rose could tell that he too had been laughing outside the door. There was about him—perhaps in a glint of the eye, a subdued curl of the lip, even in the very way he held himself—an uncomfortable hint of mockery. It was as if he were pretending, playing a part. Perhaps this was because he was so young and good-looking and was still not used to the solemn business of doctoring. Nevertheless, when he came nearer and had a good look at her, his face seemed to light up, just for a quick-flashing moment, like that of a man who had suddenly seen what he had hardly dared hope to find.

"Well, so this is our little patient," he said, quite

seriously but with a faint smile. He sat down on the bed, while Mrs. Hubarth remained in the background. "Is your ankle still painful?"

"No, thanks, it isn't really bad now," said Rose shyly. And then remembered that she mustn't be shy.

"Still, you can never tell with ankles," he said, smiling at her again. "Difficult and—er—dangerous things—ankles. Never quite trust 'em, eh, Mrs. Hubarth? Well now, we'd better have a look at it, eh?"

He stood up. Mrs. Hubarth came forward quickly and twitched back the bedclothes, at the same time giving Rose a sharp warning glance that said, "No shy nonsense now!" and it was she who quickly unwrapped the bandage. The young doctor bent forward, and carefully examined the ankle, touching it once or twice, and saying: "Humph! Humph! Any pain there? Yes, I see. A lesion, no doubt. Yes, yes, no real damage done, but you'll have to go carefully. Rest for a few more hours, but you could get up to-night perhaps, after dinner. Let me feel your pulse." He held her wrist, and looked solemnly at his watch. "Yes, yes. Not bad at all. No heart strain, I think. Let me see." He put his hand against her left breast, and she shrank back, and as she did, she looked up and saw quite clearly that he was not thinking about her heart or about her condition at all, but was looking her over in a queer unpleasant sort of way. She gave a little cry, and something flickered in his eyes and brought the tiniest and most fleeting grimace to his features, something that might have been shame. But the next moment, he was laughing at her, and Mrs. Hubarth was smiling, as if in apology for her, and she was covered up again and wondering if she had been foolish.

"Nothing at all to worry about," he said to Mrs. Hubarth. "More shock than anything else. A stimulant would help, I think. Perhaps a glass or two of wine with her dinner."

"You'd like that, wouldn't you, Rosemary?" said Mrs. Hubarth gaily. "And now you must stay and rest until dinner-time. Is there anything I can do for you?"

"Yes, please," said Rose, holding out the letter. "Will you have this posted, please? I'm afraid I haven't a stamp."

"Ah, the famous letter to the young man," cried Mrs. Hubarth, taking it. "I'll see that it goes this afternoon, and then he'll know all about you."

"Good afternoon," said the young man, smiling beautifully again.

They went out rather quickly, and there was something about the mere look of them as they went out that Rose did not like. She felt at once that there was something wrong. And now she heard the young man laughing again, and Mrs. Hubarth's voice raised in protest. Then suddenly all her suspicions of the last ten minutes were frozen into one solid certainty. That young man wasn't a doctor. He didn't look like one, hadn't behaved like one. They were playing a trick on her. The instant conviction made her hurry out of bed and across the room, though she had not the least idea of what she wanted to do. This time the door was not locked. She went along the short landing, to the top of the well staircase, and there she stopped, for the two of them were on the landing below and their voices were quite plain.

"My dear Violet, you're a marvel," the young man was saying. "I absolutely agree. She's just what he'll want to see, and he might go round the world again and not find another as good. Beats me how you do it."

"It takes brains—and patience, Gerald. I say, listen to this. 'She is trying to get me to work for her. I think I will too though I am not quite sure. She is very taken with me and calls me a very attractive child——' "

"Here I say, Violet, that's a bit thick, reading the kid's letter——"

"Don't be so absurdly hypocritical, Gerald. I can't possibly let the silly thing go."

"No, but hang it, don't *read* it——"

Rose heard no more. She found herself struggling with the housekeeper, who must have come up quietly behind her. The woman was stronger than she was, and not dazed and half sick. There was something in the woman's face, undisguised now, that terrified Rose, and almost conquered her. She was forced back along the landing, and almost thrown into her room. She sobbed helplessly for a moment or two, then flung herself violently against the door. But it was locked. There was another way out, through the door that led from the bathroom into the next bedroom, but that door was locked on the outside too. She flung back the curtains and looked out the window, then opened it, caring nothing about the rush of cold damp air, though it began to chill her at once. It was almost dark now. The windows of the house opposite did not show a single light, and there was something desolating in its great blank face. She leaned far out, and could see a distant street lamp, but desperate as she felt, she could not scream to a distant street lamp. And it was bitterly cold. She closed the window and the curtains, and sank down in front of the gas-fire.

A terrible contempt for herself burned through her cloud of fear. She was sure now that everything she had been told, and had promptly swallowed, had been a lie. Mrs. Hubarth had not taken a sudden fancy to her and wanted her as a maid; she had not spoken to Lady Holt-Ibstock; the young man had been brought in to see what she looked like with nothing on but these transparent pyjamas; her letter to Edward—and this was easily the worst thing of all—had been read and laughed at and torn up; and here she was, a prisoner. This was a bad house of some kind, and all the people in it were bad. Those drawings were not an accident. Nothing here was an accident. She ought to have known from the first that it was all rotten, as something had kept on telling her that it was rotten. She ought to have known last night when those two women stared at her. Decent women didn't stare at strange girls like that. She ought to have known this morning when she could not find her clothes. And all that business with the pretending doctor! Very attractive child! Burning with self-contempt and shame, she went into the bathroom and fiercely rubbed off every trace of the woman's filthy rouge and lipstick.

"She's just what he'll want to see," she kept repeating to herself, wondering what kind of nastiness they hoped to trap her into. Whoever "he" was, he was obviously not the young man who had pretended to be the doctor. They were going to serve her up to somebody else, and clearly that had been Mrs. Hubarth's idea all along, from the moment when she saw her, through the window of the car, last night. And nobody knew she was here. Edward, who had been looking for her ever since she left Haliford, would be looking for her again now. He would feel as if the city had swallowed her up, as if she had run away from him at night in some great dark wood and instantly been lost. It was this feeling of being lost, far more than any immediate danger from any of the people in the house or anybody who might come to the house, that made her feel so small and frightened. And then she remembered that the police were still looking for her, because of that silly Beatrice Vintnor business. She remembered too how the night before this horrible Mrs. Hubarth had looked very sharply and queerly at her when she had confessed to using two different names. How she wished the police could find her! The blue ogres of her imagination had vanished now, and in their place were large, kind, decent men.

Even in the most desperate of our plights, we are not safe from the usual ridiculous embarrassments. Returning to the bedroom, washed and clean, Rose found that she felt cold, too cold to sit about. On the other hand, she did not want to go back to bed, for she would feel more helpless in bed than out of it, and in addition there was something too passive and unprotesting about merely going back to bed. She felt she could not touch any of the odd wraps and things in the wardrobe. So finally she had to compromise by wrapping herself in one of the blankets off the bed, and then sitting forlornly on the edge. She seemed to sit there quite a long time.

This period came to an end when she heard somebody outside. She rushed at once to the door, stumbling over her blanket, shook the handle and beat upon the panel, crying: "Let me out! Let me out!"

"Now listen to me," came a cold clear voice. It was Mrs. Hubarth. "I know all about you. That doesn't matter so long as you behave sensibly. But if you imagine you can get me into trouble, you're quite mistaken. You can only get yourself into trouble. That's if you're stupid. If you're sensible, you can have quite a good time. Are you listening?"

"No," shouted Rose, and beat upon the door again. She did not hear Mrs. Hubarth go away, but when she stopped her drumming, she knew there was nobody now on the other side. She wrapped the blanket round her, and sat on the edge of the bed again. But it was too cold there, so she pulled one of the nasty little gilt chairs near the gas-fire. Even then she did not feel very warm. Actually the room was stuffily warm, for the gas-fire had been alight in it now for hours, but Rose was chilled by fear. It was not a definite fear of this thing or that, but a terror vague but vast, like that which seems to freeze and darken the whole universe in bad dreams. It numbed her, and she felt that very soon, after a little more of it, all her power of movement, all her will, would go, and she would be helpless. She was cut off by a rising tide of evil. It was seeping through the walls. There was nothing to mark the passing of time inside that room. She did not know how long she remained crouched achingly on that chair, her mind wandering blindly round a beaten track. It might have been hours.

Then the door opened. She jumped up, gave a little scream. It was Sam, the negro chauffeur, no longer in uniform but dressed in a brown sweater and flannel trousers; and he was carrying a tray with a dish on it and a bottle of wine. He put the tray down on the floor, put a hand outside the door, then withdrew it and carefully closed the door behind him. Meanwhile, she had retreated and was standing near the window, tightly huddled in the blanket, watching him. He picked up the tray and put it on the table by the side of the bed. Then he looked at her. His face shone, as if it had been made of some polished dark metal. He had big dark swimming eyes. He looked enormous in that room. To Rose, who had seen very few black men and had never spoken to one in her life, it was as if a great animal had entered. And something about him—his movements, the rolling of his eyes—told her that he was not quite sober. After a moment, she caught the reek of rum. She was terrified. The utter strangeness of him, the deep racial gulf between them, the instant conviction that there could not possibly be any communication between this man-animal and herself, enormously heightened her terror. She could not speak.

But when he spoke, it was different. Most of her terror vanished. The very fact that he could talk at all meant that he no longer seemed an animal. And then his voice, which was deep and droning and hard to understand, was not at all frightening, but had a sort of heavy sweetness and slow melancholy about it.

"You's 'fraid o' Sam," he said reproachfully, wagging his head.

She nodded, not able to find her voice yet, even though her terror was going.

" 'Fraid o' everything here, mebbe?"

"Yes, I am," she whispered. "I want to go away."

He looked at her with a sombre speculation. Then he nodded, as if convinced now that some suspicion of his had been right. "You's not that kind, Ah guess. Dey tell me bring you sumpen t'eat an' drink, an' dey put plenty salt in so's you drink plenty wine. Den you don' care. Ah'm drunk dis minute, yes, suh," he continued in his deep melancholy voice. "Big night to-night. Somebody comin' here. So dey say, 'Help 'self, Sam. We want you to-night.' So Ah'm drunk, an' later Ah'll be drunker an' den Ah don' care what Ah do, honey. Jesus, but Ah don' know what Ah've done plenty times."

There was something quite childlike in his ruefulness, and Rose was quick enough to see that she had caught him in a half-way stage of drink, when he lost the cautiousness he might have when completely sober, but was still a long way from the fierce bestiality and mindlessness that full intoxication might bring. As he was now, he was the only person she had met in this house who was frank and friendly. He had had just enough drink to wash away the influences of the last years and to restore him to the manner and tone of his childhood. And Rose felt that he too, this great black man, had somehow been caught and held here just as she had. She could not understand exactly what he meant, but she gathered he was telling her he was not really a bad chap and that they had to make him drunk to do whatever it was they wanted him to do. And Rose saw, in a flash, that whatever he had done, he was not one of these evil people, he was as innocent as she was, at heart an enormous and bewildered child.

She came forward a little, to show him that she was no longer afraid of him, and whispered urgently: "Can't you let me go? My clothes must be somewhere about. Just my coat would do. Let me go, please."

He shook his head solemnly, and then explained, not very coherently in his thick drowsy voice, that he dared not do that. He was, it seemed, trying to save enough money to get out of the country, back to America, and until he had the money, he was afraid of Mrs. Hubarth, who would tell the police about him. He seemed to accept without question the melancholy fact that while Mrs. Hubarth could tell the police about him, he could not tell the police about her. He was a black man among white people.

"Ma Grampa who could fix charms an' conjures down in South Carolina," he concluded sadly, "tol' me when Ah was a li'l' boy never to go 'mong white folks."

"But what am I going to do?" asked Rose, in despair.

He brooded for a moment. "You jus' better stay right here," he announced finally. "An' don' come out to-night no matter what dey say, honey. Stay right here."

"I can't. You see——"

"Bes' you can do. Mebbe later Ah'll be drunker'n a hog. But now Ah tells you to stay right here."

He held out a hand, palm upwards, and glittering in the palm, which seemed so oddly pink, was a key. It was the key of her door. He tossed it on the bed. "Now Ah don' know nuthen," he said slowly, "but lock your door, chile, an' stay right here. Ah's li'l' drunk now, but Ah don' wish you no harm." He gave her a last look, a last wag of the head, then humming in a deep bass, he shambled out of the room, and out of her life, so that soon the very memory of him seemed hardly real, nothing but a face and a voice out of a dream.

She locked the door. If she could not get out, then they should not come in. She even tugged at the chest of drawers and managed to bring a corner of it against the door, as additional security. Her former lethargy had disappeared now. She was fearful and excited, but no longer in a cold state of terror. It was hours since she had eaten, but she ignored the tray that Sam had brought. Nothing that came from those two vile women was fit to be touched. Once or twice she felt ready to unlock that door and make a dash for freedom; but she did not know where her clothes were, had nothing on but the flimsiest things, and saw that she might easily run straight into their hands. Sam, who seemed to know what was going on, had hinted that if she could keep them away from her that night, all might be well. Then she would stay here, as he suggested, out of their hands for this one night. In the morning it might be better. Before Sam came, she had begun to feel lost in a new and menacing world, but now she felt better, if only because Sam himself had suddenly turned from a figure of black terror into somebody innocent and friendly. If even he could help, then more help might come to her. She did not feel lost now.

It might have been half an hour after Sam's departure, it might have been a full hour, when she was suddenly startled by a slight sound coming from the bathroom. The door into the bathroom had no lock on her side of it, and she had forgotten that the bedroom could be entered that way. Without considering any possible danger, she rushed to the bathroom door and flung it open. The girl who was in there turned round. She was not much older than Rose, was fair and fragile but stony-eyed, and she was half undressed. For one insane moment, Rose felt she was staring at another version of her own self. She tried to speak, but the other girl, after one hard look, turned away, picked up some things, and hurried into the opposite bedroom, slamming the door behind her. Recovering slowly from that shock of seeing almost a damaged duplicate of herself, Rose did not follow her into the bedroom but stepped forward into the bathroom and shot the bolt on the far door, thus making herself safe on that side. Whoever this girl was, she felt, there was no friendliness about her. She belonged to the enemy.

For another unmeasurable interval of time, during which Rose flitted uncertainly between her two locked doors, nothing happened; there were a few vague sounds coming from the rest of the house, footsteps along the landing, some raised voices from downstairs; but she was left alone. The first interruption was not of much importance. Somebody tried to enter the bathroom from the other bedroom, and rattled the door impatiently. Rose did not take this very seriously. The second attempt was very different. There were several voices outside, and among them she recognised Sam's, which was loud and incoherent, a sort of deep howl, suggesting that now he was really drunk. The door was shaken violently. Fists banged and drummed against it, making a terrifying din. Rose fled into the bathroom, shut and bolted the door leading into her own room, to be doubly secure, and sat shivering on the edge of the bath. She felt that she could not stand this much longer, that if it went on she would be compelled to open the door to them. The place seemed to throb with the ungovernable beating of her heart. She felt weak and sick.

When at last she crept back into the bedroom, there was no sound from the landing. She went to the door, put her ear to the crack by the hinge, and listened hard. They had gone. Such sounds as she heard came from downstairs, and they were only faint, distant voices, laughter. Evidently they were having their "big night" without her. It looked as if she were safe for this one night, and at the moment that was all that mattered. To-morrow could look after itself: it could not be worse than to-night. Relieved, her confidence returning, she found that she was unpleasantly hungry, and looked at the tray that Sam had brought. The food was a kind of scrambled egg dish on toast, and of course had long since gone cold. She nibbled at it dubiously, and found that Sam had been right when he had said it was heavily salted. She did not touch the wine, a bottle of champagne that had been opened and then corked again, but drank several glasses of water in the bathroom. Even this ghost of a meal made her feel better. If she could not leave this room, she could make some protest, and did. She took the foul drawings and tore them savagely into small pieces, and then threw them out of the windows, into the darkness where they belonged. She stayed a few moments at the open window, closely wrapped in her blanket, and breathed deeply of the cold but refreshing night air. Then, leaving the light and the fire on, she took another blanket, rolled herself in it on the bed, and closed her eyes. Several times she had to open them again and glance quickly round the room to reassure herself. Once or twice she was startled into complete wakefulness by noises from outside, probably from downstairs. But she was very young, and she was exhausted now, after such a long stress of emotion, and gradually her mind wandered away. She did not spend much time in the untroubled depths of sleep; she was nearly always in that twilight borderland where the world outside is not completely lost but is dimly heard and felt and immediately translated into fragmentary dreams, memories twisted into uneasy fantasies, vague broken dramas in which to play a part seems more wearing than a day's hard work; but during this long lunatic film show, she lost the house and all the people in it, moved in dimensions unknown to them, and the night went by—not quickly, for on that borderland every minute of our time is unravelled and pulled out into shadowy hours—but it passed, and morning took its place.

When she awoke properly, fully conscious of everything, including her own heavy eyes and aching stiffness, she felt at once that more than time had passed, that the whole situation had suffered a profound change. This was not the same house it had been the night before. She had not the least idea what had happened, but something, she was positive, and something very important, had happened. She drew the curtains. It was a grey damp morning, and she was certain that it was several hours old. She felt dirty as well as stiff and aching. She turned the hot water in the bath full on, and was surprised to find that it was only lukewarm, and as she ran it, the stream became colder. She had a quick, shivery, goose-fleshy sort of bath, and rubbed herself very hard with the towel. She did not put the pyjamas on again, but did her best with the wrap and a blanket as a cloak. She pushed the chest of drawers away from the door, cautiously turned the key and opened the door a few inches, and then listened. Somewhere below a clock ticked. Not another sound. The whole house was lost, drowned, in an immense silence. She pushed the door further open. The silence was still there, waiting for her. She took a step out on to the landing. The clock ticked away, her heart went beating, and that was all. And now she knew what had happened. The certainty came flashing. There was nobody else in the house. They had all gone.

At the far end of the landing, away from the stairs, was a white wardrobe cupboard. Some instinct directed her towards it. There, at the bottom, in a rough bundle, were her clothes, where the housekeeper must have thrown them after she took them from the bathroom, the night before last. Rose dressed hurriedly in front of the gas-fire in the bedroom, and then turned it off. It was extraordinary how much more confident she felt, how the helplessness of the last twenty-four hours vanished, now that she was fully dressed again. Nevertheless, she returned along the landing and began descending the stairs very slowly and cautiously. She knew very little about the house. Her remembrance of it from that first night was very vague. She could only remember the first flight of stairs, then the little sitting-room where she had rested and had her ankle attended to, and then of course that section of the top floor which seemed to have been her whole world for so long. There would be no difficulty about finding her way out. These stairs could only curve down to the hall. And if she had been given the chance of getting out of the house yesterday that she had now, she would have run down these stairs to the front door. But she was so certain that they had all gone, that she was alone there, that she could not help lingering, being curious about this strange house that had kept her a prisoner. Why had they gone? What had happened?

At the top of the first flight of stairs, on the same floor as that little sitting-room, there were odd signs of disorder and sudden flight. Not only had the place not been cleaned up since the previous night, but people had been leaving in a great hurry. There were even some small articles of clothing spilled on the floor, as if they had been thrown out of bags that had too much in them to shut properly. Rose looked along the carpeted landing at these things, wondering. It was then that something rubbed against her leg, giving her a little fright. The tortoiseshell cat, who appeared to be lonely and puzzled, looked up at her, as if to ask for her explanation of what had been happening. It was a beautiful cat, and Rose, feeling her own loneliness and bewilderment shared, bent down to stroke it. The cat closed her fine eyes for a moment or two the better to enjoy this exquisite sensation, then walked daintily along the landing, stopped at one of the closed doors, turned and mewed. Rose followed it, and after a little hesitation, opened the door. This was obviously the chief room of the house, a drawing-room even larger than that in Cumberland Square. It was the strangest room Rose had ever seen. The immense carpet and all the walls were dead black, but the upholstery, including the coverings of three big divans, was scarlet. Very vivid against the black and scarlet was a long table covered with green baize cloth, on which were scattered coloured counters. In the near corner was an ebony grand piano, the top of which was crowded with bottles, glasses, fruit, and plates of sandwiches. Probably it was this food that the cat had smelled. They were both very hungry, it seemed. Rose gave the cat the meat out of one sandwich, and ate another herself. She could now see the whole of the room. She walked slowly down it, eating her sandwich, glanced at two cabinets filled with Eastern carved things, tiny men and monsters writhing for ever in ivory. There were some glasses and plates on the floor, and a lot of cigarette ash about, all very plain to see against the black carpet. The place smelled dreadfully stale. And Rose soon felt that the vague evil of the rest of the house had its core and being here, where the faded pink of the bedroom changed to a deep scarlet. It was lit by imitation shaded candles on the wall, and now Rose realised that they were burning and that she herself had not turned them on. They must have been left burning all night. No windows were visible, but she saw that they must be hidden behind great black curtains, indistinguishable at first from the wall itself. She drew the curtains nearer the door, and a grey foggy daylight wandered in, and seemed to give the room an even more evil aspect than it had worn before. It was as if it had forgotten what daylight was. She drew the second pair of heavy curtains back, and was now nearly at the end of the room. In the corner was a great scarlet sofa, with a large silky rug thrown over something lying on it. She went nearer, and then stared and stared. From the lower edge of the rug there hung two patent-leather shoes. And higher up, hanging down over the edge of the sofa, was a bit of black sleeve, a cuff, and a limp hand.

She knew at once, without going a step nearer, that the man under that rug was dead. She had not been alone in that house. A dead man had been there all the time. She felt suddenly cold, she was shaking. A noise behind her made her give a little scream. It was the cat mewing again. There was something terrible about a cat mewing like that. In another moment, she would be screaming and screaming. She put her hands to her face, pressed them hard against her cheeks. Her cheeks were cold, colder than her hands. That man's hand had a ring on it. And he was dead. That's why they had gone. They had left her with a dead man. She ran out of the room, heard the door bang behind her, then collapsed against the opposite wall, and began sobbing. She was quite unable to control herself. She could not think, she could only sob. It was silly.

When she was quieter, she heard a scratching against the

other side of that door. A dead man wouldn't crawl from under his rug—would he?—pull himself over that carpet, and then scratch against the door, asking to be let out, not to be dead any more. No, it would be the cat, of course. She couldn't leave the cat in there, if it wanted to come out. She let it out, and it had a piece of meat in its mouth. It must have climbed up itself and got at the sandwiches. Cats were awfully clever at stealing things. Now it was eating the meat, keeping close to her, though, as if it must have company as well as food.

With her little green hat screwed in one hand, Rose walked slowly down to the hall, and then dropped down on a high-backed uncushioned chair there, only a few steps from the front door. She was trying to think, and she couldn't think. She didn't sob any more, but somehow she couldn't collect her thoughts at all. They just went whizzing round, wouldn't stay to be sorted out. She could hear little noises from the outside world now, the first she seemed to have heard for ages. Cars were hooting away, men were hawking things, out there, just the same as ever. The cat was washing itself, and when it saw that she was looking at it, it gave a little miaow, and came nearer and then rubbed itself against her. She stroked it again. Time passed. She could hear it ticking itself away in the large clock on the landing above. But still she couldn't think properly. The cat went away. This narrow hall was very cold and desolate. A deathly chill seemed to creep down from that figure upstairs under the rug. There was a table near her chair, and on that table was a telephone. You could talk to people through that telephone. But she couldn't talk to anybody yet, couldn't even think. It was very quiet. No cars hooting now. What morning was it? Thursday? Thursday had always been a nice sort of day. She had said that—hadn't she?—only last Thursday. . . .

The bell behind the front door brazenly shattered the silence, stopping her very heart. Its clamour was immensely insistent, impossible to be denied, as if the whole world was ringing there, asking for its dead men. But in the equally immense quiet that followed, she did deny it, desperately refusing to move from her chair, trying to hold herself rigid in its embrace. The bell summoned her again; less startling now as a mere sound, but equally clamorous, and doubly insistent. It pulled her out of the chair. She fumbled with the little knob on the back of the Yale lock, with no sense in her fingers at all. At last the door swung back at her. Nobody? Yes, a figure now moving slowly away. At her cry it turned and became a blurred and wavering image of Edward. . . .

"There can't be," said Edward, still holding her close. They had not moved from behind the door, where she had collapsed into his arms.

"There is, I tell you, really there is," cried Rose tearfully, not letting him go.

"A dead man?"

"Yes. I'm sure he's dead. I—I didn't see his face."

"I'd better go and look."

"No, no. Don't leave me."

"Well, couldn't you come with me?"

"Oh no—I couldn't."

"But we ought to have a proper look at him. I mean

—he may not be dead——"

"I know he is."

"Well then——"

"All right, Edward. I'll show you where he is. Keep tight hold of my hand. Oh—I've had a horrible time here. But how did you find me?"

He explained how clever little Mr. Scawton of Mr. Finland's Foreign Legion had found the garage that knew Mrs. Hubarth's car well, and how he, Edward, knowing that no message had come from her to Lady Holt-Ibstock's, had thought something must be wrong and was determined to ask for her at once. As he explained all this, they walked slowly hand-in-hand along the hall, up the stairs, and along the first landing, and everything they passed was so remote from the young life in them, so decayed and mummified already, that they might have been walking in another and more evil museum. The whole house was sinking, before their very eyes, their young and innocent eyes, into the unhappy past, seemed nearly ready for the clear little labels and catalogues that would coldly indicate to thousands of future Roses and Edwards its sad luxury and obscenity. Life, with its current running sweetly through the clasped hands, was moving slowly through Death.

"There," said Rose, stopping and pointing.

"This is a rum sort of room, isn't it? Looks completely barmy to me."

"It's bad, every bit of it. I know it is. Edward, I'll wait here."

"All right," said Edward, who felt immensely brave,

ready to look at twenty dead men. He walked rather carefully to the other end, had a good stare at the rug and the protruding hand and feet, then very gently pulled the rug back. He did not touch the body, for he had read a lot of detective stories and knew that the bodies of murdered men must not be touched. He felt sure the man had been murdered just as he felt sure that the man was a foreigner. There was nothing foreign about his evening clothes, for he wore an ordinary dinner jacket. Nor was there anything very foreign about his large clean-shaven face, his indeterminate features, his putty cheeks, his staring jellied eyes. In his last struggle he must have flung one side of his coat back, for the inside pocket was visible, with one or two long envelopes sticking out of it. Very gingerly—remembering the detective stories all the time—Edward removed one of these letters, with his handkerchief covering his thumb and forefinger. It was addressed to some foreign hotel, and the name on it was Ferdinand Antill.

"Edward," Rose cried, alarmed, "you're not touching him, are you?"

"Only looked at a letter. I've put it back. I'm sure he's been murdered. But I don't know how. You'd have to turn him over——"

"Don't touch him, don't touch him," Rose cried. "Please, Edward, please."

"I'm not going to. Do you want to look at him? I mean—it might be somebody you saw here."

"No, I know it isn't. I—just—saw his face. Edward, please, come away. Let's leave him alone." And as he approached, she ran forward a few paces, took him by the arm, and hurried him out of the room. Then they stood looking at one another on the landing outside.

"What are we going to do?" asked Edward, after a long pause.

She did not reply at once. One hand played feverishly with the lapel of his coat. The clock ticked away at them. "Let's go," she cried, finally. "Edward, let's go away. Let's go back to Haliford."

"Yes, I want to do that. But——"

"No, let's go now. This hasn't anything to do with us. It's not our fault and we don't know anything about it. And nobody knows I've been here, except those horrible people, and they've all run away. Edward, come on, let's go."

"But listen, Rose. Wait a minute——"

"No, no. I can't listen and wait. You don't understand what it's been like for me in this house—I've only told you a bit of it—and I can't stand any more of it. And I hadn't anything to do with it. I don't know who that man is, don't know anything about it. And nobody'll know I've ever been here. We can go back to Haliford to-day." And she began pulling at him, and he gave in, and they went down to the hall again. But there he stopped, took her hands firmly in his, and looked hard at her. He seemed older, altogether more grown-up, than he had been before. Even while she was wondering desperately what he was going to say, she noticed this. Perhaps that other night in Trafalgar Square had changed him.

"Rose, we can't go like that," he began gently. "I know

it's not your fault. This is some kind of bad house they got you into. But the police will understand that."

She cried out at that. "I don't want to start talking to the police, Edward. I'm frightened. Oh—can't you see I'm frightened?"

"You're thinking about that other business now," he told her. "But that doesn't matter. We know you were innocent, and if it all comes out, then Beatrice What's-her-name must take her chance. It's not important. But this is—very. A man's been murdered in this rotten house, and we must tell the police about it."

"Why? Do you think they'd find out about us being here? I'm sure they wouldn't."

"I don't know whether they would or not," said Edward firmly. "That's not the point."

"It is."

"It isn't, Rose. Honestly, it isn't. The point is—we must help them. This man's been killed——"

"I'll bet he deserved to be," cried Rose fiercely, to his surprise. "He was probably the one they were expecting, the one that Sam—oh, I don't know!—something horrible——"

"I dare say he did. But that's not it either. That isn't what matters——"

"All that matters," she retorted quickly, "is that you love me—you do, don't you?—and that I love you—and that if we go home, we can get out of this terrible mess—we never ought to have left home, either of us—though I know, that was my fault—but then we can start again, properly, just us, and it'll all be different."

"I know. That's what I want. We'll do that, Rose."

"There you are then," she cried, brightening. "Let's go."

"But we can't start again properly, if we go now, without telling them about this. It wouldn't be a clean start. People can't go fighting and killing other people—I thought that the other night when they were all at it in Trafalgar Square and then the police came to clear up the mess—and we say it's no business of ours, and they probably deserved it, and all that. The police have got to know about the murder, and about this house too, or else we'll never get any further. I don't mean just us—though I do mean us—but everybody. And I want to know," and now his voice rang through the long narrow hall, up through the whole house, disturbing the dust that was already beginning to settle on its polished antique woods and silken hangings, "I want to know why this house was here, why this man came here, why somebody killed him—what it's all about. We can't go on like this," he continued—strangely, it seemed to her—"with you being lost, and then me lost, looking for you, and both of us lost, and things just happening to us and we don't know why. What's it all about?"

"Edward, I don't understand," she said sadly.

"Rose, I love you. Do you trust me?"

For an answer, she came closer and raised her face to his, and he kissed her, with great tenderness.

He pulled the chair to the table with the telephone on it, sat down, and she went and stood close to him, her arm about his shoulder. "You know, Rose, that detective chap who came to see me about you when I was at the Belvedere Trading Company—what was his name?—MacMurray, that's it—seemed a decent sort of chap. I'll ask for him." Her arm tightened round his shoulder.

"That's lucky," he said to her softly, a moment later. "He's in." He waited. "Hello, yes. Detective-Sergeant MacMurray? Well, I don't suppose you'll remember me, but you came to see me at the Belvedere Trading Company about a girl called Rose Salter. Yes. Well, I do know where she is, but that's not it. No, listen. We're both in a house in St. John's Wood—I'll give you the address in a minute—and we've found a man here who's been murdered. No, of course, I'm not. It's true. I've just seen him. Yes, we'll wait. This is the address. Are you ready?"

When he had done, he said: "They're coming now," and did not get up but put his arm round her, and she leaned against him, bending her cheek to his, and they said nothing for a long time, but kept close to one another, and waited.

THE END